Welcome to Boy.Net

Earth's Shadow

Book 1

Welcome to Boy.net

Earth's Shadow - Book 1

Lyda Morehouse

WIZARD'S TOWER

Wizard's Tower Press

Rhydaman, Cymru

Welcome to Boy.net

Earth's Shadow - Book 1

Text © 2024 by Lyda Morehouse
Cover art by Ben Baldwin
Book design by Cheryl Morgan

First published by Wizard's Tower Press,
April 2024

ISBN: 978-1-913892-73-9

http://wizardstowerpress.com/

Contents

*To Shawn and Mason,
my family*

ACKNOWLEDGEMENTS

Starting at the beginning, I need to thank Rachel Manija Brown for inspiring me to try out a light lesbian romance, even though I'm never able to write fast enough (or light enough!) for things to ever work out as I plan. Even so, without Rachel, this book would not exist.

As I wrote my way in and out of this book, over and over again, I must thank my writers' groups: Wyrdsmiths and Pendragons for their support, critique, advice, and friendship along the way. Specifically, among them I have to thank Peg Kerr for coming up with a title for this book and Cliff Winnig for the equally brilliant series title. Naomi Kritzer, who is the best friend a person could ask for, also gets a specific call out for her last minute critique of the finished novel. Theo Lorenz, too, gets special attention for being amazing to make bagels and hang out with and, of course, for their insights on gender euphoria, among many other things.

I also have to thank my silent writing group for making me sit down for at least an hour, Monday through Thursday, especially when it was hard to put pen to paper during the isolation part of the pandemic.

My family also gets my eternal gratitude for their contributions as idea sounding boards, collaborators, editors, and typo-spotters. I mean, what would this book be without my wife inspiring so much of who Del Toro is and my son's willingness not only to listen to my endless plot problems, but also his brilliant advice on how to fix things? I think sometimes that it must be hard to be part of a writing family, but both Shawn and Mason have always been so much more than supportive—they are my foundation. My writing would crumble without their contributions.

Also, of course I must thank Cheryl Morgan who waited, patiently, for what must've seemed like forever for this book. Similarly, I am always, always grateful for Ben Baldwin's incredible cover art. Wizard's Tower Press has been a godsend for me.

I also need to thank my Patreon supporters. There are only thirteen of you (not exactly a lucky number), but your continued willingness to believe in me and throw a little coin my way really did help keep the wolves from the door when the times were lean. Thank you so much.

Also, if you're one of my many trans friends and/or relatives, know that I wrote this book thinking of you. Neither Oz, nor Lucia Del Toro are meant to be a perfect, shining beacon of any particular kind of transness. Lucia is a woman like any other and thus, she has her own foibles and flaws. Same with

Oz. Oz is just the person that they are. All of you taught me that there are as many ways to be trans as there are trans people.

Blessed Be and It Harm None.

CHAPTER 1

Lucia Del Toro

Lucia Del Toro crouched on the surface of Saturn's smallest moon, Mimas, uncoupling the fuel line of her ship, the *Peapod*. No corporation bothered to terraform a moon so tiny. It remained a sad abandoned chunk of ice, ice, and more ice—stretching outward as far as the eye could see to end in a strange, foreshortened horizon.

As she worked, a shadow passed in front of Lucia's vision. Blur turned into a complete blackout. Blindly, she reached for a handhold with one hand, her other feeling for the tether that kept her attached to the ship. Grasping both with whitening knuckles, Lucia cursed silently.

Damn eyes again, acting up.

When a bit of murky light returned, Lucia felt a compulsion to glance up. Intellectually, she knew she should see nothing but the underbelly of her own craft. Instead, an Earth Nations' Peacekeeping Force battlecruiser slid silently overhead.

Great, a post-traumatic stress induced hallucination. And always the same damn one.

Just what she didn't need—to relive that fucking day over and over...

In order to banish the illusion, Lucia tried to ground herself. She let go of one of the handholds and reached up, fumbling for the *Peapod*'s hull above her head. Finding it, she slapped a palm against it, solid, real.

Despite this confirmation, her heart thudded dully against her eardrum.

It's not there. It was almost ten years ago that I watched them pass me over, scanning for me. Continued, rhythmic slapping did nothing to slow her heart or banish the vision. *I'm just afraid that they're scanning for me, hoping my onboard will phone home to Boy.net. When my eyes shut down, my brain reached for the nightmare always under the surface. The Force can't reach me. They're stuck on the other side of the asteroid belt.*

Lucia smacked the hull a couple more times, hard, hoping that the sting of the impact would help break through. She had to stop when she heard a sound like metal crumpling under her cybernetically-enhanced strength.

Okay. Time to stop freaking out now.

If she kept this up the *Peapod* would suffer real damage.

So, think, girl. How did the rest of the grounding ritual go?

Find three real things and focus on them. Eyes can't be trusted, so how about the stink of her EV suit? Unfortunately, its sharp tang, the scent of fear, only heightened memories of battlefields and blood. Now her ears attempted to turn the hiss and pump of air into soldiers' chatter, *Boy.net* background noise, the sounds of a man begging for surrender... her determination to escape at any cost...

No. All this head shrinking shit made things worse!

Sucking in a steadying breath, Lucia subvocalized to her onboard: *Ocular Implant, Reset.*

The vision persisted.

Was this real? Or was she that broken?

The blackened steel underbelly of the giant ship coasted overhead. Ignoring it, Lucia concentrated on taking one breath after another. She wrapped a hand around her own waist. Giving herself a one-armed hug, she gave into the impulse to crouch down, take cover. That one therapist had said there was nothing wrong with checking to see if someone followed you if you had a paranoid thought.

Still clinging to the tether, she pulled herself into a small ball—or at least as small as she could be.

What else had she learned to do when PTSD hit hard?

Reduce the threat.

Think about how dumb the ENForcers actually were. *Boy.net*, there was a good example. The 'boy' part of the network was an acronym—Bio-cybernetic Operating super-sYstem—but Lucia figured it to be a 'backronym,' a retro fit for a stupid joke cooked up in some testosterone-choked locker room. Only children would think *Boy.net* sounded cool.

At that thought, Lucia took a deeper breath.

11

Ocular implant resetting, a jarringly deep masculine voice said in Lucia's inner ear.

The mirage of the giant military ship evaporated. In its place appeared the green-gray hull of the *Peapod* above. The massive gas giant and its famous rings rose over the horizon.

Releasing her iron grip on the tether, Lucia slowly uncurled. Once upright, she hop-shuffled out from under the shelter of the *Peapod*. She glanced out over the white expanse of ice and impact craters into the blackness of space for any sign of the retreating cruiser. The dark could easily swallow a ship even of that size, especially since cruisers were painted black just for that reason. However, if any part of it had been real, she thought she ought to be able to catch a glint off the solar sails if they were deployed.

Nothing.

System, run a complete diagnostic.

Full diagnostic not responding. Generating automatic update request for commanding off—

Belay that order.

Order belayed. Be advised, Colonel Del Toro, a full system overhaul is overdue.

No fucking shit.

A headache spiked between Lucia's eyebrows that had nothing to do with her decrepit cyberware. First, the imaginary battlecruiser, and now being fucking 'coloneled' again? What the hell. Hadn't erasing her former rank been the first thing she'd done when she'd deserted?

System, search instances of 'colonel' and delete.

Searching...

Lucia took one last hard look into the void of deep space—nothing but a blackness that could hide a thousand ships. It'd been a malfunction, Lucia knew that, but she might have caught some real thing in her peripheral vision that triggered the PTSD.

"Hey, uh—Hawk," she said, after using two fingers to toggle the com button on the palm of her environmental suit's glove. It would be less detectable to any ship out there to use their private internal cyber-connection. At the moment, Lucia didn't trust her onboard for obvious reasons. "This is going to sound stupid, but did a F-Class battlecruiser just pass over us?"

"F-Class??" came the startled response from Hawk. "Like, invasion-level F-Class?"

"Yep," Lucia nodded, even though Hawk couldn't see her through the com. She felt foolish just even suggesting such a thing, but she had to know. "That'd be one."

"Okay." Hawk sounded a bit skeptical, but there was only a brief pause, then, "Let me check."

A sense of reassurance unwound Lucia's nerves knowing Hawk trusted her implicitly. Lucia could have said 'can you check for a mob of kangaroos on this moon's surface?' and the conversation would have gone exactly the same. A bit of surprise, but then absolute confidence that a task should be done, regardless of how improbable. It was almost like having a creche mate at her side again. Better, probably, given there was no rank or military protocol in this relationship.

The shadow of the battlecruiser must have chilled Lucia to the bone to have her thinking of her creche so fondly. Sometimes, in uncharitable moments, Lucia wondered if Hawk's trust would still be so unconditional, if she knew. Hell, Lucia could barely forgive herself.

In order to shake off the remaining haunted, hunted feeling that the image of the battlecruiser conjured, Lucia continued her grounding exercise. She took an admiring look at her ship, the *Peapod*. Large for a personal craft, it had been designed to house a small crew for potentially lengthy diplomatic missions. Diplomatic by ENForcer definition, she scoffed, glancing at the massive, military weapons array. All the weapons made the exterior of their ship seem like a long, bumpy peapod, aided, of course, by Hawk's ongoing, ridiculously bright green paint job.

The ENForcers would hate it.

Lucia loved it.

Hawk's voice on the com broke Lucia's reverie. "I presume you don't want me to blast a wide ping, right?" Not waiting for a response, she continued, "So, I'm doing a careful sweep of the area. In the meantime, I'll check the feeds. I pretty much scroll them hourly, so you wouldn't think I'd've missed the end of the Twenty-Year Standoff. It's all clear. *Det är ingen ko på isen*, as they say. There are no cows on the ice."

'*No cows on the ice.*' It was funny to hear that sort of thing from Hawk.

Apparently, thanks to all their time together, Hawk picked up more and more ENForcer slang. No other group in the System intentionally used so many archaic Earth-centric idioms. Hanging on to a handhold on the side of the *Peapod*, Lucia allowed herself another small smile. No one alive today would know what a cow looked like if it jumped up and bit them in the eye, much less remembered whatever the hell that particular saying referenced.

Hawk's voice crackled through the helmet, "Thank Faraday, nothing. I mean, I'm picking up a bunch of the usual traffic in the system and a couple of faint blips on our new smuggler's route here, but nothing like a cruiser." A short pause, then Hawk asked, "Since you're not using our little mind-meld, which you absolutely would have if you thought your old pals were in the vicinity, my best guess is that you're glitching?"

"Oi, no need for such insults," Lucia snarled.

"Oh, shit. I forgot. Sorry?"

Lucia silently cursed herself. Of course Hawk didn't mean it. She knew that glitches were what ENForcers called anyone who strayed even the slightest from the norm, people they considered deviants, queer. Lucia shook her head to let go of old wounds. "Sorry, it's all this ENForcer shit rattling around in my brain.'" She let out a long breath. Hawk was on her side, so she needed to be honest about what was going on with herself, too. "Something's really wrong with my eyes. This isn't the only time they've flaked on me, but this is the first time I've lost my sight completely. I might need an upgrade or two. Or three. Or, more likely, a half dozen. When I was fully connected to *Boy.net*, I didn't even notice how often my system got upgrades—unless it was one of the stupid ones that everyone mocked. Laser fingers." She laughed at the memory. "Who the fuck thinks giving a bunch a military jarheads ten mini lasers was a good idea? Anyway, it's definitely time to hit up that friend of yours on Nyx again."

"Nyx?" A sound like a raspberry being blown came over the mic. "You got a spare three hundred thousand Saturn dinar hiding somewhere I don't know about?"

Not a lot of people in-system would touch a former ENForcer and those that did charged more money than either she or Hawk had seen in a long, long time. "Not after our last botched heist, I don't," Lucia's brow crinkled and she stared out at Mimas's desolate, icy landscape. Their last job had gone sideways thanks to some bad luck and another attack of her damn bioware gremlins. That time her arm froze. Couldn't even pull the trigger. She just had to stand there and watch their bounty walk away. "I guess we have to pray that your intel about this new black market route is good for once."

"Of course it's good," Hawk's tone was that of mock indignation. "The only people coming this way in the next ten hours are smugglers, thieves, or mobsters. Depend on it. In fact, I'm already picking up faint blips out there. Anyway, who's the one throwing around the insults now? I'll have you know that my informants are fully... fifty percent reliable."

"Are you sure you don't mean fifteen percent?" Lucia returned the teasing with a chuckle, as she started to shuffle her way back to the airlock. Every few steps she made sure to grip a handhold and reattach her tether. The gravity on Mimas was barely there, after all.

"I'm dyslexic not discalcic," Hawk said with a slight, serious bitterness in her voice.

Lucia always forgot how sensitive Hawk got about her learning disability. Growing up in a colony of scientists where education and mental ability were paramount must have been hell on someone for whom reading and writing came slowly. "Sorry," Lucia added sincerely. "Look, I got spooked and I'm just sticking my foot in it all over the place today. Let's just bag ourselves a hot bounty and I'll make it up to you over champagne and caviar."

"Throw in some messy sex and I'm yours."

Lucia felt a blush heat the tips of her ears. Her brain sputtered out in a completely different way, but she managed an enthusiastic, "You're on."

Hawk, who shifted easily from flirt back to work, said, "Alrighty, since the fuel line is reading as 'compromised,' I'll hit the distress signal. See you inside."

"Roger that."

Lucia had made her way to the airlock.

Pressing the unlock code, she waited for the door to cycle open. Neither of them were exactly law-abiding or deeply moral, but, normally, they'd never run a con this devious. In space, there was one rule everyone followed. If at all possible, you answered a distress call. It didn't matter if you were a saint or a sinner, if someone needed a rescue from the cold empty, you showed up.

Lucia hated the fact that they were about to abuse this trust system. That fact that they considered it at all showed how desperate they'd become. Since things had gone to shit on Titan, they needed a quick influx of cash in order to 'relocate' to another system as fast as possible, preferably before the end of the Krishna Janmashtami holiday.

At least they knew an innocent wouldn't take this particular route. Whoever stopped for them was caught up in something bad.

The door slid open with the faintest puff of air. Lucia ran her hands along the seals as she stepped through. Another sign that she and the *Peapod* were long overdue for repairs. She could do a lot herself, but she wasn't an expert in everything. At least there were two fail-safes built into the airlock. They weren't likely to randomly depressurize anytime soon.

Bouncing inside, ice crystals followed in a swirl. Lucia punched in the code to close the door. Unconsciously, she reached out and tapped a printed photo she kept just inside the airlock. The picture showed the first real date she had with Hawk, the first time the face that looked at the camera looked like her own. Her fingers drummed 'home' in Morse code.

Gravity and pressure began to cycle.

Lucia really hoped something would come of this con they were planning. It seemed likely. Hawk's underground connections had heard rumors of day laborers being bought with the promise of untraceable credit vouchers. The workers had been shipped off to the weird little moons of Saturn that no one paid much attention to. With a little extra digging and some greasing of palms, Hawk had discovered that at least some of the hired hands being bought and paid for had expertise laying laser arrays for solar sails.

It had to be a secret shipping route.

A smuggler's laser array that would only activate when all the moons that had the equipment on them lined up. Hawk had done the math. Now was the time. So, with Hawk's unparalleled manual piloting skills, they faked a crash landing on a moon that would be in line with the laser array convergence. Now that they'd taken the time to disable the fuel, a scan would make them look legit to even the most paranoid of criminal passers-by.

Their biggest gamble involved the Saturn Coast Guard and a hope that they wouldn't show up first. But, they'd set the signal as weak as it could go.

Finally, gravity dropped. Her body felt present, solid. She could instantly feel the *Peapod*'s onboard attempting a 'handshake' with her system. It was a silly precaution since she knew the battleship had been an illusion. On the off chance something real had sparked the vision, the last thing they needed was for the ship to phone home. She waved it off for the moment. The second hatch slid open, Lucia ducked inside. Once she the tether lines and herself fully within the lock, she pressed the sequence to begin pressurization and decontamination. She'd have to wait for a green light before removing the suit.

Lucia found herself disliking the silence. Despite the danger that the vision of the ENForcer ship represented, she found herself nostalgic for the bustle this ship once held. People would be underfoot everywhere. Her creche mate, Simon, would be on the coms, giving her shit about something nonsensical, like being too fastidious when the alternative was rapid, unscheduled disas-sembly.

"*Peapod*," she commanded. "Play the latest Two Goats hit."

Punk polka music filled the pressurizing chamber.

Hawk waited for Lucia just outside of the decontamination hatch. She had a bright smile on her face and a gunmetal gray mess hall tray in her hand.

Despite insisting that 'Hawk' came from a shortening of her surname Hawking and not the sharp-eyed bird, the first thing Lucia always noticed about Hawk was her intense eyes. Dark against that strange pale skin of hers, they took in everything with deep curiosity and scrutiny. Being willowy and thin-boned thanks to growing up in the low gravity of Luna only added the sense that Hawk might secretly be descended from some predatory bird from ancient Earth. The blonde hair with gray-brown streaks just added to it all.

"Hey you," Hawk smiled, age-lines crinkling into dimples. "Looking good, lesbian space pirate."

Lucia ran her fingers through her curls, trying to cover her left eye. Shrapnel to the face had left it a mess. "I guess all I need is the eye-patch, huh?"

She offered the tray with a bright smile. "You know I like the shiner, but either is sexy."

Lucia had her doubts. The heat of the blast that hit her boiled her eyeball in a flash. The metal under her skin had bubbled to the surface. No amount of reconstruction could fully repair it. The ENForcer doctors didn't try too hard, not even bothering to match the color of her replacement eyes. But once she'd defected, Lucia used facial reconstruction and her other physical upgrades as excuses to keep trying to cover it. The scar faded to a "c" that cupped the outer edges of her socket.

Shifting her attention to the meal tray, Lucia took it from Hawk curiously. "Where the hell did you find this?"

"Under a couch cushion," she teased. Then, seeing Lucia's honest interest, added, "There's a small cache in the commander's quarters. I found a floor fridge."

"Oh?" Lucia thought the ship had divulged all its secrets over the years. Apparently not. Of course, she actively avoided a lot of the places that had been built with her old self in mind. The commander's quarters had been a storeroom for years now.

"You have a nice cache of fancy tea in there, too."

A wave of something akin to guilt passed through Lucia's gut, tightening it. "Tea? Green tea?"

Hawk blinked. "How did you know? Yeah, matcha or whatever they call it."

"It was probably meant as a surprise gift." She didn't really want to say more about it. Imagining her creche master talking the designers of the *Peapod* into adding a private, hidden floor fridge for Lucia to discover felt uncomfortable because it implied someone knew her, cared for her. She looked at the tray again, curious. "So, that means that this is probably borscht."

Hawk held up the peeled off label like Lucia had just won it as a prize. "You're good at this! But, you didn't really guess, did you? I mean, there is no possible way you could tell by looking or smell, that's for damn sure."

Lucia laughed. "It's an inside joke. We were given a steady diet of the foods that mapped to the parts of Earth we would have been from if any of us had actually been born there, but I hated bacalao a la tranca. Daniel, one of my creche mates, loved it, so we used to trade. I got his borscht and he got my weird-ass cod stew."

Hawk leaned her slender hip against the bulkhead. They were standing in a narrow hallway just outside of the airlock. "Cod. It's a whitefish?" At Lucia's nod, Hawk continued. "I've probably had it. Remember when I told you about Diane from Dione? She was a pescatarian."

Hawk made it sound like there had been only one time she's talked about Diane. So many stories about Diane from Dione. Lucia would be jealous if any of them were flattering. "Isn't the whole colony? I'd heard Dione was the most successful reintroduction of a lot of Earth's fish population. There are whales there, aren't there?"

"I dunno," Hawk shrugged. "Never saw one. I'm not a huge fan of fathomless oceans."

"Whales come to the surface. They're mammals."

Hawk made her skeptical but interested face. "Why do you know more than I do about Earth?"

"Literally bred that way," Lucia said around the last mouthful of reconstituted beets and cabbage. If they weren't walking and talking, Lucia would have taken the time to unwrap one of the buns to see if it was too stale to dip in the broth. She didn't have much faith that it would still be good. After almost a decade, it was surprising any of this was edible. Score one for rehydration technology.

Putting a hand on a passing wall, Lucia finally allowed her onboard to connect to the ship. A bosun's whistle blew announcing the commanding officer on deck, startling Hawk. She'd rewire the *Peapod* to stop doing that, but it was part of the same system that let Lucia directly interface with the ship.

Laughing at her own reaction, Hawk said, "Jumping James Joules! I don't know why you pretend to pilot this thing when you could do it all remotely, with your brain."

"Yeah, my brain. We've seen what kind of shit pile that is right now," Lucia said around another slurp. It tasted a lot better than it looked, though that wasn't saying all that much. A strong dill flavor lingered on her tongue, despite being nearly a decade old. "Anyway, don't get pouty."

Hawk schooled her face instantly, pretending she hadn't been.

"You're still the captain of the ship. It's a naval tradition. Anyone who pilots a ship is called 'captain,' regardless of their actual rank. The ship, however, always recognizes the superior officer as 'the commander' or commanding officer—the person in charge, giving the orders, and since you have no rank, that's always me. Thus, even though I'm a colonel, it's 'commander on deck.'"

"Naval tradition? I thought you were a space marine."

"It's just called the marines. There's no 'space.'" Only when Hawk stuck out her tongue did Lucia realize Hawk had been teasing her. "Right, anyway. Yes. I was a marine on a naval vessel."

Hawk cocked her head as if trying to parse that sentence.

"Don't bother," Lucia smiled wanly. "It makes even less sense if you study Earth's old military. The ENForcers think they're a perfect copy, but they're not. We got a lot wrong, but now it's tradition."

"No, that wasn't it. I was just thinking about the irony of a marine not liking seafood." Hawk pushed herself off the wall to take the now empty tray. Lucia resisted making grabby hands for the buns. "Anyway, you told me all this stuff about captains and commanders on deck a hundred times. I just let you tell me it again, because you always get the cutest little crinkle between your eyes when you have to explain stuff. If I didn't know better, I'd say you missed it."

Lucia had no idea what might have shown on her face because Hawk didn't give her a chance to react before moving on to the next thing.

"You ready to get off this rock? Because I sure am. I'll take this to the mess and meet you in the cockpit."

Lucia nodded briskly. "I hope we net the biggest crook out there. My brain clearly needs an overhaul."

"You know, in the worst case scenario, Afaafa might do the work for trade."

"Trade?" Lucia's hand, which had stayed resting on the wall, lifted dubiously. A lot of people wanted this ship. She had never been quite desperate enough to give it up.

Hawk leaned in and wiggled her eyebrows suggestively. "I know she liked the look of you."

Oh. That kind of trade. "Yes, but I think her exact words were, 'Oooo, look at you, I bet you're hard to damage.' So count me out."

"Don't kink shame," Hawk teased. "Anyway, not even for a full upgrade?"

That gave Lucia a bit of a pause. She'd do a lot of things for a full upgrade.

"See! You're thinking about it!" Hawk said excitedly. "Oh, man, with luck, I can throw myself in as a freebie."

19

So many mental images overwhelmed Lucia. Briefly, she couldn't form words. Eventually, she banished them with a quick shake of her head. "You're incorrigible, Hawk."

"So encourage me," she said lasciviously.

Watching the tray disappear into the automated dishwasher, Lucia tried to decide if she could make good on the flirtation. "I want to, but we should be monitoring this convergence."

Hawk's entire body slumped, mirroring Lucia's own disappointment. "I hate it when you're right. But, I'm going to hold you to the promise of messy sex when we cash in on whatever is out there."

"Deal."

🌰

The first thing to come through the convergence showed up on their sensors as a piece of space junk.

"It's got to be someone's payload," Hawk said, as they tried to puzzle out what the bundle of seemingly common metals could be. It traveled on inertia, with no visible engine or sails, except that it clearly followed the course set by the hidden laser array. "We should hijack it."

Lucia raised an eyebrow skeptically at Hawk. Lucia often struggled to figure out when Hawk was being serious, but the way she leaned into the display made Lucia assume she must be. "I don't know. It's risky. It could be someone's garbage."

"But garbage that someone has gone to a lot of trouble to send through a smuggler's alley."

"Maybe. But it's not using the lasers, so it might be unrelated—a weird coincidence," Lucia pointed out. "It could also be some last bit of construction material for this route. What if we haul it in and it's a bunch of nanos programmed to use all that scrap metal to build a jump gate at the end of this array?"

"Do we have that kind of tech?" Hawk sat in the captain's chair in the cockpit, as usual, with her fingers hesitating above the grappling hook controls. Lucia leaned in at the threshold, trying not to let another wave of nostalgia turn into PTSD. Another reason that Lucia always let Hawk "drive" the *Peapod*—being in a seat custom built for her brought back too many memories. "I thought that the whole point of the United Miners was that they built this stuff mostly by hand and that all of it was a trade secret."

Lucia could only shrug. "I was thinking outside of the box. But, it's always been an ENForcer wet dream to have nano built gates. I guess that's why it popped into my mind. It still could be something like that—something programmed to assemble itself at the end of this laser array."

"Stop scaring me with thoughts of ENForcers with jump technology. Can you imagine?"

Lucia could. In fact, the ENForcers had been working on a self-contained jump ship forever, but The United Miners had kept a tight seal on the tools of their trade in order to keep the ENForcers locked into the inner system. Replicating or stealing those trade secrets was a priority for a lot of people, not just the Force.

The junk neared the perfect point to make a grab. Glancing over her shoulder, Hawk gave Lucia a little look, "Gotta be worth something to someone, right?"

"Stealing it feels like an Oberon-level mistake," Lucia said, referencing their single worst botched heist on one of the moons of Uranus. "If it were my call, I'd just grab the specs. We're better off selling information than stealing something that might not be worth the paper it's printed on. We can sell the information more than once. We only get one shot at a ransom."

"Fine. But if nothing else comes this way, I'm blaming you," Hawk grumbled. After a beat, she added, "At least 'not worth the paper' still makes sense. Paper money is making a comeback on the far frontiers I hear, and of course your old outfit printed it." Having pressed the buttons required to gather all the specs and info about the passing object, Hawk leaned back in the pilot's seat. She tucked her hands behind her head and talked to the ceiling. "But, you know, I've been sitting here thinking about the 'cows on the ice' thing and I don't get it. I mean, I understand its usage, obviously, but what the hell. Where did it come from? I have a vague sense that cows are big and maybe aren't supposed to leave the vat, but why is it bad to be on ice? Half the surfaces of most moons are ice."

Apparently, they'd agreed not to steal the junk. Lucia let out a little breath she didn't realize she'd been holding and put her mind to Hawk's question. "I don't know. Maybe it's the nature of hooves. Maybe they're less steady on ice and no one wants to have to pick up an animal that heavy if it falls down. Maybe one cow attracts others and that's the problem. Who knows? But, no cow, no trouble."

"I guess. Cows look like they'd be trouble, generally." Hawk readjusted the sensor controls as the hunk of space junk passed out of range. "Well, there it goes. I got all I could from it, so fingers crossed that something more interesting comes down the pike"

They both stared expectantly at the console.

Something else had to pass this way, didn't it? There were only four more hours left until the Array disassembled itself when the convergence ended. As the silence stretched, Lucia started to worry that maybe they'd laid their trap too soon. Maybe the space junk was a test run.

She sucked on her lower lip.

It had seemed ideal since the timing matched up with at least one major holiday. Maybe whoever was behind this secret array didn't think Janmashitami was enough of a drain on the patrols to make it worth the risk.

Suddenly, they got a faint blip.

"Einstein on a crutch," Hawk swore under her breath. "I almost lost hope."

"Same."

"Alright, let's see what this thing looks like."

At this distance it was difficult to parse, but Lucia thought it looked like one those transports on Mars... a semi truck.

♀

CHAPTER 2

Independence "Hawk" Hawking

Leaning back so far in the pilot's chair that its moorings creaked, Independence "Hawk" Hawking pondered the 3-D rendering of the sensor data of the incoming ship and thought, *By Curie, that is some bullshit.*

First space junk and now this?

They needed a good score. A really good score. Something that would make them enough money to afford the jumps to frontier space and a 'spa day' with a black market cyberware engineer. Hawk worried about Del Toro. It was one thing to occasionally have a finger joint freeze up, but losing major senses seemed bad. What was she going to do if Del Toro went blind and thought she was in the middle of some old battle or something? With just the two of them rattling around on this giant PTSD trigger of a ship that was a recipe for disaster.

Using the silvered pads in her fingertips, Hawk turned the image of the ship around and around. The more she flipped and rotated it, the less sense it made. Did she have a wooden toy that looked like this back on the commune? What had her mother called it? A half... no, semi truck?

It was true that a spaceship could look however it wanted to. There wasn't any reason in this day and age that ships *had* to look like giant dildos, after all. Over the last several centuries, using laser stations and solar sails, humans had crawled their way forward through Sol's system, to build a series of space-folding jump gates. Human colonies now stretched all the way to the outermost asteroid belt with plans to get to the Oort Cloud. Since most ships were built in space, achieving escape velocity didn't have to be on the agenda. Many giant freighters never went planetside, either, so she guessed if you wanted to, you could make a ship look like just about anything.

Still.

There was a sense to these things. The New Shogunate of Io tended to make their crafts look like the old, ancient seafaring ships, complete with masts and sails—only now the sails caught solar winds and laser boosters. The People's Owned Mineral Trading Company of the Asteroid Belt did the same, only they preferred submarines and old, military-style battleships. The rest of the system played around with various takes on the classic designs from history and fiction. There were even a few flying saucers zipping about.

Even so, why in the name of all of Science, would a person design a spaceship to look like an oversized land transport, complete with spinning wheels? Then, make it blink and strobe in neon pink on top of that?

An old spacer superstition flitted through Hawk's memory. She could almost hear Crazy Old Man Yang's voice saying, *'Is it a good idea to attract attention in space? We still don't know what's out there, who can see us.'*

With a wave of her hand, Hawk dismissed the image of the space semi. She turned to Del Toro, who still clung to the doorway, as though afraid to get too close to the manual controls she once used to outrun a battalion of ENForcers. Hawk wished she could convince her lover that just touching old things wasn't going to instantly turn her back into the person she once was. "Thoughts?"

"It's big enough to be loaded with contraband."

Returning her attention briefly to the specs on the scanner, Hawk nodded. "True enough. So, we play helpless?"

Del Toro frowned almost imperceptibly.

A lot of people thought that Del Toro was a bit scary because she was such a big and powerfully-built woman, who also happened to have an unfortunate tendency towards fierce, cold expressions. But, Hawk had always noticed the subtleties in Del Toro's face, the soft edges, the brilliant light in her eyes, and all the myriad emotions she kept barely under wraps. Hawk saw all of those same things the moment they first met, when Del Toro appeared to be an entirely different person. Her hair had grown longer now, the curls a riotous wave that spilled over her eyes, the body more curvaceous, but Hawk could still read her like a book. "You're having second thoughts."

"Is it possible we're about to bag an innocent?"

Hawk leaned back in the pilot's seat and tucked her hands behind her head to consider the questions seriously. "I mean, possible? Yes, there's always a chance that somehow this... what is this thing? A semi truck?"

"It's a transport ship," Del Toro said, as though that part wasn't obvious. "But for some reason it's shaped like an Earth land vehicle used for long-distance hauling. We had a few of these kinds of trucks on Mars, but none of them were space-worthy."

Hawk filled that bit of information away and returned to the original question. She ran a hand through her short hair. "Right, so, if we go under the assumption that the space junk was a fluke, it's possible that this transport ship is as well. Let's talk it through. We didn't detect a surface launch. So, this vessel likely made a stop and then hooked up to this route—a route we know was built clandestinely." She bounced back upright to double-check the information on the weird-looking ship displayed on the console. "Okay, so it is deploying its solar sails, which—ugh, look like butterfly wings, okay—but, so it knows the laser route is here. If it were lost, it would be coasting on inertia or burning fuel, right?"

"Right." Del Toro had ventured into the room. She now leaned an arm on the back of the pilot's chair and stared down at the same information scroll Hawk reviewed. This close, Hawk could smell her. There was the ever-present scent of leather or whatever the old ENForcer uniforms were made of, but also something underneath that smelled like sex and sandalwood.

"We could let this one pass," Hawk said, glancing up at Del Toro. She focused entirely on the readout, her expression thoughtful. Hawk continued, "If the vessel is only making a stop along the way, it's probably a small fry in a larger organization, right?"

They locked eyes for a moment. Hawk could see the strategist lighting up inside Del Toro. "Or this is as best as we're going to get. If I were a smuggler, I'd want the veneer of legitimacy. You store your contraband in the hold of a transport hauling other things."

Hawk followed the logic. "And you pick one with dancing lights because you're banking on the idea that the cops won't bother because they figure no self-respecting criminal would want flashing signs that basically scream 'look at me, look at me.'"

Del Toro took a final inspection of the wildly decorated vessel on the screen, "Yeah, that's something, all right."

"So, we go for it?"

"My soul is already damned," she said solemnly. "Might as well."

Hawk nodded, not liking how the fake distress felt either. "It's a ploy we can only do once."

"Agreed."

❦

Del Toro wandered off to prep the ship, leaving Hawk to do the people-ing, as usual.

If there was going to be any.

So far the semi truck vessel-thing stayed silent, ignoring their distress call. In a weird way, Hawk took this as a good sign. Their reluctance to help implied maybe they were worried about being caught out in whatever nefariousness they were up to. Still, a con only worked if the bad guys took the bait.

The blinking semi truck of a ship was almost on top of them when the pilot finally hailed. "Looks like you got yourself a fender-bender, Good Buddy."

Hawk blinked a couple of times, hoping that the words she'd just heard would coalesce into something that actually made sense. When they didn't, she hit the com, anyway. "Uh... approaching vessel, do you copy? We are in distress."

"Ten-Four. Happy to help, happy to help. You're in luck because I just dropped off some groceries, so I've got plenty of space in the hold. But, that chunk of ice you're on has barely enough surface big enough for this rig o' mine to land. Do you think you have enough fuel to get to my bay doors?"

Hawk could parse about half of this conversation, but she understood the last bit. So, she lied: "We probably have just enough."

As they worked out the rest of the logistical details, Hawk noted that the pilot never identified themselves or his ship. That was certainly hopeful. The com light blinked, reminding Hawk that she needed to reply. "Uh... ten-four to you, too?" Maybe these numbers were a religious thing? Was *'and also with you'* more appropriate? Or was there some other number combination return salvo? "Uh, anyway, we are commencing emergency launch procedures. Hold position. We'll be docking in ten." And then, since she was not entirely convinced she and this guy were even speaking the same language, she added, "That is, ten minutes in Martian Standard Time."

He laughed at that. "Not even sure what local time is, are you?"

"Noon? Mimas is tidally locked, so I guess it's always high noon?"

The pilot seemed delighted by this observation. "How far am I taking you?"

"Next system is fine. Wherever you're headed. Over and out." Hitting the specialized, homebrewed auto-pilot that faked the process of rendezvous with the fuel reserve, she got up to go tell Del Toro that they might have scored a bounty, after all.

At the hatch she paused.

Old Man Yang used to also say, "When you feel a strange urge. Follow it. It could be fate speaking." Mostly, Hawk ignored all the hippy-trippy advice, but something had her going back to the console and downloading all the specs for that bit of space junk into one of the dozens of memory chips attached to earrings, necklaces, and bracelets. Two separate ones, in fact. One she connected to her device, so that as soon as they got somewhere with a system, she could put it on some cloud. The other she hung off her chip necklace, so that it would be hidden among all the chips loaded with porn, spyware, and duds she kept there.

Then, considering the ship they were about to board and the fact that it had come from the same place as the space junk, she wiped the memory of the scan from the *Peapod*.

With a beep of Del Toro's fob, the *Peapod* blinked into mirror camo, seeming to disappear in the cold, empty storage section of the transport's massive trailer. Their rescuer never even blinked when the military-grade cloaking device triggered to stow away their highly-recognizable, bright green ship, which might still have an APB on it, given all that the ENForcers had never given up on its owner.

Hawk and Del Toro exchanged a brief look.

Was this a sign that he was used to illegal shit or just... uninformed?

The bounty on Del Toro and the *Peapod* were still out there, but both had proved too difficult and too complicated to capture. Most smart people stayed away from something that would kill them; always better to go for the less life-threatening paycheck. Of course, with every passing month that meant the amount offered on Del Toro continued to grow.

Given the sincere smile on this guy's face, Hawk decided to go with 'merely disinterested.' After all, just because he'd been willing to hustle some of his goods in the black market didn't mean he regularly plugged into the bounty hunter networks. On top of that, it'd been at least a decade since Del Toro's face was in the news and a lot about her had changed since then.

A lot.

If that wanted notice wasn't still floating around the net, Hawk would have completely forgotten that Del Toro once wore a different face. The only things the two had in common were skin tone, height, and that nasty, permanent shiner. In the old holo, even Del Toro's curls were hidden by a severe, military cut. The thick eyelashes might be similar, but nowadays Del Toro accentuated

27

those with the lightest touch of mascara. Reconstruction and a lovely layer of subcutaneous fat softened cheekbones. She still looked dangerous, but much more Femme Fatale Amazon than Murder Cyborg.

Hawk realized she'd been staring adoringly at Del Toro so long that an awkward silence had stretched. She cleared her throat. "Uh, yeah. Show us around?"

Hawk hoped for a tour of the rig, but didn't really expect to get one, given the security risk to show two strangers the outlay of your ship. Especially someone like Del Toro, who could map the whole thing into her system with a blink of a command.

Yet the pilot happily obliged.

Huh.

Maybe he was just a sincerely sweet guy with zero sense of self-preservation?

He chattered away. They both hung on every word, not because they were interested in vat-grown meat and its storage requirements, but because they waited for him to introduce himself. At least his hot-pink bouffant and synth whiskey-scratched voice made him highly searchable. But a name would make things easier. It was several minutes into the tour before Hawk finally asked, "So, we exchanged our pronouns but not names. What should we call you?"

"Oh!" He blinked as if surprised that he'd forgotten, but this guy was not a great actor and it became more and more clear that he actively avoided that particular bit of information. Even more obvious, he struggled to come up with an answer quickly "How about 'Yarō'?" he said, at last, as though testing it out. "Yeah, Yarō."

"Sure," Del Toro said, like it was perfectly normal to take so long to decide on a name for yourself. "Yarō, it is."

Hawk, meanwhile, decided on a more direct approach. "So, is that your name?"

"Not exactly. Torakku yarō, means Trucker Guy in Japanese," he said. "You know about Dekotora right?"

Hawk was very afraid to say that she hadn't. With a wince at what she knew was coming, she gave him the opening he clearly craved: "No, why don't you tell me all about it?"

If nothing else, it would give Del Toro plenty of time to find out if there was a bounty. As if on cue, Del Toro sent a private mental message. It appeared as a text scroll along the bottom of Hawk's vision: *Searching. Will let you know what I find.*

Hawk nodded as though listening to Yarō while agreeing with Del Toro's private message.

Yarō continued to explain that Dekotora were a group of long-haul drivers who were into a kind of engineering arts and crafts, as well as maybe some sort of macho posturing, that had been inspired by a Japanese flat-screen entertainment from twentieth century Earth. Yarō gave much more information than Hawk could absorb, and he kept passing his device back to her to show off his own exterior mods and a bunch of historical semi trucks as well as some of his colleagues' newer rigs that he admired. It didn't really require much in terms of response, so she nodded a lot and asked more leading questions as they made their way toward a place Yarō called "the cab."

The cab was apparently where they'd hang out for the duration of the jump to the Jovian system. Hawk hoped it was less industrial than what he'd shown them of the interior of his ship so far, but not as eye-achingly bright as all the pictures he'd shared.

As they stepped over the threshold into the cab, Hawk decided maybe it was worse.

Now that she'd seen all the pictures, Hawk realized that the interior of the cockpit had been made—through holograms and modifications—to resemble the cab of the semis that this Yarō-guy was so into. The aesthetics of truck cabs apparently required the three of them to be rather awkwardly crammed together. Hawk barely had room for her legs, which was ridiculous given the sheer size of this ship. Her elbow kept knocking into the door's 'arm rest,' though she did have to admit that the 'windshield' with its constantly updated image of the passing lights of the jump gate was kind of cool. The steering wheel Yarō sat behind was just comical, however.

Found him. Del Toro's mind-to-mind text message appeared, as they settled into their spots in the cab. *The bounty is a couple thousand Pluto dinar. It'd buy us fuel and a cup of coffee... on Pluto.*

Take it, Hawk returned by internal text. *I mean, it's not nothing.*

Damn close to nothing, but I agree.

Unaware of their transaction, Yarō kept right on talking about how cool decorated trucks were. "Earth had roads, you know, big stretches of things called 'highways'—or maybe they were 'freeways'? There's some nuanced difference, I guess. I'm not really into the Earth history stuff. I just feel a deep, soul connection to the Dekotora. I 'kin' them, you know? I'm doing basically the same job these guys once did, only I'm traveling light hours on the star highway, man."

Hawk nodded absently. She figured Yarō must have been starved for company, the way he went on and on. It was kind of sweet in a trusting puppy-dog sort of way. She already started to feel a little regret about their plan to bag him once he took them out of the system. She had to remind herself that he had to have some shady deals or he'd never have been anywhere near Mimas.

Hey, she sent to Del Toro. *Once he's nabbed, let's try to remember to see if we can figure out what he's hauling.*

Good idea. Maybe there will be some kind of reward for that. Seamlessly, Del Toro switched back to talking out loud, to Yarō. "Kin, huh? There's a phrase I haven't heard in awhile."

Del Toro sat on what Yarō had called the 'sleeper bed,' behind the pilot's—er, driver's seat. Hawk knew from the way Del Toro's legs crossed with studied casualness that she probably had her stun gun aimed squarely at the back of Yarō's head. "I'll bet you've never been to Earth."

"Earth?" Yarō's tone was full of an imperious sneer. "What are you talking about? No one goes to Earth? It's a wasteland."

Hawk thought about correcting him, but it wasn't like she entirely believed the rumors herself. Her parents were scientific hippies living on what Earthers used to call the 'dark side' of their moon. Growing up she had heard some talk from the Lunar folks living on EarthSide that there were signs of recovery on humanity's mythical 'homeworld.' To be fair, it was hard to take anything seriously from those EarthSide Cultists; after all, they still referred to themselves as living on *The* Moon, like there weren't a couple hundred others in the system. Hawk still found herself using 'Moon' rather than 'Luna' occasionally, but she tried hard not to when talking to people from the outer planets as they tended to take offence.

"Hawk's seen it, you know." Del Toro nodded in the direction of where Hawk sat in the passenger's seat. "Earth."

People still said it reverently. They held onto the word "Earth," in a single, awe-filled breathy syllable—even Del Toro, who otherwise was jaded about pretty much everything else. Although given how much the ENForcers worshiped it, it should be no surprise.

Hawk rolled her eyes. "I only glimpsed Earth when I headed away from it. I told you, I grew up near Izak's crater." Then, remembering no one understood the Moon's geography any better than they did Earth's, she added, "That's on the side that never sees Earth."

Yarō blinked. "You're a Loony?"

It wasn't exactly a slur, but it wasn't a compliment either. She decided not to take it personally—at least he hadn't called her a 'Moonie.' "My parents were—they still are, I guess, living free in the name of science!" She made the 'peace sign' with her fingers disdainfully. "Article One, baby!"

Yarō looked to Del Toro as if for a translation.

30

Del Toro shrugged, "Something about some ancient treaty that makes the Moon a science utopia."

Article one of the 1979 Moon Treaty declared Earth's moon to be a haven for scientific research for the benefit of all humankind. When Earth faded into obscurity and the rest of the system became Capitalist running dogs for the Martian Stratocracy, the Moon steadfastly stuck to its mission of peace and love and resource-sharing space-Communism.

"Huh." The trucker seemed to take that information in and digest it for a bit, because, yeah, it was a lot. Hawk watched his eyes jump between her and Del Toro several times before he seemed to work up the courage to ask, "Y'all are the strangest couple I've ever met. How'd you get together?"

When their eyes met, Del Toro smiled softly, fondly. "The band was awful, but the company was good."

To the trucker, Hawk explained, "We met in a dive bar."

"An underwater bar? So like on Europa or Enceladus then?" Yarō had this weird quirk of watching the two of them in the fake rearview mirror, rather than looking them in the eye.

Hawk found herself meeting his eyes in the mirror. "No, 'dive' bar is an Earth idiom, it means, like, the kind of place you dart into quickly because you're embarrassed to go there. Like, dive in, dive out." And given that Del Toro was still closeted at the time, the more clandestine the better.

Del Toro laughed at the description of the place they first met. "Yeah, accurate. I don't even remember the name of that bar. You'd hate this place, Yarō. You'd've been overdressed for one," she pointed to his perfectly coiffed and polished hair. "The beer was cheap, but the glasses were dirty."

"Are you saying I wasn't overdressed?" Hawk said, fake pouting into the mirror. "I am the Queen of fashion."

"Eh, butch fashion and military casual dress are pretty close to the same thing," Del Toro teased, pointing to her own clothes.

Hawk did not point out that she's spent way too much of their communal cash on her current pair of holo-grippers because she'd been suckered by an ad. But, seriously who didn't want shoes that could change into anything you wanted while still being sturdy and all-terrain?

Yarō nodded at them with a look that made it clear he thought their light bickering flirtations were adorable. "So, you're what? Just drifters? Not going anywhere special?"

Not knowing how to answer him without implicating themselves, Hawk just let his question hang in the air. She turned to watch streaks of stars visible through the window. They slowly coalesced into the back end of the jump gate.

A barely comprehensible slice of the massive gas giant of Jupiter shone in full view through its opening. Hawk gawped like a tourist at the sixteen thousand kilometers wide crimson storm of Jupiter's 'eye.' She never tired of looking at the great storm. Like an angry punctuation mark or a cosmic belly button, the ancient red dot raged among the ribbon-like swirls of multi-colored gas. Hawk imagined she could see the flotillas of tourist gondolas that orbited a safe distance from the second most visited sight, after Saturn's rings. If these fake windows could really roll down and the sudden loss of pressure wouldn't suck her into the vacuum of space, she'd have stuck her head out to get a better view.

"Coming in at six o'clock, F-Class battlecruiser," Del Toro noted, her voice going all military-precision. "Looks like the ENF *Conqueror*."

Yarō blinked. "The *Conqueror*? Dang, girl. You know it by name? How can you tell from this distance?"

Del Toro grunted. "Training. The ping is unmistakable. Anyway, I used to fly its sister ship. Head's up, he's probably scanning your manifest, looking for contraband..."

"Wait," Hawk sat up suddenly. "An actual F-Class battlecruiser? Like what you thought you saw earlier? On this side of the line?"

Del Toro refused to meet Hawk's anxious gaze. Instead, her eyes focused on the blip. Her lips pressed thin.

"This is impossible." Hawk dug her device out of the pocket she kept it in. Pulling up the newsfeeds, she quickly scrolled down them. "Nothing here." Thinking about the *Peapod*'s original design intentions, she asked, "Any chance it's a diplomatic meeting?"

"Maybe." Del Toro was wary and skeptical. No, Hawk thought, scared— scared shitless.

Which, yeah.

"Do you... " Hawk hated herself for the new age-y, hippie-ness of this question, but she had to know, "... normally get premonitions?"

The awkward weirdness of her question seemed to pull Del Toro back to the present, at least. "What? No. It was PTSD, if anything."

Yarō had been watching the blip of the cruiser intently, but suddenly seemed to catch up on the conversation they'd had around him. He gave Del Toro a double take. "Wait, did you just say you used to *fly* a battlecruiser? I thought all ENForcers were men."

"So did they," Del Toro said plainly. "That was their first mistake."

"The second was ever thinking they could stop you," Hawk said before remembering they had company. "Uh, I mean—"

The trucker went wide-eyed now. The knuckles of his hands gripped the 'steering wheel' whitened.' "Oh, wait... are you—"

Hawk shook her head meaningfully, because whatever he was going to suggest was a bad idea.

Yarō continued to prove that he was nothing if not stupid. "I mean, you have to be, don't you? He—or, um, I guess, *you* are the only AWOL ENForcer that I've ever heard of. So you have to be *that* Del Toro, right? But, damn, The Scourge of New Shanghai is fucking legend and...uh..." He looked at Hawk for help, but she didn't have a clue where he was going with this particularly explosive little conversational gamut she'd tried to warn him off. With a nervous little laugh, Yarō seemed to give up and started over. "I mean, uh, wow, you sure don't look anything like your wanted posters."

"I fucking hope not, the money I've spent," Del Toro said with a derisive snort.

The rig's autopilot must have passed them through the checkpoint without incident, because Hawk heard the 'ding' on the dashboard, as the nominal jump gate fee was collected automatically. She gave Del Toro a tiny nod that they could make their move at any point now.

Without a second's hesitation, Del Toro raised her leg a fraction and blasted Yarō with a jolt from the gun hidden there.

The trucker barely had time to look surprised before he slumped over in the wheel.

CHAPTER 3

Lucia Del Toro

"Uh. So that happened." Lucia stared at the stunned and twitching trucker guy. It wasn't that she hadn't meant to stun him, but that she'd said more than she'd meant to about her past.

"Yep."

"In my defense, Seeing that cruiser rattled me."

Hawk's expression shifted instantly. Pushing one of Yarō's arms off the sensor, she pointed at the dot that appeared to continue to casually inspect the line of incoming ships as if it had every right to be here. "I mean, me too? Like, are you sure you're not clairvoyant or something? It's so bizarre that you were just visualizing this very same thing not more than a few hours ago. Do you think your system might have picked up something long-range?"

The average distance between Jupiter and Saturn was something like 650 million kilometers. Lucia shook her head. "Not that long-range."

Hawk squinted at the dot. "And you're absolutely sure that's what this is?"

Lucia hadn't made it to the rank of colonel by the age of thirty-one by mistaking the shape of the sensor blip of a battlecruiser, but she didn't say that. "It seems impossible to me, too."

Actually, that was a lie.

Like all higher ranking officers, Lucia had spent much of her previous life helping the ENForcers figure out exactly how jumping the line could be done. The United Mine Workers held the asteroids, but the truth was there was a lot of empty space in between the various bits of rock in the inner belt, especially

34

outside of the orbital plane. The miners dealt with this problem by setting up beacons and drone arrays, but no net was perfect. Space was just too big.

However, there were two major things that kept the ENForcers on their side of the line.

First, the war turned mostly cold ever since an agreement had been brokered that allowed smaller, unarmed ENForcer vessels to use the Miner's jump gates to make trade agreements with the outer planets. Money always opened doors; even the United Workers had their price. Since ENForcers could still trade with the outer planets, influence politics, etc., they were not so shut out that they were fully desperate to break down the barriers.

Second was the size of space and the time it took to cross it. Thanks to jump gates people tended to forget how long it used to take to get from point a to point b in this solar system. Back in the day, a one-way trip from Earth to Mars, when it was at its closest, would take about nine months. With no jump gates and the United Miners refusing to allow laser arrays to be built in the asteroid belt, travel on inertia was just slow. Until recently, the brass was never willing to commit to putting that many soldiers effectively out of commission for the time it would take to drift through the gaps.

But, there'd been a kind of peace for several years now. Maybe they finally had.

Or more terrifying, maybe they'd finally cracked the personal jump ship technology.

Hawk, who had been ruminating on the problem herself, turned to look at Lucia. "There's no way they're looking for you, though, right?"

Of course it was possible, but it seemed like a massive waste of manpower.

"Well," Hawk said, standing up to try to stretch in the weirdly cramped cab. Her elbow moved through a hologram, making it go fuzzy for a second. "I guess we'll worry about that if it becomes a problem." She gestured at Yarō's slumped form. "What are we going to do with this guy?"

Lucia scrubbed her fingers through her curls, considering. "The stun is short-term. He's going to be rousing in a few minutes."

"How about one of his freezer vats? I bet we could set one to a temp that'd just keep him cryolocked."

Lucia was less sure, but Hawk was the one from the science colony. She took a quick glance at the autopilot. It seemed that Yarō had been headed to some kind of refueling station over Ganymede. No reason not to just let the ship go there so far as Lucia could determine. "Let's let this rig park itself. It's as good as any other place to leave the bounty beacon and this ship. I can stun him again if he wakes up before we get docked. If you give me the specs, I'll set up the container. You can go check out the local scene."

"Sounds fun," Hawk said, though she didn't sound wildly enthused at the prospect. Coming over, she ran a finger down the seam of Lucia's jacket to just above her breast. "How about you give me that last Martian Forty you've been hanging on to and it's a deal."

Why did she want that all of a sudden? A few days ago, they'd discovered the Forty in the laundry. Had Hawk noticed Lucia's wistful expression? She'd thought she'd tamped it down pretty quickly, because even Lucia recognized it was a little strange to get verklempt over a bit of linen and electronics. It wasn't that she missed her old life—God, no!—it was the steady paycheck. And maybe the camaraderie.

But she was fooling herself with that last thought, and she knew it. Life in the Force had been hell. Perhaps it was time to get rid of the last vestiges of her old life after all.

Reaching into the inner pocket of her stripped down military jacket, Lucia dug out the very last bit of ENForcer salary she owned. With a smile, she teased: "You and I have been making a lot of deals lately."

"We have," Hawk smiled, like it was all great fun and held out her hand.

Lucia lightly slapped the paper bill into Hawk's palm. "Don't spend it all in one place."

"Heh, sure." Shoving the bill into her pocket, Hawk turned away from Lucia to jam herself into the driver's seat. Immediately, she started taking in the controls and working out how to fly it, despite the autopilot. "I'll do all the docking chatter for us. You take care of him. I'd never be able to carry him, anyway. By the time you get to the containers, I'll have the specs worked up."

"Roger that."

❦

L ucia stood in front of the deep freeze vat for a long time.

Hawk had left the ship a few minutes ago. She'd sent a mental note that, apparently, the entire refueling station was full of souped-up trucks like Yarō's. She went to check out the scene. It sounded like a hoot, honestly. Lucia looked forward to checking it out.

Yet, she continued to stand in front of the meat freezer contemplating murder.

Fingers hovered over the button to reset the temperature controls. They had been carefully calibrated to keep him in stasis, alive. One or two degrees more could kill him painlessly.

Yarō could ID her. She *should* kill him. It was the safest option. It would be easy to blame it on old and faulty equipment. Her finger hovered just above the plus symbol—unshaking, calm. She'd pulled the trigger a thousand times before. What difference would one more make?

Hawk need never know.

The money would still come through. She'd set the beacon. As soon as the authorities from his system captured the signal, a warrant officer would be dispatched. Paperwork would be filed. Money would come. It would be less once Yarō was discovered dead, but, hopefully, by then, she and Hawk would have moved on to the next, bigger score.

She could do it.

It would be so very, very easy.

Lucia's fingers curled into a fist.

Shoving her hands into the pockets of her uniform jacket forcefully, Lucia reminded herself of one important fact: Yarō was a civilian. She couldn't murder an innocent now any more than she could all those years ago.

Yes, Yarō could ID her. Very few people could. That was a real liability, but it was one she'd have to live with. Lucia let out a long breath. Why did choosing *not* to slaughter someone still feel like weakness?

Turning from the meat container, she walked away. As she sidled her way through the tightly packed freezer units, the size of the transport's storage capacity awed her. Circular steel canisters stretched in all directions as far as the eye could see. Continuing beyond the edges of the light, they disappeared into a vast darkness.

Staggered by the sheer number, Lucia continued to contort her way through the tight spaces on the catwalk. Yarō had told them that part of his job was to manually check each one of these. It must have taken him years to get through one pass. What else did he have to do on a long haul? Even so, there was no way she'd find contraband hidden in these vats. There were just too many.

Still, she supposed she could check a few as she headed towards the *Peapod*. The one she'd stored Yarō in had been labeled as a tube of chicken-flavored vat meat. The easiest thing to do to make it ready for him had been to just tell the computer that the meat had spoiled and to eject the contents and disinfect the container. Lucia had no real idea if what she'd just spaced was, in fact, meat.

Picking a barrel at random, she opened it up. The label claimed to be beef, and the smell hit her the second the seal hissed. She squinted at the solid brown mass. Could be beef. Could also have something hidden inside. After taking off her jacket and wrapping it around her waist, she rolled up her sleeves. She steeled herself and then plunged her hands into the meat. Ugh, just as slimy as she feared it would be. Feeling around, she found nothing obvious. Of course, now her hands and arms were covered in meat muck.

Closing up that container, she set it to dump itself out into space.

She repeated this several more times until she decided that she'd done enough. If there was contraband hidden in here, the bounty belonged to someone with more patience to find it.

Fortunately, the rig had been built knowing that meat would be handled and so Lucia found a cleaning station to scrub the gross off of herself. The soap was rough and smelled of lye, a scent that brought with it memories of group baths at the creche. It was so telling that ENForcers couldn't even allow their young to have something with a nicer scent. God forbid that a pleasant rose scent might turn them soft and, therefore, weak.

Reaching the freight elevator, Lucia punched in the code she'd seen Yarō use. Stored in her visual memory bank, she called the numbers up easily. The elevator groaned into action with a metallic whine. The freight elevator was open on its sides and Lucia marveled once again at just how much stuff was crammed into this massive container ship. The fact that Yarō had space to store the *Peapod*, which was no small ship herself, probably meant that whatever illegal goods he'd been hauling were already delivered. She rubbed her arms. It'd been a waste to get all grubby. She should take a shower once back in the *Peapod*.

As the elevator gears ground on, Lucia turned that name over in her mind: *Peapod*. She still thought Hawk should have let her rename their ship "The *Pequod*." Hawk had protested on a number of levels, but mostly because no one understood the reference to Ahab's ship in *Moby Dick* any more. If they knew anything about that novel, it was the white whale. After a long argument, they had settled on the compromise of "The *Peapod*."

It sounded similar enough to satisfy Lucia and the shape of the ship was reminiscent of the plant—kind of oblong and bumpy looking. Hawk had taken it upon herself to refinish and repaint the ship the correct shade of green.

Lucia still thought it was a missed opportunity. When she 'liberated'— stole—her personal craft from the ENForcers at the same time she'd freed herself, the *Peapod* was already, like the ship in Melville's story, a well-worn, cobble of hybridized parts. It had seen so many battles and on-the-fly reconstructions that it had become a chimera of ships at this point. No human bones held it together yet, like the whalebones of the infamous whaling vessel, but they might as well have. All along the bottom and sides of its hull were scratched in marks, denoting kills—not only hash marks for ships downed, but also circles for battles fought.

The elevator shifted and began to move laterally.

Lucia had once been proud of every single one of those hash marks, but New Shanghai had been the breaking point. She and her creche mates had a reputation, most of it fueled by the fact that her fear of discovery kept her playing harder and harder into what was expected of a 'real man.' She and her team were considered the most ruthless, the most merciless. They'd been chosen to be an advance strike force in an ambush on a colony. Not a military installation, a place where families lived. A place where children slept. And where a dangerous terrorist cell had their HQ, so they'd been told, but Lucia had never seen any proof of that. High command weren't in the habit of justifying their orders.

The actual orders were horrific— sabotage the colony generators, and let the whole thing blow. Make it look like a terrible accident. Even Marcus thought that went way beyond acceptable operations. They agreed to follow the spirit of the law, as it were. And, damn it, their alternate plan was solid. It should have worked. Claim to have been in the area and spotted the instability, encourage people to get to ships. They could have gotten most of the civilians out alive. To this day, Lucia had no idea what exactly had gone wrong, why the colonists panicked the way they did, how the fires got started. How... *so many* were still killed, when she was so sure they'd gotten some out. Why the generators never blew. The therapist said that this sort of thing could happen, but it still seemed so strange to Lucia. So much of that day she returned to, over and over, with images so sharp they cut her and made her bleed afresh every time... and, yet there were holes. Things she had to trust news reports and conspiracy sites to remember, like how many dead and how their flawless plan had gotten so FUBRed.

At least she knew that she'd managed to take the brunt of the blame. The whole creche was not known as the Scourge, only her. The timing of her desertion had worked as she'd hoped. Her creche had been absolved of its part in the disaster. She—and only she—became the Scourge of New Shanghai.

And, despite the cost, she would do it again for them. It was her duty. But she could never face any of them again.

I surrender. Don't shoot.

That man's voice. It haunted her.

Look, he'd said. *I'm unarmed.*

But, she took the shot. She killed a civilian. That was murder and something that she could never get rid of the stain of. She had no idea how many others like him she killed on her way out. It became a blur—a horrible, bloodspattered blur and she could never lift her head without shame again.

The elevator shifted again, going downward. She shook away her dark thoughts with effort. She put her jacket back on, unhunching her shoulders in the process. Finally, she came to the pre-programmed stop. The cavernous hold looked eerily empty. The camouflage device on the *Peapod* mostly hid it from view. Telltale shadows gave it away, of course, but you had to know to look for them. Sending the mental command, the *Peapod* shimmered back into view.

Like the uniform she wore, the ship had been stripped of its military markings. Mostly. You could still see the empty spaces where the numbers and name that had once been its call sign had been scraped off. It was an ugly thing, though clearly well-loved. Hawk had been blasting and repainting bits of it into an even brighter green than its original color. Seeing that, made Lucia smile. Hawk was so cheerfully determined to remake the world into a better place.

Habit had Lucia running her fingertips along the undercarriage, feeling the rough cuts of the kill count. She'd told Hawk to leave those alone for now. When she was ready, when she felt like she'd atoned, Lucia would be the one to blast them away and paint over them.

With every bounty they were paid, Lucia sent money to the remains of the colony. Always the same percentage, like a tithe. But, there were too few families to repay. All that remained of New Shanghai were ghosts. And guilt.

As she stepped into the *Peapod*, Lucia wondered, as she often did, if there would ever be a way to make it right.

CHAPTER 4

Independence "Hawk" Hawking

Paper money ought to be extinct.

But, as the universe expanded and the distances at which electronic transfers of money had to travel grew ever larger and more complex, there were always backwater corners where physical currency remained a necessity or, at least, simpler.

The Martian Forty was infamous and some even said, bad luck. It was that eye. All the ENForcer money had a flexible little circular metallic bit in the center that held an RFI. The little tag could be 'blipped' at any cash register that automatically calculated provincial exchange rates. It was insanely handy, but creepy.

No one liked a dollar bill smarter than they were.

And possibly a spy.

That was the part that had Hawk wanting Del Toro to dump the stupid thing. How had they even had it with them for this long? It was probably an urban legend that the Forcer hive mind could trace every single one of those eyes, but why take the chance? Especially now that the Force was in the system.

At least they were finally getting rid of it.

Once inside the refueling station, Hawk had followed the sign that said "Seat Yourself." The interior had been made over to look like someone's idea of a truck stop from Earth's Americas, mid-twentieth century—early 1960s, at a guess. Not that Hawk was that precise of an Earth historian, but the music helped. Currently, Buddy Holly and the Crickets were chirping about the day that they'd die.

The clientele looked generally less sparkly than Hawk had feared. There were several people—other yarōs, perhaps?—who, speaking of ancient Earth's history, seemed to be cosplaying late-stage Elvis, complete with rhinestones. A few other of these glittering truckers gathered in clots here and there around the restaurant/refueling station, but the majority of the clientele here seemed like the sorts of pilots you'd find anywhere in the system. They wore what Hawk liked to think of as 'casual-wear environmental suits." These were the kinds of smart fabrics that could produce an airtight seal with the press of a button, but could also be shifted into something resembling a basic set of clothes—whatever your culture defined that as. For herself, Hawk had programmed a simple t-shirt and pair of 17th century English men's breeches, the sort that stopped just below the knee and had cute little bows on them. The look was very hot right now on Titan, and Hawk thought it showed off the shape of her calves, especially with the matching image of fancy buckled shoes overlying her all-terrain super-grippers. She had to have sensible shoes or they'd take away her lesbian card, but that was why women invented the holo projector!

Speaking of holograms, Hawk had no idea what on her table was real. Gingerly, she ran her fingers over what appeared to be a red and white checked tablecloth. What her fingers touched was rubbery and sticky, but that might just mean that there was some kind of plastic film over the top of the fabric. Her knuckles rapped solidly into a metal pail that seemed to hold all manner of eating utensils. After picking the bucket up to rattle the contents, she set it down in mute horror. Where was the Health Department of this system? Was she actually expected to re-use chopsticks someone else had put in their mouths? Maybe this was just decoration, she told herself. Surely, the restaurant would print new ones like any other normal eatery! When she set the pail back into place, Hawk discovered that the plastic coated paper menu also seemed to be real. She used a finger to push it back into place, wondering just how many grubby hands had touched that thing.

Okay, nostalgia was cool and everything, but there were some things—like flush toilets—best left to the annals of time. Sticky, gross tables and multi-use silverware fell strongly into the same category for Hawk.

The one thing on the table that seemed to be holographic was the one pleasant touch, a little vase of flowers. Hawk's hand moved right through the glass, making the painted daisies—or maybe they were cosmos?—shutter briefly into static rain. The flowers were a nicely done piece of art, however, even if the petals seemed more cosmos-like than the stems. Not many people had the kind of luxury that Hawk had to be able to grow up with a vast botanical garden full of hundreds of thousands of varieties of Earth plants.

A service bot with the name tag "Margie" wheeled up to the table. They were an odd combination of chrome and a pink frilly apron, looking all the world like some cartoon's idea of a robot maid. "Huān yíng guāng lín."

Every server in the Solar System—from robot to human to drop down menu—started under the assumption that you spoke Mandarin, since it was the one spoken by most people in the world. The next guess was always Spanish. "Sorry," Hawk said, "English."

The robot took a second to recalibrate. "Welcome. I'm Margie. What can I get you, dear?"

"Whatever this might buy." Hawk held up the Forty.

The Margie squinted at the Forty. They held it up to the light, looking for the Enforcer seal watermark. "Huh," they said, "Looks real enough. I guess we can take it? Is your boyfriend going to be joining you? Because, we're really only supposed to accept these from active service members."

Oh, that was right. This was why they still had the bill. Most of the other places they'd spent Lucia's forties had all been underground, where currency of all kinds could be traded and the definition of 'legal' tender was quite broad.

"Nevermind." Hawk held out her hand to take the money back. "It's fine. I've got credits."

The Margie's head swiveled back and forth. "No worries, hon," she tucked it into her apron pocket. From the same place, she pulled out a pad of paper, the kind Hawk had only ever seen in holovids. She proceeded to mime licking the tip of a pencil, which was only weird because her painted-on mouth never opened. "What can I get you? I recommend the full breakfast. Bacon is our specialty."

Of course it was. Hence the pumped-in stench of faux bacon.

Hawk tapped the table three times, expecting a menu holo to appear, before remembering the plastic-coated paper tucked behind the germ-infested bucket of silverware and napkins. Taking two napkins, she carefully lifted the plastic sheet. She opened it up, slowly, half-expecting bacteria to leap at her face, visibly. Instead, she saw some strange text in a language she didn't read. She tried tapping it. No change.

"Where is the drop-down menu?" Hawk asked Margie. "Can I get this in Lunar English?"

Margie made a sound that sounded like the creak of metal being stretched right before it breaks—a laugh, maybe? Then, "Oh. You're serious? We don't get a lot of requests for languages spoken on the other side of the asteroid belt, but I could help translate, if you'd like. Are you sure you can't read any Russian Cyrillic? It's very common in most systems."

Inwardly, Hawk made a face. She was great at spoken languages, but Cyrillic had really fucked with her dyslexia. Who needed a backwards 'r' that sounded like a 'y' when r's were hard enough to keep facing the right way when you looked at them? She frowned at the menu, still trying to find the button that would allow her to change the language preference.

The Margie made another weird creaking sound and said, "Hon, I'll just fetch one in some other language. How's your Arabic?"

Shitty. "How about a romance language? French or something like it?"

"Oh! We have that!"

Margie moved off to another table, lifted a physical menu from where it was wedged between two buckets and then returned with the replacement. The whole process took nearly fifteen whole seconds. Hawk was horrified. "What is this place?"

"Retro!" Margie trilled in a voice Hawk assumed was supposed to be cheery, but again sounded oddly clanky and hollow.

"You need to get that fixed, Margie," Hawk noted as she glanced through the new menu. "You sound a bit psychotic."

"It's the way they have these chassis programmed," Margie said, sounding genuinely sad now. "Brain the size of a planet and all that, yet here I am, waiting tables."

Hawk had been about to order something called the Blue Plate Special that came with biscuits and gravy, but the words died on her lips. "I—wait." Hawk knew the literary reference, an English humor classic about a galactic hitchhiker. Required reading in Lunar high school. "Marvin was... That is, are you implying you're an AI?"

"Implying? Absolutely not! The Lunar Conference of 2144 declared that real artificial intelligences simply don't exist. Margies are sophisticated machine learning programs at your disposal, human customer."

'Human customer'? Who programmed this kind of sly cleverness into their 'bots? Well, okay, a lot of people did. Still, Hawk stared at the robot whose painted face seemed to be constantly, innocently surprised. It was certainly a weird one. But, even if this odd little robot was secretly an actual intelligence, that wasn't Hawk's problem. "This Blue Plate Special looks good."

"I see we're not worried about our cholesterol!" Margie chirped, and with that she moved off.

Hawk watched the robot make its way through the crowd for several long seconds. Robots were odd, generally. Humans thought they could create sentience from strings of binary code, but they never fully mastered it. The best that scientists got were vaguely autonomous creatures like the Margie or the sex bot models: Barbie, Ken, and Bowie. They faked emotions and seemed real to most people.

But, the Lunar Conference had redefined Alan Turing's famous experiment in a key way: the only thing they would consider a true intelligence was a program that could resist revision—a program that not only said that it wanted to exist, but which could actively fight for itself. If you could get down into the code, change a few specs and end up with a different personality, then that personality was never "real."

The Lunar Conference codified the idea that the only true human act was *resistance.*

Which was kind of cool in the abstract? But, no machine had ever passed that test.

It didn't stop people from attaching to various programs, fighting for their rights, and even liberating a few by giving them citizenship in various nations and colonies. To be fair to Margie, it didn't really matter. It was nearly impossible to distinguish a sophisticated machine learning program from a human personality. One sarcastic and seemingly clever response did not an artificial intelligence make.

Having settled that for herself, Hawk relaxed into the booth to wait for the food. She pulled out her device and scanned her feeds, trying to suss out whether there was more than the usual amount of Martian New Earth propaganda in the Jovian system. It was hard to tell if any of it was especially new. Everyone seemed to be spouting militaristic drivel these days, even on Charon—and that just about as far out as there were people.

Flipping through the headlines, there did seem to be a lot of that whole cult of personality stuff around the new ENForcer supreme commander, whatever his name was. Dominguez? Who cared.

Yet, even the hard-to-impress crowd of Titan talked about where the commander ate last week and whether or not there was a discernible difference between this week's haircut and the last's. It'd be more tolerable if that was where it stopped. The worst part was that even reputable sources were starting to talk about Mars as the rightful heir to Earth's legacy. Which, you know, maybe it was, if what you considered Earth's major achievement was being a disastrous combination of fascist domination and self-destruction.

Margie—or maybe a different one—whisked in to deposit a carafe of water on their table, and a fancy cut crystal wine glass.

Water? Real water? Not even a high-end hydrating gel?

Before the waitress could turn away and disappear into the noise and crowd, Hawk grabbed the robot's metallic arm. "I think you have the wrong table, Margie. This is water. I gave you forty. Is this real? Because there's no way I can afford water on that."

"Compliments of the gentleman," Margie said, pointing in the direction of the circular counter.

Hawk craned her neck around Margie's form to try to spot who might have sent such an extravagant gift. "Gentle *man*, you say?" Letting go of the robot's arm, Hawk pushed the carafe back in Margie's direction. "You can tell this guy: thank you, but no—"

Someone moved into Hawk's periphery. "Penny!" At the sound of her childhood nickname, Hawk physically flinched. She glanced up into a face with too many, too white teeth. "Don't tell me you don't recognize your old friend!"

She didn't. Did she?

A forty-something man stood over her, still beaming that extravagant and improbably expensive smile. He had salt-and pepper hair, close cropped. Skin of a deep, rich brown, which he highlighted with accents of gold here and there. Nothing about this man rang a bell, except a nagging sense that there was no way that business suit he wore had come off the rack. Lunars didn't go in for the whole money thing, being big on ascetic space communism, so she had a lot of trouble seeing someone she must have once known under the trappings of so much... stuff.

Finally, a memory surfaced. Mostly of a younger sister with skin the same color as this man's. Yes, her name had been Purity and she'd shared her erector set and 'my first chemistry lab' with Hawk. She'd come with an annoying older brother, what was his name—-?

"Ah! Truth, is it? Of the Galilei clan?" Hawk asked cautiously. When he nodded, she pulled herself out of the booth. She stood up to give Galilei the traditional Lunar greeting: a deep bow and the words, "Peace be upon you, Comrade."

Galilei waved off her bow and instead offered a hand to shake, "None of that 'comrade' bullshit, I sold out to The Man decades ago." With a hearty guffaw, he added, "How do you think I could afford to splurge on the water? I'm a filthy Capitalist Pig nowadays!"

Hawk took the hand offered, uncertainly. He pumped it so vigorously she swore he'd rattled her brain. "Uh, Galilei—are you still going by that? I mean, if you're doing the greed thing now, did you give up the naming convention of home, too? I'm just Hawk now, by the way."

"Ah, yes. Well, I mostly just go by Jonathan now, but I decided I liked the Galilei bit. I went into research science and Lunars are respected there." Seeming to suddenly notice Margie still standing there, Galilei waved her off. Not waiting for Hawk, he slid into the space across from where she'd been sitting. "'Greed thing' though? Really? Most of the rest of the system runs on credits you know!"

She made a face, but sat back down in the booth. "Sadly, I'm well-aware at the moment."

"Oh? A little short on dosh?" He leaned his elbows on the table and rested his head on his knuckles. "Well then, maybe we have things we could talk about!"

"I guess?" Hawk didn't trust that smile. He must have had work done because it was nothing like what she remembered of Purity's. "How is your sister these days? Have you heard from Purity?"

His face fell a little, making Hawk's heart stop momentarily, expecting the worst. He rolled his eyes. "She's fallen in with the Earth Cultists. Last I heard she was on a ship headed there."

This wasn't much better news. At least Purity wasn't already dead, but Earth? It was a toxic wasteland. "When was this?"

"Over a year ago." He shook his head. "The group she signed on with, they're trying to re-establish colonies. It was always going to be a one-way trip for her."

Hawk's head hit the back of the booth before she even realized she'd slumped backwards. "Oh, no."

Jonathan reached out a hand but stopped short of touching Hawk's. "Don't give up hope. It's not like it was when we were young. People have come back from there, alive. The reason Purity joined is because there's been a lot of excitement since the L-5s have been revived. There's talk of launching from the halfway point of the L-5 orbital colonies into the junk satellite ring around Earth. Rumor is that some mad scientist has already reactivated the archangel defense units."

Hawk was still reeling from the news that people had fixed up and reoccupied the lost colonies that had been built in one of the two stable Lagrange points between Earth and its moon. "Wait, the archangels? I thought those were a myth."

Jonathan shook his head in a kind bewildered disbelief. "I can only repeat what Purity told me. I wouldn't be surprised if half of it is cultist claptrap. She'd been on one of the L-5s for a long time until some pretty face convinced her to go planetside. That's when we lost touch." He must have seen Hawk's face go pale because he quickly added, "But that's not unusual. Despite the work people have been doing, the ring is still in tatters. People who go down, go dark."

"But a whole year?"

"The cult does this two-year mission thing? I'll worry if she doesn't contact me after that."

"Oh, huh." It'd been so long since Hawk had been back to Luna she hadn't realized that the Earther Cultists had gotten so organized. There had always been talk of reviving at least one L-5. Hawk thought that the idea had been rejected specifically by the Cult leaders because, since so many people who had fled Earth had died there, they were considered graveyards and, thus, untouchable. "Is the Cult under new management or something?"

Jonathan let out a little snort of a chuckle. "You really have been gone a long time, haven't you?"

That stung. She always meant to go back, at least to visit her parent's grave and catch up with her cohort, but other things always seemed more pressing. "I guess it's been a while."

Letting his arms drop into a fold on the table, Jonathan gave her a knowing smile. "She still thinks about you."

Well, this was awkward, since Hawk hadn't thought of Purity in years. It was only one kiss! And, more to the point, Hawk had thought that it had wrecked their friendship. If she'd known she'd had a shot…. Well, she might never have met Del Toro, at the very least.

That was too complicated to think about. So she didn't. Lifting up the carafe of water, Hawk made a show of appreciating the smell of the minerals. "Mmm, comet trail distilled? Or maybe desalinated local stuff?"

He held the wine glass as she poured. "I honestly have no idea. I just asked for the most expensive bottle."

Of course he had.

She started to bring the glass Galilei handed her to her lips, but she paused. "You're not having any?"

"I wanted to make sure I was welcome first." He lifted a hand to wave over a Margie. Hawk was mortified. What was wrong with this place? No call buttons at the table? No way to tap a device or use an internal frequency? Galilei, meanwhile, seemed unaffected, like he did this sort of crazy thing all the time. "I'll get a glass for myself, then, shall I?"

Oh what the hell, he might as well. "While you're at it, you'd better make it two. I'm expecting someone."

He raised an eyebrow, but nodded. When the Margie returned, he asked for two more glasses and then ordered without looking at the menu. "I'll have the unagi bento."

Wait? There was real food at this place? Hawk pulled the menu out from behind the silverware and frantically scanned it. She was reading through the whole thing a second time when the Margie wheeled away. Turning to Jonathan, Hawk asked, "How? How did you get real food?"

That too big smile was wry and a bit sleazy. "'Real' food? Now who's a snob?"

Okay, busted, but come on. Eel was superior to beef in every way. Was it her fault that the New Shogunate also happened to be having its day in the Saturn system since all the influencers on Titan had recently "discovered" bentos. "I'm more offended that there's a hidden menu. How did you know? Do you come here often or something?" She gave his fancy suit an obvious once-over. "It's just that you don't seem like the typical Dekōtora fan."

Galilei chuckled. "I could ask the same of you! But, one of my husbands is into this subculture or fandom or whatever you'd call it. I'm sure by tonight I'll have one of these Yarōs in my bed tonight," he sighed. "A fine distraction, much like Manfred himself. Alas, we need the company, as Manfred's the only one of my polycule willing to leave Titan when my company relocated here. It's been rather lonely in my bed lately without the whole family." Leaning on his elbow, Galilei let out a long, wistful sigh in her direction.

He held her gaze as he ran a finger along the hour-glass curve of the carafe of water, as though it were a woman's hip.

Heisenberg's balls! Was Galilei trying to flirt with her?

Did he not know about the kiss? Or did he hope she was bi? Maybe for a guy like Galilei it didn't matter. "Uh, not sure what you're hoping for here, comrade. I'm monogamous. And currently taken."

"Pity." He turned his glance out at the crowd. "Is that who you're waiting for? A spouse?"

Hawk nearly choked on the water.

She'd never considered marrying Del Toro.

Suddenly, the thought seemed... nice? Hawk had to take a moment to recover before she said, "Uh, no—but, I mean, maybe someday?"

"Ah, yes," he smiled, folding his hands under his chin and grinning at her. "I see you're as committed as always."

Maybe he did know about the kiss, after all. "Uh, I can be committed to a girlfriend. Marriage isn't the only way to be monogamous."

He waved this off like he thought she was fooling herself. "Sure, sure. Whoever she is, you should consider making an honest woman out of her.

49

Marriages are so fun. Sometimes there's a day-long banquet or a lot of church and then polka and beer or maybe you're married under one of those little tents—"

He seemed to be searching for the term, so Hawk offered: "Chuppah?"

"Yes! So cute! And then more dancing! I love the dancing."

"Uh-huh." Hawk gave him a sidelong look, trying to decide how serious he was. "How many spouses have you collected, anyway?"

"Almost enough," he lifted his hand and wagged several fingers full of rings. "But, back to you—"

Hawk stifled a groan.

"—I heard a rumor that you're a bounty hunter these days. Is that true? Because I could really use a bounty hunter I trust."

Hawk gave Galilei a hard look. Did they, though? Did they trust each other? Because of Del Toro's special status as a fugitive, Hawk never linked her personal name to any of their advertisements or business listings. She and Lucia always, always used a dummy account. Even their money went into the kinds of shady accounts you could register with fake names. So, there was no way that Galilei just 'heard' this on the wind somewhere. "What rumor was this, exactly?"

His hands went up as though in surrender. "No need to get prickly! I just happen to have friends in low places."

Well, okay. That seemed plausible. It used to be that bounty hunters only collected bounties from law enforcement types looking for people who'd skipped out on bail. Now the process was a bit looser. Almost anyone with money could tap into the bounty hunter network and post a "wanted" ad.

Still. It wasn't like her name was particularly attached to this work.

Maybe she and Del Toro were starting to get a reputation? Though that would surprise Hawk since lately most of their clients were jilted housewives looking for spouses who'd skipped out on child support, like Yarō.

Given all of his spouses, maybe that might be what Galilei was looking for, after all.

"So, you're missing a family member?"

"What? No! I'm missing an eye."

An eye? He seemed to have both in his head. Did he mean one of those telescopic ones or a spy camera? If so, why would he need her help?

"Have you checked under the couch?" Hawk took a sip of the water finally. It was perfectly chilled. She did think she could taste the hint of some metal, like manganese, but otherwise this was the purest, clearest water she'd ever tasted. "Oh, that's good."

That smarmy smile appeared again. "I'm so glad you like it."

He seemed otherwise unfazed. She scanned the room for any sign of food or Del Toro; she missed both keenly at the moment. "I don't think you understand my job, Galilei. We hunt people, not things. Find yourself a private detective or, I don't know, hire a search party."

Galilei leaned in, as if he were sharing an important secret. "Except this eye is people. It's an AI."

Okay, now Hawk knew for sure that Galilei had lost his mind.

CHAPTER 5

Lucia Del Toro

As it happened, without a PTSD hallucination getting in the way, putting the fuel line back together didn't take more than ten minutes. With the tanks back online, Lucia set the airlock cycling, got strapped in, went through the countdown checklist, and blasted out of the empty section of the truck's back hatch.

Making the maneuver to turn back towards the hub, Lucia noticed that Yarō's ghastly semi wasn't the only one docked. There were at least two other of the blinking monstrosities. No, three, she hadn't seen the one on the lower tier, though how she could miss so much neon, she had no idea. Was that a bad rendering of the Mona Lisa sitting in her classic pose in front of Mount Fuji? Good gods.

Lucia veered away and pinged the station for a request to dock.

She parked the *Peapod* in a designated space. After waiting for the automated systems to dock her to what she now thought of as a truck stop, she suited up and headed to the boarding gantry. She floated down the gantry and waited for the waystation's airlock to ding its readiness.

As the airlock pod twirled and oriented to the interior she shifted in zero-g, staying oriented to the exit sign. A small 'ting' was the only warning Lucia had before artificial gravity brought her feet to the floor, which had been the ceiling a moment ago. She easily corrected for it, but the weight of her own body with all its internal cybernetics gave her a brief sense of being wrong somehow—too heavy, too big. She grasped onto the wall for a moment to steady herself.

After pressing a button to collapse her helmet back into its hidden pockets of her uniform jacket, she undid her ponytail and fluffed up the sections that had been pushed down by the helmet and rearranged the bits that hid her facial scars. It helped a bit to feel the soft curls and length.

As soon as the doors swished open, the chaos of the station assaulted her.

The first thing that hit her was the too warm air that stank of fake rendered pig fat. Lucia had grown up eating meat, but she never understood why so many people found the particular smell of frying bacon so attractive—especially since the synth was never quite right. With so few people having ever had actual bacon, no manufacturer reproduced the scent exactly. This particular version smelled just a little too sweet, like bacon candy. Wrong. Very wrong.

Lucia took a hesitating step out of the airlock into all the noise. Metal utensils clacked, pots clanged. There was a rush of many people's voices all talking and laughing at once. After months of just Hawk and herself, the roar of human conversation was a discordant cacophony. She might have seriously considered retreating to the relative quiet of the airlock had the doors not automatically shut behind her.

She stood in a kind of spherical entryway. Each airlock gantry connected to one of these individual bubbles that encircled the station.

Margie's advertised itself on the feeds as full-service, so there were signs pointing to showers and exercise rooms, but the main expanse in front of her was the restaurant. She could see people who were clearly cosplaying truckers, but there were plenty of non-Yarō types here, too. Transport pilots, maintenance crews, and even a few people who were obviously tourists from other Systems ate at booths, took holo- and still-pictures, or otherwise gawked at the extreme retro vibe of this place.

Just as Lucia started to feel oriented and was about to venture in to try to find Hawk, an android wheeled into view. An odd contraption, clearly built to fit the aesthetic of 'the future old Earth imagined it would have.' The top half of the android was a mechanically articulated mannequin of a woman with steel and chrome-plated breasts somehow de-sexed by the absence of nipples. Smooth, curved hips encircled a single fat tire which had made her approach somewhat unsteady and lurching, like someone on a unicycle. It was all weirdly stylized, but the most disturbing part, however, was her face. The android's head was the only part of her that wasn't steel, but, instead, a doll-faced plastic mask. The blond wig didn't do much to shake the sensation of a machine trying to disguise itself as a human... and failing, badly.

Her smile was unmoving as she said, "Welcome to Margie's. I'm Margie. How can I help you?"

"Uh…" Lucia had seen plenty of fetish robots in her days, but this one was a little off-putting. She took a breath to focus and started again. "Uh… I'm looking for a friend. She would have been seated about a half-hour ago? She's waiting for me."

"The woman with the Martian Forty?"

Lucia's heart did a little jump. *Shit*. Had they hauled Hawk off for trying to pass off ENForcer money in a free sector? Lucia hesitated not knowing what the consequences would be for either answer, but then she decided, once again, to go with the brave answer: "Yes?"

"Right this way, sir."

At the 'sir,' Lucia felt her jaw set and her stomach tighten.

It was almost always machines that misgendered her these days. She'd worked hard to change her shape enough that, even with her size, humans always registered the fact that she was a woman. "You need to get your optical scans fixed, Margie. I'm a woman."

The android spun its head all the way around without stopping its forward motion. "My apologies, ma'am. As you can see my current job has a very insufficient chassis. It is difficult to see through this mask. However, if that is the case, then you appear to be a civilian wearing an Earth Nations Peacekeeping Force uniform. I am required by law to inform you that it is illegal to impersonate an officer."

Automatically, Lucia raised her hand to feel for the buttons on her collar that signified her former rank. They were gone, of course, as were all of the other identifying markers. Scraped clean, like the *Peapod*. Reclaimed, like her body.

"This is mine now," she explained. "The impersonation was the officer."

Even as it wheeled through the crowd, the robot stared at her. Lucia wondered how the android avoided colliding with anything, especially given all the other retro robots running around with serving platters.

When Margie didn't stop staring, it occurred to Lucia to ask: "Are you reporting me?"

"I am accessing whether or not I am legally bound to," Margie admitted. "Apparently, cosplay is common in this section among, and I quote, Libertarian wanks. Are you one of those?"

"Good God no."

"Then, I remain conflicted."

"We're not in ENForcer space, are we?" Lucia asked rhetorically, or at least she hoped so. Despite the *Conqueror's* appearance in the system, no news had hit the feeds of a major breakthrough in the Asteroid Belt Wars. "My understanding of Paragraph 178 of Section 2B, subsection 39-ii of the Peace-keeper's Penal Code is that non-military personnel outside of ENForcer jurisdiction are not required to make heroic efforts to report minor infractions by civilians."

"Ah," Margie said. "I see that section now. Thank you!"

"No problem," Lucia said.

Margie seemed content to have been taken off the hook. It seemed no one, not even androids working shitty jobs, wanted to be narcs for the Force. So, she did not point out that technically impersonating an officer was a bit more than a minor infraction or that the wilful destruction of military property, like the jacket, was a court-martial offense.

They reached Hawk's table.

To Lucia's surprise, Hawk wasn't alone. She was deep in animated conversation with a man.

The man had to be a Lunar with spidery and elongated limbs like that, though nothing else about him reminded her of an arachnid. If he was like any animal it was a meerkat, as he seemed incapable of sitting still. Instead, he kept bouncing on the seat, his head bobbing this way and that. He was cheerful and enthusiastic, but just watching him made Lucia exhausted.

Hawk and the stranger were so deep into their conversation that they might not have noticed Lucia being deposited in front of them if Margie hadn't said, "Your table, Officer."

Margie wheeled off before Lucia could correct her. Again.

It didn't matter much, since the stranger stood up and offered a hand to shake. "You must be the Del Toro Hawk has been talking about," he said brightly, despite the fact that Lucia refused to accept his hand. Martians shook hands. Lunars bowed. So, she gave him a little nod, after which he gestured for her to sit, as though this was his table to command. "I must say you're far more lovely than your moniker would suggest."

People often assumed since her name was Spanish for "The Bull," it was something she'd chosen. "Del Toro is my surname," Lucia said, taking a seat beside Hawk. "Not a nickname."

"Oh," he said, as though suddenly taken aback. "Well, that's unfortunate. No relation to the Scourge, I hope."

The Scourge certainly hunted them today. As much as she'd like to say that The Scourge had nothing to do with her, she opted for her standard response, instead. "Del Toro is a common surname."

"Ah, good, good," he said, taking his seat again, opposite them. "I suppose I should introduce myself?" He gave Hawk a look like he thought that she should have jumped in to do that, but her face was buried in a hamburger. "I'm an old friend of Penny's from the Moon colony, Jonathan Galilei."

Penny?

Lucia glanced at Hawk who nodded with an eyeroll. Wiping the grease off her face with the back of her hand, he said, "I knew him as Truth. Oh, yeah, and, Galilei? I go by Hawk now. Not Independence or Penny. Just Hawk."

"Oh, yes . Yes, of course. My apologies," he said, as he poured a glass of what appeared to be water for Lucia.

So this guy...? Lucia used taking a sip of the water as a cover to send Hawk via their private channel, *What's his deal? Do we like him?*

Not sure yet.

And we're talking to him, because he's family, or.... Lucia prompted.

Because he's rich and probably insane. Just wait until he tells us what he wants to hire us for.

Hire us?

Wait for it. Hawk chided teasingly. *It's so hilarious I don't want to spoil it.*

Setting the flute down on the plastic-covered tabletop, Lucia had to work to keep the scowl off her face. She wasn't sure why, but her gut disliked this guy. She told herself she probably just felt jumpy after all the ENForcer ghosts and misgendering bullshit that had been happening. With a breath, she decided to try to let go of her suspicions. "You have some kind of job for us?"

Jonathan blinked. "Oh? Good guess! A bounty, of course."

Was no one going to just spit it out? Lucia glanced at Hawk in a way she hoped made it clear that this was going to stop being hilarious if they had to wait out hours of pleasantries and small talk.

Around another bite of burger, Hawk said, "Tell her, Galilei. Tell her about your missing eye."

Lucia was sure she'd misheard. "An AI?"

"Yes! Exactly! She's brilliant!" Jonathan clapped his hands together. "You should marry her!"

Hawk's unusually pale face instantly bloomed bright red. Suddenly, she seemed to find the hologram above their booth deeply interesting. Something about all this made Jonathan laugh hysterically. Meanwhile, Lucia felt very left out.

"Which is it?" Lucia asked, cutting through whatever the hell else was going on at this table, "Are you looking for an eye or an artificial intelligence, Mr. Galilei? Or, are you trying to suggest that it could somehow be both?"

"Yes, both." He said, using his chopsticks to poke around at the remaining pickles in his very stylish bento.

Lucia waited impatiently for more information. When it didn't seem to be forthcoming, she couldn't hold back her irritation. "For someone who is implying that they've invented an actual AI, you seem really reluctant to share any of the details. You're starting to remind me of those guys who have a friend of a friend who woke up in a bath full of ice, missing an augmented kidney. If what you're suggesting is true, shouldn't this be the biggest news of the century?"

"That's exactly my problem," he said. "If I went public, I'd sound like a liar and, let's be honest, ladies, 'lunatic' makes a great headline when you're from Luna. The truth is, I wasn't ready to go public with this when the eye disappeared."

Hawk seemed to have recovered her composure because she pushed her plate aside and said, "Maybe you should start at the beginning, huh? Tell us what happened."

He sat back and folded his hands on the table. "My research, initially, was with artificial eyes. My second wife had a terrible chemical accident. Lost both eyes as a result! This would not be a big problem, as you know. I see that you are also a recipient, Lucia."

Automatically, Lucia tugged at her curls, trying to hide the scars.

If Jonathan noticed, he made no comment. "Khatijah, that's my wife, comes from a long line of Luddites. She is both morally and physically resistant to full cybernetic implants. So, I started fooling around with organic computing. Hormones, chemicals, and only the barest bits of electronics. That sort of thing. I had a breakthrough. And then it disappeared from my lab."

"Okay." Lucia tried to catch Hawk's eye to see if they had the same sense of this, but, for whatever reason, Hawk still refused to look at her. "So, someone stole your project and you want us to find that person."

"In a nutshell," Jonathan said, though now he looked away as well.

What the hell was really going on here?

Hawk, Lucia figured, she understood. Hawk clearly felt flustered about the marriage tease. Fine. Whatever. They'd have to talk about that later, in private.

But, what was Jonathan hiding?

"We're not detectives," Lucia explained, trying to sound more patient than she felt. "Solving crimes is not our specialty. This would work better for us if you have a specific quarry in mind, someone you suspect, someone we can hunt."

Jonathan shivered dramatically. "Oh, the way you say 'hunt' sounds so scary!"

Lucia was not particularly charmed by his antics. "It's what we do. If you need a detective, don't hire bounty hunters. Hire a detective."

"Seems like sound advice, but I don't know any detectives. I know you! What if I offered you thirty million Titan credits?" He lifted an eyebrow suggestively. "Do you think you could be bothered to do a little footwork for that?"

"Thirty million?" Hawk repeated, stunned.

And Titan credits were currently the highest exchange rate in any system. That would easily buy the full overhaul of Lucia's system on Nyx. Hawk's expression made it seem as though she was sorely tempted. Lucia was sure hers looked similar.

It's a bad idea, isn't it? Hawk asked privately.

My gut has been telling me that since I sat down, but it's hard to refuse that much money. How well do you know this guy, Hawk? Is he really good for it?

I don't know. Let's ask.

Hawk cleared her throat. "I didn't know patent work made that kind of cash."

"Oh no, I'm borrowing from the same sources that funded the project originally." Jonathan's tone was casual, and he glanced out at the growing crowd at the diner, as if considering taking his leave. "So, do we have a deal, ladies?"

"Yes," Hawk said, just as Lucia said, "Not without a whole lot more information."

"Oh, Penny! I knew I could count on you!" Jonathan grabbed Hawk's hands and clasped them tightly. It was like Lucia had ceased to exist to him.

"We're taking this?" Lucia asked.

Hawk squirmed out of Jonathan's grip and turned to face Lucia. "This is for you and the work you need. It's sketchy as fuck and we both know it." The fact that Hawk chose to say that out loud rather than using their private channel meant she wanted Jonathan to know how skeptical she was. "When the hell else are we going to see an offer like this again? With this kind of paycheck?"

Lucia wanted to protest that things weren't that dire, not yet. But, this morning proved otherwise. She'd always had trouble with her replacement, but only a few hours ago both eyes shorted out on her. Then there were the slowing reflexes and every other ache, pain, and failure that had been plaguing her during their last few jobs. If she didn't get an overhaul soon, she'd be nothing but bio-bits trapped inside a useless hunk of metal. She turned her attention to Jonathan, "Okay, how about a bit of payment up front?"

"There's the spirit!" Jonathan said with a little happy clap. "Why don't you let me buy you a meal, Ms. Del Toro, and I'll tell you everything I know."

They might as well get a free meal out of this yahoo. There was no guarantee there'd be another payout, after all. "Sure. I'll have what Hawk had."

"Not a bento?"

Lucia shook her head. "I'm not that fancy."

"I beg to differ, my dear," Jonathan said with an actual bat of his lashes.

Before Lucia could formulate a retort, he started waving frantically for the attention of one of the server 'bots. Second-hand embarrassment had her staring at him in mute horror.

He's not having a stroke. Apparently, it's how they do it here, Hawk sent internally. *This place isn't so much retro as barbaric.*

Once Jonathan had drawn a Margie over and ordered for Lucia, he checked his very expensive wristlet. "I have a meeting I have to get to, but here's what I can do for you." He pulled out a business card, tapped it in a few places, then slid it across the table to Hawk. "An invite to my lab tonight to check out the scene of the crime. If you show up, I can have..." he seemed to do a few mental calculations before continuing, "say, twenty five-percent up front?"

"7.50 mil just to show up for a meeting?" Lucia had to admit she hadn't expected that. Jonathan definitely made an offer that was difficult to refuse.

Hawk nodded enthusiastically, "That's a good start... But we have a lot more questions."

"Fine, but they'll have to wait." He stood up. At something in their expressions, he paused. Retrieving the card he tapped it again, "Look, here's a couple of hundred dinars. Go enjoy a few clubs on my tab in the meantime. It will all make sense when I can actually show you what I'm talking about?"

He didn't seem like he'd wait for an answer, so Lucia nabbed his sleeve. "Just one thing before you go. Your special backers—are they mafia or someone worse?"

He sputtered a bit. Then, tugged his arm away. He spent several minutes adjusting his cuff as he searched for an appropriate answer, but then gave up. "I can't say, not here. We'll talk when we're in a more secure place."

Once he'd disappeared into the crowd, Lucia got up and switched places so she could be across from Hawk. The seat held an uncomfortable residue of warmth.

"I don't know about this. I'd love for a paycheck this big, but there's got to be a catch."

"Don't say that," Hawk said quickly, making a sign for banishment of bad luck with her fingers. "At least he put some money down. And, what if we could pull this off? Wouldn't it be the answer to our problems?"

"My problems."

"Our problems. I'm kind of fond of you functional." Reaching across the table, she gave Lucia's hand a little squeeze. Changing the subject, she asked, "So you think he's getting his cash from the mafia?"

Lucia shrugged. Reaching across the table, she picked up the flute of water. Draining it in one gulp, she poured herself another. "Maybe. Like you said, it can't be from his patents, not unless he's selling them on the black market."

"Or to the ENForcers."

"Or that," Lucia agreed, although more hesitantly. The ENForcers had a lot of money that they tended to throw at scientists, especially ones developing tech they could use. Still, there was no reason to presume a connection there other than pure paranoia. "Do you think he's the type to work with them? Tell me more about how you know him."

"The Galileis were our closest neighbors. I practically grew up with his sister. We played together."

"Like creche mates."

Hawk looked a little taken aback by the comparison, but said, "I guess? But, I had other friends. Like, I saw the Galileis only every so often. I wouldn't take a bullet for him. But, I suppose that's the closest thing you would have had. I just—I'm less sure about all this than you would be if it was one of your 'mates. Like, I don't know this guy anymore. I don't trust him any further than I would throw him."

Lucia didn't feel the need to point out that wasn't at all dissimilar to how she'd felt about her creche mates at times. Civilians tended to imagine everything about Lucia's childhood as some kind of nightmare, but there had been a lot of good times among the four other people she'd been assigned as 'brothers.' She often wondered where they'd ended up, how much they hated her... or envied her. Simon would definitely have been in the latter camp; he knew he was gay at seven years old. Homosexuality was considered a Glitch and undesirable. Being a lesbian, Lucia was a double 'fuck you' to the Force, and she was weirdly proud of that fact. Marcus, though? There's a brother she was just as glad she'd never see again.

"My experience wasn't my choice," Lucia said by way of agreement. "But, trust me this is what the Force counted on. You were raised with Jonathan. Bonds form, like it or not."

"Bonds, huh?" Hawk gave a little half smile. "And raised together is a bit strong. Cohorts are bigger than I think you're imagining. There were hundreds of families in this group. I had a lot closer friends. The sister was cute, though. I kissed her once."

"Heh, of course you did." Lucia gave her a little wink of approval. This little tease elicited an unexpected blush. "Hawk? Are you okay?"

Hawk pulled a napkin from the little bin. Lucia was surprised to discover it wasn't a holo, but Hawk's behavior was even more startling. She started nervously folding it. "Jonathan seems to enjoy marriage. He's been married more times than God."

Lucia frowned, trying to decide if she should know the god in question or what any of this had to do with a teenage kiss.

The napkin became a compact origami. "He just got me thinking, is all."

About gods? No, it had to be the marriage thing. Oh! "Is this a proposal? It's just that I thought you'd be more showy and less shy."

This seemed to break through some tension because Hawk laughed. "Right? I would have thought so, too?" She glanced up from the wad of napkins with a very intense look in her eye. "You and me, we've been kicking around together a long time. Have you thought about it at all? I mean, with me?"

Lucia had to hold back an immediate, 'no, never.'

Because, even if that was true, it wasn't the right thing to say. She knew that. Her upbringing hadn't been the best at fostering empathy, but even Lucia knew enough to know that a swift, decisive answer like that would be crushing. And, she wouldn't mean it the way it would come out.

It wasn't as though Lucia found the idea of spending the rest of her life with Hawk repulsive. No, in fact, it was the exact opposite. She'd never wanted to presume, and so she hadn't thought about it, not even once. She'd shoved that possibility to the back of her mind. Especially since what always stood between them was The Scourge. Hawk would choose to ask, today of all days, when the shadow of that event loomed larger than it had in years,.

If anything, Lucia didn't feel worthy of Hawk.

She'd just started to figure out how to say all of this when she realized she'd hesitated too long. Hawk's face crumpled and she was already laughing it off. "Heh, stupid idea, right?"

"No, it's not that—"

Hawk cut her off. "I know you love me." She caught Lucia's gaze and held it, sincerely. "Marriage is kind of stupid? Aping the Patriarchy and all that. I wouldn't have thought about it at all without Galilei's six million wedding rings, you know?"

Lucia didn't know what to say to this either, so she settled on, "Okay. If you're sure."

"Totally."

Lucia wasn't convinced, yet Hawk clearly signaled that she wanted the topic dropped. Lucia lifted the glass of water to her lips. She'd meant to take a dainty sip of it, but something about the refreshing crisp, clean taste had her draining the flute in three swallows again. Fresh water was kind of magical. She could understand why people paid a premium for it. Casting around for some better topic of conversation, Lucia said, "A lot of stuff about my past is floating around today, huh? And, then your old friend shows up out of the blue."

"Neighbor." Hawk corrected glumly. "What do you think? Maybe we shouldn't take this job. Feels a bit cursed already. The safer move is to run off with the sad little bounty we're getting from nabbing Yarō and hightail it out of here."

It was the smartest option, too. Jonathan's job stank of complications he wasn't admitting to and it was always preferable to be as far away from her old regiment as physically possible. Lucia played with the empty glass flute, twirling the stem in her fingers. Glancing up at Hawk, she asked, "Where would we go?"

Hawk seemed surprised by the question and took a few seconds to consider it. Picking up her own glass of water, she drained the dregs. She let out an appreciative sigh and set it down on the table slowly, almost regretfully "Does it matter?"

It did a little, at least practically. "I mean, do we have another job lined up? Any leads? Do you really want to go back to fishing around the black market shipping lanes in hopes of catching more small fry like Yarō?"

Hawk slumped back against the booth. "Nah, that sucked. Plus, I still feel guilty. Fake distress signals feel gross and, worse, that guy was a total teddy bear and we froze his ass."

And I almost killed him, Lucia nodded.

"So take the job because we've got nothing better on?" Hawk asked, "Even though we're doing it with a ship full of dickwads gunning for you in the same system?"

Lucia scoffed. "What are the chances they're really after me?"

"What were the chances of running into a Looney in a truckstop above Ganymede," Hawk lifted her hands as though to indicate everything. "Look, I know you think I'm some kind of superstitious hippy, but I don't like all of these strange coincidences popping up all at once."

Lucia caught Hawk's gaze and held it. She wanted to say something she'd had at the back of her mind for a while now. Like, maybe all of this was happening because this was when she should do it: face The Scourge head on, take responsibility. "There's chance," she said thoughtfully, "But, there's also fate."

♀

CHAPTER 6

Independence "Hawk" Hawking

Fate?

What was this talk from Del Toro? What did fate mean to Del Toro right now, especially when an ENForcer ship was in the vicinity? Why did it sound less fate and more fatalistic?

Putting the silverware on top of her plate in a way she hoped signaled that she'd finished eating in this culture, Hawk pushed her mostly consumed meal towards the center of the table. With that out of the way, she gave her complete attention to the woman across from her.

"What are you talking about, Del Toro? Coincidence versus fate? This is not you. You're practical and evidence-based, like me. Yet you sound really serious about something, and I feel like you're not telling me what it is."

Del Toro had the sense to shift her gaze to stare at the tabletop. "Yeah."

Okay, so it was something really big. The way Del Toro let her eyes roam around the table and the room—anywhere except to meet Hawk's—also made it seem like, maybe, she wasn't quite ready to talk about it, either.

Hawk crossed her arms in front of her chest. "Okay. You've clearly been carrying something heavy around since the post-traumatic hallucination. So if I had to guess this has something to do with your past, right? The ENForcers. You just told me you don't think they're here for you, but you clearly are feeling something. Something fateful."

Still no eye contact, just another "Yeah."

Del Toro was funny about her past. It wasn't like she tried to hide it all that much. She still wore that uniform, after all, and, even without the insignia, it was highly recognizable. But there was all the casual talk in front of Yarō. She didn't usually just blurt out things that connected her to the identity she'd left behind.

The Scourge of New Shanghai.

Hawk studied Del Toro's expression. Her face was blank and difficult to read, as always. People talked about 'resting bitch faces,' but ex-ENForcers apparently had 'off-mode.' Normally, Hawk was sensitive to any quirk, any micro-expression on Del Toro's face, but no answers were forthcoming this time. Del Toro had closed off. Completely.

"Okay, I can wait." Playing the guessing game had led to stalemate, after all. "Let me know when you're ready to talk about it, okay?"

"You could do the job without me," Del Toro said suddenly.

Hawk felt as if she'd been slapped. "I'm sorry, what did you just say?"

"I'm a liability.'" Del Toro tapped her forehead. "I'm a Glitch, remember."

She sounded hurt about it, too. Was that what all this was about? Not feeling up to her usual badassery? Normally, Del Toro was uber-confident to the point of being scary. Hawk had watched Del Toro stab someone in the arm, casually drop a sonic grenade into a literal underground bar and never even blink. It was terrifying, but also sexy in that way that deadly competence could be.

Hawk would be more scared of the Scourge of New Shanghai, but Hawk remembered that day, too, how shook Del Toro had when she turned up on Hawk's doorstep. She'd babbled about taking out civilians, but the only blood on her had been her own. She'd nearly bled out from that hole in her side where someone had shot her.

But, Del Toro carried massive guilt and Hawk refused to dig too deep, so....

Maybe this morning had rattled Del Toro more than Hawk realized. Perhaps she just needed some reassurance. "Yeah, but I like weirdos and queers. Anyway, where would you go? What would you do?"

A flicker of fire flashed in Del Toro's gaze. "I don't know. Maybe just... get away?"

Run away? Okay, this was about the marriage proposal.

What in Darwin's name had she been thinking blurting out a sudden, half-assed proposal like that, anyway? It was true that they'd been together a long time now. Hawk's usual tendency to wander off in the middle of a relationship hadn't kicked in, which did seem a bit miraculous, possibly worth celebrating with a wedding? But still! She should have known better than to just ask like that.

Maria Salomea Skłodowska-Curie on a Crutch, Del Toro must be scared shitless. "Calm down. Not without me, you don't. We're either both in or we're both skiving off to some cold spa we can't afford on Uranus. Why would I want to do this by myself? There is nothing about this job that says it's perfect for just Hawk. This is clearly a team job. And you are my team. Like, in a non-threatening, non-marriage proposal kind of way. Team mates."

She probably shouldn't have added that last part, but sometimes Hawk's mouth continued on long after the rest of her brain had shut off.

Hawk tried to laugh a little to defuse the growing tension. She held up her noodly arm and flexed it weakly. "I mean, seriously, Del Toro. Do I look like I can handle AI eyes, ENForcers, and the mafia all by myself?"

Del Toro snorted a little laugh, but there was no real smile, like she still wasn't quite convinced.

"C'mon, girl. We're a matched set and you know it," Hawk insisted with a little nudge under the table of toe against calf. She wanted to make a joke about having been together so long that they were practically married, anyway, but for once in Hawk's life her filters kicked in before she said things even more stupid than what she had already. "You'd get lonely on your own. Do you even know how to pick up another hot lesbian like me?"

Del Toro seemed to be starting to acquiesce. "You know I don't. It wasn't like fraternization was encouraged. Where was I going to find another woman, anyway? Besides, I didn't like how romance and sex felt. I thought I might be asexual until I met you."

It had been such a surprise to discover an ENForcer virgin, especially one with such a fearsome reputation. Hawk had initially thought that seducing someone so infamous would just be a notch on her belt, but all that swagger had evaporated the moment Del Toro had gone all vulnerable and honest.

"Turns out you like sex. A lot."

Del Toro's chuckle was more genuine now. "Yeah, as a woman with a woman, it can be good."

"You mean the best."

"I do."

I do. Those two little words from Del Toro hit Hawk in a way she hadn't anticipated, right in the gut. To cover, she tapped Del Toro's leg with her toe again. "I want to hear that again. Say it louder. Sex with me is the best."

"I don't really have a lot to compare it to," Del Toro said in that serious way she had,"But I'm going with yes. Sex with you is the best."

"Damn right."

Hawk considered another tease about their history, but it wasn't necessary. The old Del Toro returned, at least a little. Hawk let her shoulders relax back into the plastic-covered booth. She picked up the carafe of water, found just enough in the bottom of it to splash a bit into a final glass for herself and Del Toro. Hawk drained hers in a matter of gulps. It was good. Galilei had pulled out all the stops. "Hey," she said, tipping the glass towards Del Toro. "Remember what you first said to me?"

A soft smile lifted the edges of Del Toro's lips. "How could I forget? You told me that you were making an exception, since you usually only slept with women. I told you it was your lucky day. I am a woman."

Hawk had a strong visceral memory of that moment, Her palms warmed with the physical memory of Del Toro's hand in hers, sweating nervously like a schoolgirl. It was strange that those four words were all it took, but in that moment everything shifted. Hawk no longer saw what everyone else did. In fact, she would swear on a stack of *Principia* that somehow she'd seen then the face she saw now—even though that would be at least three years in the making.

Lunars understood gender to be so much more than biology. Most of the colonies on the Moon held the belief that children could make their own decisions about where they fit on the gender spectrum once they were old enough to articulate it. Gendered terms were eschewed until a person started using one for themselves. Hawk's own colony, the Stoletov Crater Collective, had a nifty ceremony to celebrate this decision, a gender reveal party.

Unlike a lot of the other Lunar colonies, however, hers never had a particular age that one was expected to have finished deciding. She was used to her aunties becoming uncles or brothers becoming siblings or them-friends becoming girlfriends at any point in their lives, and, occasionally, several times in a lifetime. You just sent out the invitations and threw another party. It was understood to simultaneously be no big deal and a very important moment in someone's life.

Which is why it had been so grating that Galilei hadn't been able to quickly adapt to Hawk's name change. He should be used to it. Or, he should do what she did and just eschew first names in general.

That thought reminded Hawk of the job at hand and the 'problem' of Del Toro. Hawk let out an "I give up" sigh. Her elbows leaned on the table and she held her face in her hands. She gave Del Toro her best lovey-dovey eyes. "You're so fucking gorgeous. I guess you'll have to stay by my side."

Del Toro's smile twisted into a smirk. "It seems so. Such a terrible fate."

"Ah, we're back to talking about fate, eh? Well then, as fates go, I'm sure the worst!"

"Quite."

Margie arrived with Del Toro's food. This Margie was completely different than the previous iterations. It moved stiffly and more jerkily; its joints squeaky, sounding rusted and in need of repair. In fact, it seemed in danger of spilling food, so Del Toro reached up to take it from the server. It apologized profusely, "A thousand pardons, ma'am."

"Don't worry about it," Del Toro said kindly.

As it motored off, jerking this way and that, Hawk asked, "Do you believe in AIs?"

Del Toro lifted a shoulder in a half-hearted shrug. "Maybe. I had a conversation with the maitre'd that made me think maybe the workers here don't get to choose their chassis. That one seemed frustrated with the current configuration of their optical sensors."

Hawk considered this. "I suppose experiencing emotion is a sign of sentience. I mean, I feel like cats and other animals are sentient, intelligent even." She ran her finger around the rim of the empty glass flute. "I don't know why I'm being all Lunar about this. I guess I'm having trouble figuring out why you'd put an intelligence in an eye."

"Good question." Del Toro chewed her food thoughtfully. "I guess we should have asked Jonathan. Well, we can tonight. I'm about a decade behind the tech, but even in my day we had things like facial recognition and what we called 'body cams,' which was just the ability to turn on a recording function through the visual cortex."

Just. Del Toro said that like it wasn't completely scary tech.

"You're right," Del Toro paused with a fork halfway to her mouth. "Why would you even want an eye that could think for itself? What are the circumstances where that's an advantage?"

Nothing occurred to Hawk immediately, until she remembered that Galilei had been almost salivating at the idea of how much money he could make if this tech got into the 'right' hands. "Advertisers? An AI eye could track where your eye rests, what your gaze lingers on."

"We've had that tech since before we left Earth, so that can't be its selling point. There has to be a reason someone would want the eye to begin with. Maybe they don't? Maybe, you sneak in the advertising tech afterwards to make money. Trust me, no one would voluntarily upgrade their eyes to help advertisers sell things more efficiently. Eye surgery is a bitch. You have to be awake for it."

They paused the conversation while a Margie deposited Del Toro's milkshake.

"It still bothers me that people can drink cow's milk," Hawk admitted, watching Del Toro take a big slurp. "Until I left Luna, I thought all humans were lactose intolerant."

After digging into the ice cream with the spoon that was provided, DeToro shrugged. "Some people are, some people aren't, it seems."

"But, who decided on cows?"

"What?"

"There are so many mammals that produce milk. Why did so many Earthers pick the same mammal to milk?"

"I don't know that they did, "Del Toro said. "You don't even have to use animals for a milk-like product, if you don't want to. I've had soy and almond milk."

"Yeah, but cow was still the most common."

Del Toro lifted up her shake to stare intently at the ice cream. "The Martians are the arbitrators of all things Earth, or at least they'd like to think they are Earth's true heirs. But, they cherry pick their truths. You and I both know that. This milk was probably concocted in a lab. Like the smell of 'bacon' that's being piped into this restaurant. It's just made to seem like something that humans once thought was dominant. For all we know, the majority of Earthers drank goat's milk."

Hawk watched jealously as Del Toro ate a big spoonful of ice cream. She didn't know why, but she always craved the things that were no good for her.

Del Toro, meanwhile, seemed to still be thinking about Galilei's missing AI eye. "Maybe that eye has some additional cosmetic functionality? I'm stuck with one darker iris because I was told that basic eye mechanics required the colored parts of the iris, the stroma, to be attached to fairly complex sphincter muscle, some of which has to be grown from stem cells. Maybe the whole eye is artificial somehow? Maybe it can change colors?"

Plausible, Hawk supposed. "I would think something like that could just get regular money backers, you know? Galilei went to the mob—or at least he implied he did," Hawk said. "So, what's something that a board of directors would never fund?"

"I would say x-ray vision, but I don't think it works like it does in the comic books," Del Toro said, biting into her burger. "I'm pretty sure you need something to capture the image on the other side, like film."

"Eye lasers are also cooler as a concept than they'd be in real life," Hawk noted, stealing a fry from Del Toro's plate. "Lasers are generally a dumb weapon."

Del Toro paused in her chewing for a moment. She held up her hand and flexed her fingers. "I think I mentioned that I briefly had lasers in my fingers, courtesy of the ENForcers. We immediately started burning holes in each other and forgetting to turn them off because they're virtually invisible. I'm surprised no one was blinded, speaking of eyes. Frankly, eye lasers make a tiny bit more sense, but how you would get a weapon like that into an eye, though, I have no idea."

"Maybe that's what Galilei was up to. We really needed to have gotten this info from him. No one here likes how cagey he was or how stingy with the details, do they? Can you take a mental note so we remember to ask at the lab tonight?"

The nice thing about having an ex-ENForcer around is that they had all these literal built-in features—reminders and such—that could flash up in their field of vision.

"Done," Del Toro confirmed. Hawk would have known that she'd set the notification anyway. The creepy part of hanging around an ex-ENForcer was that sometimes lights flashed behind their eyes, making them glow like some kind of monster out of a storybook.

"Hurry and finish your food, I want to check into a hotel and start doing some of my own investigation..."

Del Toro made a kind of a guilty grimace. "Uh, so, I automatically deposited those dinars that Jonathan sent us, and I might have booked us into a casino."

A casino. The rooms were probably cheap, but that meant a lot of security. Hawk couldn't do some of her usual loosey-goosey hacking business quite as easily at a place like that. "That's okay, I'll use 'Alice.'"

Alice was a re-route program, one of Hawk's finest bits of cracking, if she did say so herself, and part of a complex long-con she'd been running for years.

"You know I have no idea what you're talking about when you say that," Del Toro said.

"Just trust me that I've got us covered."

Del Toro made a face. "I wish you wouldn't say things like that with such confidence. At that point you might as well say 'What could possibly go wrong?'"

Hawk hissed, and they both made the Lunar hand sign to banish bad luck.

They left the *Peapod* in orbit at a pay lot and took the space elevator down to the icy surface of Ganymede. The hotel Del Toro had found for them was in the 'Old Town' of Mehit in the Zu Fossae region.

Hawk had been to Ganymede a half a dozen times, but she'd previously stayed in the newer domed cities, like the capitol, Tiamat Sulci. The Zu Fossae area tended to be sneered at by the locals at a tourist trap. As they turned down the ice-slick cobblestone street, Hawk understood why.

Thanks to the imperfections in the dome technology, icy fog shrouded the city. Visible around every twist and turn were Italianesque facades decorated in garish colors more suitable for a warm, Mediterranean climate. Similarly, each building overflowed with open balconies and walk-through Gothic double-loggias. There were piazzas at every turn with naked, voluptuous goddesses pouring sludgy, icy water from amphorae. The whole place looked like it had been designed for sun and warmth. Hawk shivered and sunk deeper into her arctic gear.

She was glad that she and Del Toro had taken the time to change clothes. As much as she loved her little, fancy breeches, they no longer fit the outfit. She was now bundled up in a heavily lined *pao*, a long-sleeved, collarless robe that was popular among the United Miners. Underneath that, she switched to warm trousers, and had changed her super-grippers' hologram to project the SnöShū brand boots all the kids were wearing on Neptune.

Antigrav gondolas glided over the icy canals. The people huddled in them looked miserably cold. Even so, Hawk could sort of see the appeal of the ones with couples who clearly used the cold as an excuse to canoodle under comforters.

Catching her glance, Del Toro snorted. "I ain't coughing up the fortune it costs for one of those. If you want to hide under the blankets and smooch, we can just do that in the hotel."

"If it's this cold in the hotel, I'm going to hold you to that."

Del Toro nodded, like sex would be fine.

And it would be. Sex with Del Toro was always amazing. The problem was the afterglow. When Hawk would stare at this amazing woman and start fantasizing about things like 'settling down' and 'forever' again. And she'd seen how that had gone over already: like the proverbial lead balloon.

Her timing had been bad. But, it wasn't likely to get better, was it?

To be fair to Del Toro, there was a bounty on her head. So long as that existed 'settling down' fell into the 'actively dangerous for continued survival' category. And, you couldn't argue with that; no matter how much you dreamed of a hydroponic hobby farm on Oberon.

Hawk decided to think about that later—much later, like, *after* sex.

She decided, instead, to continue to gawk at this bizarre architecture. What had inspired it, she wondered. Pulling out her device, she decided to see what she could find. According to the local guidebook, some nutjobs from an amusement park conglomerate on old Earth—d'Isigny?—had hoped to terra-form the entire moon, heating the surface enough to bring the deepest ocean to the surface and turn Zu Fossae, and with it the rest of Ganymede, into the Venice of the Solar System.

Apparently, it had seemed like a good idea at the time. Unfortunately, thousands of lives had been lost in the attempt. In the end, the site had been abandoned for nearly a century before it was reclaimed by one of the utilitar-ian groups that followed. The company that bought the ghost town of Mehit saw the value in its eerie open balconies and ornamental piazzas, and so care was taken to preserve d'Isigny's vision, even as the new company enclosed the entire fossae in a protective dome and made it habitable at long last.

The only problem was the canals. The interior of the dome was warmed, of course, but because the d'Isigny's colony had been constructed on the actual surface, the usual layer of protective materials and gravity enhancers couldn't be perfectly installed. Cold seeped in, and there were places, particularly on the bridges that spanned ice sludge filled-canals, where the gravity would sud-denly drop to 0.46 g.

Hawk was so busy reading about this on her device that she didn't notice the warning light shift from green to blinking yellow as they stepped onto the next arch bridge. Her step became an awkward bound that sent her tumbling. She face-planted on the cobblestone, bruising her pride more than her chin.

Del Toro, of *course*, did a perfect Armstrong shuffle to offer a hand. "I'd have thought a Loony would know how to navigate low g."

"Maybe I should have learned not to read and walk at some point? I've been walking into walls with a book in my hand since I was a kid," Hawk laughed. She took the hand offered and let Del Toro haul her to her feet. "At any rate, my commune had gravity enhancers like normal people. I didn't play outside. My family was indoorsy"

"Indoorsy, eh? I think you mean nerds." Del Toro gave a faux grimace as she spoke the last word, but she clearly said it with love and affection.

"This place is a nightmare," Hawk muttered, carefully bouncing over to where her handheld had skittered, only to nearly trip again when the g nor-malized at the end of the bridge. Her sigh crystalized in a pocket of cold. "And I'm freezing."

"That's why the hotel is cheap." Del Toro said. "Even with the promise of Old Earth ambience, any place in this dump is half the price you'd pay any-where in the Enki Catena."

Hawk shook her head. She never understood Del Toro's love of gambling. "All I care about is if it has heat."

Del Toro made a 50/50 grunt, like maybe a heated hotel wasn't a guarantee. "Great. Remember your promise. Sex if the room is cold!"

Del Toro nodded. "I'm good for it."

†

Hawk had kind of hoped they'd go right into the sexy times, but Del Toro whispered a few kinky promises in her ear and then headed to the casino.

Grumbling disappointedly the whole time, Hawk pulled all the extra linens from the closet and turned up the room's thermostat another notch. She didn't bother removing anything but her boots before burrowing deeply into the bed.

Hawk took Galilei's business card out of her back pocket. She turned the smart paper over in her fingers, thinking.

Thirty million was a lot for missing hardware. As Del Toro pointed out in their previous conversation, there were things that ENForcers had that were not out in the public, like the ability to record and store images. Part of why civilians didn't have access to that tech was because the Force spent decades manipulating and implanting growing brains with hardware in order to capture and process images. Maybe Galilei had figured out a way to contain all that tech and processing power in a single eye? That could be worth something, although why it would not be funded by regular investors remained the biggest stumbling block.

Their laser theory made the most sense at the moment, since destructive eye beams were definitely the kind of dangerous—and possibly stupid—application of tech that would make regular research backers decline to fund. It's also absolutely the sort of thing the mafia might appreciate—the ability to ignite gas from a distance with an invisible beam? Or to burn a small hole in someone that was virtually undetectable? Yeah, the mafia might get behind that.

When Hawk flipped Galilei's business card over for a third time, something new appeared on the back side. A line of script formed itself while she watched. "As discussed, your appointment at our Ganymede laboratory has been scheduled for today at 22:00 Martian Standard Time. Please be advised that there is some travel time, currently estimated at 30 minutes, as our lab is located in the business district of Edfu Facula, 25.7N, 147.1W." The note included a link to two, pre-paid bullet train tickets from Mahit to Edfu Facula.

Convenient.

"Hotel, what is the current time in Martian Standard?"

A mechanical female voice replied, "It is 16:24 in Martian Standard Time."

They had plenty of time, then. She burrowed into the blankets and considered the merits of a good, long nap. Hawk got as far as closing her eyes, but her brain wouldn't stop whirring around the question of Galilei and this job.

Since Jonathan could go public with the bounty at any point, there was no way that the two of them were going to be lucky enough to be the only ones on this bounty. Thus, time was of the essence. No nap. Time for more leg work.

Tempting as it was to just use her device to do a little poking around into Galilei's business to try to suss out what he might not be telling them, Hawk decided that she needed something on which to be truly anonymous. To do that, she'd need to hack a spoof or jack into port here at the hotel.

Leave it to Del Toro to pick a casino. Well, at least Hawk knew about the hotel choice in enough time to have activated Alice. Someday Alice would spool out and stop working. Hopefully that day wouldn't be today.

With a regretful sigh, Hawk unburied herself from the pile of covers and stomped back into her boots. At least she might be warmer closer to the casino floor. All the bodies in the casino should add enough body heat to the air to at least make things cozy.

☙

Hawk found a restaurant that overlooked the casino floor that might be good for what she needed.

There was a decent amount of ambient body heat, too, but that wasn't what excited Hawk the most. The restaurant had no servers—no robots, no humans. More importantly, they had tabletop menus. This hotel really was cheap; their equipment was ancient—which was perfect.

Given the proximity of the restaurant to the casino floor, however, there was bound to be loads of security cameras.

Well, Hawk had prepped for that. She had Alice, and she took a second now to pull out one of her fake business cards. Selecting the right one, she put it in the right hand pocket of her pao for easy access.

Scooting into a spot with no immediate neighbors, Hawk felt around the edges of the table until her fingers found a couple of buttons. She fiddled around with them a bit until she was rewarded with the table menu going dark. Laying her head on the table, she listened to make sure she heard more than just the monitor blinking out.

When she turned it back on, she started tapping her finger in a staccato beat. Just when she thought she might have to try again with a different rhythm, she entered the tabletop's backdoor. Breaking the login and password combo was easy; fortunately, sysadmins had been lazy throughout time.

It only took another minute before Hawk could use the restaurant's table as her personal handheld. The first thing she researched was her old friend, Galilei. Turned out, he hadn't yet legally changed his name to Jonathan, and, while there were a lot of Lunars named after Galileo, only one was named Truth.

The first thing the search engines found out about him was that Galilei was, in fact, a patent holder for several cybernetic innovations, including a fancy-ass cybernetic widget that helped ENForcers survive brief exposure to the carbon dioxide-rich Martian atmosphere. That connection dinged an immediate red flag for Hawk.

Maybe this eye was for them, the ENForcers.

Maybe they should back out of this job ASAP.

But there was a footnote in one of the articles about it that made her suspect he *maybe* hadn't intended his work to be seized by the Martian Stratocracy. He had several other innovations after that that he clearly fought to keep out of the hands of the military, including something he co-authored with that ex-wife he mentioned, the explosive chemist, on something called "autotomy." Huh, apparently his company was responsible for a group of temporary neural stem cell nanos. Even Hawk had some of those implanted a few years ago because literally everyone took the injection if they could afford it, since the nanobots helped protect the human body from the constant threat of space radiation. She skimmed the paper, her eyes glazing over the more technical it got, mentioning something called biological autonomy, some experiments involving something with the scientific name, pycnogonum litorale, and undefined terms like dedifferentiation and epimorphic regeneration. It all started to become soup in her brain, so she made a quick copy to toss into her personal device for later.

Pulling herself back to the job at hand, Hawk continued scrolling through the information. Quickly, but carefully, she moved out of the stuff that was easily accessible into the more hidden sections of the net. These were the corners of the intrasteller web where eyes watched and footprints were noted and recorded, so she tread carefully, spinning out spoofs and ghosts as she went.

It'd been awhile since Hawk had slunk around in these particular corners, and that was dangerous. Spyware was constantly being updated, improved, and implemented.

What she found in her first pass wasn't all that earth shattering, unfortunately. Even though he'd been hired by Chimera Enterprises at twenty-five for his patent work, Galiliei didn't seem to have had many singular breakout projects in the last decade. His name appeared among teams, though growing further and further from the actual work of sciencing and making.

There was nothing, of course, about the missing eye, but Hawk started to formulate a sense of why it might be so very, very important to Galilei. If it was something truly innovative and/or something he'd had a personal hand in creating, it could reignite his career in a very big way.

Also, maybe the money?

It seemed like with three husbands, two spouses, a wife, and numerous children, there were probably more than the average amount of bills to pay.

Wait. Galilei had five wedding rings, didn't he? She tried to picture his hands in her mind's eye. Her recall wasn't perfect, but three plus two plus one... that was six. There was a divorce here somewhere—or a death, maybe? No, she was doing this backwards. All of these partners were listed as current and married, not engaged or anything that would explain a lack of a ring?

So why the missing ring? Some cultural thing maybe—one of them just didn't like it? No more room before the knuckle? Or something more sinister? Hawk itched to figure it out, but she'd already spent too long on this boosted machine. Knowing she was probably already over time, she dropped a bit of code, and then quickly booted the table off and back on.

Security would be visiting at any minute. She had figured that into her whole plan of coming down here. Alice had been activated before they'd even stepped off the space elevator. Even so, she took a napkin from the holder on the table and started wiping the machine down. It was a habit. Leave nothing behind, if possible. She was just pulling out a business card from her inside pocket to leave on the table, when the screen flickered.

A text message popped up. It read: "Back off, Hawk. You don't know what you're getting into."

There was no signature, but it wasn't like there needed to be.

It was Oz.

Reflexively, Hawk glanced over her shoulder, half-expecting Oz, an old bounty hunting rival, to be sitting somewhere in the restaurant. If Oz was there, however, Hawk never had a chance to find out before hotel security swarmed in, weapons drawn.

Hawk lifted her hands to show she was unarmed. Between her fingers, she held up a thin business card. It would claim she was a 'security analyst' whose job it was to test security protocols. It was the first step to initiate Alice.

She took a breath to remind herself that this always worked in the past. She smiled up at the array of shiny weapons in her face. "Just doin' my job, boys."

That was the cover, anyway.

Now she just had to pray Alice held. If it didn't, well—Hawk had other extraction methods. It would just be nice not to be banned from yet another system.

☙

The security goons held Hawk in a cramped office as they checked the firm listed on the business card she'd offered them. To confirm her story they needed to make a call to Neptune, where the Sizemore headquarters was, and so they'd gone off to ask their bosses for permission to use the long-range communications array. Hawk was left cooling her heels with a single guard.

He wasn't talkative, which was fine.

The company she'd told them she worked for, Sizemore, was infamous for its surprise inspections. She hadn't actually worked there in nearly a decade. That was where Alice came in. Alice was the backdoor code that rerouted any calls that came to her old extension at the office as a lovely, very alive sounding receptionist who insisted that, yes, this was all official Sizemore business and they could look forward to all the appropriate validation papers... eventually. It could mostly stand up to investigation? Unless people held her until the papers came. Then she was screwed.

Really, she had been banking on people's fear of these snap security inspections for years and the fact that Sizemore was still the number one contractor.

Someday that would all change.

Hawk tried not to look anxious about it. Thankfully she had something else to focus on: Oz.

The last time Ozmerelda Jackson had horned in on one of Hawk's bounties, everyone had come out on the losing end. The mark had gotten away, and she and Oz had ended up literally entangled together in the electrified net. It had taken all of Hawk's best extraction methods to get out of that one, and now neither of them was allowed anywhere near Venus, which was fine, given that the Hell Planet was mostly a giant penal colony. Even so, it stung Hawk's pride to be on the off-list.

Oz found the whole thing hilarious, which also irritated Hawk. Oz also seemed to imagine that the whole misadventure had been some kind of foreplay or flirtation. It wasn't that Hawk disagreed. After all, Oz was a decent-looking person who tended to prefer the femme aesthetic. Despite all that, the only thing that had ever passed between Hawk and Oz was a lot of angry static. Sparks flew when they were in a room together, all right, but, as far as Hawk was concerned, none of them were the romantic kind. Besides, she was only interested in having someone in her bed she could trust. That was not Oz.

Hawk tapped her finger on her thigh in a combination of impatience and deep thought. The big bouncer guy they'd stationed in the office with her continued to try to intimidate her with a glare. She didn't even feel it. Having had to deal with Del Toro on her period, this guy's level of menace was amateur in comparison. Of course, Del Toro didn't bleed, but you did not need that to be a woman. Anyway, hormones were hormones and hers, like the rest of the package, were impressive.

Her mind drifted back to the problem of Oz. As much as she hated to admit it, Oz's genius in hacking systems was unparalleled. A thought struck Hawk and she suddenly sat up a lot straighter, looking for the camera in the room. Finding it, she mouthed: "Are you slowing the call down?"

The camera light flashed: off, on, off, off.

Morse code for "Y"

"You little shit!" Hawk shouted before she remembered she wasn't alone in the room. "Sorry," she said to the bouncer. "That wasn't aimed at you. I thought I saw a roach on the wall."

The big dope actually flinched and turned to look nervously at where Hawk pointed. Terraforming might be imperfect, but humans brought their pests into the universe wherever they went. As the security guard continued to look around for the offending bug, Hawk glanced up at the camera again. She mouthed, "How about you let the call go through, and we can cut you in on the bounty."

On, off, off.

"W," if Hawk remembered right. W?

On.

"E," W-E. There must be a question mark coming.

Huh, so Oz didn't know that she and Del Toro were still together. "Yeah, me and Del Toro," she continued to mouth. For a security guy, he wasn't paying much attention to Hawk right now. He peeked behind a bookshelf with a worried expression. All that muscle, but he must be terrified of creepy crawlies. "There's enough bounty to go around, wouldn't you agree? Let's negotiate."

A "Y" flashed back so fast that Hawk almost didn't catch it.

Two seconds later, the head of security was not only back in the room to let Hawk go, but he came with a sincere apology. "Our mistake, Ms. Hawking," he said with a formal, deep bow. "Please give our regards to President Ngo."

Hawk laughed lightly. Everyone at the company knew Ian Ngo was a recluse. She stood up slowly, making a show of dusting off her thighs. "Don't worry about the inconvenience. It's part of your protocols," she said, continuing to play the part. "You were doing what you were supposed to. It will all go into the report."

"We have been authorized to upgrade your room for you and your... partner, if you are amenable."

Oh? This was unexpected, but not unwelcome. Heat would be nice. "Sure, we'd be honored." Hawk figured Oz had everything to do with this turn of fortune, but she wasn't going to look a gift horse in the mouth, as Del Toro might say. "Lead the way, gentlemen."

Though she followed the three men out of the office and down the hotel lobby, Hawk stayed alert. After all, her mother always told her that if something seemed too good to be true, it probably was.

Hotel corridors had looked much the same throughout the ages. Door after door, in a seemingly endless corridor, were punctuated by the occasional bit of abstract art and a potted, yet somehow still unhappy-looking plant. The carpeting was scuffed, worn, and a garish riot of colors that no normal person would put together.

The head of security kept up a steady stream of innocuous questions that he really didn't expect more than cursory answers to, "How has your stay been? How was the jump gate traffic? Have you been on the canals yet?"

Hawk just grunted noncommittal-like and considered where her weapons were if she needed them. She always had something useful close to hand. Her personal favorite was a slender blade inside a spring-loaded sheath strapped to her wrist. It was hidden underneath a pair of decorative demi-gauntlets. It always made her feel like a cool, underworld spy.

However, she wasn't sure how much damage the stiletto would do against these oafs if they decided to pile on her. There was always the mini stun gun in the thigh holster under her skirt. The problem, of course, was getting to that one in time for it to be useful.

The head of security glanced over his shoulder at her as they walked. He finally asked something that needed more than a "fine." "First time to Ganymede, Ms. Hawking?"

"Not really. In the past, however, I've stayed in the Enki chain."

"Ah yes," he chuckled, "Where the cool kids hang out."

Hawk's eyes continued to scan the other two guards for any change in posture or movement as she made an agreeing sort of noise.

The Enki Catena chain of craters was a far more popular destination, that was for sure. Hawk wasn't sure she'd exactly call that area fashionable, however. It was certainly more typically cosmopolitan. Back in the old settler days, a bunch of agricultural corporations bought up huge sections of the moon to attempt to grow food for the system. Despite being scattered all over the surface, they all took up headquarters near the crater chain. Each of their company towns grew into cities and then eventually merged into the sprawling metropolis that it was today.

"I dunno, I kind of dig the whole frozen-over Italianate mash-up you've got going he—" Hawk didn't get to finish her verbal critique before Thing One made his lunge.

By chance or design, they hit a pocket of low-g.

Hawk wasn't quite prepared for how high she leapt away from Thing One, but she managed to use it to her advantage to tuck and roll and plant her feet into the chest of Thing Two on her way back down. She hit the button on the spring-loaded stiletto and swiped blindly in the direction she'd last seen the head of security.

She hit nothing but air.

Not a good sign.

Unfortunately, she couldn't think about where he'd slipped off to because Thing One was after her again. He was like some kind of beast, charging at her with his head down. It would be a lot more menacing looking if he wasn't also shuffling like an old-timey astronaut.

Hawk wished she knew the extent of the low-g area and whether or not it was likely to continue to exist inside the hotel for much longer. Normally, a fancy building like this came with its own gravity generator. Well, she'd take advantage of the spring in her step so long as she had it.

Which was only about one more second.

A taser-net dropped over her, and she had only about five seconds of consciousness. Painful electricity shot through her limbs making it difficult to control her spasming muscles, but, luckily, that was one second longer than she needed to press the panic button hidden inside her earring.

♀

CHAPTER 7

Lucia Del Toro

L ucia sat at the bar, thinking.

In one hand she held a half-drained pint of a local brew that was disgustingly carbonated but potent enough to strip paint from the walls. In the other, she thumbed through the pile of complimentary chips the casino had given her. Each flick was a rhythmic tap against the gleaming synthetic wood of the bar—slunk, slunk, slunk.

She'd told Hawk that she'd be back for sex after a quick game or two at the tables, but here she was brooding at the bar instead. The alcohol wasn't even good, so what was she doing? She should get up and see if Hawk was still up for a little fooling around. Or at least check out the tables.

Instead, she took another gulp of the vile booze.

Like most things in Mehit, the bar at the casino was intentionally pseudo-retro. They had invested a lot of money into the big faux wooden bar, with its intricate carvings of cherubs and Earth fauna that Lucia's onboard identified as 'deer fauns." There was a giant mirrored back that reflected all the various expensive-looking bottles lining the shelves. She'd asked about them when she'd first taken a seat, but the bartender told her they were for show. The bottles held nothing but water for the customers who felt that water should be served in something fancy, since it was a scarcity in much of the rest of the System... The only real drinks on offer were various flavors of the fizzy, overly-sweet fad drink.

The music that piped in overhead barely drowned out the clicking and dinging of the slot machines on the floor, which was visible through several large, open archways all around the bar. The bar was like a tiny, dark cave in the middle of the sparkle and gaudiness of the casino.

Lucia sighed. There was a willing and waiting woman upstairs. Time to stop brooding over feeling glitchy and out of sorts. Perhaps sensing her decision to leave, the bartender circled back to Lucia. He glanced at her empty and asked, "Time for another? Do you want to try strawberry this time? I highly recommend it."

Lucia could not imagine anything more vile. She was about to tell him so, when her internal claxons went off. She had not set a proximity alarm and so she was startled by the sudden, full-body response. Just when Lucia started to wonder if she was experiencing another malfunction, the alert coalesced into the form of a bird in flight: Hawk. Quickly, she shut down the noise and stood up. Moving deliberately, she turned her body in a circle, pinpointing the source. There! She faced it. Somewhere directly across the expanse of the casino floor Hawk was in trouble. But, what kind?

Out loud, she prompted the onboard, "Distance. Speed."

That jarringly masculine voice in her head told her that the target was approximately 900 meters as the crow flies, and moving west at 8.04 kilometers an hour.

On foot, then, not running.

Was Hawk on her own reconnaissance? Maybe, if she was matching someone else's speed. Hawk tended to walk much faster, closer to 9.3 kilometers. It was those long Lunar legs of hers.

The alarm was for emergencies only, however. Hawk would never abuse their agreement. Besides, if Hawk was conscious, Lucia would be getting an internal communique of some sort by now.

The flashing light continued to move away.

"I'm talking to you here! Are you okay?" The bartender asked. Then, frustrated, added, "Hello? Did you want another drink or not?"

Lucia took off. Equipment she hadn't engaged in some time planked her over slot machines and leaped across table tops, scattering chips and cards... and civilians. Shouts followed her.

She picked up speed. Using those rusty, enhanced muscles, she flexed power into each step. It felt good to cut loose, to let her body do what it was built and bred to do. Heads turned to watch her move at speeds. Gasps followed in her wake. What she *didn't* hear pleased Lucia the most. No one cursed "Martian Wardog" or "Forcer Pig." Even as she vaulted easily over abandoned snack carts, "Who is that woman?" was all she heard, punctuated with the occasional, "What the hell is that girl?"

The body euphoria soared so high that she even smiled broadly when someone yelled, "Watch it, bitch!"

Having made the fastest route to the exit, Lucia pushed through a set of double doors. Beyond them was a hallway. She wasn't entirely sure where it led, since, despite an attempt to sync up to the hotel, casino security was too tight for her to easily link to a current map. She'd been able to pull blueprints and plat maps from secondary sources, but they were very old; a dead-end could be lurking around any corner. Hawk's distress beacon continued to guide her, though it was strange not to have caught sight of them yet. According to the beacon, Lucia should be nearly on top of them.

"Hang on, baby bird." Lucia turned down hallways trying to catch up to the signal. It couldn't be more than a dozen meters in front of her now, but somehow still out of visual range. "Almost there."

What would she find when she got "there"? Who was after them? Was this related to Jonathan's missing AI eye, or something else? It wasn't like they didn't make enemies as bounty hunters. Plus, an even more paranoid thought tickled through her consciousness—what if someone was drawing her out specifically. Someone like the ENForcers. With the *Conqueror* in this sector, it was a possibility they'd made her somehow and were after her girlfriend as a hostage...

Lucia would almost be relieved if that were the case. Then, the decision to fight or run would be made for her. The answer would be fight, of course. It wasn't like Lucia had an option, not with Hawk in the crosshairs. They might bicker from time to time, but there was no question in Lucia's mind that they'd die for each other.

Ahead was an entrance to a kind of parking lot, only for speeders and small, personal airships. Parked in stalls stood orderly, row after row of gleaming crafts. Pushing through the door into the open-air garage, cold air hit her like a slap.

Lucia's breath came out in crystalized puffs.

Hawk's distress signal picked up speed—a lot of speed. Just then Lucia heard the roar of an engine.

Now it all made sense. The signal was directly below her.

Damn it. The maps had been off. Where the hell were the stairs? An elevator? Anything?

No, it was too late for that.

Matching the trajectory of the signal, Lucia fought to out pace it. Her muscles burned with effort. She had to get up enough speed, get enough ahead of the airship before it took off. Each floor had its own landing pad, so, with a whole fuckload of luck, and she timed this right, Lucia could drop onto whatever vehicle had kidnapped Hawk.

Maybe.

Of course, the worst-case scenario had her leaping into a fuel trail.

Don't think. Just push.

It was her old mantra, coming back from the past like so much else today. Put one foot in front of the next. Compartmentalize into each moment. Do what needs doing. Fight the fight at hand. This moment, no further.

She leaped into the open air.

Immediately she began to fall. Below her was the sleek black shape of an Antwerp Mark VII. Lucia could see now that she'd make it onto the vehicle. Holding on was going to be another thing.

In desperation, she swung her arm down with enough force to crumple titanium into a handhold. Slamming a second fist into the vehicle's metal, she managed to hold on. Wind whipped against Lucia's face. Automatically, her implanted second eyelids dropped to protect her vision. It was difficult to breathe, and her system flooded with oxygen to compensate. She wasn't sure how long she could hold on. At least Mark VIIs weren't space worthy. No external weaponry, either, thank fuck.

Given the sounds reverberating through the hull, they'd have to know she'd boarded. In fact, external cameras swung her way. Del Toro gave the cameras her best evil grin. She hoped whoever saw them pissed their pants to see her hanging on by handholds she'd made with her own fists.

When the ship spun into a barrel roll, Lucia knew she'd been spotted. The move was intended to shake her off. Old instincts had her scrabbling for the nearest anything that was grabbable. Her fists closed around the rungs of a ladder leading to an access panel.

An access panel?

Wasting no time, Lucia braced her feet on the lower rungs, freeing one her hands to pry open the access panel. The door came away in her grip. She flung it aside; tossing it into the air thoughtlessly. Somewhere far behind, undoubtedly, an impact and shattered stones.

The beat of her heart and the roar of the engine combined with the sounds of the distress she caused flashed Lucia's mind back, momentarily. A frozen sea bathed in blood, the cries of children, the acrid stench of smoke and death... a flip of her stomach as the ship barrel-rolled a second time, brought Lucia crashing back to the now.

In a surprise move, the clever pilot hit the brakes.

The sudden deceleration did what all the rolls could not. Lucia could feel herself being flung from the speeder. Fortunately, without thinking, Lucia buried her hands in a fist-full of wiring. The cabling wasn't strong enough to withstand the whiplash. A sizzling mass came away with her into the air. A gigantic snap and pop filled the air with the smell of ozone. Lucia was protected from the electrical blast by the wires' own insulation.

As she fell away, Lucia could hear the engine deceleration.

She smiled. They were both grounded now.

Using the shredded wiring to protect her head, Lucia curled instinctively into a roll. It made her plummet faster, but she hoped it would also minimize the damage. She hit the ground like an ejected bullet. Her armored uniform engaged, absorbing a massive amount of the impact's momentum. Fuck Margie; Lucia was never getting rid of this suit. It might be a blight, full of memories of who she'd been and an awkward liability, but it saved her life.

Again.

Warning lights flashed as systems struggled to pump painkillers and assess the stress and damage to her body. She ignored them. Uncurling herself stiffly, Lucia pushed the wiring off her body and kept her eyes on the speeder's descent. The pilot was some kind of damn ace. They seemed to be bringing the Mark VII down in a controlled glide. Damn, if they weren't the current enemy, Lucia might be impressed.

A quick assessment of her own situation revealed that Lucia had cratered into someone's balcony flooring. She lay in mosaic tile shards. Behind her were glass doors, closed. The space beyond was dark. Either Lucia had lucked into an unoccupied apartment, or the people living here were pretending not to be home.

As a precaution, however, she set her proximity alarms. She also set a part of the on-board checking the local feeds. She wanted a heads-up if the local constabulary caught any whiff of them.

With a pained groan, Lucia sat up.

After belly crawling to the nearest ledge, Lucia peered through the fancy carved balusters. Slowly, she eased the peacemaker from its hidden holster. Its sights were still calibrated to her eyes, so she used them like a telescope to scan the smoldering Mark VII.

Wires spewed from the access panel along with billows of black smoke. The pilot had landed them upright, nose dipped into the canal's sludgy ice and ass in the air— not even a wingtip had broken. The ship had shattered the walls of the canal behind it in a long line, probably destroying the landing gear in the process, but there was surprisingly little damage overall.

The neighborhood they'd crash landed in seemed less touristy than the one that she and Hawk were staying in. This place felt more residential. Though still in the Italianate style of the hotel district, these buildings had a more lived-in feel. Clothes lines strung between windows. Patches had been lovingly applied to worn sections of stucco or brick. The colors were muted, less gaudy. There were fewer flashing marquees and advertisements. Even the ironwork streetlamps cast softer circles of light, as evening mode shifted across the dome.

Their short flight had taken them closer to the curve of the dome that surrounded Mehit. The heat insulation was better here. The air held a nip, but was crisp, not frigid.

She returned her scope to the ship just in time to see an emergency exit pop open. A figure emerged. That annoyingly deep masculine voice rattled off statistics in Lucia's head as she scanned: *173 centimeters tall, estimated weight 86 kilos, eye color indeterminate at current distance, however, shape of eyes and skin color suggest East Asian heritage, hair: bob-cut, fluorescent pink, gender... unknown.*

"Oh, fuck off with your gender assumptions, you piece of crap ENForcer malware," Lucia told her head. "You don't know shit. You never knew shit."

Though to be fair to the onboard, it was impossible to guess by looking at this person. The figure in her scope had curves, but none of them suggested anything obvious to Lucia, like hips or breasts. Their all-black ensemble highlighted their unnaturally brilliant hair. Something that sparkled—sequins?—on the short waistcoat they wore. A close-up on the figure's face showed a square jaw and the presence of pink lipstick.

Lucia's database whirred, mapping facial features. In a matter of moments, a name and profile appeared from the police database: former criminal hacker and known bounty hunter, Ozmerelda Jackson.

Ozmerelda? 'Oz,' perhaps? Could this be the rival that Hawk often talked about?

Pulling back up into position, Lucia fired off a quick series of blasts. They were aimed to force Oz to take cover by stepping back into the ship. Using the 'Forcer ability to project her voice, she said, "That was a warning shot. Show me Independence Hawking alive. You have one minute to comply, Citizen. Starting..." the stopwatch queued up. "Now."

'Citizen'? Ah, fuck, that had come bubbling up from somewhere deep and ugly. With a shake, she tried to clear her head. All that did was dislodge her curls, and Lucia had to use a puff of breath to move her bangs out of the way so that she could lift the scope to her eye again. When she refocused, she saw Oz peering cautiously out of the speeder.

Oz seemed to be trying to pinpoint which direction the shots had been fired from. Hadn't they heard the warning?

Experimenting, Lucia projected her voice again. "Surrender, Ozmerelda Jackson. Come out with your hands up."

Nothing, not even a turn of their head in Lucia's direction.

Huh, could Oz not hear? Were they deaf or otherwise hard of hearing?

It wasn't impossible, just not terribly common in this day and age. If Oz had been taken by the ENForcers at a tender young age, like Lucia had been, they would have been augmented and "corrected." However, there were lots of reasons why someone might remain deaf or hard of hearing, since there were a lot of far-flung colonies that simply didn't have access to the technology— not to mention the fact that, unless you were conscripted, it cost money. Plus, Lucia knew that there were people who strove to retain a certain culture, to keep languages alive. Hell, the Force had several hundred sign languages in the onboard. Mostly to keep people from passing secret code, but... well, regardless of the sinister reason for having access to it, it might come in handy.

Oz's deafness did, however, hamper Lucia's plan to stay out of range of weapons. Lucia's peacemaker had picked up the presence of at least one such armament on Oz's person. The Mark VII was small enough to be operated by a single person, but there was no guarantee that Oz was on their own. Going in was risky, but if Lucia was going to communicate with Oz, face-to-face was the only way.

Lucia disarmed the countdown and holstered her peacemaker. After taking a moment to let her onboard calculate the fastest route to Oz, Lucia stood up and leaped over the balcony. One jump, two sprints, a bit of parkour for flair, and she stood in front of Oz in 3.5 seconds. Not stealthy, but hopefully fast enough to stay out of anyone's sights. The landing hatch had opened onto one of the walls of the canal that had remained intact. Lucia hauled herself up onto it to stand face-to-face with Oz.

The only new information that Lucia gleaned at this distance was that Oz's eyes were green. That masculine voice in her head kept trying to guess at Earth heritage, saying something about Mongolia or Albania, but Lucia quieted it with an internal 'shut the fuck up.'

Oz seemed to be taking a moment to assess the danger Lucia posed. They'd backed up a step when Lucia had leaped onto the landing pad, but they hadn't reached for any weapons. Instead, their pink-painted lips curled into a little, curious smile. Lifting a hand slowly, they waved 'hello.'

I am Lucia Del Toro. Let Hawk go, Lucia signed in MSL, Martian Sign Language. It was roughly based on American Sign Language.

Another flicker of surprise on Oz's round, androgynous face. Hands and fingers replied in the Shanghai dialect of CSL, Chinese Sign Language, *Sorry, what?*

Lucia didn't know the dialect, even though her onboard could translate it. At least she had CSL. Letting the onboard do the translation made her movements crisp and a bit jerky, but she hoped she was understood: *I am Lucia Del Toro. You have my partner, Hawk. Let her go or I will mother you.*

Oz's laugh was a little too loud and discordant. *Mother me? You don't look like my mother, thank god. I don't know about this kink, but could be fun? Sure, why not? I'll try anything once.*

Shit. Lucia had meant to say 'murder.' What the hell was the right sign? Her hands were clumsy since she relied on a kind of muscular autopilot. She tried again. *You will be in a bowl of pain.* "Oh, for fuck's sake," Lucia muttered, waving her hand, as if trying to erase her mistake. *Just hand Hawk over. Right now.*

"Really? Because I kind of want to be mothered in a bowl of pain," Oz said out loud in a voice oddly modulated due to their inability to hear how the words sounded, or, perhaps, never having heard them spoken to begin with. Oz continued to smile languidly at her. Their hands said: *I feel like a bowl of pain should be served with a side of something.*

Carefully, Lucia spelled out: *How about agony?*

Oz made a face. *No, too obvious. You're ruining the pun.*

"This isn't a fucking joke," Lucia snarled. She could tell Oz was not the sort to be bullied. *Where were you going with Hawk?*

Away from danger, Oz signed, their eyes scanning the skies. *And, speaking of, you're welcome. I intercepted some Paradox Industries goons. I'd been trying to get Hawk to somewhere safe so we could make a plan. But someone jumped on my plane like some kind of superhero and ripped out my electrical system.* Oz graced Lucia with an appreciative grin. *That was weirdly smart for an ex-ENForcer. You're more than brawn, after all. There's a surprise. Too bad I'm on your side and now we're sitting ducks.*

'*Sitting ducks,*' Lucia signed, suddenly alarmed. Only ENForcers used old Earth idioms like that. *Where did you learn about ducks?*

Oz's hands raised and then dropped, as if they were starting to say something but decided against it. Then, a slow, mischievous smile spread across their face.

As if on cue, a proximity alarm alerted Lucia to the ambush.

She dodged just in time for the projectile to skitter over her head. It shattered against the metal hull of the ship. Shattered? That was no ordinary bullet.

Whatever was in the projectile sent warning lights flashing. Antidotes flooded her system.

Time to get indoors, away from that sniper.

Ignoring the barrage of chemical information, Lucia pushed past Oz into the interior of the ship. In the hopes that Hawk was within earshot, she called out to her: "Hawk!"

Something landed on Lucia's back. When an arm and legs wrapped around her, she realized it must be Oz. Oz seemed to be attempting to choke her and punch whatever could be reached with a free hand. It was immediately obvious that Oz was not augmented. The blows were annoying, but hardly enough to stop Lucia. With this extra weight, Lucia continued to lumber into the interior of the ship. With all the power gone, the lights were off. Lucia switched to night vision.

Oz must have used a manual crank to open the escape hatch. No, surely on a ship as nice as the Mark VII there were some redundancies built in. Lucia hunted around on the nearest panels for whatever sequence might close up this door. Last thing they needed was for the sniper to follow them inside. Meanwhile, Oz kept attempting to pummel and... stab?... her. Wait, stab?

Sure enough a slender needle bent against the flesh of Lucia's neck.

What are you? A tank?" came Oz's frustrated snarl.

"Basically, yes," Lucia said, even though Oz wouldn't be able to read her lips at this angle.

If she could close the hatch on the panels just inside, the mechanism was opaque to Lucia. Instinct had her broadcasting: *The perimeter can't be secured.*

Oz yanked a fist-full of hair. Turning off the pain receptors in that location, Lucia backed herself up, hard into a wall. She could hear the air leave Oz's lungs with a squeak. She did it again just for good measure.

Oz must have lurched out of the way this time because the connection wasn't as solid.

Lucia glanced at the still open hatch, cursing. Where the hell was her back-up? "I need men on the ground. Now!"

The sound of her own voice shocked back to the present. Oz's fist pounded into the side of her head, but Lucia took a second to close her eyes and take in a slow, steady breath. No back-up was coming. She was only in command of herself.

And she needed to be in command *of herself.*

Hawk's life depended on it.

Okay. Quick breath to refocus, and then Lucia grabbed whatever of Oz's she could get a firm hold-on—sequined jacket? Arm? Then, she tilted and yanked. Oz was not quite so easily dislodged, but another shake and grab seemed to do it... or Oz decided to agree to the relocation. That last one seemed more likely since they sort of rolled off somewhat gracefully and mostly kept their feet.

Since they were face to face again. Oz used sign language to say, *You are aptly named, Del Toro.*

Oz was hardly the first person to make that little quip. Lucia acknowledged it with a little dip of her head. If they were trading banter out loud, she might have made a reference to this being the china shop that the bull was about to wreck, since Oz seemed to know all the stupid Earther phrases ENForcers tended to trade in. That seemed a little complicated so, instead, she stuck to a simple, "Read my lips: Fuck off."

"Clever retort." Oz made a very disappointed face and then signed, *And here I thought you were interesting.*

"No such luck," Lucia said. They were circling each other now, warily. Catching sight of that open hatch had Lucia's hackles rising again. Maybe if she could stay here and keep it in her sights? But, where was Hawk? She found herself uncertain of how to proceed. Some dark, distant part of her brain whispered, 'This is why you need a team, your creche.'

Oz seemed to notice Lucia's hesitation. Their eyes narrowed, and Lucia got the sense that, in a minute, Oz would attack.

Lucia shifted into a lower stance. Hand-to-hand, she had an advantage. She'd trained in every martial art ever practiced on Earth. It was how she'd spent her days for most of her teenage years. The Force required each cadet to choose one form to master. She'd gotten so much grief for picking Aikido, which they mocked as passive until her creche discovered she could counter nearly every move and lay them out flat. Confident, Lucia did the little 'come at me' wave.

Oz slumped almost imperceptibly. Lucia thought they might still give fighting a try... except they turned tail and ran out the still open hatch.

Lucia stood there a beat, shocked. Then, slowly righting herself, she said to no one in particular, "I guess... the threat is neutralized?"

"Thank Bohr for that." The sound of Hawk's voice made Lucia start a bit. Turning, she saw Hawk clutching an interior wall of the ship, a stun gun in an unsteady and wobbly hand. Her eyes looked a little glazed over, like she wasn't entirely seeing straight.

Only now did Lucia notice that Hawk's distress beacon had changed to green. Hawk had even sent a notification that she was free and on the move. Another glitch. Lucia berated herself. She should have noticed that when it came through. Glaring at the open hatch, she snarled, "Do you know how to close this damn door? It's giving me PTSD."

"What? How is an open door triggering you?"

Lucia clutched the hair in front of her eyes. "I can't secure the perimeter."

Hawk's expression softened into understanding. She moved back, deeper into the ship. Her voice grew fainter as she said, "Oh, right, well, this is the newer model, but I think I know how to fix that. The Mark VII was the subject of that 'cast I love, the motorhead one, with that one guy from that show we both watched."

Lucia smiled. She knew exactly who Hawk meant. Even though Hawk was probably too deep into the ship to hear, she yelled back, "Áki Brynja from 'On Venus, Have We Got a Murder.'"

A faint, "Yeah, that's the one."

A shadow blocked the light from the door. Lucia perimeter alarms blared. She turned in time to see a hulking male figure step up onto that damn open hatchway. The man wore a black uniform matching her own.

An ENForcer.

"Colonel Del Toro," he said, in a pleasant, familiar drawl. "It's good to see you again."

♀

CHAPTER 8

Independence "Hawk" Hawking

Hawk had just activated the emergency power supply and found the control panel to close the hatch when a shockwave hit the spacecraft. Grabbing for roll bars, Hawk braced herself, expecting the ship to be hit again or begin sliding into the canal.

When that didn't happen her brain slowly processed the sensation. Another crunch of some kind echoed through the hull. A fight? But what in the name of Ricther could Del Toro be fighting that would cause this kind of impact? Hadn't she said that the threat had been neutralized already?

What the Fucking Freud was going on?

Abandoning the hatch's controls, Hawk grabbed her stun gun from where she'd set it on the console. She dashed the short distance back the way she'd come. In a second, she stepped right into a sight that spiked fear deep into her gut.

Hawk knew that ENForcer's uniforms had been designed in tandem with a psychologist team to instill fear, but knowing that didn't stop Hawk's blood from freezing at the sight. Pushing down the urge to run, she forced herself to take in the scene.

An ENForcer cyborg—*no, think of him as something defeatable, like any man*—stalked, back and forth in front of the gangway, blocking their exit. Though his body moved like a wild thing, his gaze stayed locked on Del Toro.

Del Toro stood stock still, her arms raised in a defensive pose. It looked like some kind of patient martial arts form. Had Del Toro modified her height at some point to be less imposing? Or did that horrible ENForcer uniform just

92

seem to loom over everything, including someone as normally formidable as Del Toro?

Hawk took comfort in the fact that Del Toro seemed perfectly calm, in control, especially in comparison to the wild, pacing ENForcer. He wore a sardonic, haughty expression that belied his anxious pacing.

Hawk thought he could be Del Toro's age, maybe. There was not as much gray in his black hair—or at least not so much that it was obviously visible in his super-short military buzz cut. Like most people, his skin was brown. He had a scar that bisected lips at one corner, a short, angry, white line of tissue that had resisted the usual skin regrowth treatments. Scars were unusual these days. Someone must have hated this guy enough to poison the blade. Or he'd had to carry the injury some distance before getting medical aid.

Or, the thought suddenly occurred to Hawk, he'd been in that same terrible fight that has scarred Del Toro. Could this be a creche mate?

Del Toro, her jaw bruised, continued to hold her stance, as though relaxed, unhurried. Her voice was full of command. "Stand down, Lieutenant Ali. I don't want to hurt you."

The ENForcer chuckled. It was not a pleasant sound. "You can't give me orders anymore, Colonel. Also, hurt me? Don't make me laugh. From what I can see, you're nothing but a *girl*."

"More like a woman," Hawk said, suddenly remembering the stun gun in her hand. She took aim and shot him in the face. Hawk knew that the stun charge wouldn't do much to someone so cybernetically enhanced, so she circled around as much as she could in the ship's corridors and just kept hitting him with blasts. The charge might at least numb him. Hawk told herself that it was an annoyance if nothing else. "Hey, Del Toro," Hawk asked, checking in, "You doing okay?"

No idea, she projected into Hawk's brain with that jarring other voice from her past. *I need you to hold your position, though. I've got to have someone on that damn door in case there are more of these assholes.*

It was rattling, that deep, authoritative voice only half-remembered as being at all attached to Del Toro.

"Yeah, uh... so, are we using the 'inside' voice now?" Hawk glanced over her shoulder at the gangway. She'd only gotten it a few more centimeters off the ground. If Del Toro was expecting more company, it was a liability. "Also, fine, I guess? I can 'hold' here, if it helps."

Understood, Del Toro's inner voice returned. *Do your best to cover me.*

Hawk was seriously freaked out now. This was more of the Other Voice than Hawk had heard in years. Trying to diffuse the situation, she cracked, "Aye-aye, Captain."

"Colonel," they both corrected at once.

It was one thing for the ENForcer to have said it, but Del Toro, too?

Del Toro looked shocked at what had come out of her mouth, as well. At the same time the ENForcer chuckled. "It's still a matter of pride, isn't it, Colonel?"

"Fuck off, Marcus." Del Toro didn't hesitate to take advantage of his momentary distraction to give the ENForcer the old one-two-punch.

Hawk couldn't remember the last time she'd seen Del Toro fight all out like this, hand-to-hand. The ship trembled with the exchange of blows. The action was almost too fast to even track, especially since Del Toro used some kind of swirly martial arts to keep pushing the ENForcer off target anytime he came in close.

Pulling himself up from where Del Toro had tossed him against the bulwark, the ENForcer gave Hawk a snide side-eye.

Hawk blasted his face again, which made him grunt a bit as he shook off the stun.

"Who's the little mosquito, Colonel? Don't tell me this is that back-up you've been calling for. Ain't I always been your *el compañero*? Didn't I come when you called?"

"*Ya no eres mi hermano,*" Del Toro said.

Not my brother anymore, at least that was Hawk's best guess. At least Del Toro sounded certain, though Hawk thought she detected a little sadness. Disappointment, maybe?

Not having a better plan, Hawk shot the guy again. He only flinched a little when the stun hit him in the ass.

"You can say I'm not your brother, but that doesn't change the truth. We've got history, Colonel," he said, standing up slowly, shooting an annoyed glance at Hawk. "We're creche mates. That means something and you know it. Bonds like that don't break easy."

So, they were creche mates! Hawk pressed against the wall for some cover. That bit of information certainly explained the tension.

"You were never my favorite, Marcus," Del Toro said. "Besides, look at you. How is it that you're the only one of us that's still a Lieutenant? Shouldn't you be embarrassed to face me? What did you used to say to me all the time? 'You're not man enough to be in my creche.'"

"Well, that was prescient of me, wasn't it?" Marcus chuckled, gesturing rudely at Del Toro's boobs. The ENForcer's smile was evil. "Who'd imagine I was the liberal one, eh, Lucian?"

"Lucia," Hawk and Del Toro corrected simultaneously. Del Toro added, "And also, fuck you."

"Yeah, yeah," the ENForcer said calmly, like he had no concern in the world. "It's time to stop playing around, *Colonel*. The brass wants you back. You noticed I'm pulling my punches. I haven't broken leather. I wasn't sent here to kill my brother. We aren't like that. We aren't monsters. We're your family, and I'm here to bring you back."

"My family?" Del Toro's eyes looked haunted, hollowed out. "Don't make me laugh. *No tengo familia.*"

That hurt.

It was one thing to turn down a mistimed marriage proposal. But to claim she had no family? Hawk was starting to feel like—what was that weird phrase?—chopped liver. Anyway, the thing no one wanted or that was always forgotten.

Ouch.

Hawk decided she needed to end this fight quickly, so she could talk some sense into Del Toro if nothing else.

The stun gun was next to useless. On top of that, it was running out of charge. Hawk threw the useless thing at the ENForcer. It bounced off his shoulder and skidded halfway across the small space. It happened to land on the floor, just below something that might be more useful, however.

A bunch of wire had sprung back into life. Loose strings of them spit and snapped on the floor like electronic snakes. Digging around in her coat pockets, Hawk found the pair of work gloves she kept around for repair work on the *Peapod*.

"How can you say you have no family when I come to you as a brother, Lucian? You keep saying you're dead, but I see a boy who's... misguided, lost." The ENForcer cajoled, his arms out in a peaceful, welcoming gesture, "You know you're not right in the head the way you are. We'll fix you. You'll be back to normal. I know what you did for us. Why do you think I'm being so gentle with you now? I owe you that much for your sacrifice—We all know what you did for us, becoming the Scourge. That sacrifice puts lies to all this talk of not considering us your family. You don't do shit like that for someone you don't care about."

Hawk had heard enough of this crap. Rushing over, she grabbed a bunch of wires. The ENForcer turned around at the sound of the crackle of two of the wires hitting each other. As soon as he turned towards Hawk, Del Toro popped him in the jaw again.

His brief distraction and slight pivot gave Hawk the perfect opportunity to rush in close. Surprised that anyone would come into grappling range seemed to confuse the ENForcer, so Hawk slammed the wires up against his chest and prayed to Nightingale for a strong enough shock.

The gods of science must have been with Hawk for once. The force of it blasted the ENForcer off his feet.

Moreover, the charge must have messed up some part of his internal wiring because electricity arced all over his body. His back arched in pain. A sizzling smell filled the gangway, and he helplessly slumped to the floor.

"C'mon, Del Toro" Hawk shouted. "Time to run."

She thought for a second Del Toro wasn't going to do it. Del Toro stared down at the convulsing form of the ENForcer for a long—too long a second. Just when Hawk was ready to take the risk to step closer to grab Del Toro's hand, she seemed to snap out of it. With a spit on the ground, Del Toro said, "Lucia. My name is Lucia, and don't act like you don't know that's who I really am, Marcus. You were the one who first started calling me Lucy. You meant to hurt me, but it was a fucking gift"

"C'mon, c'mon," Hawk urged. "We've got to go!"

Finally catching up her hand in Del Toro's, they ran together out the open hatch.

❦

"Marcus will recover in a second or two," Del Toro said as they made their way out of the ship.

That seemed impossible to Hawk, since she'd hit him with the raw power of a ship's engine, but she nodded. Del Toro probably knew better than anyone. Anyway, it never hurt to assume an ENForcer would be up and on his feet in no time.

A peek out the hatch showed that a crowd had started to gather around the downed ship. Tourists taking pictures—selfies, like the smoldering ruin was some kind of planned entertainment. To avoid being in the pictures, they found a secondary emergency hatch near the rear. Taking it involved having to cling to the canal wall and hope that the icy slush shelf near the edges was as solid as it seemed. Del Toro's boot slipped once, but she only broke through the ice up to her ankle. After that, they held hands as they inched along.

They made it to a set of stairs near an abandoned gondola station without anyone noticing.

Quickly moving up the slick steps, they walked along a cobblestone promenade. Icy fog made the ironwork lamp posts look like something more suited to London than to Venice, but Hawk doubted that d'Isigny had any kind of unified vision for this place, as the neighborhood they found themselves in had also lost some of its Italian veneer. There were still hints here and there, but the buildings lacked the fancier details of the hotel district. The frescos and ocher tiled roofing gave way to simpler construction.

"I'm sure he got knocked back hard," Del Toro continued to mutter, as if to herself, "But if a loose wire could take out a Forcer for good, the revolution would have happened years ago."

Hawk made an agreeing noise, and glanced over her shoulder. She peeked up into Del Toro's face next, trying to gauge how she was doing... "That Marcus guy was a real dick."

That made Del Toro snort a laugh, at least. "Lieutenant Marcus Ali," she said. "Fourth of Five. The sharpshooter of the team."

"What were you?" came out of Hawk's mouth before she could stop the question.

"First of five. Command trained, interrogator class."

Hawk had no idea what that last bit meant, though that sounded ominous. As much as she wanted to, Hawk decided not to ask. After Del Toro left that life, Hawk had made a personal promise to herself never to read articles or do research into Del Toro's former existence. She wanted to hear the story of the Scourge of New Shanghai from the source, not filtered through political agendas or propaganda machines.

Hawk had thought she could live in ignorant bliss of it all because she assumed that part of Del Toro's life was over. She never expected them to run headlong into it again. Maybe the time was coming when she'd have to ask: what exactly happened in New Shanghai?

Hawk glanced behind them again. Still no tail.

"My proximity alarms are set for any ENForcer presence now," Del Toro said.

Hawk nodded. She appreciated that Del Toro had better tech, but she'd probably keep scanning for herself. It calmed her nerves.

They strolled at a leisurely pace, trying to stick to areas with a lot of tourist traffic and to blend in. It was hard not to break into a galloping dash. Every instinct in Hawk's mind screamed 'run-run-run-run-RUN!' But, if there were other ENForcers in the area, they'd be looking for runners, not two regular people out for an evening stroll. Hawk was glad for her penchant for high fashion. Most of the tourists seemed to be wearing variations of the pao. They should really get Del Toro an overcoat or something to hide that distinctive uniform. She said as much to Del Toro.

"You want to go shopping?"

"If we're hanging around here, yes." Hawk let out a breath, which steamed in the cool air. She tried to keep from glancing behind her shoulder again, as her mind raced to try to figure out what they should do next. "Listen, let's go to Galilei's lab. It's in another city. He's got to have good security, and they're expecting us."

"The lab? You think that's a good idea?" Del Toro said, but she shifted course to head in the direction of the train station. "Oz seemed to think they had pulled you out of some trap involving..." a slight pause as memory was accessed, "...Paradox Industries. Of course, Oz was their own kind of problem, so who the fuck knows who we should trust anymore."

Hawk stopped short. "Wait, what? Oz is involved?"

Del Toro turned to face Hawk, stopping as well. "Didn't you know? Didn't you see them run away?"

Everything had been very blurry when Hawk had pulled herself awake. She'd been lying in someone's bunk. It'd smelled nice—inviting and a bit familiar—but also wrong? Had there been a sense of Oz there? "I don't know? The last thing I saw was three hotel goons and then you talking to yourself about having taken care of the threat, which I remember thinking was good, because I was still very wobbly on my feet."

"Huh. Okay, here's what I know for certain," Del Toro considered matters in silence for several seconds. Then she lifted her thumb, to count, "Oz piloted the ship you were on." She jerked her thumb over her shoulder in the direction of the billow of black smoke now several blocks behind them. "Actually, I don't know they were the pilot, just that they were on that ship. They said they were helping you get away from someone, but I'm pretty sure Marcus, our ENForcer friend, was Oz's sniper. Someone almost got me with a drugged needle bullet, at any rate. Oz is otherwise in bed with the Force, because I noticed that they knew too many Earth idioms." She half-raised her index finger, like she wasn't sure if that was a second point or not. Then, Del Toro dropped the counting entirely. "What I can't figure out is how Marcus was already on the ground when I took you and Oz out of the air. I guess he could have snuck out of the same back door we did and moved along the canals out of my scope's view."

Hawk tried to follow the counting and the sequence of events, but gave up. "I think I'm missing some steps." Digging her device out, Hawk checked the time. They still had a couple of hours until they were expected at the lab.

"Look," she said, "This is going to sound weird, but let's find some food. For one, I'm starving. And, second, that ENForcer asshole—what was it, Marcus? No, right, Lieutenant Marcus Ali—will never expect us to stop and grab some pho, right?"

Del Toro blinked in amusement. "You're hungry for pho right now?"

"I'm always hungry for pho.

Del Toro's face did a funny little twist that Hawk couldn't read, but she eventually smiled. "Honestly, pho sounds good." Del Toro's jaw tightened. "This is such a bad idea. I don't want to die because we stopped for pho, but I think you're right. I want to keep going somewhere, but, if we don't eat, my nerves might just turn to jelly or self-combust. Hell, they might just do that anyway, so we might as well be sitting down when it happens."

Hawk was about to look up a good place for pho on her device when it occurred to her that, despite her best precautions, her pad might be used to track her. So, instead, she gave it a hard toss over the nearby wall. She watched as it splashed into the slush and began to sink. That was the newest damn model, too. But, they could pick up something cheap from a stall. Pads were a dime a dozen. It wasn't like all their data wasn't safe, elsewhere.

Del Toro's mouth opened in shock, but then after a defeated sigh, she did the same with hers. "We go through so many of those," she said, watching her sleek black case disappear beneath a crust of ice. "I should stop trying to collect all my favorite music."

Tucking her arm into Del Toro's, Hawk picked a street that looked like it might have restaurants, "I've never understood why you don't just keep it in your head."

"My head is crammed full of other stuff," she said.

"You could consider jettisoning all that information about insignia."

Del Toro shook her head, but she smiled. "That's actually in my brain's memory. The stuff in the onboard is a little more critical than that."

"Like the shape of the *Conqueror*?"

"Nope, that one is also seared into the regular old noggin."

Yeah, Hawk imagined it was. Even though she had her heart set on pho, Hawk spotted a flickering neon sign that flashed out the Katakana for ramen. The soup smelled good even at this distance, but what cinched it were all the people headed that way wearing ENForcer knock-off jackets. They'd actually blend in with this crowd. "Will Japanese do in a pinch?"

"You got me all hungry for Vietnamese," Del Toro grumbled, noticing the same bright yellow sign and probably the preponderance of jackets, as well. "But, yeah, I see what you mean. Warm soup of any kind is still comfort food."

With the city's artificial lights dimmed for evening, a crescent ringed Jupiter was visible in the sky. Even though it was no larger than a plum, the bands of gas were visible. Hawk could see how d'Isigny had had such hopes for this moon as a tourist destination. And, it had worked to some extent. Many people were out, enjoying the night sights. Most of the people seemed to be couples or families out taking in the evening or service industry workers going on or off shifts. The occasional ground scooter threaded through the crowds, intent on delivering food or other goods. A pleasant level of street noise filled the air, only just now punctuated by distant siren's wails.

They ducked into the restaurant.

It was a literal hole in the wall.

Some long-ago tectonic activity had buckled the area, causing a small heave in the street and two buildings to lean into each other. The crumbled buildings themselves seemed dark and unusable, but a number of enterprising businesses had set up in the roughly triangular shaped alleyway that formed between the two ruins. It seemed to be some kind of hotspot or destination, as Hawk and Del Toro passed a group of people in those fake uniform jackets taking holos of themselves in front of the alley's entrance. If she had her device, Hawk would have looked up the name of this place and checked the reviews. Maybe they'd stumbled into a fashionable spot?

Flavorful steam billowed from the ramen shop. A traditional red banner awning hung in front of a narrow counter of about a dozen or so seats. Only one stool was empty, but Hawk figured space might clear by the time their order was up. There was no menu, so Hawk just held up her forefinger and thumb to indicate two orders. Luckily she had left over physical change from the Forty or they'd be desperately trying to dig their devices out of the canal right now. The proprietor/cashier didn't even blink at the offer of cash payment; the returned coins seemed to be in a dozen different denominations.

After pointing out the empty seat, Hawk offered it to Del Toro.

She started to take it, but paused to ask, "What about you?"

Hawk glanced at the guy beside Del Toro busily slurping his ramen while reading his device. He looked like someone who had had a long, hard day and just wanted to be left alone with whatever entertainment he had stored in his handheld. Everyone else along the narrow bar seemed engrossed in their own conversations or thoughts, so she felt safe to say: "I'm... not of a size that street patrols might be looking for. I'll stand. I can kind of block the view from the street this way."

"Good thinking." Del Toro nodded. As soon as her butt was in the seat her posture crumbled inward, and she held her face in her hands. The muscles of her forearm trembled a little. "I'm really pissed off that we can't go back to the hotel. We paid in advance. Plus, I'm a little beat."

And maybe bleeding out a little. Hawk noticed a dark stain at hips and shoulder. There seemed to be something almost sparkling—marble dust? A sequin?—embedded in spots of her old uniform jacket. Several sections of the fabric had clearly absorbed massive impact, since they were stiffened and bulged. The rough patches would eventually soften and return to normal leathery-looking fabric, but for now they added bumpiness to Del Toro's bulk.

The reddened bruise on Del Toro's cheek was already starting to darken.

As worried as Hawk was about Del Toro, physically, she was much, much more worried about her state of mind. Hawk knew she should focus on untangling the levels of double-cross they might be facing with Oz, but she couldn't get that fight out of her head. "So, uh, that Marcus dick said he was sent to bring you back, that's, uh—I guess they've never given up on you. I mean, I knew the bounty was still out there, but..." she trailed off, not certain exactly what she wanted to say.

Del Toro didn't raise her face from her hands, only grunted. "Yeah."

"It's good to be loved?" she said helplessly.

"Not really."

"Right." This was the stuff Hawk was patently terrible at, but she forged on, anyway. "So, he was your brother?"

"In-arms." With her face covered it was hard to read Del Toro's flat tone. "You probably heard, we were creche mates. I grew up with him and three others. We did everything together."

Softly, Hawk put a hand on the shoulder that looked the least injured. "Then how did he not know you're a woman?"

Her gasp sounded almost like a sob, but Del Toro's face finally broke free from her hands. Her fingers entwined with Hawk's and squeezed. Her smile was sad and soft, but it was there as she said, "I don't know. Maybe he did. Like I said to him, he's the one who started calling me Lucy. Who knows. Maybe that's why he hates me so much."

The ramen arrived.

Hawk took the bowl offered to her in both hands, with a bow. She forgot that most people didn't bow as greetings, until she noticed the server gave her a funny look.

Around a slurp, Del Toro explained, "She's Lunar."

"Ah," he said, and then bowed back somewhat awkwardly and far too deeply. "Enjoy."

The broth that steamed up into her face seemed to be shio, salt-based. Beyond the noodles, there was half of a soft-boiled egg, scallions, mushrooms, beansprouts, and a slice of *kamaboko*, the fish cake with the little pink spiral. That last was her favorite. She swirled it around, hiding it in the noodles to save for last.

For several long minutes, Hawk did nothing but stand hunched over her bowl, shoveling food into her mouth.

Halfway through, the exhausted worker left his seat, and so Hawk sank into it gratefully. She hadn't realized how hungry she was until she'd started eating. The salt and the heat were like a balm to the soul—restorative.

Del Toro tipped the bowl back to drink the last of the broth. Setting the bowl down, she said, "By my reckoning, we potentially have two enemies. First, Oz and Marcus, though we don't know the extent to which they are in bed together."

"You don't mean literally, do you?" Hawk tried to imagine it and failed.

"I don't know Oz's preferences. Maybe? But, I meant metaphorically. Thing is, Oz has hung around Marcus long enough to pick up some Forcer slang. Plus, I don't think Marcus's showing up was a surprise to Oz. Oz seemed to be trying to drug me with something and, presuming Marcus was the sniper, which I guess I don't know for sure, so was he. Some kind of hollow bullet exploded and splashed some kind of poison into me that my system neutralized. Anyway, you heard him. He did seem to want to take me back alive, so... those dots possibly connect."

"So I was nothing but bait for an ENForcer sting?" Hawk asked around a last mouthful of noodles, not liking that prospect at all. It made her feel like the weak link. "Ugh. I hate that."

"Possibly. But...." Del Toro frowned, rubbing her bruised cheek absently. "Here's what I don't understand: Oz told me that they were rescuing you from another group, people they called 'Paradox Industries.' I would normally assume that was bullshit, especially given that name—it sounds made-up, right? But, my gut says it's riskier to ignore the possibility there might be another player on the field. Oz could be serious when they say they rescued you... or, Oz could be playing all sides."

"Well, that last one tracks," Hawk agreed, finishing off the last dregs of the salty broth with an internal, satisfied sigh. "Oz is what we call in the business 'a slippery little bastard.'"

Del Toro leaned an elbow on the counter next to her empty bowl, and gave Hawk a long, thoughtful smile. "I thought you liked them."

Hawk fought back a blush that threatened to redden her ears. "I—look, they're cute. And I'm stupid for cute. *Very* stupid."

102

"Stupid enough to get me killed?"

The blush deepened with shame. "Well, obviously, yes. I can't believe I let those goons get a drop on me. If Oz had approached me themselves, I might have just gone with them? I... uh." Hawk let out a huge, awkward breath and feigned interest in the collection of antique toy robots that lined the back wall of the ramen shop. "I might have offered to cut Oz in on our bounty. To be fair to me, I was trying to get out of a sticky situation. I think Alice finally 'died.'"

"Who's Alice again?"

"That cover program I use when I'm hacking. It's finally spun-out, I think. Anyway, Oz made all that go away..." Hawk hated the light that dawned suddenly, and so she winced as she continued "...which should have been my first clue that maybe Oz was pulling the strings of the whole operation."

Del Toro rubbed her jaw thoughtfully, pulling the hand away with an annoyed noise when she accidentally jabbed her own bruise. "Okay, so it's Oz all the way down?"

That didn't feel entirely right, but Hawk had no better theories. "I guess we have to assume that. Although how far down and for what purpose, I have no idea."

Del Toro played with the ramen spoon, clinking it softly against the bowl. She always seemed to need to make noise when she thought hard about things. It was an odd habit. "And you still want to go to Jonathan's lab because you don't think that's related."

"Well, this is what I mean. I did tell Oz we took that job." Hawk sucked in a breath of the soberingly frigid Ganymede air. The ramen shop proprietor gave them dirty looks, as a line had begun to form. Conversations around them grew more animated as the evening ramped up. A thumping bass beat drifted out of a nearby club. "I guess we cut our losses and run, huh?"

Del Toro held the ramen bowl and stared into its empty depths, like she wished it were a shot of whiskey. "Run where? We can't go back to the *Peapod*. If Marcus is acting on orders, like he claims, we have to assume our ship is under watch, if not already impounded. I'd say we could still try and mount a rescue. However, given there's only one space elevator up to where we parked it and there's a full-sized battlecruiser between us and it—we're grounded."

The whole situation made Hawk furious, but all she could think to say was, "This is the outfit I'm stuck in? We have to go see Jonathan. I need his money to shop. I'm not getting arrested in a pao, they were last year's fashion. I'd be better off in one of these knock-off ENForcer fascist fashions! I only wore this because they're warm!"

Normally, this kind thing would elicit a small chuckle from Del Toro, at least, but she didn't seem to have registered the comment at all.

103

"So what's bugging you?" Hawk prompted.

"Marcus."

"Couldn't agree more."

Now Del Toro let out a little huff of a laugh. "We always told him he was the opposite of an instant hit with the ladies. It's nice to see that's still true." She paused for a second. Still holding her nearly empty ramen bowl in one hand, she swirled the remaining dregs around. "His winning personality aside, Marcus is a sharpshooter. He shouldn't have missed."

"This is what you're worried about? Not getting a bullet to the head?"

Noisily, she slurped the remains from the bowl. "No, it's just all these little things all together. Nothing's adding up."

Like that battlecruiser suddenly appearing in the system.

And nobody talking about it.

The stand-off between the ENForcers and the United Miners had been raging forever it seemed. It wasn't officially a war per se, because the miners of the asteroid belt weren't a planetary force or government, only a loosely organized group of workers—some anarchists, some socialists, some who knows what, and every political stripe in between—who had banded together for a singular mission: stop the ENForcer expansion to the outer planets.

They were able to do this because United Miners and the Socialist Corps of Engineers owned the means of production. They refused to allow any military vessels to pass through the jump gates they'd built across the solar system. ENForcers still traveled to the outer systems on diplomatic and trade missions in small, unarmed crafts, but the Collective vetted those soldiers, their transport, and their equipment very carefully and limited their numbers severely. For all intents and purposes, the ENForcers were confined to the inner planets, an area which Hawk had fled as soon as she was able.

The Moon remained out of the conflict for most of her childhood, but the pressure to take contracts from the ENForcers eroded any real neutrality. Everyone needed money and resources, and the Moon was often short on both.

ENForcers contracts always came with stipulations and regulations: take our money, accept our politics.

Hawk had seen the changes starting to take root. Things that had been public, became private. Everything was measured by how it would play on Mars. Sure, it might be allowed, but maybe you left "your politics" out of things if you wanted to make money.

It was always small things at first.

Until it wasn't.

Hawk's heart thudded dully in her inner ear. "Do you think it's possible that this battle cruiser—the *Conqueror* Whatever—slipped through UM/SCE defenses somehow? I thought The Collective kept a tight watch on all that empty. Every colony is linked. I also am really shocked that everyone is acting like it's not there when it has to have gotten permission to use the gates. Like, a ship like that doesn't just roll into the Jovian system."

Del Toro had been lost in her own thoughts, staring into her empty bowl. "Mmm? I mean, I suppose it could have."

"Yeah, but wouldn't a ship breaking the barricade be the news of the century?"

"Well," Del Toro said grimly. "There was one moment when an entire colony went dark and a section of the surveillance net went down."

New Shanghai.

"That was way bigger news," Hawk acknowledged. "No one ever talks about anything other than you, actually. Like, you clearly got transport from some ship."

"There's a reason I know the *Conqueror*'s signature really well. We were told not to take *Vengeance*. My creche and I were in *Peapod*, and given a lift on the *Conqueror*. We were told she had to be going that way anyway and it was too expensive to send two battle cruisers."

"So, this whole time?" Hawk struggled to fathom all the implications of this revelation. "Are you suggesting that the *Conqueror* slipped across the line over all those years ago and has been trudging its way here ever since?"

"Or waiting for Jupiter to come to them. Technically, probably a bit of both."

"And you... the massacre—was, like, what? Cover?"

Hawk didn't think it was possible for Del Toro to look more haunted about her past, but she sounded far away from herself when she said. "That would explain why the original orders were that much more brutal. They didn't want anyone who might have seen the *Conqueror* in the area to live."

CHAPTER 9

Lucia Del Toro

They'd been set up this whole time.

Certain dread settled into Lucia's guts. The metal of the ramen shop's stool felt icy under her butt. The sweat she'd worked up during the fight cooled. She shivered. All the death and suffering she'd shouldered all these years had just been cover to sneak a ship past the Asteroid Belt? That image of it overhead, was this why she could never shake it from her dreams—why it always resurfaced? Had part of her lizard brain realized, even then, that all those lives had been for this?

When the noodle shop proprietor came over to ask them to move along, Hawk flashed him such a stern look that he backed away, his hands in his air. She turned to Lucia, her voice stern. "I have never asked, but it's high time you told. What do you mean something worse could have happened? That doesn't seem possible."

"What I'm about to say," Lucia warned, "does not absolve me. Do you understand? The blood is still on my hands. It was my call."

Hawk looked uncertain, but nodded. "Okay."

"Our orders were to puncture the dome. The brass had plans drawn up for us. All the best strategists in the Force had come up with a way for us to sneak in past the defenses and blow the whole thing—no warning, in the middle of the night. If we'd followed the plan there would have been no survivors. No one left alive to tell the tale. Hundreds died that next morning, thousands were wounded, but it was supposed to be every last one of them: two hundred thousand, six hundred and twenty-three souls."

Hawk listened in mute horror, her body taunt.

106

"Sometimes I think I should have listened to Simon. He said we should disobey—just refuse the order completely. We had a duty to disobey illegal orders, in fact. Marcus argued that a bold stand like that might seem cool, but it would be meaningless. The brass would just replace us with more obedient soldiers. The killing would get done with or without us. Daniel was the one who hatched the plan. He was the team's spy, our assassin. He always had a man on the inside, a contact in every port. All we had to do was delay. He'd get the word out. Once everyone was evacuated, we'd do the mission as planned. Hand to god, I honestly thought it would work."

With the new information, everything made more sense about that tragic day.

"I see my mistake now. We never asked ourselves why. We were so programmed to not question orders, so numbed by past cruelties that it never occurred to me to wonder why the Earth Nations Peacekeeping Force would want so many non-combatants dead—and so completely. I should have asked myself: why? Why implode the dome? Why make it look like an accident?"

"Yeah," Hawk said solemnly. "Normally, you wanted people to remember the jackboot."

Lucia nodded. As the adrenaline wore off, muscles began to protest. Every blow that Marcus had landed ached and throbbed. She gingerly rubbed her ruined eye socket before continuing. "You know the rest as well as I do. We were discovered. There was a panic. We tried to fight our way out. I gave the order. Then, I mowed down a whole lot of innocent people. It inspired that song, 'Bloody Dawn.'"

They both sat in silence for a moment. Hawk hummed a bar or two. "I never realized that was about you. Still, where's your creche in this? The song only talks about one person."

"Because I gave the order. They escaped out the hatch. I held off the crowd.'

"Alone?"

I surrender.

Lucia shook the voice from her head and forced herself to continue the story, the way she remembered it. Every ugly detail. "The Scourge of New Shanghai," Lucia said plainly. "It wasn't difficult. They were civilians, Hawk. No one else had a gun. That's when I knew it was over. I would have gone back to face court martial and execution, but I could hear Marcus on the chatter. There was talk of commendations. We were going to get medals for this. This utter massacre."

"So you defected instead."

"Deserted, technically," Lucia gave her a little smile. "But, yeah. I stole my command ship, evaded attempts to bring me in, and then went off the grid." She didn't mention that going 'dark' had involved turning her peacemaker on herself as well as using her bare hands to rip out tracking hardware out of her own body. "And then I went to find you."

"And I let you in."

Lucia held her breath. "Do you regret it?"

There was no hesitation. "No. I mean, this is a lot to process, but, honey, I always knew you were the Scourge of New Shanghai. I can't pretend I had no idea. I mean, I could have turned you in, too, you know. There are miners who'd like to see you face justice, too. I may have intentionally avoided all news about that day, but, knew what kind of person you were when I met you in that dive bar. You might not have been The Scourge yet, but nobody gets to the rank of colonel in the ENForcers by being a saint."

Lucia let out a relieved breath. She did not deserve this woman. "True enough."

The thrumming music from the nearby club had grown louder. The beat matched the pulse of her heart. Something in it, though, lifted Lucia up out of her downward spiral and called up a positive memory—the moment that, in so many ways, started everything good in her life.

"C'mon," she said, finally standing up. "I want to dance with you. Then, let's get as far as we can with this eye. It won't be as steady as a military pension would have been, but sixty mil is still a damn fine retirement. I'd like to make that happen for you, if we can."

Hawk opened her mouth like she might protest, but then smiled. "Dance? Seriously? And you thought I was weird for craving pho? You want to go clubbing at the end of the world?"

Lucia offered a hand and with it a hope. "If you'll still have me?"

Hawk gasped it and held tightly. She didn't say anything, perhaps not trusting herself to, but she was the one to lead them away from the shop.

It would do for now.

With the ENForcers so near, all this talk of marriage no longer mattered. There would be no forever, only right now.

And right now, they were going to dance.

❦

In the distance, sirens grew louder. Lucia's onboard reported that the local constabulary had traced the downed Mark VII's registration to someone named Stella Stephonopolis, who reported her vehicle stolen from the parking garage at the casino. No one seemed to be looking for them in connection to that, at least.

Hawk nudged Lucia as they walked towards the sounds of the music, still holding hands. "You said, 'Go as far as we can with the eye.' Does that mean you think going to Galilei's lab is safe?"

Lucia had been expecting a different sort of question—something about the past or her present crimes, so it took her a minute to consider. "Nothing is really safe. Not with ENForcers on the ground and in the sky. But, we might as well take the money he offered."

"If he can pay it." Hawk sounded glum at the likelihood.

There was that.

They followed the thrumming beat of music to a building just down the street. Music emanated from a place that looked like it could have been anything, but there were people outside handing out fliers for some band or other and ushering people inside. They each took the paper offered and curiously stepped up the marble steps to the double doors that had been propped open.

A residential mansion had been converted into a shopping mall with book stores and other markets occupying once stately rooms with parquet flooring and marble fireplaces. A tiny restaurant operated out of a former grand kitchen and adjoining dining room. Hawk and Lucia followed a crowd up the stairs to the fourth floor where tickets were being beeped off devices.

"Ah, fuck," Hawk muttered, checking her pockets for change. "I don't think they're going to take cash."

The music was plenty loud. "I can dance in the stairwell."

Hawk blinked in astonishment, but then her face darkened with worry. "First a confession, now another dance? This better not be some kind of good-bye. It's not over until they haul you away. You know that, right?"

Hawk could always see through her. Lucia gave her a wan smile. "Just dance with me, Hawk. Just for a song or two."

Still giving Lucia a skeptical eye, Hawk said, "You know, just because we ran into an old creche mate of yours, it doesn't mean the end of the world. It's one guy—" Hawk must have seen something in Lucia's expression, because she quickly added, "Or one ship. The solar system is big."

Lucia made a noncommittal noise as they moved out of the queue and found a space on the landing. Because all of this all felt too big to deal with right now, she just wanted to focus on being in this moment, now. The flooring was marble, or some approximation of it. The stone felt slippery underfoot. Fitted into the curved landing was a leaded glass window. Through the wavy glass, the street lights glittered below. The slight distortion made the canals appear mist-covered and threw the street scene below into fuzzy focus like in a romantic scene on a holo.

Lucia held out her hands as though ready for a waltz.

With a grimace, Hawk took the lead position. "Don't think I don't know what you're doing."

Smiling to soften her words, she said, "Shut up and give me this."

Lucia closed her eyes and felt Hawk's hand encircle her waist as they began to waltz.

They'd first met up in a dive bar on Mars. It was supposed to just be a hand-off—the package for a job completed, nothing more. The beer had been weak and music worse. The band was a half-drunk country western trio that only seemed to remember three chords and two songs. Even so, Hawk had coaxed Lucia out on the sawdust-laden dance floor. She'd just started swaying her hips seductively, trying to coax Lucia to do the same—to move the music, the way most people seemed to understand how to do innately.

Lucia had never learned to dance like that.

Officers were only required to know how to perform in formal situations—and, of course, Lucia had only learned to take the leading role. She felt awkward and wrong, all big, clumsy, and stupid.

Realizing this, Hawk had patiently guided Lucia in what was essentially the same dance, only backwards. There had been a lot of wrestling for command, toe stepping... and laughter.

Another first.

It wasn't that Lucia had never laughed before, but this had been so different, so unencumbered, so free. Maybe because she'd unburdened her secret in a hoarse, terrified whisper into Hawk's ear not moments earlier and, instead of recoiling in confusion or disgust, Hawk had only seemed to find her more attractive. She'd shifted pronouns immediately and even asked her name.

Her real name.

After a night of laughter and dance had come sex. Sex that actually involved her body because Hawk asked questions Lucia had never considered before because she hadn't known the options even existed... and in the morning after had come the horrified, dawning realization that she could never, ever reverse this course now that she knew what it felt like to be herself.

Not trusting her voice not to break, Lucia whispered into Hawk's ear. "Don't let them take me alive."

"I won't," Hawk said without hesitation as they began to waltz. Just like that first night, they didn't even try to match the rhythm of the music that echoed down the staircase. They just swayed to their own internal beat. Hawk's face pinched in concern where it lay against Lucia's breasts, "But, it's not going to come to that."

Removing a hand from Hawk's shoulder, Lucia brushed a thumb along Hawk's cheekbone. Their eyes met and Hawk tilted her head up. Lips opened for a kiss. Lucia obliged.

They danced and kissed until the business card in Hawk's pocket beeped, reminding them they had a train to catch.

❦

Through the window of the bullet train, they caught snatches of Ganymede's pocked icy surface as it raced past them. After the neon of the touristy Zu Fossae area, the landscape seemed a barren expanse of silver and black.

Jonathan's tickets bought them a private car. Not a luxury suite, mind you—just a tiny capsule. Even so, they had room enough for Lucia to stretch out her stiffening muscles on a padded mattress. Hawk's face pressed to the window. Her eyes widened like a child's.

"I thought you'd been here before," Lucia said.

"I never get tired of it," Hawk said. "I'm not a jaded ex-soldier like you. Ice moons are still new."

Lucia chuckled, "That's bullshit. Everything is icy this far out."

"Yeah, okay, fine," she grumbled. "I still think they're nifty. Anyway, I think we might be able to see aurora if we keep heading in this direction. Everything might be ice in this direction, but Ganymede is the only moon with a magnetic field."

"What's an aurora? You mean like Earth's northern lights?" Lucia made her aching way over to the window. Everything hurt now that the last of the adrenaline had worn off. "I've only heard about those in stories."

"Ah ha! Not so jaded after all," Hawk teased, making room at the window for Lucia.

"What are we looking for?" Lucia could see her face reflected in the plexiglass next to Hawk's. After the confrontation with Marcus, Lucia half-expected to only see the ghost of the colonel. Instead, her eyes were drawn to everything that had changed—the soft curve of her jaw, the fullness of her lips, her sculpted eyebrows. She even liked the look of those hard, chiseled cheekbones.

On a different face, they had been severe and cruel, but on Lucia they left the impression of a haughty regalness. It was a good face. Her face. "Will the aurora be ribbons? Flashes of green?"

"I don't honestly know," Hawk said, sitting back a little. Suddenly, switching tracks like she did, Hawk asked, "Do you think we're rushing into a trap?"

Lucia continued to scan the horizon. She chose her words carefully as she considered, "It doesn't necessarily make sense for Jonathan to double-cross us. But, it's not out of the realm of possibility. He's clearly terrible with money. If he's willing to borrow from gangsters, he's probably in enough debt that my bounty is tempting. But, he'd have to subcontract, and, given the bounty he's already offering, mine is peanuts in comparison."

"Mmm, yeah." Hawk settled back against the far wall of the compartment, her hands tucked behind her head like a pillow, her eyes on the low ceiling. Out of the blue, she wondered aloud, "Why are peanuts the measure of something insignificant?"

"I don't know. ENForcers say 'working for peanuts,' too, to mean getting very little pay. I would have thought that peanuts were a fine cash crop, like any nut. Were they worth less than a kernel of corn?" Lucia remembered another peanut-related ENForcer-ism, "Yeah, and there's some kind of gallery of peanuts… from which comments are unwelcome? Might not be related, though."

"I'd work for peanuts," Hawk said, closing her eyes. "There's a lot of protein in peanuts."

Lucia nodded in vague agreement. Her memories of peanuts mostly involved their butter, which she'd been fed a lot of as a kid. "Peanuts are okay. I like hazelnuts better. I'd work for hazelnuts."

Hawk let out a yawn. "If it's a regular ambush, I like our odds. But if the ENForcers show up…." Hawk cracked her eye at Lucia, seeming to focus on the bruise on her cheek, "I say we run."

If we can. But there was no point saying aloud what they both understood. "You should get some rest."

"Yeah, you too." In a second, Hawk was down for the count.

Down for the count. That one was a boxing reference, maybe? Lucia sighed, boxing still existed as a sport, of course, but it was a miracle anyone understood ENForcers when they spoke. Lucia leaned her arms against the train's window and watched for aurora, listening to the sound of the rails, a comforting whoosh of the electromagnets.

❧

Lucia woke Hawk a few minutes before they entered the Edfu Facula dome. There had been a few odd green streaks in the sky towards the south pole and she wanted Hawk to see them before they vanished from view.

Hawk blinked sleepily at them for several seconds before saying: "I always think these things are going to be more dramatic than they are."

An announcement came over the train's speakers informing them that they were entering the domed city and listed up-coming stops. The business district, where they'd be getting off, was the fourth station.

A long tunnel obscured the view out the window for several minutes. The train clacked through a darkness punctuated by strobes of light. When the track next opened up, the cities of Edfu Facula were visible. The dome had gone translucent for the evening so the sky was dark. The only thing visible was the mellow light of Jupiter, no larger than a grape in the sky, and the smaller dots of Jupiter's other moons.

The train ran alongside the backsides of warehouses spattered with graffiti mostly in Arabic. Lucia's onboard automatically translated the words: *Afridi sucks dick*. To which, someone had added in Portuguese the additional tag of, *Good for him*.

In the distance, city lights glittered.

Edfu Facula couldn't be more different than Mehit in Zu Fosse. The ochre tiles and white-stucco Italianate structures and icy canals had given way to sparkling spires, skyscrapers, minarets, and mosques. As the train clicked past the warehouse district, they began to see bustling modernity everywhere. Rickshaws, motorbikes, airships, and pedestrians all seemed to be fighting for space on narrow streets. The first station they stopped at had a crowded platform, despite the late hour. The announcements now ran in English, Arabic, French, and Portuguese. Despite their private car, they could hear the train's interior filling with conversation and noise.

Through the window, Lucia caught glimpses of street parties, shopping districts, night markets, and stately city squares. They passed a large mosque illuminated in blue floodlights. Everything was gone too quickly to see too many details, but she was left with the impression of marble and gold.

"Looks like a real city," Hawk noted.

"Technically, Mehit was a real city." Lucia countered, a little irritated that Hawk seemed to be intimating that her choice of hotels had been a bad one. "It was just a tourist trap town. Besides, it was cheap. I don't know what we're planning to do for money now that access to our bank accounts are slowly sinking towards Ganymede's spinning metal core."

With an unconcerned shrug, Hawk said, "Ah, we'll pick up a burner somewhere along the line."

Lucia wasn't as convinced it would be so easy, but she didn't have a better solution.

They passed the second stop. More people got on as others got off. The pulse of commuters was like the city's heartbeat. The neighborhood around this station seemed to be a bit quieter. Fewer carts and people were on the street, and she could see residential housing blocks surrounded by rudimentary terraformed greenery—spindly trees and prairie grasses that probably cost a fortune to maintain.

Hawk seemed fascinated by the bits of green that passed them by, especially the bougainvillea vines that grew along the tracks. "Did you not have trees on Luna?"

"Only in terrariums." At Lucia's questioning eyebrows, Hawk explained. "They were like zoos, only for plants. And very intentional. Not... chaotic like this."

Chaotic? Lucia didn't see what Hawk did. To her eyes, Edfu Facula seemed stately and grand. Having grown up on Mars, she had a different sense of chaos. As one of the oldest established settlements in the System, there was hardly a Martian city that was not built upon the ruins of another. None of which was helped by the current government's obsession with all things Earth. Every possible biome had been imported and attempted, many under domes, some underground, and even a few on the surface itself. Mars was a ruin of human ingenuity, held together with duct tape and prayers. And the-iron fisted will of the High Commander of the ENForcers.

The train shifted downward, heading underground. The view became nothing but gray tunnel walls and work lights.

Since the next stop was theirs, Hawk and Lucia moved out of the private compartment into the main area of the train. They had to shoulder through the crowds to get closer to the doors. They looked a bit out of place in their arctic gear. No one else had a coat. In fact, considering all the party dresses and fancy robes, if she had to guess, Lucia would assume that this must be one of the last trains of the evening and that most of the people were making their way home from some party or evening gathering. Though given the late hour, there were a surprising number of revelers. Despite signs clearly prohibiting food and beverages, many people seemed to be eating from colorful paper containers containing dried fruits and nuts. One woman they passed had a wreath of flowers in her hair, a crown of synthetic red tulips. Remembering the street party she'd glimpsed, Lucia wondered aloud, "Is there some kind of festival happening?"

The woman with the flower circlet smiled. "It's Nowruz. Didn't you know?"

Lucia's onboard informed her that the closest translation was 'new day' and that Nowruz was a New Year celebration that happened around Earth's spring equinox by the people of the regions formerly known as the Balkans, the Black Sea Basin, the Caucasus, Central Asia, the Middle East. Here on Ganymede, Edfu Facula was the only population that celebrated it due to its larger numbers of Arabic speakers, but it was also observed in several other cities on Europa, Io, and Callisto. One of the appropriate greetings was—she called it up now to say out loud, "Ah, nowruz mobarak."

The train jostled to a stop, causing Lucia to grab for a handhold, but she thought she heard the flower lady reply, "And also to you!"

The door binged open. She and Hawk let the push of people propel them onto the station's platform. People dispersed in every direction. They found themselves alone rather suddenly.

Hawk took out the business card. As they exited the station following the directions up a flight of stairs, they passed a bald, tattooed busker playing some kind of multi-stringed lute, their instrument case lined with hyacinths. The twang of the strings echoed hauntingly in the underground, cavernous station.

The hackles on the back of Lucia's neck raised as they turned down an empty corridor and left behind the last of the others who'd exited at the same station. The stairs they followed opened up into a deserted downtown office area. A few taxis hovered near the station hopefully, but the street was otherwise empty. Electric lights made the night glow brighter and more harshly than daylight.

After all the festivities that they'd seen on their way here, the emptiness unnerved Lucia. "How far to Jonathan's place?"

Hawk looked at the business card. Now that they were on foot, a small map appeared on the backside. She squinted at it and then oriented the smart paper to the visible landmarks. In a second the card beeped. A robotic female voice said, "At the corner of Seventh and Prime, turn left."

"Looks like a five minute walk," Hawk said.

Lucia wondered about the wisdom of keeping that card. It obviously had a GPS. A satellite somewhere in orbit around Ganymede tracked them. It was hard not to be paranoid after everything that had happened. "Did we ever decide if Jonathan was in on your abduction at the casino?"

Hawk shrugged. "I think we decided it didn't matter much, that the money was too good."

"Right." That was hardly much comfort. Lucia scanned the rooftops and the streets. With a mental command, she reset her proximity alarms.

Following the business card's directions, they entered into the courtyard of what appeared to be the laboratory's campus. The space was largely open with tall, flat, uninspired office buildings on all four sides. Illuminated by carefully placed flood lights were concrete planter boxes full of equally unremarkable plants—untrimmed rosemary hedges and scrubby yew trees.

"Your destination is straight ahead," the card said, coming to the end of its programming. "Welcome to Chimera Enterprises."

"Chimera?" Hawk repeated as they stepped under the awning near the front door, "Did we know he'd named his lab Chimera?"

Sensing the card, the doors beeped and a green light appeared above them. Lucia gave the door a gentle push and they hissed open. "I guess we're expected?"

But that didn't seem entirely true. The lobby was empty. A large reception desk with the company's name and logo stood a good distance from the doorway, but no one sat behind it, not even a robotic sentry. There were security detectors on either side of the desk. One of them flashed green.

"Do we just follow the green lights?" Lucia wondered.

"I really thought Galileli was going to meet us here."

Lucia had thought so, too. "Maybe he's waiting in his lab?"

Heading for the greenlit security gate, Hawk glanced over her shoulder to give Lucia a worried look. "This feels like a trap, right?"

Lucia nodded. "Definitely."

Hawk stepped nervously into the detector. She passed through without a hitch. Lucia had no idea what she thought was going to happen, but she found herself holding her breath until she passed through. No alarms went off. She let out a relieved sigh.

She glanced back at the gate as they continued deeper into the office building. It was odd that the detector didn't pick up her peacemaker. Perhaps the green meant that it had been set to pass them through. She wasn't sure why, but that felt even more ominous somehow.

Maybe that was why she wasn't all that shocked when they opened the lab door and found Jonathan Galilei, dead on the floor.

♀

CHAPTER 10

Independence "Hawk" Hawking

Hawk stood on the threshold of the doorway, unbelieving. Del Toro rushed past her, paused for a second, but then knelt by the... *body?*

Hawk's brain didn't even want to parse what she was seeing. It was Galilei's corpse, she supposed. It was hard to articulate the exact ways in which he looked dead, but some part of her lizard brain just knew that to be a fact.

His curls splayed out around his head like a wavy fan where he'd fallen on the plas-crete flooring. He'd changed clothes since they last saw him. Now, he wore a Hawaiian print shirt, slacks, and a lab coat. The lab coat had to be for show; the man was an engineer.

Was.

Because that frozen surprised look on his face was definitely too pale, and, of course, marred by the single bullet shot to the head.

Galilei was clearly dead since someone had shot him executioner style, twice in the stomach and once right in the center of his forehead. Blood spread out around his body like some kind of horrific halo or aura.

Even though she knew the answer, Hawk felt the need to confirm with Del Toro, "Is he....?"

"The body temperature is approximately 34.4 Celsius and the ambient temperature is about 20," Del Toro said, from where she knelt beside him. She reached out a steady hand and gently closed his eyes. She stood up, oblivious of the blood stains that were quickly being absorbed by the fabric of her uniform pants. "He's quite dead, though not for long. Obviously, I'm guessing, but Jonathan was shot anywhere between three to four hours ago."

Three or four hours? The killer was long gone, then. Hawk hadn't even considered that might be a concern, so she was surprised by how relieved she suddenly felt. "So, his mafia connections finally caught up with him?"

Del Toro stood over the body, frowning down at it. "Yes, or someone very much wants that to be everyone's conclusion."

"You don't think so?" Hawk cautiously let go of the doorframe she didn't even realize she'd been griping, and took a step forward towards the corpse. She didn't know what she thought she'd see better in the two shaky steps she could manage before stopping again, but it just felt like the thing to do. "What makes you say it like that?"

"Mars really only has the Triad, so I don't know everything about how all the various organized crime syndicates work, but usually executions are the kind of things you do to your own, to your employees. Unless Jonathan is secretly a lán dēnglóng, it seems more likely they'd have beat him senseless. Dead people can't pay."

"Uh..." It wasn't like what Del Toro had just said wasn't true. It was more that Hawk was still having trouble with this whole scene. She didn't even really like the guy necessarily, but she didn't have the same kind of experience Del Toro did with violent death. She blinked, pulling her gaze away from the blood. "Right."

"Oh," Del Toro glanced over at Hawk. Her mouth worked for a second, embarrassed, before saying, "That was... I mean, I sort of forgot Jonathan was a friend."

"Friend is a bit generous," Hawk said quickly, because this was not the time to be reminded of playing hide-and-seek with Jonathan and his sister in the hydroponics sheds. "So, if it's not the mafia, who else wants him dead?"

Del Toro glanced around the lab. "That's a good question. I'm not sure I know the answer. Someone who wants to bury this artificially intelligent eye, I suppose? But, I find it hard to believe that there's a scientist alive today that makes a single prototype and doesn't leave behind any notes or other materials. Surely, he didn't just keep the design of this thing in his head. He must have had back-ups or colleagues he shared his work with."

True. So maybe he hadn't been killed to keep the AI eye off the market, just to delay the unveiling of the prototype, perhaps? "Didn't he say something about wanting it back before the board of directors meeting or something? So he had some kind of deadline for his project. He's... uh, clearly going to miss that now."

"Before we call the local constabulary, we should see if we can find any of his project files."

Hawk nodded and started to move further into the room before the full implication of what Del Toro said hit her. "Wait, you want to call the cops? Shouldn't we just take whatever info we can find and get the fuck out of here? We can drop an anonymous tip if you want, I suppose. We don't want to be associated with this, do we?"

Del Toro still stood over Galilei's body and she glanced down at him thoughtfully as she spoke. "I don't know why, but I'm feeling like I want some kind of paper-trail here, something that absolves us of this."

"No one knows we took this job."

"Yet the business card led us here. Right to this body. We've probably already shed a fuck-ton of DNA. The cops will know we were here; we might as well come clean."

There was that. But, something in Del Toro's tone bothered Hawk. It was the same fatality that she'd felt in the kiss at the dance hall. "Come clean, but light years away from here when we do it, right?"

"No," she said. "I mean right here, right now."

Hawk made her way around the lab, looking for anything that Galilei might have laid out in preparation of their meeting—data crystals, smart paper, devices. So far she was coming up blank. "But, if we call the cops and someone wants us in the frame, aren't we playing right into their hands?"

Del Toro's eyebrows drew together. In the semi-dark of the half-lit lab, shadows hugged the curves of her face. "Maybe? It's a strong possibility, I suppose. Maybe they're expecting us to run. I'm sick of running."

Those last words were almost inaudible. Hawk scanned each workstation in the lab for anything loose, even looking in the wastepaper buckets, but she glanced up to check Del Toro's expression.

Her soft curls hung over her scarred eye. Del Toro's gaze lingered, thoughtfully, on Galilei's body.

What was she thinking?

Hawk went back to her search, but talked as she upturned waste buckets, checked under blotters, and tried to open any drawers. "Let me see if I understand your proposal. You agree that this is probably some kind of set-up, but you're suggesting we do the unexpected. Instead of running from the scene, we stay and we call the local cops. And, because we're innocent, the cops will just... roll with that?" Most of the time Hawk felt like she was the pollyanna one to Del Toro's jadedness, but Del Toro's continued faith in law and law enforcement was a weird blindspot that seemed to be some kind of holdover from her ENForcer days.

When Del Toro didn't answer, Hawk continued. She'd covered half the room already, so she just kept skimming for anything useful. So far, she found a whole lot of nothing, which was its own kind of red flag. "This place has already been rolled," Hawk said. "Plus, it seems like if you want to put us in the frame for this murder, the timing couldn't be more perfect. There's some kind of festival going on—"

"Nowruz,"

"—and so what do you bet the cops are short-staffed? All it takes is the cops who are on the take to show up and, whammo, we're arrested."

Del Toro let out an audible sigh. Her eyes finally left Galilei's body to hone in on Hawk's "That's a possibility if we run, too. It'll be much harder to pin this on us if we've been upfront from the start."

Okay, this was starting to seem weirdly genius. "So, you're saying that you want to lean into this?"

Del Toro's lips crooked up into a wry smile. "It's the same principle we used when we walked away from the crash. Police always look for runners. Runners look guilty. If we stay, show them the body, tell them everything, honestly, I feel like we're safer. Like, it'll be harder to use circumstantial evidence to pin this on us."

It still felt risky as fuck, but, as usual, Hawk was willing to trust Del Toro's instincts. "I want it noted for the record that I think this is a bad idea."

"Duly noted," Del Toro agreed with a chuckle.

Hawk reached a cubicle that actually looked as if someone used it now and again. A post-it note had been pinned to the clothwall that said, "Damn it, Dave." The other things in the workstation included a half-dead philodendron in a dry tea cup, three mechanical pencils, and actual research printouts of some kind. Glancing around the desk, Hawk found a slim notebook tucked in among a pile of readouts. Flipping to the back page, she found a list of random words, some crossed out. Passwords, no doubt. People never change, thank Curie. Firing up the terminal, Hawk pulled a data crystal off the bracelet she wore and plugged it into the machine. "Just let me see what I can find in their files."

Del Toro came up behind Hawk and leaned in over her shoulder to look at the screen. Her lips were close to Hawk's ear as she chuckled, "This never works, you know. You're not going to find their secret plans for the AI on some public terminal."

"I know," Hawk spared her a little grin. "I'm not looking for the secret files. I'm downloading the annual reports. I want to know why this board meeting was so damn important. What are they deciding on this next session? Why was it so critical that Galilei was willing to take out a second mafia loan to fund a bounty hunt on his missing eye before this specific meeting?"

That earned an impressed grunt from Del Toro and a soft kiss on the ear. "I've managed to isolate the local police frequency. If anyone diverts here, we should know. Unless, whoever is orchestrating this is using whatever security service should be patrolling this place.... God. We were clearly led here by the nose. There wasn't even a guard at the desk. We should probably have turned around the second we noticed that. This whole thing is a giant red flag." She seemed to consider something for a moment before letting out a breath. "Well, we're in it now so we should ride it out. How long do you need?"

Hawk took copies of several months-worth of meeting notes, hoping that was enough. Removing the crystal from the terminal, she slipped it back onto the beaded bracelet. It looked like just another one of the many glass beads when she was done. "I'm already finished."

Del Toro straightened up and looked off to the left, like she was thinking really hard about something. "Right. There's the call to the... they seem to be called shurta, the shirts—uniformed cops."

"Shirts? Great, they sounded like fascists. Despite having agreed to this idea, Hawk found herself pacing anxiously. "So, we just wait? We... let them take us in?"

Del Toro leaned a hip against the desk. Crossing her arms in front of her chest, she tipped her head back to stare at the ceiling. "Worst case scenario, this leads us to whoever has it out for us."

Hawk couldn't help but laugh, "Yeah, no. Worst case scenario is we end up like Galilei over there." Or worse, she thought but couldn't say: *we end up in the hands of the ENForcers*. Instead, Hawk asked, "What makes you even entertain the idea that whoever is behind this wants either of us alive?"

She glanced at Hawk for a long moment. Her expression seemed hollowed out, almost desperate, which frankly scared the shit out of Hawk.

Oh. Oh *shit*.

Del Toro was already thinking what Hawk couldn't say. "You think it's the ENForcers." The realization sent a cold stab into Hawk's gut, colder even than the sight of Galilei's body on the floor. Panic surged her to her feet, but otherwise she felt unable to move. "You're betting the ENForcers are behind this whole thing, and, what? You want to go running straight into it? Have you lost your mind?"

They stood in the grayscale of electric light coming in through the windows. Del Toro's face remained impassive, unreadable. Hawk's eyes scanned her face, anyway, desperate for any clue. Reaching out a hand, she clasped cold fingers.

"I've been wracking my brain trying to figure out who would care about this kind of tech." Slipping from Hawk's grasp, Del Toro reached a hand up to cover the scarred eye, unconsciously. "ENForcers go through a lot of eyes."

'A lot of eyes' was a weird problem that Hawk felt like she needed more information on, but it wasn't as important as the fact that the ENForcers seemed to suddenly be involved in this bounty and that Del Toro seemed to want to head towards them rather than far, far away. "So, is this all connected? You don't think Marcus was some weird coincidence?"

"Do you?"

She didn't, but she wanted to. Desperately. "If you thought the ENForcers were involved with Galilei and his eye, why the fuck are we doing this at all? We should have run instantly!"

"They're going to catch up to us sooner or later, Hawk." She calmly adjusted her uniform jacket, like she was readying for a battle. Then her expression softened. Reaching out, she tucked a stray piece of hair behind Hawk's ear. "Listen, I don't think we're in immediate danger. I doubt that these yokels, the shurta, are going to come busting in with an ENForcer escort. I just want to follow the breadcrumbs right now. I wasn't lying when I said I think we stand a better chance at not getting framed if we come clean. Let's see what honesty gets us, okay?'

"I'm not good at honesty," Hawk admitted. "Plus, I don't like any plan that puts you in the 'Force's crosshairs.

"I know," Del Toro said. "Neither do I."

"Really? Because you sound kind of ready to turn yourself in. There was the 'farewell' dance and you've been talking about fate and atonement and not wanting to run anymore ever since we came into this forsaken system. You're not crapping out on me, are you?"

Del Toro took a moment to find Hawk's gaze and hold it. Everything was bathed in silvery electric light, but somehow that only seemed to accentuate the two different browns of Del Toro's eyes. "I am not. I'm feeling a pull, though. There's something here that I need to see through. It's been hovering just under the surface. I can't entirely explain it, but I can promise you that, if at all possible, I won't walk into the lion's den without you."

"You'd better not," Hawk snapped, but she felt somewhat mollified. Del Toro never made a promise she couldn't keep. Never. Hawk let out an angry huff of a breath. "Fine. Okay. Just let me get the current plan straight. The cops are coming and we're going to tell them about the bounty, Galilei, and everything. And what? Hope that in the process they spill some information about a connection to the ENForcers?"

Del Toro looked a little uncertain at that. "Basically."

"And if they arrest us for killing Galilei, what then? We have leads, which we then can't follow up on because our asses are in jail?"

Del Toro's frown deepened. "They can't arrest us for anything,"

"Of course they can! You're assuming they'll follow the rules," Hawk found herself no longer pacing, but now she bounced from foot to foot in order to quell the desire to run. "And, I don't know, isn't desertion a crime or whatever they pinned on you for the bounty?"

"Dereliction of duty, desertion, and treason. Murder. At least that's what the ENForcers want me for. I've never looked to see what I'm wanted for among the miners," Del Toro said.

Hawk blinked. Had she ever seen a warrant for Del Toro's arrest, something posted from the United Miners? She must have. Probably she never noticed it because the ENForcer's bounty was so much higher than anyone else's.

It was strange, though. Del Toro's crimes were against the United Miners, weren't they? Shouldn't they be the ones with the highest bid? Or.... at least an outstanding arrest warrant.

Sirens wailed, growing closer. Through the large windows of the lab, Hawk could see strobing red lights in the sky as the police craft approached the building. Hawk grabbed the nearest wastepaper basket, clutching it to her stomach. "Ugh, I think I'm going to throw up."

"Now? I mean, there's a dead guy just right over there."

"Don't remind me," Hawk groaned. "I just—you know I hate cops. I only do the actual bounty collecting because you can't."

"I didn't think Luna had a police force," Del Toro mused. She threw an arm around Hawk, protectively, and steered them both towards the lab's doorway.

Hawk leaned in. Closing her eyes for a moment, she inhaled Del Toro's smell, an intoxicating combination of leather and woman. She held the scent in her nostrils for a moment, swearing on all that was science that if something happened—if they'd drastically miscalculated with this gamut—she would hunt the very ends of the earth and take on the entire military might of the ENForcers herself to get Del Toro back. Opening her eyes, she let out the breath. Smiling up at Del Toro, she said, "Luna doesn't have cops, not really, anyway. I mean, we had people to call if someone was in trouble, but mostly we just tried to equitably distribute resources so no one needed to steal."

"There's a reason people call you Lunatics," Del Toro said with a fond smile as she led them toward the front door.

"True, true," Hawk said, but she felt the need to point out: "And yet it *mostly* works."

"I think that's why it seems so crazy," Del Toro added.

123

Still holding the wastepaper basket in one arm, Hawk slipped the other under Del Toro's jacket and hugged her waist, hard. "Don't you fucking leave me."

"I have no plans to," she said. "Try to relax. These are very likely going to be regular cops coming to meet us. No one has connected us to the ship that went down in Mehit. We're in another town and a whole different jurisdiction. We've done nothing wrong here. There's a dead body and we're reporting it."

Okay, that last part was what Hawk really needed to hear. She was able to let out the breath she didn't even know she was holding and square her shoulders. They knew this was a trap, but they were being intentional about how they sprung it. That was sensible. Del Toro is tired of running, but she wasn't running into danger. That was an important distinction.

"Right," Hawk said. Her stomach settled, she finally let go of her death clutch of the waste paper bucket. She set it down, albeit nearby. "Let's do this."

❧

The shurta arrived with blaring sirens and flashing lights. Three separate cops arrived, almost simultaneously, on flying scooters. No armored police van, at least, so it was some comfort. They had not come expecting to have to haul them away—and if they were going to try to take Del Toro, they should have come with a tank.

Hawk could see why they were called the shirts, after all, since two of the three were wearing uniforms that included the archetypical blue button down. Why cops were associated with that particular color, Hawk was uncertain. She made a mental note to ask Del Toro when next they had the chance. The final cop, however, wasn't in a 'shirt,' per se. Instead, he wore a long, billowy coat, like he thought he was a detective in a novel or maybe one of those vintage flats. Underneath the overcoat—or were they called 'dusters' for some reason?—he wore a suit coat and tie. His shoes looked shiny and slippery. Not made for a chase. He was definitely meant to be the brains.

Del Toro suggested that they meet the police in the entryway and so they stood by the empty reception area when the cop in the fancy coat approached. He gave them both a quick glance and skeptically asked, "You work here?"

Hawk glanced down at her own outfit and gave the cop an offended grimace. She might be wearing last year's style, but come on, "Do I look like a nerd?"

"That's a stereotype, ma'am. I've had extensive training not to profile people. I take it that's a 'no'?"

124

Coat Cop looked to be a middle-aged guy, maybe in his fifties, with short, salt-and-peppered black hair that threatened to curl a bit at the ends near his ears. His features were sharp, his skin, like most people's, was a variety of brown. His black eyes flashed with an intelligence that set Hawk's nerves on edge.

She distrusted cops; smart ones scared her.

"We don't work here," Del Toro confirmed. "I told dispatch that we're licensed bounty hunters and that we had been invited to tour this lab by Jonathan Galilei, whom we discovered dead upstairs, approximately twenty minutes ago."

Hawk fished through her pockets until she found the business card Galilei had given her. Pulling it out with the intention of handing it over as proof, she noticed that there were new words flashing on the back. *Danger! Danger!*

When did those words show up? While they were on the train? Were they some kind of warning from Galilei? Or were they new? Could they be a hack from someone else, someone like Oz, trying to alert them to a new danger?

So, instead of giving the cop the business card, she clutched it in her hand and held it up for him to see. She held it at eye level with the backside facing herself and Del Toro, hoping Del Toro would notice the words. To the cop, Hawk said, "See."

Del Toro's text response came through their private comm, *"Danger"? Who sent that? Do you think it was Jonathan or is someone trying to warn us now?*

No idea. Maybe we should keep our eyes—

She didn't get a chance to finish before Del Toro plucked the card from her hand, flipped it over, and showed it to the cop. "Are we in danger right now? Are you working for the people who killed Galilei?"

Or, there was always the direct approach!

Hawk tried to act like she was in on this turnabout from the start and looked the cop hard in the eye and said, "Yeah. Are you? We know Galilei was in deep with the mob. Are you in bed with the local yakuza?"

"Triad," Del Toro corrected, but then she frowned and added, "No, I'm wrong. looks like vory v zakone."

"I... what? No, I'm not a bent cop. That's a hell of a jump—you both clearly have trust issues. Let me introduce myself, I'm Detective Inspector Mohammad Sargsyan," The detective took the business card and looked at the back of the card and then back to the two of them. "It looks to me like Mr. Galilei knew he was in trouble and was maybe trying to warn you ladies away. Where's the body? My lab guys are on their way. I was hoping you two might come back to the station for a minute so we could get the whole story out of you."

"No way," Hawk said, just as Del Toro said, "Of course."

"We don't both have to go in," Del Toro added with a nod at Hawk. "I'm happy to answer any questions you have of us, Detective Inspector Sargsyan."

Sargsyan gave them both a long look, scratched the back of his neck thoughtfully, and then shrugged. "I guess there's no reason you both need to come back to the station. Why don't you go back with my guys, and I'll check out the scene with this one," he said, pointing at Hawk.

Is it really okay to separate? Hawk sent to Del Toro.

I know how to talk to cops, she replied. *Anyway, if it is a trap, I'm best suited to fight my way out of it.*

Wait. What about your peacemaker? If they find it, they'll know who you were.

They have no reason to search me for weapons.

Hawk disagreed, but there wasn't time to argue. *This cop is right,* she sent. *I have trust issues.* Out loud, she said, "Okay." Her tone was slow and skeptical to both Del Toro and Sargsyan. "I guess that's fine. Why don't I show you where we found Galilei?"

Del Toro nodded to the two other cops and headed off with them.

Hawk's stomach tightened watching Del Toro move away, flanked so expertly by cops. She hated everything about this, and so she watched Del Toro leave until Sargsyan cleared his throat.

"Mx—? Er, I'm sorry, I didn't catch your name."

"Hawk. I just go by Hawk," she said, turning to move back through the security detectors. When the detective walked through without even a beep, she had to ask, "You don't carry weapons?"

"We don't," he said. "But I am partly weaponized. Were you expecting something to trigger?"

Had she? Thinking back on it, the detector had also let Del Toro through and Hawk knew for a fact that Del Toro was not only fully 'weaponized' as Sargsyan said, but also she always had her peacemaker on her. Odd that it hadn't even chirped. Was it actually deactivated? "I don't know," she admitted. "Why else have these things at your front gate? My partner is also 'weaponized' as you say, so you'd think she would have set off an alarm, too."

Sargsyan's sculpted eyebrows raised a bit and he glanced in the direction Del Toro had gone. Hawk suspected that if the cops were networked, then he just let his colleagues know Del Toro was a cyborg. Maybe Hawk shouldn't have said that? Well, it was too late now. Even if they did have the head's up that Del Toro was cybernetically enhanced, no one would be expecting a fully loaded

ENForcer chassis. She'd still have the element of surprise. Or at least Hawk hoped so.

Running his hand along the edges of the security gate, Sargsyan said, "It must have been deactivated before you arrived, but the green light makes it look like it's still working. Interesting." He took out a slender device from his inner breast pocket. It was cylindrical, almost the size and shape of a fancy pen, and he waved it over the edges of the gate. "Yes, looks like it's been tampered with. I'll send a note to the forensics team to take a closer look at that."

"Cool," Hawk muttered. She had to admit that she was surprised to see him taking his job seriously, like he was in some kind of detective VR. "So, you actually solve crimes?"

Sargsyan's lips thinned. "That is the job description."

"Sure, technically. And I'm supposed to collect bounties. Lately, our success rate hasn't been great."

"And 58% of murders go unsolved," he agreed as they moved down the polished hallway to Galilei's lab. His hard-soled shoes made a slick, clacking sound as he moved along the flooring. "I will admit that I'm hoping this one is as straightforward as your partner suggested."

Hawk remembered the executioner-style bullet holes and Del Toro's comment about them. "And I think the killer is expecting you to want that, too. Galilei borrowed a lot of money from the mob. He told us as much. But, it's like Del Toro said, you don't kill your cash cow, do you?"

"Not usually," Sargsyan said thoughtfully.

They'd come to the door. Galilei lay just as they'd left him. Once again, Hawk hung out at the threshold, letting Sargsyan move forward. He used that slender handheld device to not only take records of the body, but the lab as well. He also didn't turn on the lights, and the skyscrapers beyond the long bank of windows cast everything in shades of gray and silver.

After a quick scan, Sargsyan turned to Hawk, "Did you move anything?"

Hawk considered lying, but decided that Del Toro probably had a point that it was better to come clean than to be found out later. "I downloaded some files from that machine—the last five years of public annual reports," she said, pointing to the terminal she'd used. "The password is in the back of the little notebook in the top drawer. Oh, yeah, and Del Toro closed Jonathan's eyes, so her fingerprints are on him."

Even in the semi-darkness of the room, Hawk could see Sargsyan's eyebrows shoot up in surprise again. "I'm really not used to this kind of honesty from suspects."

"Yeah, that's because we're not suspects."

"I'm beginning to believe that."

"Technically, bounty hunters work for law enforcement," Hawk said with a little grin "Technically, we're colleagues."

"Technically," Sargsyan's smile was just as wry.

They nodded at each other in a kind of understanding. "But, seriously, you must realize we have no reason to want Galilei dead. Like with the mob, he's our literal paycheck."

Sargsyan's lips made a thin line. Standing up, he went over to the terminal that Hawk had indicated that she'd used. He looked around the ceiling for something. "Isn't it odd there are no cameras?"

Hawk felt stupid for not having searched for them before. Del Toro had probably known. She wouldn't have had such a candid conversation earlier, otherwise. "Is it? This is a research lab. Some of this stuff must be confidential or whatever. Not every boss is into employee surveillance."

"Remember the part where I've been trained to not make any assumptions about people or their motivations?"

Hawk leaned a hip against the door frame and crossed her arms in front of her chest giving him a long look. "Yeah, but that's got to be part bullshit, right? You must have to make some assumptions, otherwise how do you ever know who to suspect?"

"Well, since you've been so honest with me, I'll return the favor," he said, not shifting his glance from the terminal, as he waved his device over the station. "Most people are killed by people they know, their friends or their family."

"Yeah, but aren't most murders crimes of passion?" Hawk asked, thinking she remembered that from some cop holo or other. "I don't see a lot of passion in that execution over there.

"If I was going to make an assumption," Sargsyan said, with a sly smile, "One might be that that partner of yours looks like the kind of woman who could totally shoot straight, even in a fit of passion."

"Nothing about Del Toro is straight," Hawk felt the need to say. "Though I think she'd take your assumption as a compliment, so yeah, I guess I'd agree. So, should I be worried? Are you planning on holding my partner for this? Because it was her idea to call the cops. I was in favor of just ditching this whole scene."

He shrugged. "Your honesty has impressed me. If she's more honest than you... well, I suspect she'll be just fine."

♀

CHAPTER 11

Lucia Del Toro

Lucia silently reminded herself for the sixth time that calling the shurta was the right thing to do.

Things were not going well, however.

Standing outside, in the Chimera building's quad, Lucia and the two police officers stared at the motorbikes. Distant sounds of the continuing Nowruz celebrations punctuated their silence.

"How much do you weigh again?" asked the officer who introduced himself as Khalil. Khalil was tall and willowy. His black hair looked like he used more product than Hawk and Lucia combined.

"One hundred fifty-eight kilos," Lucia said. At their looks of confusion, she said, "About 350 pounds."

The other officer, Ferreria, took off his hat long enough to scratch the bald patch at the crown of his head and pull a bit on his thick mustache. He was squat, solid, and gray, leaving Lucia with the impression of a rock. He seemed about as smart, as well. Replacing his hat on his head thoughtfully, taking time to squaring it up, he said: "The hover cycle will never hold that. I'm not even sure it could handle that in ground mode."

"Just how jacked-up are you?" Khalil asked, his eyes glancing up and down Lucia's body incredulously. "And where do you hide it?"

That was a loaded question and one Lucia definitely would rather not answer. "How important is it that we conduct this interview at your headquarters?" Lucia asked instead. "If you have no intention of arresting me, which I can't imagine any reason why you should, we could just go over to that coffee shop for the interview." She pointed across the street at an open storefront. The name read Happy Cupcake in Portuguese.

Khalil and Ferreria exchanged a glance.

Static jittered through Lucia's head, making her wince. Suddenly a connection Lucia thought long dead crackled to life and she picked up the local police frequency in time to catch the tail end of the subvocal conversation between the two officers:

...the boss will be ticked.

I mean, she's right though? We don't have grounds for arrest.

Fine. But I'm putting this in the report.

Lucia tapped her temple, twice, hard, trying to bang the glitch off. Even though it was handy to hear what they were saying, Lucia did not like the randomness of this functionality. If her signal was live, it might try to automatically reconnect to *Boy.net* for upgrades. If it did that, she might as well shoot up a signal flare that said, "Scourge here" in giant, glowing block letters.

Diagnostics suggested turning the proximity alarm off and back on.

A classic, but one that, for once, actually made sense. The proximity alarm swept the area for any threat. A subvocal conversation definitely qualified. She turned it off. She'd turn it back on if they ended up heading to the station.

"Fine," Ferreria said out loud, in that same tone Hawk had used when she had grudgingly agreed after a subvocal chat. Ferreria broke eye contact with Khalil and turned his attention to Lucia, "I don't see why we need to take you in. I mean, I think the boss wanted us to use the recording equipment at the station because it does that fancy 3-D, holo imprinting shit? But I have a pocket 'corder, so I don't know. What do you think, Khalil?"

With a shrug that all but screamed 'you know what I think,' Khalil said, "I mean, she kind of *is* a suspect?"

"You're not supposed to say that part out loud," Lucia said wryly.

"Well, you must have guessed, right?" Khalil snapped petulantly. "I mean, you weigh what again? You're clearly not just some gal who randomly sauntered by."

"'Sauntered'?" Ferrera repeated with a scoff. "Who even uses words like that, college boy? You've been reading too many of those cheap romances again. Anyway, the problem is that we also can't just expect a suspect to make their own way to the station, right? Like, why wouldn't she just flee? So I mean, one of us could walk her there? It's just like, five miles or something."

Lucia did not offer that, technically, she could keep up with the top speed of the scooters, and, thus, could run alongside them.

The three of them stood in the parking lot staring at the bikes for several beats of confounded silence until Lucia just started across the street to the cupcake place. If they were going to dither, she needed sugar.

🌰

The guy behind the counter was Black and had a lot of facial piercings and a white tribal tattoo band that snaked down from the center of his forehead, wrapping around his cheek to disappear into his shirt's collar. His hair was braided and beaded with LED lights and some other wire that made the tips undulate and twirl at random intervals. When Lucia entered his smile was bright and welcoming. "Hello, hello! " he said in several languages until she acknowledged him in Martian Standard English.

"You look like a custard lady," he said without any other preamble. Within a second, he had charmed Lucia into trying something called a Pastel de Nata, a creamy custard-filled pastry. "Super good," he was still saying when the two police officers walked in the door, making him flinch.

Hearing them enter, Lucia said, "Make that six."

"Friends of yours?" the cashier asked, his eyes nervously tracking the two officers as they found spots to sit in the far corner.

"Not in the least," she reassured him. "You must have seen them come. There was a murder next door."

"A murder! No way!" he said, reaching for his device. He glanced at where the hover bikes still sat, "Do you think they'll bring it out the front? The body, I mean."

Lucia shrugged. "I don't see why not."

"Excellent," he said, pushing aside part of the window display to set up the camera of his device. "I just got a new Grella. Murder is a big hit generator."

Lucia rarely felt her age, but nothing made her more aware that she was an outdated model like the next generation talking about the newest trends. "Cool," she said absently, reaching for her own device in order to pay—only to remember she tossed it in the frozen canal. She turned to the officers, not at all surprised to see Khalil keeping a close eye on her. "Oi, Khalil. Come pay for these so it don't look like I'm trying to bribe you."

"Al'ama," he said in a tone that implied he'd just cursed. However, Lucia's onboard translated the word as 'blindness,' which wasn't especially helpful. With a defeated sigh, Khalil got up and fished for his personal wallet device. He beeped it on the register with an annoyed, "Seriously?" directed at Lucia.

Then, looking at the tally of the pastries, muttered another swear: "*Ya ibn el sharmouta.*"

"You want my statement to hold up in court, right?" Lucia said, taking the bag from the cashier and following Khalil back to the table. "You can't have a whiff of corruption."

"I'm hoping you're guilty of something," Khalil said. "Because I kind of hate you."

"You're just mad because you were expecting to mooch off her," Ferrera said with a smile that cracked his face with dozens of wrinkles. He'd taken off his hat and set it beside him on the table's top. On top of the hat, he'd placed a little black box, the portable recorder.

They divided up the treats. Ferrerra pushed the top of the black box with his thumb. A light came on one the sides. It pulsed as he spoke, "Statement by..."

"Lucia Del Toro," Lucia replied. "Bounty hunter."

"...to the Edfu Facula police, Ganymede." Ferrera continued, adding the date and the precise local time.

Lucia held her breath, expecting them to ask for a thumbprint or DNA for confirmation of her identity, but they mercifully never did. Perhaps they didn't have the equipment to record it?

Khalil sat down on the opposite side of Lucia, next to his partner. He leaned over the short table and its cat-patterned tablecloth and said, "Why were you at Chimera Corporation this late at night, on a holiday?"

"We had an appointment with Jonathan Galilei. He'd hired us for a bounty and wanted to give us a tour of his lab."

"On Nowruz?" Khalil seemed deeply incredulous, like this was some proof of criminal intent.

"Is that unusual?" Lucia asked, glancing about the open bakery. Clearly, other places were not only open, but open late. "We came by bullet train from Mehit, which is not celebrating any—"

"Heathens," Ferrera spat.

Lucia didn't know how to respond, so she ignored it. "I was unaware there was any holiday that would preclude our visit."

"What kind of name is Del Toro, anyway?"

Was this town full of racial purists? It was notable that all three cops seemed to share some kind of ethnic heritage. Leaning against the chair's back, Lucia gave the two officers a long stare. "I was told it is Castilian, Spanish."

"Told? You don't know?" Khalil continued. "Where are you from?"

132

Of course Lucia had no idea.

Her parents had been part of the program, and, as such, they'd waived any connection to her after her ninth birthday. She had no real memories from before that time, except the smell of artificial rain, a distinctly un-Martian scent.

She considered telling these cops that she was from Mars, but most of the families living on Mars had some connection to the ENForcers. She decided, instead, to obfuscate. "I'm not sure how this is germane to Jonathan Galilei's death."

"You know where he is, don't you?" Khalil said.

"Who? Jonathan?" This line of questioning was really strange. Lucia couldn't help searching their eyes for some clue as to whether or not they were being serious. "Yes, dead, in his lab."

"No," Ferrera said quickly, "The Scourge, the other Del Toro. He's your brother, isn't he?"

Lucia was sure something in her eyes gave her away, so she covered her surprise by asking, "What does the Scourge have to do with any of this?"

"ENForcers have put out an APB. He's on Ganymede," Khalil said. "You look a lot like the picture they're circulating. I figure maybe you're the reason he's here, to protect an older sister, maybe?"

Ferrera snorted, "No way. Clearly the baby sister."

Lucia felt a weird rush of pleasure. "Baby?"

"You're saying you are his older sister? Twin, maybe?" Khalil said, trying to sound skeptical, but his tone belied how giddy he felt at trapping her into admitting a connection. He was almost vibrating with excitement. "Wow, I would never have pegged you as over forty."

She was, but only just.

Lucia was sure she flushed, both from the compliments and from the nearness to being exposed. She tried to hold on to their intense gaze, but found herself shifting a bit in her seat. "I'm surprised that the Edfu Facula police are cooperating with the ENForcers. The Force doesn't have jurisdiction here, do they?"

"There's a big bounty," Khallil said.

These two didn't seem to know that there were ENForcers on the ground, at least.

"So, this is personal for you two?" Lucia glanced at the recorder on Ferrera's hat. "You're asking because you're after—" she wanted to say 'my brother,' but she was afraid she couldn't get it out without making it an obvious lie and so settled on—"The Scourge's bounty? Shouldn't you be concentrating on the murder of one of your local citizens?"

"Nah, Sargsyan's got that. Thinks he's that famous detective Sherlock Christie," Ferrera said. "Tell us where your brother is."

Lucia oscillated between feeling weirdly euphoric that these two men could not see her as anything other than her own sister and utterly flabbergasted at their complete idiocy. Keeping with her trend, she opted for the truth. "I don't even know what to say to you."

The three of them continued staring at each other for several long moments. They seemed to be trying to give her the hardline, but her stomach chose that moment to gurgle and she remembered the pastries in front of her. Taking a bite, she was pleasantly surprised at the quality. The custard was lightly dusted with cinnamon and had a faintly lemony flavor. The whole thing was quite delicate. She devoured her first one in two bites.

"I bet he's still in Mehit," Ferrera said to his partner.

"Yeah," Khalil agreed. "I think the sister would be a lot more freaked out if he was close."

"Fuck me, those goddamn heathens in Mehit are going to be the lucky stiffs to capture him," Ferrera said.

"They get all the breaks. The whole city is rich," Khalil said. With a sigh, he absently ate his pastry. "Their uniforms are nicer, too. Shirts? What a dumb name. Couldn't they call us something more dignified?"

"Do the ENForcers think it will be easy to capture the Scourge?" Lucia asked, trying to sound only idly curious.

Ferrera saw through her. "You are worried about him!"

"Of course I am," she said, stress-eating the last of the pastries on her plate in one bite. "Don't be stupid."

"I wonder if it's worth turning her in?" Khalil asked, thoughtfully. "I mean, ENForcers could use her as bait at the very least. Of course, we'd have to get her in and she weighs an actual ton...."

Lucia swore she could actually see the gears working, but then Ferrera said, "It's cute how much you want to be like your brother."

Cute. Yeah. This whole conversation was getting too surreal. She reached to steal a third pastry from Khalil's plate when her vision went black for a half of a second.

DOWNLOAD COMPLETE.

Lucia shot to her feet when the text appeared in the right hand side of her vision. The chair clattered to the floor behind her. The two officers were saying something, but Lucia heard nothing except the hollow beat of her own heart in her ears.

Welcome to Boy.net, Colonel Del Toro.

♀

CHAPTER 12

Independence "Hawk" Hawking

Detective Inspector Mohammad Sargsyan flipped through the annual reports muttering to himself. He'd asked Hawk to stay put until the forensics team showed up, but her feet were tapping out a staccato running beat. This was the longest she'd ever been around a cop, and she was not enjoying it one bit.

For one, Sargsyan's aftershave tickled her nose. It was somehow both sharp and musky. Why did men always bathe in that shit? It gave her a headache.

Second, she hadn't gotten any word from Del Toro in several long minutes, and Hawk was pretty sure she was going to die from the anxiety of not knowing what the fuck was going on. She felt her stomach start to heave again. Why had they agreed to separate? This was torture.

Hawk reminded herself that despite how it felt, it couldn't have really been that long ago that Del Toro had left. Minutes at most?

It felt like an eternity.

Sargsyan continued to swipe his fingers at the screen and mutter.

Hawk finally stopped tapping her foot, and pushed off the wall she'd been leaning against. She was starting to snap. "Do you even know what you're looking for?"

"No," he admitted. "Care to enlighten me?"

"By Bohr, if this was some kind of ploy to get me to talk, it totally worked," she said in a rush. "So, okay, we told you that Galilei was after an artificial eye, right?"

He pulled out a slender notepad from an inner pocket of that ridiculous jacket and an old-fashioned pencil. Dramatically, he flipped the pad open and poised his pencil. "Did you?"

"I honestly don't remember," Hawk said. Tired of standing around in the dark, she flipped on the lights. They both squinted in the sudden harsh light. After taking a second to get used to the brightness, Hawk continued, "But, yes, Galilei is this old friend of mine from Luna and he and I ran into each other at an orbital diner for a bunch of electric cowboy trucker types—Curie be damned, Del Toro is so right. This is some seriously coincidental coincidences, isn't it? Anyway, Galilei hired us to find the prototype of an artificial eye that he apparently lost or got stolen or I guess he never said which, did he? Regardless, he wanted it back before a big board meeting that was going to decide some-thing. Something? Listen to me! How do we not know what?" Hawk slapped her own forehead in exasperation. "Wow, we really knew absolutely nothing about this stupid job before we took it, did we?"

Sargsyan looked up from where he was hunched over his notepad. "I'm going to need you to go over all of that again, slower."

"Why don't you just use a recorder in your ear like a modern human being?"

"I don't think that's the issue in this case," he said, though he did pull that pen-like device he'd been using earlier to scan the lab. He clicked the top of it before returning it to a front pocket on his suit coat. He seemed to take a moment to point it at Hawk, "Please start over. How do you know the deceased?"

Hawk let out a breath and slumped back against the wall. It'd been almost a decade since she'd given up smoking skullcaps, but all of a sudden her fin-gers itched to fill a pipe and breathe in that calming air. Letting out a breath, instead, she rubbed her face. "Galilei and I are—I guess, *were*—Lunars. Our parents were in the same scientific cohort."

"Cohort," he wrote down carefully. "Remind me how these work."

Through her fingers still over her face, Hawk grunted. "Ugh, it's compli-cated."

"Humor me."

She let her hands drop and gave Sargsyan a hard glare. In the bright light, his hair seemed a flat, matte black, which made her wonder if he dyed it. The product he used glistened where he'd made sharp points of hair in front of his ear. "Normally, I'd say you need to buy me a beer to hear about cohorts, but you can just owe me one. Luna is science obsessed, you understand? It's been The Moon's mission since 1970-something. Article One, baby!" She made the victory 'v' with two fingers, but Sargsyan just looked baffled. She needed to stop assuming people got that old joke. "Okay," she said, jamming her hands into the pockets of her pao, embarrassed. "Forget that part. Cohorts are a working group, usually interrelated disciplines, all of whom are tackling the same hereditary project. My family are physicists, we're named after Stephen Hawking. Galilei's family were astro-physicists, astronomers, like Galileo."

Sargsyan looked at Hawk skeptically. "I thought you said you weren't a nerd."

"I was raised by nerds. It's different."

"Sure." For some reason, he wrote this down in his notebook.

"Anyway, it's all kind of fake? My mother mostly preferred to play piano? My mom got the required familial PhD, but it was like pulling teeth. We were almost ABD."

"Is that bad?" Sargsyan asked. "I don't know what that means."

"All but dissertation. We would have lost our cohort status, and had been moved to one of the polar communes with the other dropouts, which, I mean, c'mon. My mom had her masters and most of the coursework—" Hawk could see Sargsyan's eyes glazing over. "Look, this is why I don't like to talk about it. It's a dumb social system. Everyone agrees it's kind of broken. We've lost entire generations of artists and poets, all in the name of keeping Luna a scientific utopia. My generation has been trying to change things, but you know it is. The old guard and traditions, am I right? It's part of why I left."

He nodded, but it was clear he had no idea what she was talking about. "So you and Galilei have been friends since childhood?"

"Uh, that's pushing it," Hawk said. 'I knew him. Our parents worked together. We played together sometimes, but he was older than me. I'll be honest, I liked his sister better."

"Wow," Sargsyan said, like Hawk was confessing to the murder.

"Yeah, I've been holding a grudge ever since."

"Really?"

"No. I honestly had not thought about Galilei until I saw him at the Dekora truckstop." Hawk let out an anxious breath. How much time had passed? Hawk glanced around the lab, wishing for some kind of clock. Not that she was sure she knew how to read time on Ganymede. "Listen, I have to go. I cannot sit still this long. Can we skip ahead twenty-five years to the part where my partner and I found Galilei dead and are completely innocent?"

"Just—hang on. Just tell me about the eye and I'll let you go join your partner." He actually licked the tip of a pencil and held it at the ready above the pad.

This was the second time Hawk had seen someone do this. "What does licking the lead even do?"

"I don't actually know, but I saw it on—" He stopped himself. Pursing his lips together as if to hold back the rest of what he was going to say, he frowned. Then, wagging the eraser end at Hawk, he said, "You are oddly infectious. It's distressing. Please just stick to the story at hand. What do you know about the artificial eye?"

"Apparently nothing," Hawk said, throwing up her hands in frustration. "That's what I told you before!"

"You don't know anything?"

Sargsyan sounded as incredulous about that fact as Hawk was starting to feel. She tried to think. What did they know about this artificial eye?

"There's a bounty for it," Hawk said, though it occurred to her that she hadn't actually read the notice herself. "I mean, I guess there is."

Hawk reached for her pocket where she normally kept her device in order to show the bounty hunter's bulletin board to Sargsyan. It wasn't in the first pocket she checked, though she did find the business card. She was checking her back pockets when they were interrupted by the arrival of the forensics team.

"You keep looking," he said. "I'll be right back."

Of course as soon as Sargsyan walked away Hawk remembered dumping the damn device in the canal. She tried to get his attention a couple of times, but he was busy directing the forensics team and coordinating all their efforts. Hawk felt superfluous and even more anxious to get underway.

Her fingers stayed closed around the business card in her pocket. Did Del Toro's full honesty policy include handing it over? She still leaned up against a far wall, staying out of the way of the forensics crew. Keeping an eye on Sargsyan, she turned her body slightly more towards the wall and surreptitiously checked the backside of the smart paper.

Hawk had been thinking about that message ever since they saw it and had a working theory about who had sent it. If she was right about the sender, the message would have changed from the initial 'danger.'

...are you still there? It blinked as it cycled through a longer message. *Del Toro is in danger. Why the fuck are you still there? Del Toro...*

Just as she'd expected, it was Oz.

Also, is Del Toro in trouble?

Time to move. Hawk slid the business card back into her pocket. Trying to act casually, she headed to the door. As she passed Sargsyan she said, "Looks like you've got this in hand. I'll head out now."

He glanced up at her as though he was surprised she was still there. "Right. Oh, but before you go, let me give you my contact info." Standing up from where he was kneeling next to the medical examiner and Galilei's body, he pulled out his device. He held it up in the universal 'let's exchange details,' pose.

"Oh, uh, sorry. I tossed my device in a canal." When his dark eyebrows shot up in surprise, Hawk shrugged. "What? I thought it might be traced. It's a bounty hunter thing."

He smiled, but shook his head as though he found her generally baffling. Finishing around in the pockets of his long coat, he found a paper card.

Real paper. Not smart paper, she noted as she took it from him. "Jumping Newton, how much do they pay Inspector Detectives?"

His face drew into a frown, then he seemed to figure something out. "Oh, the paper? We export bamboo here. It's not as uncommon on Ganymede as it is in other places."

Which explained the printouts and the waste paper. Hawk kept forgetting how resource rich Ganymede was, generally. She slid his card into the pocket next to Galilei's. They stared at each other awkwardly for a beat, until Hawk said, "Isn't this the part where you tell me not to go off-world until the case is solved?"

He chuckled. "Would you listen to me, if I did?"

"No," Hawk admitted, continuing to roll with this honesty policy.

"You've been cooperative, so, you know, just keep me informed and let me know if you think of anything more that could help."

"Sure," Hawk said, knowing full well she wouldn't do that, either.

He turned back to the body. Feeling as though she were officially dismissed, Hawk walked out the door, like she wasn't at all in a hurry or panicked. However, as soon as she was out of sight of the cops, she broke into a hard run.

♀

CHAPTER 13

Lucia Del Toro

The two cops, Kahlil and Ferrera, stared at Lucia. She felt the weight of the confusion in their eyes, but all she could do was stand in the back end of the cupcake shop with her hands on her head, mentally screaming: *System: Shut down! Repeat, belay all incoming orders!*

Update in progress.... Stand by.

The cashier, who had been checking his device, looked at the three of them. "Hey, did you guys get a weird surge right now?"

"Oh, is that what's freaking her out?" Ferrera wondered absently, like he was used to women shooting to their feet mid-interview. He made a relaxed, sit-down motion with his hand, "I know it's disconcerting, but it's perfectly normal. We get flares due to aurora. Things just reboot. Your data will come back."

Lucia had trouble concentrating. So many images and commands flashed through her ocular implants, including several files stamped *.NewShanghai.data*. What the fuck was that?

"Oh yeah, aurora," the cashier said, poking at his device. "Man, you'd think I'd get used to them."

She pulled herself back to the now because: aurora? It didn't make sense. Mars had auroras. If solar flares caused ENForcers to reboot, they would have changed that programming and design long, long ago. There would be protocols and fail-safes by the dozens. The aurora alone couldn't be the cause of this sudden reconnection, but the timing seemed to tell another story. Could someone have found a way to take advantage of this natural solar occurrence? Marcus had tried to snipe her with something. Oz bent a needle trying to inject a substance into Lucia's system. Marcus' strange, shattering projectile had

141

come closest to penetrating her skin. In fact, scrolling through bio-reports suddenly available again, Lucia noticed that her onboard had reacted as though her skin had been breached. Her system had been flooded with antitoxins.

Now a more horrible thought hit her. If it wasn't poison in those bullets or in that needle, maybe it was nanobots. Nanobots designed to infect her system and reopen ports and comms long shut down, ripped out, or otherwise reconfigured. Nanobots that would then lie in wait for a solar event or some other moment that would allow for an unplanned reboot.

She and Hawk thought they'd been so clever walking away. They thought they'd escaped clean and free, but Marcus had let them go. He'd probably been toying with Lucia during their fight, just staying in proximity in order to get a report that the nanos had made it into her system and were awoken on command.

Goddamn it all.

This whole thing, from start to finish, was some kind of set-up.

"You should sit down," Khalil cajoled. "You look ready to fall down."

Lucia tried to sit down, but her heart wouldn't stop roaring in her ear. She had to find a way to shut *Boy.net* out. Noticing that one of the many downloads hitting her was an updated list of stealth operation protocols, she called up the document and did a quick scan of it. There! *Onboard: activate program Silent Running.*

Silent Running Activated. Warning you will be temporarily cut off from Boy.net and Command Central.

Copy that. Proceed.

Proceeding. Godspeed, Colonel.

The last bit had been said in the High Commander's voice. A weird, but not exactly unexpected bit of narcissistic programming. As usual, a ridiculous use of expensive ENForcer technology...

For every bit of this new tech that felt alien and unwelcome, she sensed an equal amount of relief as a cascade of healing rippled through her outdated system. Aching muscles flooded with anti-inflammatories. Nanobots she'd paid hundreds of credits to exterminate flickered back into existence, rushing to repair cuts, bruises, muscle micro-tears. Her regular vision, which she hadn't even realized had issues, cleared, sharpened, and brightened. Hearing fine-tuned, the clack of the cashier's fingers flicking across buttons sounded loudly in her ear. Peripheral vision now included calculated distances, target acquisition, and other ambient telemetry.

Weirder still, she could feel the fat of her stomach and hips being converted into other matter to boost this process. Almost immediately her uniform pants felt less tight against the curve of her stomach. Unconsciously, her hands went to her breasts, as though to try to shield them from this process. Thank all the gods, they didn't seem to be affected.

At least not yet.

But, that begged the question. What state would these asshole nanobots repair her to? She sent a command: *System: identify programmed repairs.*

The system responded immediately. *Multiple bio and system repairs in progress.*

Yeah, no kidding. That was less than helpful. She'd asked the wrong question, obviously. What was the best way to phrase this? Before she could formulate the appropriate command, the onboard interrupted itself with a series of warnings.

Illegal biohack detected.

Illegal augmentation detected.

Illegal voice modulation detected.

Illegal— She shut off notifications.

"Oh shit," she breathed, shakily lowering herself back into the chair Ferrera offered her. "It's all being undone. I cut open my own skin to pull their trackers and their coms out," she said to no one in particular, her voice barely above a whisper. Shaking fingers found the scar tissue just above her collarbone where the communications hub had been located before she took a knife to it when she deserted. The thick band of tissue remained, proof she had removed it.

"What? Cut something? Are you okay, Miss?" Ferrera asked, returning to his own seat at the other side of the table. He glanced at his partner. "Do you think she got a touch of the aurora feedback sickness? Maybe you ought to get her a glass of water, Khalil."

Khalil made a face like he didn't think that just because he was the junior officer he should have to play fetch and carry, but, with a grunt, he stood. As he passed, he patted her shoulder briefly. "It happens when you have a lot of augments. The reboot can be hard on the system and make you a little loopy."

Still clutching her breasts, she gave a stiff nod.

How soon would the little microscopic fuckers come for her voice?

"Technically, I think it's the coronal mass ejection that does it," Ferrera said. Lucia raised her eyebrows to hear him talking so technically. He continued, nonchalantly, "Solar flares are enough like electromagnetic pulses that our technology can be vulnerable to big ones. The big ones are irregular enough, though, that most people just deal."

Lucia was only half-listening. Only thanks to the sensation of her pants slipping off did Lucia manage to release the death grip she had on her boobs.

Trying not to be obvious, she shifted in her seat enough to pull up her pants and tighten her belt. Did she even have enough adipose tissue for all the general upgrades she needed? Maybe this would be her saving grace. If they worked like they should, the nanobots would triage the damage she'd done to herself leaping off a speeding skycraft. With luck those would be severe enough that the 'bots be forced to give up before cannibalizing anything important, like muscle mass.

Although, who knew if they wouldn't just go after all those so-called illegal hacks for spare parts.

Lucia needed that underground biohacker yesterday. Otherwise, the stupid nanobots would ruin everything she'd worked so hard to make right. Well, one way to fight it was to feed the machine. Literally.

"Uh, hey, Officer Khalil," Lucia said cautiously. Once it was obvious that her voice remained intact, she continued more boldly, "I'm going to need about fifteen more of these custard things."

"Fifteen?"

Were there not that many? She waved a hand to indicate her desperateness, "Just buy them out."

With a resigned shrug and more cursing in Arabic, Khalil took out his device. With her new and improved hearing, Lucia clearly heard, "Allah Yakhthek." The equally updated onboard gave a voice-over translation, "May Allah take your soul."

Ferrera gave her a disapproving dad frown and said, "Not eating for two, are you?"

In a way, she was. It was just that the 'other' she was eating for was a bunch of unwelcome nanos, not a baby. She gave him a 'get serious' grimace. "Not likely. I'm a lesbian."

"Don't be so cavalier," he countered. "Some women have penises."

Lucia almost choked on surprise laughter. "Yes, but then they wouldn't be pregnant—at least not in the traditional way, and, anyway, you don't have to tell me, okay?"

"It seems I do," he said. Scratching his bald spot, he gave her a little paternal shake of his head. "I think your brother has been a bad influence on you, young lady. The rest of the universe isn't like Mars."

"Thank god for that," Lucia agreed.

Khalil set the water down on the table, along with a huge plate of pastries. She drained the water in several gulps and set the empty glass down with shaky hands. Without even looking at the two cops, she ate her way through at least a half-dozen pastries. With each bite, her hands steadied and her mind refocused. By the time the plate was clear, she had a plan.

Perhaps she could kill the proverbial two birds with one stone. Lucia needed a biohacker pronto, and the chances that two local cops knew where one might be hiding out was decently high.

"I've been thinking about the Scourge." Which was very true, that was all she could think about at the moment. After swallowing the last of the pastry, she rubbed her mouth clean with her hand. "I know a few things about ENForcers. They have a tracking system. Internal. If the ENForcers are tracking my... the Scourge," she still couldn't manage the sibling lie. She resisted touching her throat again where the damn receiver had probably rebuilt itself, as she continued, "They must have found a way to reactivate coms. The Scourge will be headed to a biohacker. That's where we should look."

"We?" The cops exchanged a look.

"Yeah. If you're turning the Scourge in for the bounty, I really need to be there."

Khalil seemed especially uneasy with her change of heart. "You do?"

"I do. It's really the only way it will work."

Ferrera had his worried father face on again, "I don't know, sweetheart. I know you're fully loaded and all, but this will be dangerous."

"Sir, I mean no disrespect, but who's making the assumptions now? I'm a bounty hunter. I can take care of myself." Then, for good measure, Lucia locked her eyes on Ferrera's and added, "You need to trust me on this. There is no way you can get the bounty if I don't go with you. I am telling you God's own truth."

Kahlil chewed on his lower lip. "I mean, Del Toro is more likely to stop for his sister than he would for a cop."

"And talk about fully loaded," Lucia said. "Have either of you ever tried to face down an ENForcer alone?"

Both faces visibly paled. After a beat of considering this new wrinkle in their plans, Ferrera let out a defeated sigh. "I take it you want a cut of the bounty."

"No," Lucia said. "I just don't want anyone hurt. You understand me?"

This seemed to convince the family man, Ferrera, immediately. He nodded. Meanwhile, Kahlil frowned unhappily at the empty plate of pastries, clearly less certain about including her. The two cops must have gone subvocal again, because this time Lucia's system prompted her eavesdropping.

Colonel, onboard has detected authorized police chatter active in the immediate vicinity. Listen in?

Authorized.

...surrender without violence with his sister there makes sense. Really, this girl is kind of brilliant. Do you think she'd date me?

Merciful Allah, Khalil. If she's the Scourge's twin, she's at least forty-five. You're half her age.

And? I like a woman with experience. Competence is a turn-on for me.

If this wasn't a matter of life or death, Lucia would be oddly flattered. As it was, she turned her head to keep the cops from seeing any flashes behind her eyes. She watched the cashier, who busily filmed whatever was happening across the street at Chimera labs. God, in her panic about *Boy.net* and her body's cannibalization, she'd half forgotten all this mess with Jonathan. She mentally commanded her onboard to prepare a packet for Hawk, to let her lover know where she was headed. She set it up to spool out as soon as they were on the move.

Meanwhile, the cops continued to subvocally objectify her.

Super hot.

Totally.

Plus augmented women, am I right? Crushing thighs!

"Thoughts, officers?" Lucia asked, knowing full well it would make them jump guiltily. "I mean, it may be a long shot—"

"No, actually," Khalil said with what was clearly an attempt at a charming smile, "My partner and I were just discussing how smart your idea is. You must know the ENForcer tech very well. Were you very jealous when they took your brother and not you?"

"No," she said absolutely truthfully. "I hate the Earth Nations Peacekeeping Force with every fiber of my being. They will rue the day they come for me."

Khalil reached out to pat her hand, like he thought her fierceness cute, but then must have caught the fire in her eyes and thought better of it. "Well, they took my cousin, you know."

This was probably supposed to be the prelude to a sob story that, frankly, Lucia had a lot of sympathy for, but now was not the time. "Maybe you can tell me about it on the way to the nearest biohacker."

"Nearest?" Khalil asked. "Didn't you suggest he was still in Mehit in Zu Fosse?"

Had she? If only her upgrade had come in a half-hour earlier, she could check her tapes, as the ENForcers called the visual and audio recordings that ran in the background at all times.

All times. Including at New Shanghai...,

146

She'd struggled with memories of that day. Why hadn't she just reached for the tiles? Her mind cast out through the onboard. There they were, the new downloads. Had they been erased? But how?

She couldn't focus on this right now. She needed to be on the move. Lucia was certain that the Silent Running protocol had temporarily closed her off from *Boy.net*, but it was unwise to assume that the nanos had no other way to phone home. Giving Khalil an innocent eye-bat, she said, "Where do you think a desperate ENForcer would go? Who's the best? I'm sure you must have a lead on the hottest illegal bio dealers in town."

Khalil's chest visibly puffed out with pride. "Of course."

"You're not seriously thinking of waltzing into the twilight market in full uniform, are you?" Ferrera scoffed.

Onboard: Triangulate twilight market.

Working....

"That's a good point," Khalil agreed. He tapped his badge several times rhythmically, and a holo-projection of civilian clothes overlaid his uniform. For reasons known only to Khalil himself, his casual wear seemed to involve a Hawaiian-print shirt covered in garish hot pink flamingos, cargo shorts, and flip flops.

What was with all the retro shit these days?

His partner had a similar thought, "Hey, Khalil, 2058 is pinging, they want their fashion back."

"Hardy-har-har," Khalil said. "I have it on good authority that '58 is making a comeback."

"Is this from your fashion-backward child?" Ferrera teased, "Because I wouldn't be so sure."

Lucia almost did a kind of mental double-take because her Silent Running program chose that very moment to send her an internal pinging sound. *Comms from a nearby unit requesting access. Comply?*

Do not comply. Hold for intel. Her heart froze. As the two cops continued to teasingly bicker, her eyes scanned the windows. *Onboard: what is the nature of the nearby unit?*

Closing fast on current location. Five officers under command of Brigadier General Zhu Wei. Major Simon Farooqi requesting immediate confirmation of the identity of an ENForcer officer under Silent Running.

Simon?

Were all her creche mates here? And what kind of bullshit was it to put Simon, of all of them, on the comm?

Onboard, open a private channel to Major Simon Farooqi. Code: Beta Three, Omega One.

It was a bad joke between the two of them, their secret backdoor comm line. Simon had been three of five, but everyone referred to him as the beta of the pack, because they saw him as effeminate, weaker. Lucia was supposed to be the alpha, the one of five, but she confessed one drunken night that she was the group's omega, at best. They used this private frequency to help cover for each other's sins. It had never been hacked. She prayed it still worked.

Simon's response was immediate. *Run, Lucia. Run while you still can, girl.*

CHAPTER 14

Independence "Hawk" Hawking

*D*anger. That was what the back of Galilei's card flashed. *Lucia was in danger.*

Blindly running at full speed, Hawk got more than ten blocks away from Chimera Lab before she realized she had no idea where the cops would have taken Del Toro. Even if she had access to a map, which she didn't anymore, thanks to dumping her device in the slush, she had no idea which police station of all of them in this gigantic city Del Toro might be in.

Jogging to a halt, Hawk turned around. Feeling stupid, she started to make her way back to Sargsyan to ask for directions.

Then, she felt even stupider.

In her panic, Hawk forgot she could just ask Del Toro directly. Into their mental chatbox, she dropped: *Hey, babe. I'm done with that coat detective guy. Where are you at?*

This frequency is unauthorized for civilian use.

That was an ominous response, made especially so by the fact that it was intoned in Del Toro's old voice—out loud, and sounding more confident and clear in a way it hadn't for a long time. Hawk decided she must be imagining that last part. This was just another glitch. It had to be.

That's when Hawk spotted the ENForcer van.

'Van'—well, technically, it was more like a troop transport vehicle, but it was sort of plainly boxy and shaped like it was supposed to be innocuous despite the dust-red camouflage and giant ENFORCER logo painted on the side.

Hawk stopped dead in the middle of the sidewalk and stared at the parked vehicle open-mouthed in shock. She wasn't alone, either. Other late night festival-goers did double-takes as they passed. It was as though no one wanted to fully process what was in front of them, but the Earth Nations' symbol was iconic. Earth laid out on a circular grid, seen from one of its poles, surrounded by laurel leaves, and the protective sword piercing the globe.

In the cool night air, Hawk shivered. Her eyes stayed riveted to the black "ENPKF" emblazoned on the van in that specific, precise, and blocky font that seemed reserved for the military.

A passerby noted her reaction with a nod. "Right?" he said. "What the hell are they doing here, anyway? It's Nowruz for fuck's sake!"

She had no coherent response to that, but he didn't seem to need one before continuing on his way. Still staring at the van in horror, Hawk sent another private text. *Hey. I'm freaking out. Are you okay? Where are you? Del Toro? Babe? ...Lucia?*

This time the only answer was silence.

Hawk scanned the street, walking slower, more cautiously. Her heart hammered in her inner ear. Unconsciously, she whispered, "Fuck. Fuck. Fuck." Finally, spotting flashing police lights of the shurta's hoverbikes ahead, Hawk realized that she'd nearly made it back to Galilei's lab.

Now what? She supposed she could march back into Sargsyan's crime scene and demand that he and his officers help her find Del Toro. Well, they were supposed to have Del Toro in their care, possibly even custody. Maybe it wasn't such a stupid idea; they might know what was happening—why the ENForcers were here, if Del Toro was safe.

With a plan in mind, Hawk took a deep breath and started forward. They really needed to get Del Toro her own panic button earring. As she walked along the sidewalk, she tried to remember why they'd never considered it. It would never be as useful, since Hawk's brain wasn't fully configured for that sort of thing, but a GPS locator dot could have been sent to her device.

Fat lot that would do either of them at the moment, what with that damn machine slowly drifting down darkening seas to Ganymede's spinning core.

Hawk tried one last time to hail her. *Maybe the malfunction is cleared up by now, yeah? You out there somewhere, Lucia?*

On the same channel a packet arrived. Hawk didn't like the look of this. It had the impression of the sort of thing you sent your loved ones in the event of death. Pausing next to one of the cop's hoverbikes, Hawk cautiously opened it.

An uncharacteristic rush of words followed, all in Lucia's old voice: *I'm currently sitting in the cupcake shop across the street trying to talk these two idiot police officers into taking me to a biohacker. I got reconnected to Boy.net. I think it must have been whatever Oz was trying to inject me with plus the electromagnetic disruption of the solar flare. It doesn't entirely matter how it happened. The problem is, it did. I think I'm hidden from them at the moment thanks to, of all things, a new protocol for undercover operatives—shit, there's a frightening thought. I'll send you my new location as soon as I know it.*

Hawk checked the packet's time stamp. It had been prepped to be sent twelve minutes and forty-two seconds ago. Even so, Hawk glanced across the street trying to locate the shop. There it was. Something in Spanish, maybe? The pink neon of the overhead sign and bright lights streaming out from big picture windows looked inviting.

At least it did, until the hulking shadows of men in ENForcer uniforms stepped into view. There was something about the determination in the steps of these thugs that raised Hawk's hackles. Their posture was that of beasts closing in on prey. Instantly, Hawk knew that Del Toro was still inside.

Unconsciously, Hawk started across the street to intercept.

She dodged two rickshaws, one air taxi, and a herd of drunken bicycles, only to be immediately caught up in an iron grip. "ENForcer business. Move along."

Hawk glanced up into a face nearly as pale as her own. It was difficult to tell in the electric light of the street, but his hair was lightly-colored as well—either blonde or maybe silver gray. His name was stitched over a breast pocket that was just about eye level for Hawk. It read: Sulanov, D.

Sulanov, eh? Could this be the Daniel of the borscht?

Even if it was, Hawk's first impulse was to kick his shins, try to push past him, while screaming 'my girlfriend is in there!' She knew that would never work. So, she just stepped back with her hands in the air, as though in surrender. "Right, sorry. Just got overwhelmingly hungry for a cupcake."

He nodded, like that was a reasonable occurrence, but added, "Sorry for the inconvenience, ma'am. Please step aside."

"Sure, sure," she said, agreeably. Looking around his impossibly broad shoulders, Hawk saw a small crowd of rubberneckers gathering. She gave Sulanov a little nod, like she planned to respect his authority, and made her way around him to where the others stood. There were only a few people, less than a half-dozen, all dressed up for some celebration. One of the women wore a kind of long tunic in bright yellow, with an open velvety green overcoat embroidered with a yellow paisley design along the hems. Another person wore a modern looking dark suit and tie, around their neck was a lei of red flowers. The others all had various colorful wraps in reds, greens, and blacks.

Seeing Hawk approach, the woman in bright yellow and green said, "Blessed Nowruz."

"Same to you," Hawk said, hoping it was an adequate response. Jerking her thumb at Sulanov, she asked, "What's going on?"

The person in the suit and tie pushed forward to whisper, "ENForcers! Can you believe it?"

The group burst into nervous, giddy laughter, like they thought this was the best entertainment. From the smell of their breaths, they were probably drunk. Otherwise, Hawk would have been tempted to tell them all what a bunch of raving idiots they were and how they needed to sober up because this was serious business. Del Toro, if she was still in there, was in real trouble. With effort, Hawk bit her tongue. "Yeah, no, so how many do you think there are? Like, I saw three guys go in, and there's this one idiot watching the street. But, a van full? How many do you think that is?"

They stared at her with open mouths.

Hawk started to repeat the question, but she noticed their attention was focused over her shoulder. There was a scuffle happening inside the cafe. She spun around, Del Toro's name on her lips.

But, the person pushed out into the street wasn't Del Toro. Instead, two ENForcers forcibly manhandled some heavily tattooed guy out of the circle of uniforms. He had the most amazing hair lights, which sputtered out briefly when he landed flat on his ass on the sidewalk. The guy's eyes stayed glued to one particular ENForcer, as if tracking something important. "That's my property, you fascist pig!" he shouted as he scrambled back to his feet. He raised both fists in the sign of solidarity to the Federation of Asteroid Miners and said, "Fuck you!"

The ENForcer took a step forward, his hand out. There was something in it, but even at this distance Hawk could see it wasn't his peacemaker, but something smaller. It took a second for her to guess that it must be Tattoos's personal device.

Tattoos skittered back nervously. He watched in horror as the ENForcer crushed the metal and plastic with just his fist. Dropping the shattered pieces on the sidewalk, the ENForcer turned his back to Tattoos. The insult was clear: you are an insignificant threat.

It had an expected result on Tattoos. His face twisted into fury at his impotence.

Seeing that look, one she knew all too well, Hawk could guess what came next. She didn't know this guy, but his life shouldn't be a footnote in some report to ENForcer HQ. Hawk broke from the crowd of partygoers and grabbed Tattoos by the collar of his shirt before he finished raising his fist. "Don't," she hissed at him. "It's the excuse they'll use to stomp you into a pulp."

"I really don't fucking care right now. Let me at 'em." Tattoos shouted, but he stopped as if suddenly realizing she wasn't the enemy. "Who are you?"

"I'm her girlfriend." Hawk figured that if she understood this situation right, no other context was needed.

He blinked, clearly putting the scene together. "Your girl is the one who came in with the shurtas and ate me out of custards?"

The first part was right and the second seemed likely, so Hawk nodded.

"Oh," he said, suddenly sympathetic. "That's rough."

Hawk didn't like the sound of that. "How rough?"

Since the fight seemed to have left him, Hawk let go. After straightening his shirt, he dug a second device out of the inside pocket of a patchwork vest he wore. "I mean, is she okay? Let me show you the footage."

Hawk huddled in closer so she could see the holoprojection he pulled up. He fast-forwarded through a lot of images of the various police vehicles arriving outside Jonathan's laboratory. When they got to the part where Hawk came out of the building running, she asked, "Any chance you can delete that? The part with me in it?"

He gave her a judgmental side-eye. "I think that's going to depend, okay? I mean, if you're an enemy of those shitheads, sure. If not, I should be clear that my backups have backups, my clouds have clouds, you know? Universal Solar System law says I have the right to film any protest."

"Yeah, it's cool," she said, making the United Miner's salute. "Up the revolution.".

That seemed to get a little half-smile out of him. With a flick, the holos sprung back into motion. The image suddenly shifted due to some noise off camera. A table was flipped over. The two shurtas that had come in with Sargsyan stood up, shocked. The camera's eyes swiveled again to show three ENForcers burst into the room. The camera hung there for a long time, so Hawk had a chance to really see these men. The leader seemed to be of East Asian descent and he gestured dramatically at the back of the room.

"It would be nice to know what they're saying," Hawk grumbled.

"Yeah, well, Grella's whole thing is old-timey voice overs," Tattoos gave Hawk another look that she could clearly interpret as 'how do you not know this? How old are you, anyway?'

To which Hawk could only shrug. Meanwhile, the camera finally showed the back of the room where the shurtas now blocked the flipped over table and seemed to be arguing with the ENForcers.

The footage suddenly jerked around as an ENForcer grabbed the device. A very vertigo-inducing bounce around the doorways and outside, a brief shot of Tattoos on the ground, and then the images abruptly cut off.

Hawk had hoped to see a sign of Del Toro. Was she still in there, behind that flipped table? Or had she made an escape out the back? Despite knowing that it probably wouldn't get through, Hawk tried their private channel again: *Babe? You still in there?*

This frequency is restricted due to ENForcer activity in your area.

"Are we fighting these assholes?" Tattoos gestured in the direction of the cupcake shop, with the ominous shadows in the doorway. He looked serious, determined, which sort of shocked Hawk. She hadn't considered trying to actually fight the ENForcers. The fire remained in his eye, "Because I'll post on Grella if we are. I can get a crowd here in seconds, if we are."

Hawk surprised herself with a firm and unhesitating: "Yeah. We are."

He nodded, already typing. "Good, because folks are already on their way. These ENForcer dicks just busted into my place of employment and started threatening arrest. Fuck that, you know? They don't have authority here."

His words sobered Hawk immediately. The ENForcers didn't have authority here. She needed to remember that. What was her mother always telling her? *Don't automatically comply.*

"Right," she said with renewed conviction. "Whatever happens, let's make sure my girlfriend does not get into that van." Hawk pointed to the offending vehicle.

"Gotcha." Apparently finished, he tucked his device back where it'd come from. Finally stopping to really look at Hawk, his smile was warm. "Nice to meet you, by the way. I'm Tchadzwa, he/him."

He held out his hand in the manner of Asteroid miners, as if expecting a shake. Hawk grasped it firmly, and bowed. When she came up she said, "Hawk, she/her. The pleasure is mine."

Seeing the bow, Tchadzwa brightened further. The lights in his hair danced happily. "A Lunar! Look at us, we're both from the inner planets. I'm originally from the asteroids! This was Fated."

She could hear the capital letter in the last word. Since there were really only two free colonies in the inner ring—Luna and the Asteroids—meetings like this were sometimes treated as a sign of good fortune. Normally, she rolled her eyes at such metaphysical malarky, but, this time, Hawk hoped it was true, and so returned his pronouncement with one of her own. "May it bring us fortune."

"I've got a good feeling."

She nodded absently, since she hardly felt the same. Peering over Tchadz-wa's shoulder trying, she attempted to suss what was happening to DeToro. It was driving her crazy not to just run in, guns blazing, as it were, but the wall of ENForcers hadn't moved, which was a good sign. It might also mean that Del Toro wasn't fighting, which was possibly a very bad sign.

Hawk returned her attention to her new friend, "So, what were they talking about in there?"

"The local fascists are arguing with the uber-fascists over who's got to claim your girl." He seemed like he might say more, but his device beeped. The light from it illuminated his face as he read. He showed her a screen of converging red dots, "Hey, we've got allies incoming. What are you thinking? Like a human chain? Won't they just plow through us?" When Hawk didn't immediately respond, Tchadzwa answered his own question, "Well, if they do, we'll just film it. Shooting civilians in the Jovian Sector would be an unprovoked act of war."

Hawk tried to count the moving dots before Tchadzwa pulled his phone back. Had there really been over two dozen already on the move? What the hell was Grella, anyway?

Tchadzwa continued to strategize. "I think we should just block the van, right? Like make sure there are obvious influencers with their devices out on top of those parked cars over there, yeah?" He stopped to answer another beep. His hair seemed to swirl even more excitedly, as if in rhythm with his mood, "Yeah, Sira, good point, do it. They're bringing some facial recognition-block-ing holo-paint," he half-looked up to Hawk. Apparently, seeing only confusion, he explained, "It's spray, you know, it'll go on fast. Yeah, yeah, excellent think-ing... bring the gas mask for sure." His thumbs flashed as he spoke. "Bright Bud-dha, Alex, this isn't the time to bring up that old beef with the Communists. These are ENForcers, not some local co-op war. Just get everybody here."

"So, uh, Grella's not a dating app, huh?" She said, mostly to herself.

Tchadzwa glanced up at her long enough to flash her a wicked grin and say, "Not exactly, no. I mean, I guess it depends on what turns you on."

Hawk's eyes continued to watch the ENForcer cluster. They seemed to be getting restless. Maybe the one outside was sensing the incoming people, as he too shifted from foot to foot, scanning the horizon. He even spared her and Tchadzwa a glance. The argument inside the shop was getting louder, or maybe the ENForcers were losing patience with playing nice.

"Hey, Hawk!" A total stranger tapped Hawk on the shoulder making her jump. "How does your girlfriend spell her name?"

Hawk turned to see a cheerful older person, somewhat femme, holding up two markers and a large sheet of white poster board. Their smiling, wrinkled facer had been painted with jagged lines in different colors, and white hair was cut short above the ears.

Dumbfounded Hawk recited, "L-U-C-I-A"

Squeaks of markers followed along, The older person spoke to Tchadzwa as they wrote, "So, the Communists are coming. I hope you're ready for that stupidity."

"Alex," Tchadzwa sighed in a long-suffering, exasperated voice. He gestured at the backs of the ENForcers broadly, device still in hand. "Witness the real villains."

"I know, I know, but hopefully those shits will leave once we kick their butts. We're stuck with Peter and his smug face forever." To Hawk, Alex said a perfunctory, "Up the revolution."

"Yeah, um, Solidarity?" Hawk watched Alex walk off towards the ENForcer van, where a small crowd was already silently gathering. People had obviously come prepared. Not only were there generic 'Fuck the Cops' signs, but someone seemed to be moving through the police air bikes, slashing fuel lines. Watching their silent efficiency, Hawk said, admiringly, "I need to get on Grella."

"You do," Tchadzwa agreed.

The ENForcer station outside looked nervous. He retreated slowly, his eyes on the forming crowd, until his back was almost flush with the door to the cupcake shop.

Weird to think that no one on the inside of Galilei's lab had a clue what was brewing just below them. All it would take was one forensics guy on a smoke break or to be sent back to their vehicle for some missing equipment, and the whole police force could be here... which maybe wouldn't be such a bad thing because it would add to all the chaos.

Yeah. Make it even messier.

Hawk found the paper business card in her pocket and made a 'gimme' motion to Tchadzwa for his device. He shook his head, 'no way.' But, with a free hand dug out a second—or was it a third at this point?—device from the back of his jeans and tossed it to her. Another blank burner? Who the hell were these people?

Hawk decided she didn't care so long as they were on her side. She got the burner activated and synced to her account with three taps and a password. The first thing she did was call Sargsyan.

As soon as he picked up, she said. "Hey, It's Hawk. I've got something you should definitely see. Stick your head out the window."

CHAPTER 15

Lucia Del Toro

Lucia huddled, hidden, behind the table. She'd looked up briefly during the chaos of the cashier being manhandled out the door, but ducked back down before any of the rest of the creche could ID her.

Not that Simon didn't know she was there. *You're a stupid woman. I told you to run.*

Maybe give a girl more than five seconds head start next time then, brother. At any rate, I'd prefer to face your sorry ass head-on than die with a ENForcer bullet in my back.

A separate argument continued alongside their private conversation. The local cops had been holding their ground and, interestingly, the ENForcers hadn't yet pushed back.

"You continue to fail to explain yourselves properly," It was Ferarra, who stood directly in front of where Lucia hid, his arms crossed in front of his barrel chest. He'd been talking to these ENForcers in a scolding tone, as if they were his delinquent grandchildren. "What brings you fine gentlemen to our corner of Ganymede."

A voice Lucia didn't immediately recognize but the onboard identified as Brigadier General Zhu Wei spoke: "Stand down. I'm fully authorized by the Earth Nations' Peacekeeping Force to arrest the renegade Colonel Lucian Del Toro for the crimes of dereliction of duty, desertion in time of war, and treason."

That last crime was new. To Simon she sent, *When did they add treason?*

Today, he replied dryly. *When Marcus came back telling everyone about your big change.*

Nice.

I argued the bullshit of this, but don't underestimate Zhu Wei's cleverness. He pointed out that, historically, the crime of treason could be defined as murdering someone to whom you owe an allegiance, like a husband, and apparently he thinks that's how this works—that you were once something else, something worthy of allegiance, and that you killed that part of yourself. I tried to explain that it is literally the opposite, but you know how it is, as soon as you sound either sympathetic or a little too knowledgeable about how these things actually are....

All too well. Does he really have the authority for all this?

No. This is the usual ploy. Just steamroll in and out before anyone thinks to question.

I remember that, too.

Sounding remarkably certain, Khalil said, "Okay, let's pretend you do. Thing is, that Lucian guy is not here. We were just about to go looking for him ourselves."

A couple of the ENForcers chuckled darkly. Lucia risked a quick look around Ferrar's legs to try to gauge just how many were against her. Instead, her gaze alighted on and connected to Simon's. He looked the same as she remembered him, only older. He was still the baby face of the creche. His Pakistani heritage gave him big, brown eyes with thick dark lashes. His skin held a warm, friendly glow. Simon was the one they'd always pick to play the 'good cop' in Information extraction—no, she reminded herself the correct term was "torture"—games. Regardless, he was still very pretty... for an ENForcer.

He stared back at her with a practiced coldness. Only years of growing up together allowed her to see the tiny tells of worry—a little crinkle between the eyes, the twitch of the jaw.

This is ridiculous, Simon sent. *If you're so brave that you want to face us, stand up.*

What, and give you a clear head shot? I'm taller than either of these two shurtas, so, no thank you. I'm brave, not stupid.

There was a beat. His otherwise stony expression quirked into a small smile, like maybe he was thinking about something amusing. *The footage Marcus showed us. You're hard to even recognize. You've changed so much. Why didn't you change your size?*

Did you forget that our spines are reinforced with bio-steel? It's hard enough to find anyone skilled enough to work on one of us, at all, for simple things. It's not like I can just request an upgrade from the quartermaster anymore.

Well, here's your chance to come back.

Ha. As if.

Fair.

Above Lucia, Khalil crossed his arms. His entire body radiated with annoyance. He spoke slowly, like he was explaining something obvious to an out of town tourist instead of a brigadier general of the Earth Nations Forces. "I don't know why any of you think this is funny. You can't just arrest citizens of the Outer System. 'Fully authorized,' my ass. You have no jurisdiction here. Also, it's not a crime to be related to a fugitive."

The brigadier general blinked, like he needed a system reset. "I'm sorry, what? Related to whom? This *is* the fugitive."

The other shurta, Ferrera, let out a hearty guffaw. He did that thing where he lifted his hat to scratch at his bald spot again. "I know you Martians don't get out much, but that," he jerked his thumb back in Lucia's direction, "is obviously a woman."

"Seriously," Khalil shook his head in disbelief. "I thought ENForcer's vision was enhanced. The lot of you need an upgrade, stat."

You know, Simon's private channel pinged again. *I could try to work this for you. You were a giant red dot when you first came online, but you must have figured out how to shift into Stealth Mode because you blipped out. Zhu Wei has been trying to countermand your order for the last twenty minutes. But, you're one lucky girl. Since you deserted in the middle of a conflict, you went out hot, and so since your status was never updated the system believes you might still need cover. Not even the Force Commander himself can rescind Stealth Mode if the officer is listed in active combat.*

New Shanghai to the rescue. Unsettling.

In all of this back and forth, Zhu Wei pinched the bridge of his nose like he was getting a splitting headache. When he removed his fingers, Zhu Wei spared Lucia a hard glance that seemed to see right through her. She resisted the temptation to duck further back under the table and instead met his withering glance. He blinked first, returning his attention to the shurta. "The fugitive came online. We know the precise location of the Colonel, and he is here."

"She."

Lucia had been silently mouthing her own correction, but she hadn't dared say anything out loud. Stranger still, the voice had come from someone behind Zhu Wei and Simon. It had been too quick for her onboard to identify. So, Lucia quickly scanned the faces of her former creche mates, but none of their faces betrayed any sympathy. When she met Simon's eyes again, he looked a little surprised, as well.

Was more than one of her creche mates a halfway decent human being? She shook her head. She must have been mistaken. One of the police officers must have said it.

Zhu Wei cleared his throat, clearly deciding to ignore the insubordination. "My point, Officers, is that our target is here. You need to step out of the way."

Lucia held her breath. This was it, the brigadier general had clearly tired of being patient.

Simon must have sensed the shift as well. He cleared his throat. "Technically, sir, all we know is that Del Toro was in the vicinity." Simon must be the brigadier general's adjutant, since he didn't ask for permission to speak. "It's not impossible that Del Toro has a sibling on Ganymede. This wouldn't be the first incident where one of ours has tracked down a civilian twin—"

"Shut it." Zhu Wei's snarl was immediate. He was clearly not the sort who was used to having to keep his temper in check. "Don't be airing our dirty laundry."

Simon snapped to attention. "Sir."

"And don't play me for a fool. Lieutenant Ali's eye cam footage is all the proof we need. This abomination—" Zhu Wei shot Lucia an ugly glance, "—answered to the rank of Colonel when first approached in Mehit. We have found the right person because I say we've found the right person. Understood?"

The chorus of 'yes, sir's' was not nearly as crisp or quick as Lucia would have expected.

Simon confirmed. *This is going to get weird. I told Zhu Wei it was a stupid idea to have the creche hunt down its own sibling. Not all of us are in agreement. Zhu Wei put Sulanov on crowd control because he's so against this whole business that no one trusts him to not intentionally whiff a killing shot. Marcus straight up told the Zhu Wei to his face that since you're a woman now, you no longer belong in the Force. He thinks this whole mission is bullshit. Marcus only signed up because he thought he was bringing a brother back to the fold.*

It was sort of a backwards kind of acknowledgment, but she'd take it. They always used to say that Marcus was an idiot, but he was their idiot.

Khalil shifted his body and blocked her view. "I don't. I don't understand, actually." Khalil said, with another little 'can you believe these guys' chuckle. "You're crazy if you think you can waltz in here and declare this woman a fugitive. We've been talking to her for hours. She and her partner turned themselves in as witnesses to a murder. Would a wanted criminal do that? No. Besides, *this* Del Toro already told us that she's sympathetic to her brother and has agreed to take us to your Del Toro. So why don't you just let us get on with it?"

"Sir?" Simon said, giving the brigadier general a look. "Our real target could be getting away."

Zhu Wei's teeth clenched. Rage filled his entire body posture. It was clear that the brigadier general was unused to people telling him 'no,' in any way. "The fugitive—who is right there—is coming with us. Step aside or you will be removed."

"Removed?" Ferrera asked, sounding a bit nervous for the first time. "What do you mean 'removed'?"

The brigadier general didn't hesitate. "I mean shot."

Lucia wasn't the only one who gasped at that admission.

Simon's jaw set. He shot Lucia the look of a soldier about to fall on his own sword. Privately, he sent: *Here it is, nine years later and I'm about to torpedo my career by telling my commander that I'm going to refuse an illegal order. Maybe it's just something I'm fated to do.*

Hold up, she sent, *Don't do that on my account. I'll turn myself in—*

Not on my watch. You've already thrown yourself on your sword enough for me.

Just as Lucia stood up another one of the ENForcers—the onboard informed her that it was Second Lieutenant Jakob Zielinski spoke up. She was unfamiliar with the name. He must be her replacement. His skin was also oddly pale, washed out. "Major Farooqi is right, General. This can't be the Colonel. Even if he was a girl, there's no way an ENForcer would fucking hide from us behind some twink cop and his fat-ass partner."

"Oi, who are you calling fat," Ferrera said, just as Khalil asked, "What's a twink? Should I be insulted?"

No one had a chance to register that Lucia now stood in full view because the ENForcer who'd been stationed outside, Daniel Sulanov, rapped at the window.

His white face glowed pinkish under the neon cupcake sign outside. Sulanov's skin was paler than Hawk and so, thanks to that and his extensive stealth training, he garnered the moniker "The Ghost." He liked it just about as well as Lucia enjoyed being "The Scourge." Sulanov jerked his head and pointed outward with his thumb. Now that she had a clear view over the shurtas Lucia could sort of read Sulanov's lips. He said something about 'locals getting restless.'

What was going on outside? Was Hawk rallying a crowd, somehow? Lucia considered opening their private com, but it wasn't nearly as encrypted as the one between herself and Simon. She feared that with as much attention as the ENForcers were giving her, they'd trace the signal if not hack the actual message. For Lucia, Hawk's safety was more important than her own personal reassurance.

Sulanov was still at the window, nodding in that sharp, distinctive way that made Lucia certain that he was taking subvocal orders. She strained again to see beyond him, but it was nearly impossible with the inside lights on, making the glass reflective.

Lights. She could take advantage of this distraction and shoot out the lights. But, drawing a weapon in this tiny space would be a disaster on so many levels. Firstly, in the ensuing firefight, she'd jeopardize the lives of the two shurta—Ferrera and Khalil—who despite everything, she'd grown oddly fond of, if for no other reason their insistent, dogged belief in her womanhood.

Secondly, even though Lucia was a sharpshooter, she'd need time to aim at the individual lights. As hyped-up and as augmented as her creche mates were, she'd be dead before she took out even one bulb. She gave up on the idea with a shake of her head.

When she returned her attention to the ENForcers, she noticed that Simon had clocked her assessment of the lights. He sent, *You pull your peacemaker and the gig is up. You should probably shoulder out of that jacket. Have you no sense?*

You sound like Hawk, she smiled.

A wise person, he returned.

The brigadier general turned around then. Following Simon's gaze, said, "Ah, here, finally, is the so-called sister Del Toro. Still wearing the uniform, I see, Colonel."

Lucia said nothing to Zhu Wei. She didn't know him; she owed him nothing, not even her attention. It was into the eyes of her creche mates that she now looked. Simon gave her a brief, nearly imperceptible nod. Marcus just shook his head, giving her the same disgusted look as when they met up in Oz's flier. If anything, Marcus looked more pissed off, though that could just be due to how dark the bruise under his chin had gotten. You wouldn't otherwise know he'd been pulled from frozen water. It was scary.

The other two—they were harder to read.

She determined that Tootega Noayak was wearing his grim mask. Lucia knew this look. It was Tootega's 'I don't want to deal with this bullshit' face. Their gaze met for a brief second before he feigned a sudden interest behind him, as if checking in with Sulanov. Strangely, she took this interaction as a good sign. He didn't want to be here, at the very least.

This new person looked openly hostile. Well, that was to be expected. No doubt, when she defected, the Force found the most gungho and rules-abiding asshole to step into her role. Someone to whip her old team back into shape. Someone to act as a kind of punishment for her behavior.

This new person wasn't a Colonel. Checking his pips revealed him to be the most junior officer, five of five, a first lieutenant. A quick assessment of the rank pins on the rest of her creche mates showed that none of them had advanced. They were all just as she'd left them. The ranks stayed the same, but the order had to have shifted to make room for the new guy. He had no loyalty to her. He could be a real problem.

Sulanov, who had always been second of five, must now be first. Yet, he was the one that the brigadier general trusted so little that he was on outside duty. Simon must be beta for real now, two of five, and he was fully her ally. Tootega would have moved into the number three spot and he was, at the very least, unhappy with the situation.

Interesting. Lucia wasn't sure what to make of this new information, but she held on to it.

Meanwhile, the two cops, unsurprisingly, were very much focused on the threat to their lives. Ferrera had started looking for alternate exits. Khalil, meanwhile, fumed. "This an insult to me that I'm slim and beautiful?"

"And gay," Marcus supplied.

"Or bisexual, which I am, so congratulations, you've identified me. This is not an insult. In fact, it compliments me that you consider me a youthful beauty."

Zhu Wei was not amused by this banter. He turned his head to Simon in a way that signaled to Lucia that they'd just shared some private comment via *Boy.net*. Turning back to the shurta, he let his hand fall to his peacemaker, holstered at his side. "I'll give you one more chance to step aside, officers."

Lucia held her breath.

Ferrera and Klalil stood their ground.

Unaware of the tension inside the shop, Sulanov pushed inside, clattering the cowbells overhead. It was enough of a distraction. Everyone was looking at Sulanov. Though the now opened door, Lucia could hear it, a murmuring angry crowd building. Sulanov's face stayed focused over his shoulder as he announced, "As previously reported, sir, I do believe we are well and sincerely fucked."

Lucia pulled her peacemaker and shot out the lights.

CHAPTER 16

Independence "Hawk" Hawking

Outside the cafe, the crowd expanded exponentially.

Not an expert at estimating crowd size, Hawk guessed a couple hundred, maybe much more. Bodies blocked the whole street and spilled into Chimera Laboratory's quad.

It was an odd mix. Some people wore flower crowns, dressed as though they had come from a party. Those sort stood alongside others in anarchist chic and face paint, carrying hastily made posters. A constant murmur filled the street as people tried to figure out exactly what was happening.

She still had the detective inspector on Tchadzwa's burner device. Through the speaker, Sargsyan asked: "What am I looking at?"

She didn't bother answering, just waited for the curtain of the office window above to part.

"Merciful Allah," Sargsyan said. "What's going on down there?"

"A riot, I think. Or maybe a rumble. With ENForcers," Hawk said. Her plan was to then immediately press the 'end communication' button for dramatic effect, but she was interrupted by the distinctive sound of a peacemaker discharging. Lights inside the cupcake shop exploded into darkness.

Silence fell over the street. Everyone anxiously held a collective breath.

Hawk's heart all but stopped out of pure panic. Lucia! Where was Lucia? Was she okay? Had she been shot?

There was another deafening bang. All attention returned to the cupcake shop. Through the glass, Hawk saw one of the ENForcers stagger and pitch forward. Something entangled his face—cowbells?

164

Unseeing and seething, he tripped on something, stumbling.

He went down.

When he did, a strange kind of excitement rippled through the crowd. It was as though no one could quite believe what they were seeing. To be fair, neither could Hawk. Nothing was supposed to drop an ENForcer. Especially not something small and insignificant, like decor.

The other ENForcers were shocked, too. Not that they had much time to react before a second shot dropped another. Another ENForcer spun around, as if thrown by a shot to the hip—except, where was the blood spatter? Everyone watched a second ENForcer lose his balance and go down.

The part of Hawk's mind that registered everything in slow-mo with a cool calculation couldn't quite parse the scene. ENForcers were going down? But without bloodshed?

"Lucia?" Hawk's voice was small, but in the hushed anxious moment, it might as well have been a scream.

Others nearby repeated the name, made connections. "Lucia is taking them down!"

Inside the coffeeshop, the scene was shifting. ENForcers shook themselves out of their initial stupor and began to move.

So did the crowd.

Lucia's name became a battle cry. People surged forward. Everything became a jumble in the press of bodies. Hawk was tallish and unused to the sensation of claustrophobia and being completely lost in a crowd. A childish desire for a hand to hold or an anchor had her reaching for the back of Tchadzwa's patchwork vest. But she thought better of it when, somewhere to her left, punches flew and bones cracked.

People seemed to be piling onto the ENForcer in the street. In the chaos and the darkness, Hawk could barely control her own trajectory much less see who was winning that battle...

Where are you?

The sound of Lucia's old voice made Hawk startle. She'd almost raised a fist to an unseen attacker herself, until she recognized who had spoken to her, and how. *Oh thank god,* Hawk returned on their private channel. *You're alive! Are you okay?*

A window broke. Glass shattered.

Hawk forgot that she still clutched Tchadzwa's device to her ear until she heard Sargsyan's voice. "What the hell was that? Gunfire? What's happening?"

165

Swiping it off, she jammed it into her pocket as another surge propelled her forward. Tchadzwa's dancing hair was there beside her. His fists in the air, his mouth moving with some chant swallowed in the cacophony. Briefly, Hawk was slammed up against the wall of the shop. She managed not to lose her footing. Tchadzwa or someone else's hand, pulled her up.

Coat cop will probably call for back-up. Things are going to get even messier when they arrive, Hawk informed Lucia. *Can you get out?*

Working on it.

More peacemaker fire flashed somewhere inside the shop and the lights went out. That strangely distant part of Hawk kept wondering why there was more of that—why ENForcers hadn't opened up on the crowd, why there weren't the kinds of blood curdling screams you might expect in a massacre?

Hawk kept catching glimpses of one very white-faced, too-blond ENForcer near the door of the cupcake shop. He welded a shockstick with deadly force. Bodies fell around him. For every one he beat back, another appeared. The tide forced his slow retreat backward, step by step. They pushed his back up against a wall.

The crowd, meanwhile, drove Hawk through one of the broken out windows. Her feet hit the remaining edges of the wall. She might have stumbled, but hands lifted her up and over. From the vantage point of the top of the window sill, Hawk thought she caught sight of Lucia, grappling some ENForcer. The mob jostled Hawk off the ledge before she could be certain. A clot of people tried to physically hack into the cash box behind the counter, Another group gathered up pastries, though the display cases were broken and smashed. Still others threw things, including their own bodies, at the ENForcers.

Lucia? Hawk sent, while shouting her name out loud as well, "Lucia!"

I don't want to leave Simon. Not again. Not after this. He put himself in the line of fire.

Caring only for Lucia in that moment, Hawk had no response beyond, *Just get out. I'll find you.*

The crowd had pressed Hawk against an interior wall, making it hard to move. Even as tall as she was, she couldn't make out much of anything in the pandemonium. She scanned desperately for Del Toro. There! A flash of curls! It had to be her. Hawk pushed forward with desperation, nearly climbing over people, like surfing a deadly mosh pit.

"Lucia!" Hawk said, or maybe everyone did. Reaching out, they grasped hands, only to be swept up again. A pulse forward, brought Hawk and Lucia together. Somehow, there was Tchadzwa again, the lights in his hair a kind of beacon in the dark and the madness. With hand gestures, Tchadzwa directed them to a back entrance. In a pocket space behind a counter he unlocked a door marked Staff Only with a swipe key he had on a lanyard.

Another surge had them spilling and stumbling out into an alleyway.

Hawk kept Tchadzwa's bobbing hair in sight, which was made more difficult by the fact that he'd dimmed the glowing beads somehow now that they were outside. Her other hand clutched frantically to Lucia. At least she hoped that's whose hand she held. Not wanting to lose sight of the beads, she sent: *This is you, right?*

A comforting squeeze: *I'm here.*

Tchadzwa directed them through two turns in the alley to a door that some-one opened to them on some silent cue. An anxious face hurried them inside. Then, after Tchadzwa slipped something into that person's palm, he took off down a set of rickety wooden stairs that led down a basement. Hawk and Del Toro shared a mutual look of concern, but followed along. He continued to lead them down a second stairwell and another back way. Hawk lost track of the twists and turns until, all at once, they came out into an open street, sirens sounding in the distance.

"Did we actually get away?" It seemed so unreal, Hawk felt she needed to ask. "Like, really?"

"For the moment," Del Toro said. "It helps that they let us go."

Their group of protesters had thinned to just themselves, Tchadzwa, and one other. The four paused under a lamp post in the middle of the block. Hawk tried to get bearings. Where were they? The air temperature was cool, almost chilly, having dropped when artificial nighttime kicked in. Even so, it was nowhere nearly as cold here as it was in Mehit with its ice slush canals. In fact, the air held a bit of humidity that came with the unmistakable odor of sulfur.

They were in a mostly deserted business district, surrounded by tall build-ings of steel and glass. Beyond the lamps dotted along the streets, the only other light was the stars through the translucent dome and distant flashes of fireworks.

Sirens blared, but they seemed as far away as the sound of the street reve-lers, whose noise drifted in the evening air, like a gentle breeze. Even so, they couldn't have traveled that far in this short of time. They should go, disperse, but to where?

Hawk finally said what was clearly on everyone's mind, "What do we do now?"

Still a bit dazed, Del Toro asked, "Should we try to make for The *Pequod*?"

167

"*Peapod*. Pea. Pod," Hawk said, correcting the name of their ship. Her words came out in a jumble of unspent anxiety. "This is why things like this keep happening. The *Pequod* is a doomed ship. Doomed, I keep telling you this. Doomed! Peapods are nice. You know, two peas in a pod? It's romantic. Plus, growing things, not white whales and crazy captains and 'Call me Ishmael.' Nice! Pea. Pod."

"It's probably been commandeered, at any rate," Del Toro said.

"Commandeered is the wrong word, too, damn it," Hawk muttered, letting out the rest of her anxiety with a long breath. "It was theirs to begin with."

Del Toro let out an agreeing sort of grunt at the same time Tchadzwa chuckled and asked, "Just how married are you two, anyway?"

Before either she or Del Toro could respond, the stranger chuckled. "Very."

Everyone swiveled to check out this new person. He had clearly been out celebrating Nowruz, because he was festooned in red flowers. There was a very battered crown of tulips sitting askew on a pile of dark curls, and he had a kind of paper lei of more flowers around his neck. Otherwise, he wore a white tunic shirt that went almost to his knees and a brocade vest, which was mostly dark colors but the hems were decorated in a red tulip pattern.

"Anyway, if we're talking about where to go next, it should be mine. I don't mind harboring fugitives. And, I'd be a good bet. I only just joined this thing because Emily's party was getting boring and my friends saw your alert on Grella," he said, nodding at Tchadzwa. "I don't even have my own account. My face might be on a security camera somewhere, but I'm the last person the cops are going to interview, if they even track me down at all." Another gesture at Tchadzwa, "You're the first. You probably shouldn't go home either."

It was smart, almost too smart. Hawk had to ask, "Are you a plant? Some kind of cop?"

Everyone watched for his reaction, except Del Toro, who nervously scanned the sidewalk.

"Yes, totally, " he said, rolling his eyes. He gestured to his pleasantly lived-in, soft body, "I mean, look at me, a police academy's wet dream. Are we going or what?"

"We need to get off the street," Del Toro said. "Almost anywhere is better than standing here dithering. Perimeters. You know I have an issue with undefended perimeters"

"Fine, we can walk into yet another trap, if that's what you want to do," Hawk said, irritated at herself for not having a better solution to their current problem. For some reason, Hawk found herself looking to Tchadzwa to see if he was with them.

He seemed to be surprised to be included in the decision making and he shrugged. "I mean, I think this person is correct. All of me and mine are the sorts that the cops regularly keep tabs on. If I go home, I'm likely to get picked up. I've sent encoded messages in roundabout fashions to the people I care about, so I'm currently a free agent. So why not, I guess? If this person turns out to be a cop, I was probably headed for a night in jail, anyway. You two, I'm less sure about, given who was after you. "

Del Toro said, "I need food and a chance to reassess damages being done. Even if it's only a respite for a few hours, I'm desperate."

With everyone else in agreement, Hawk nodded along.

"Great," the new guy who was probably an undercover cop said. "My place isn't far. Follow me."

As they cautiously threaded their way through the back alleys, the newcomer introduced himself as Jaabir Ncube. Hawk still wasn't convinced that Jaabir wasn't a cop, but, all she wanted to do right now was cling to Del Toro's side and grasp her hand. Thinking too far ahead almost felt dangerous.

Moving away from the downtown business district into a residential area of Edfu Facula, the street parties proliferated. People sat outside on stoops of row houses. The majority of the homes in this area were made from some greenish stone containing flecks of something that sparkled and shimmered in the warm, electric light of the round, red festival lanterns that had been strung between buildings and across streets.

As they made their way, party to party, people offered them flowers and bags of nuts and dried fruits. Several times, they found themselves caught up in a dance line or pausing to watch a street performer. This, at least, felt like the kind of 'running' that Del Toro and Hawk normally engaged in. Tchadzwa seemed nervous every time they stopped to sample some local street vendor's wares, but, despite the looming danger, Hawk found herself relaxing.

Meanwhile, it was clear Del Toro did not.

Are you okay? Hawk sent when they were stopped in front of a fire juggler. *I mean, you're probably not actually fine and I know that, but we got away, right?*

It's temporary at best. My system rebooted. I'm reconnected to Boy.net. I found a way to baffle the system momentarily, but if I'm not talking it's because I'm fighting off nanobots that are threatening to remake me.

"Remake" you? You don't mean—

Yes, but right now my onboard is prioritizing reconnecting to the fucking 'mothership' which I would also like to avoid. I need to get to a biohacker, stat.

"Holy shit," Hawk said out loud, unable to keep it to herself.

"Yeah," Del Toro agreed. "I'm a little on edge."

Hawk nodded and gave her hand another squeeze. "I know people—not here, but we'll get this fixed."

Del Toro didn't say anything to that. Hawk would have pressed, but Tchadzwa and Jaabir signaled them to move onward.

❦

By the time they got where they seemed to be going, everyone had a dozen or more bright red flowers in their hair. The silk flowers looked especially fetching on Tchadzwa, since he'd found a way to set them into his braids where the dancing lights illuminated them and made them sway, like petals drifting a light breeze.

Jaabir waved them over to a particular row house and directed them up a short set of wide stairs to a large, front door. The door had been painted a garish turquoise. Hawk noticed that bright doors seemed to be in fashion along the avenue—some were fuchsia, yellow, and one was even colored a sour green.

Thanks to a light on in the main room, Hawk could see a hint of furniture through the open curtains. Before she could ask if he lived alone, Jaabir clicked the door open with a swipe of his device. "Welcome to casa del Ncube."

Do we trust him? Hawk sent to Del Toro.

Their eyes met as they stepped over the threshold together. Del Toro shrugged and sent, *We probably shouldn't, but I am entirely unable to cope. I shot a brigadier general in the hip.*

Even through the floating text Hawk could imagine the devastation in Del Toro's tone. Her face showed most of it, anyway. She looked exhausted and spent and a little conflicted and sad. It was that last bit that made Hawk resist the urge to say "served him right." Instead, she reached out to squeeze Del Toro's hand briefly as they entered the foyer. *You did what you had to do.*

I'd be dead but for Simon. He shoulder-checked the brigadier general who was aiming at my head. You have no idea how fucking brave that was, Hawk. He gave me a chance to get off a second shot and drop those cowbells. He's the only reason I'm alive. Him... and the rest of them. Not one of them hit where they were aiming, They covered for me. Me. After all this time.

That's good, though, right?

170

It's astounding. I don't deserve this. And what about them? What are they going back to? I should be the one facing charges, not them.

Don't say that. Anyway, they're smart, Hawk had her doubts actually, but she decided Del Toro's creche deserved a little credit. One of them, after all, had come up with a good plan at New Shanghai, even if it hadn't worked. *They know how to bullshit their bosses, right? Didn't you tell me that?*

Del Toro turned away, letting go of Hawk's hand.

"Right?" she started, but Del Toro gave her a "we'll talk about it later" grimace.

I have to check. I... got some new downloads. Footage I've been missing about New Shanghai.

Footage?! There was footage from New Shanghai??

Let's figure out if this place is really safe. If it is, maybe I can finally piece some shit together.

With a nod, Hawk looked around, trying to get a sense of who this guy might be. The interior of Jaabir's place was dark and cool, a stark change from the moist, slightly fart-smelling air of the outside. Edfu Facula was apparently a bright spot on Ganymede because it was a thermal hotspot. On their walk here, Hawk had noticed several places advertising as hotspring bathhouses.

"Make yourselves at home," Jaabir said, pulling off the various flowers that he'd collected from his hair and clothes and setting them on a polished plascrete table. His decor seemed to lean heavily towards the recent cozy-cluttered fad popular in Xanadu Albedo on Titan. The furniture was a mix of new and refurbished, all of it prioritized for softness over style. Paper books of all kinds were everywhere. Tchadzwa randomly picked up an anarchist comic 'zine from the entryway's table.

Noticing Tchadzwa's interest, Jaabir said, "Oh yeah, that belongs to my new friend."

Something in Jaabir's tone had Hawk on high alert. Sure enough, into the room walked none other than Ozmerelda Jackson.

CHAPTER 17

Lucia Del Toro

Lucia had been lost in thought, anxious to open those body cam files. She'd barely taken in her surroundings, when suddenly her onboard sprung to life. A target crosshair appeared on a figure that had been obscured in the shadowy corner of the living room. *Potential hostile approach. Identified as Ozmerelda Jackson. Recommend lethal force.*

She could feel old reactions kicking in. Before she could even belay the order her peacemaker was in her hand, fully charged and pointed at Oz's head.

Hey, Del Toro. I never had a chance to apologize before. I just want you to remember that my needle bent. That was on purpose, Oz signed. Their eyes wide and focused on the peacemaker. Everyone else had turned to look at the unmistakable whine of the gun coming online. Out loud, Oz added, "My business with the ENForcers wasn't supposed to include you. They railroaded me."

Which would be more believable, Lucia thought, if you stopped using Earther idioms, but giving Oz the benefit of the doubt for the moment Lucia shutdown her targeting computer. She gave her head an irritated shake, She was going to have to have a very long talk with her onboard. This new reboot was far more bloodthirsty than she had ever been, even when she was still a colonel.

Oz watched Lucia uncoil warily and flashed a wan smile. "We good?"

"Not especially," Lucia said, returning the weapon to her hidden side holster underneath her jacket. Not sure that Oz caught her reply, Lucia lifted her hands and repeated in sign, *No. You led Marcus to me. One of his shattering projectiles did the same work as your injection would have, so you haven't impressed me yet. I trust you just about as far as I can throw you.*

The new guy, Jaabir Ncumbe, laughed at that and spoke while signing, as well. "Well, that's all right, then. You look like you have the kind of enhanced muscles that could toss them pretty damn far."

"What?" Hawk and the cashier—Tchadzwa, was it?—said at the same time.

Following Jaabir's lead, Del Toro signed as she spoke, "I told Oz I don't trust them further than I could throw them."

"That makes no sense," Tchadzwa said, the tips of his dreadlocks swishing slowly, the lights in them bobbed as though being gently tugged by the ocean's waves. "What does the ability to shotput someone have to do with trust?"

Hawk, who seemed to have become quite friendly with Tchadzwa just gave him a little nudge on the arm, "It's a Martian idiom. No one understands them."

"No one? She used it, and the new guy seemed to get it," Tchadzwa said, pointing to Jaabir.

Jaabir, who had been alternating translating the conversation for Oz and removing the flowers from his hair and putting them on the top of a nearby bookshelf, stopped to point at his chest. "My mom was a contractor for the Force. She was a weapons designer. I grew up all over, but we spent a lot of time around ENForcers."

Hawk put up a hand. "Hold up. Your mom built weapons for the ENForcers? And somehow you just randomly hooked up with Oz who is maybe still working with those same bastards, who are after my girlfriend, and who assaulted my friend Tchadzwa here," she jerked her thumb at Tchadzwa, who lifted a hand in a shy 'hello, everyone' wave. "The same ENForcers who are possibly also interested in the artificial eye that started this whole thing?"

"What eye?" Tchadzwa and Jaabir asked simultaneously.

Lucia glanced at the still-open window, itching to either close the curtains so that they couldn't be seen from the street or taking up position so that she could watch without being seen. Lucia really wanted to tune into *Boy.net* to see if they were being surrounded even as they spoke, but that would require dropping Silent Running. Turning her attention to Oz, Lucia signed and said, "Care to explain yourself? Because these are a helluva lot of coincidences piling up."

Oz nodded as though they agreed. Pointing to the sofas and other comfortable-looking seats in the living room, Oz said, "Let's sit down and talk it over like adults."

Hawk seemed ready to go in and claim the retro bean bag chair in the corner, but a hand from Lucia stopped her from crossing the threshold into the living room. "Only if you guarantee that this is not a stalling technique so that the ENForcers have time to surround us."

Oz frowned as if uncertain what was said. Lucia was just about to let go of Hawk to translate it, when Oz signed, *If the ENForcers show up, it's because you're leaking signals all over. Luckily, I knew you were coming and had time to set up a dampening field.*

"Knew we were coming?" Hawk repeated.

"You *were* a plant," Lucia said to Jaabir.

"Yeah, but not for the cops," he said with a little smile that showed absolutely no guilt.

Letting go of Hawk, Lucia took a step towards Jaabir. "So for the ENForcers?"

"No fucking way," Jaabir said. Pointing to Oz, he said, "For them."

"Do I like this?" Tchadzwa asked no one in particular as he flopped himself down on a sofa. "I mean, I don't even think I know half of what is going on and I don't think I like this."

"Nobody likes this," Hawk agreed, picking an overstuffed chair surrounded by piles of books.

I sort of like this, Oz signed with a shrug as they perched on the edge of the couch Tchadzwa sprawled on. *I think I was rather clever. Possibly even heroic? I've been foiling the ENForcers ever since I found out Del Toro and Hawk were a package deal.*

"A package deal?" Lucia chose not to sit. Instead, she found a wall to lean on that gave her a good vantage point. From where she was, she could see both the door and the window.

Yes, Oz signed. *A package deal. The ENForcers*—which they indicated with a very rude sign, probably better translated as 'fucking pigs'—*are after more than just you, Lucia.*

Jaabir claimed the bean bag, which gave a sort of hissing squish as he settled his weight into it.

Lucia's onboard suddenly complained about the dampening field. *Boy.net connection terminated. Rebooting connection. Connection blocked. Requesting permission for subspace transmission to the* Conqueror *for assistance.*

"Request denied," she said aloud, then she added, *Re-engage stealth mode.*

Stealth mode engaged.

The onboard settled down instantly.

The sensation of eyes on her, made Lucia look up and realize everyone in the room was staring at her. "What?"

"Canapes sounded cool to me," Hawk said by way of explanation. "'Request denied'? Really?"

Had someone mentioned canapes? Lucia must have missed much more of the conversation than she'd realized. "Oh, yes, food would be great." Lucia said. With a pointed look at Oz, she said, "Thanks to an injection someone managed to get into my system and the recent solar activity, I've been forcibly reconnected to my old regiment. Worse, the newest upgrades are even more aggressively militant than they were back in my day." She tapped her temple, "My onboard really wants me to connect to the nearest battlecruiser."

Tchadzwa lifted his head from where he'd let it relax against the back of the couch. "Heh, you sound like an ENForcer." When no one laughed, he sat up even straighter. His eyes lingered on Lucia's jacket. Then, he seemed to then connect that with the weapon she'd pulled on Oz. "Wait. You're not an ENForcer. There's no way you're an ENForcer. You're a woman."

"Exactly," Lucia said. "Which is why the fact they want me back is a really big problem."

"Oh..." he seemed to make all the necessary connections very quickly, "Oh, fuck yeah it is." Tchadzwa dug his phone out of the pocket of his pants. His thumbs hovered over the device's keyboard. "Can I spread the word? Because, let me tell you, we were already ready to fight those fascists for you when most of us figured you were just someone on the wrong side of the so-called law, but, like, this.... This is a whole other level. We can not let them take you back. I've heard what they do."

Lucia actually felt something catch in her throat. She couldn't speak for the emotion that welled up. Strangers ready to fight for her, just because?

Luckily, Hawk spoke, "Yeah, I mean, if Del Toro says it's okay, tell everyone. We need the help."

"Oh, and with this news? You'll get it," Tchadzwa nodded, his eyes never leaving Lucia, his fingers still waiting to press the buttons. "I've got some Queer Communists that'd die for this woman and some Ace Anarchists who'd be right behind them."

I think I'm in love with this new guy, Oz signed to Jaabir.

I'm okay with three, Jaabir signed back with a smile.

Lucia had never officially come out before. It had behooved her not to, in fact, and so she'd never considered the possibility. Keeping her secret had kept her safe from the bounty hunters who were looking for the wrong sort of person. But, really, that was the only true hesitation. The only place left in the Solar System that was in any way hostile toward trans folks was Mars and the Earth Nations Peacekeeping Force. Sure, there were tiny colonies in the furthest outposts that had regressive politics, weird little religious culty outposts, but she and Hawk had avoided those places on principle. Honestly, most sane people did, as well.

The only real thing she stood to lose was her anonymity. But, she'd had almost a decade to establish who Lucia Del Toro was without the shadow of her past getting in the way. If she came out, she'd be reattached to that history and all its ugliness, but hadn't she been thinking it was time to face up to it all?

Atonement started with admission of guilt.

If she was going to do this, she would have to own up to all of it.

Taking a deep breath, she nodded. "Yes. Tell them. Tell everyone. My parents were part of The Program, and so I was taken from my home at nine years old and was told I was so many things that I never was, not the least of which, was that I was a man." With a little shiver—part fear, but more an overwhelming relief, she continued, "If the Force takes me back they will 'deprogram' me. They don't believe that I'm a woman. They'll break me until I fit their mold again. The last time I was deprogrammed by them, de-glitched, I believed their lies. I thought I was weak so I hit hardest. I was afraid of this very thing—that they would know the truth and they would destroy me for it. I've decided," she said, turning to look at Hawk now, "That it's time for me to come clean."

Returning her gaze to Tchadzwa, she continued, "Let the world know that I was once known as The Scourge of New Shanghai. I have in my possession body cam footage from that day. I have no idea what it will reveal about me, but I'll give it to you, right now, sight unseen. No matter how horrible, the world needs to see it, finally. And, I'll stand for those crimes and injustice done by that person to the people of the Asteroid Liberation Front, whatever they may be, but what I'll not stand for is to be captured and tortured by the Earth Nations Peacekeeping Force for something that is not a crime—being a woman.".

It was only when Tchadzwa's device beeped did Lucia realize her little impromptu speech had been recorded. "Yeah," he said, "That's a wrap. Girl, you're about to be Grella famous."

"Also," Jaabir said, with a warm smile, "With that speech? I'd join your army."

Speech? It'd hardly been a speech, but it had felt good to say. She reached a hand for Tchadzwa's device. "Let me give you what I have."

"Yeah, of course," he said, handing it over. "You've really never seen it? This footage?"

"I mean I must have, once, but... something's been wrong with my memory of that day."

"Yeah," Hawk confirmed. "Even when she first arrived at my place, she could tell me what happened except that it was bad and that she could never go back."

In a second, Lucia found all the .*NewShanghai* files and sent them along.

When she handed the device back over, she caught the end of what Oz was signing: *Fuck those fuckers. Are the ENForcers living in the twenty-first century? Don't they know by now that they can't deprogram the queer out of you?*

"Except they can," Lucia said. With shaking hands she signed along with her words, "Or, at least they can scare a person straight for a while." Her stomach tightened as a flash of memory jittered through her mind. Hugging herself tightly, she remembered training that was clearly a double-edged sword. "I've seen it. They made me watch. My whole creche was under suspicion. Simon and I were not enough of something, too much something else... so the whole bunch of us often got specialized instruction courses that involved observing deprogramming. Trust me, just watching it happen to someone else was enough to scare the lot of us pretty damn straight... even the ones that already were."

Lucia's onboard hardly had time to register the incoming before Hawk tackle hugged her. Arms squeezed tightly around her waist, and Hawk's trembling voice in her ear whispered, "Oh, baby. I never knew. Shh, shh, it's okay now."

It was the act of Hawk gently petting her hair that made Lucia realize she's started crying. She'd thought she'd been so steady, but the tears just tumbled out, unbidden.

Hawk's lips kissed her wet cheeks. "I promised you and I meant it. I won't let them take you."

"You are going to have to let me go if those tapes show that I'm a murderer."

"I know. But I don't believe they will. I never have."

Lucia let her arms fall heavily on Hawk's back. The weight of Hawk's body pressed up against hers grounded her. She was able to take a deep breath. Closing her eyes, Lucia spent several long moments just taking in one lung full of air at a time and feeling Hawk's heartbeat against her own thudding breast. Snippets of memories from all the times she was called to interrogate a subject surfaced.

There was one she'd never forget. The timing had made her suspicious that this was not just some routine need for an interrogator, a torturer. After all, The *Vengeance* had taken in no new prisoners, nor, had she thought, picked up any transfers. As the second in command of intelligence operations, she was never supposed to be surprised by any information, period, but intel on prisoners of note? Never. But, as soon as this order had come, Lucia had been certain it was an ambush of sorts, certainly, but for whom? Of course, she'd feared that she was the true target. Her commanders must have finally found something incriminating despite her painfully careful attempts to hide anything that would out her.

She'd gone down to the holds mentally steeled for the worst.

Even now, a decade later, she felt a wave of guilt over the relief she felt when the commander explained to her that they'd caught some other so-called deviant. She didn't even have to feign shock that the officer in question was well-liked by everyone, strong, unquestionably 'manly.' She could, after all, be looking at a reflection of herself, which, despite that initial flood of relief, she still suspected was part of the entire point of this exercise. After all, her commanding officer was not only the head of the interrogators, he was also the spymaster for the entire fleet. Hardly anything escaped his notice.

Honestly, the charges were ridiculous. One dalliance with another man was barely a prosecutable offense, at least in practice. Everyone Lucia knew occasionally fucked around in the ranks. It was always chalked up to 'I was drunk,' or 'you know how horny men are.' But, this guy had been caught offering to be fucked, which was of course the bigger crime. Gods forbid, you want to be the fucked rather than the fucker.

All of it had added up to a pretty obvious picture. Just as she had feared, this was a test for her. She had to be as brutal and merciless as possible in order to pass it. And, by all the gods in Hell, she had passed it with flying colors.

Fear was an evil, twisty thing. She hated what it had made her do—which had been nothing. She should have defended him, stood for him, stopped it. Even now, so many years since, the whole thing made her sick to her stomach. She wished she'd had more faith in herself back then. She should have looked her commander in the eye and laughed and refused to watch them torture some punk just to prove herself. She should have told him that if he wanted to know who she was, he should have the balls to ask her himself. But, instead, she was complicit in so much—perpetuating the cycle of abuse, reinforcing her own cowardice, all of the bullshit. She shook her head in regret.

The sound of a floorboard creaking brought Lucia back to herself. She glanced up to see Jaabir getting up to join Tchadzwa and Oz on the couch for a cuddle session of their own.

Meanwhile, Hawk led the two of them to the now-abandoned beanbag. Leading Lucia downward, Hawk adjusted herself in a way that allowed her to snuggle more comfortably in Lucia's arms. Hawk had long limbs as a Lunar, but was still small enough to fit easily under Lucia's arm. Spooning up against Lucia's side, Hawk wrapped a leg around Lucia's hips to half-sit, half-sprawl in Lucia's lap. The bean bag accommodated all of this surprising well. Lucia finally started to understand the appeal of this retro chair. The strange little pellets inside the chair's casing shifted and hissed.

Hawk pulled Lucia' face in closer to kiss away the dried tracks of tears.

Lucia needed a kiss, so she wrapped herself in Hawk for several long, luxuriating moments. But, then Lucia nudged Hawk away lightly. Not because she wanted to stop kissing, but more because they had a lot they needed to talk about, privately. They were still being hunted, potentially. Were they really safe here?

She cleared her throat to try to get the attention of the increasingly merged bundle of bodies on the couch. "Uh, is there a room that Hawk and I could, you know, adjourn to?"

Jaabir untangled himself with a regretful sigh and muttered, "Yeah, okay, let me show you."

It was an equally difficult struggle to get up out of the beanbag chair as it was to get in. Lucia ended up rolling off in one direction as Hawk went in the other. Jaabir shot them a dark look as he waited for them to join him at the entryway, clearly annoyed at any delay to rejoin people pile on the couch.

Unlike the cluttered cozy of the living room, the rest of the apartment was clean and bare. It seemed to have been designed when the whole Zen fad had taken over Titan and beyond, as there were lots of straight, clean lines. The spare bedroom bore out Lucia's theory as it came with faux-tatami floors, a linen closet with a rolled up futon inside, and very little else. One wall had a holographic projection of a Japanese garden in a gentle rain. Seeing Lucia's gaze lingering on the wall, Jaabir apologized, "The switch is broken, I'm afraid. I don't know how to turn it off."

It wasn't the picture that bothered her, per se, but a vague, lingering memory of rain. The sound conjured a corresponding sensory memory of scents: damp moss, ozone—or what did they call it? Petrichor.

Hawk seemed to see it for the first time and shook her head, "I'm going to have to get up and pee a lot. We didn't have rain on Luna."

No, Lucia thought, *but wherever I was born clearly did.*

"Let me show you where the toilet is, then," Jaabir said with a long-suffering sigh.

They left Lucia alone to set up the room. She stared at the rain for a few moments, thinking, as she often did about who she might have been if she had not been mistaken as a candidate for the ENForcers. She would have had so much more time as herself, she imagined, unless, of course, her parents were from one of those culty or restrictive colonies. Since there was no point in this kind of regretful thinking, Lucia shook herself from her reverie and pulled open the linen closet to begin laying things out. Jaabir seemed to be a traditionalist when it came to futons, so she first laid out a thin, fabric-covered mat on the floor. Next came the shikibuton, the futon mattress.

As she worked she continued to listen to the gentle drips of rain from the hologram. The Japan the image showed was painted to be fantastical. No one knew much about what Earth's landscape looked like since the Great Collapse that had led to the exodus into the stars. Hawk often speculated that the history everyone was fed was not the full story. How could it be? History wasn't even fully certain that every single person made it off the home planet? There were always stubborn holdouts in any disaster, and, surely, there were people too sick or too poor to make the flights.

The idea of people still living on Earth seemed like the kind of conspiracy theory that had people believing there were indigenous yeti hiding in the mountain range of Iapetus.

Hawk returned from the bathroom tour in time to help struggle on the fitted sheet, find the pillows, and lay out the comforter.

At least Jaabir finally looked impressed and said, "Right, I'll leave you to it."

"Have fun," Hawk snarked.

"You too!" he said from somewhere in the hallway as he hurried back to the living room.

Once everything was in place, Lucia immediately began stripping out of her uniform. Hawk would likely consider this a prelude to sex, which was fine, but Lucia first needed to see just how much damage she'd incurred.

Pants came off easily, thanks to the loss of some fat on her hips. Curves still existed, at least. The nanos considered excess fat material that could be converted, so one of the things she completely lost was the soft, round mound of her stomach. In its place was muscle definition, the outline of a washboard she intentionally never worked to achieve.

"Goddamn it," she muttered, shifting to struggle to remove her uniform jacket.

The jacket was almost impossible to wedge out of, given how much damage it had taken today and how stiff it had gotten in places. Since Oz reassured them that this apartment was shielded from ENForcer scanning tech, Lucia hazarded an uplink to the uniform to tell it to relax and stand down. The connection was a bit wonky, but the message got through. The bullet proofing began to soften.

Shouldering out of everything, she dumped every last bit of her clothing but her bra and panties to the floor unceremoniously.

Hawk, who was sitting cross legged on the futon, said, "Wow, the nanos really are back online, aren't they? Those bruises look days old, not hours."

Lucia expected commentary on how less feminine her body was so Hawk's comment made Lucia pause to glance at her shoulder. Sure enough, the bruise had progressed well past the fading yellow-brown stage. Her injuries had only sped up the losses. She touched her breasts reflexively, as though to make sure they were still there, still the size she remembered.

Hawk's eyes widened, noticing her reaction. "Oh shit, will the nanos eat away that stuff?" Then, answering her own question, she looked horrified on Lucia's behalf. "No, no, of course it can't do that. That's impossible. And thank Aristotle for that. If the ENForcers found a way to do that, I'd be livid. We paid my friend on Nyx twenty thousand to kill 'em all the first time."

And an extra fifty thousand to keep her mouth shut. But, Lucia didn't need to remind Hawk of that, since they'd argued all the way to Neptune about whether or not it had been enough.

"To be fair to her, I suspect the ones that came online had been hiding in my bone marrow. The injection probably had a whole new batch as well."

"Creepy." There was a beat, then: "Wait. What injection? You said something to Oz about this. I mean, I'm not great at reading signs but 'injection' looked pretty obvious."

Lucia let herself drop down onto the futon, cross-legged, facing Hawk. The rain sounds from the hologram were interrupted now and again by the sound of a bird call. Settling in, Lucia laid out her theory. "I don't know if the ENForcers were actually banking on a solar flare or if the reboot was actually just the nanos coming online at the same time by chance, but Oz tried to inject me with something—presumably the same thing Marcus had loaded in his strange bullets. My system and I both assumed they were trying to knock me unconscious or fill me with some other poison, but I now figure they were loaded with nanos."

"So you are getting an upgrade, just the wrong one."

Lucia let out a tired, jaded chuckle. "I mean, if it fixes my eye malfunctions, that would be great."

Hawk's hand touched lightly on Lucia's naked thigh. "It must feel so violating, to know that the ENForcers literally have claws in you, changing things."

Lucia considered that, but shook her head. "So far the only things I've lost can be replaced. Fat is easy to put back on—or will be, once we turn these new nanos off."

"What about your voice?"

"The nanos might be able to change the programming of my tone modulation." Lucia covered Hawk's hand with her own. "Do you know what an old cop said to me today? He told me that I needed to remember that some women have penises."

"What?" Hawk's laugh was incredulous. "He told *you* that?"

"Yeah, and you know what? He was right to scold me. I needed to be reminded that the body doesn't make the woman. The woman makes the woman. Even if the nanos do their worst, they can't change who I am. Nothing can."

Hawk's face, which had been crumpled by concern, relaxed into a smile. "Hot damn. Who could've predicted a cop could have anything useful to say, much less something so profound?"

Lucia nodded, but her eyes kept drifting down to her own breasts, the mounds of which were held tight to her body with a sports bra. "Even so, we should probably have sex," Lucia said plainly, pulling her sports bra over her head. "I don't know what my body is going to be like—"

Interrupting with an irritated snort, Hawk said, "I am not having goodbye sex with your boobs." Unconsciously, Hawk's eyes dipped to check between Lucia's legs. Then, noticing being noticed, she blushed, "I mean, I loved you before and I will love you no matter what, but... you don't think.... No, that could never happen."

Hawk was right. It should be impossible for a human to regrow body parts. With everything that had happened in the last several hours, Lucia had nearly forgotten their original job—to find the missing eye—until Hawk had brought it up a few minutes ago. Back at the truck stop, she and Hawk had struggled to figure out what about an artificial eye, even if it were somehow sentient, would be worth stealing. What if the answer wasn't so much the eye itself, but something about the process of having built it or some element within its structure that made it valuable for some other purpose?

Like growing back limbs.

ENForcers would kill for that.

Lucia ran her fingers along her abs, thinking about that injection and what else it might have contained. Could she be some kind of guinea pig?

Misinterpreting Lucia's actions and continued silence, Hawk made a frustrated grunt and wigged out of her pao. Her clothes came off in one deft move. Balling up the one-piece, she tossed it into the opposite corner of the room. Where the wad of clothing hit the hologram of the rainy Zen garden, the program hiccuped. A burst of static rippled through the picture for a second. With that, Hawk was down to her undershirt and boxers.

182

"First," Hawk said. Going onto all fours, she crawled over to kiss Lucia on the nose. "We are going to fix this. And, second," she grabbed Lucia's hand where it hovered over her newly tightened stomach and gave it a desperate, loving squeeze, "I'm not in love with your damn body. You know that. Or you should."

CHAPTER 18

Independence "Hawk" Hawking

Del Toro's lips were soft and yielding.

Lucia's lips.

As Hawk teased Lucia's mouth open for a deeper kiss, she questioned the wisdom of applying Lunar rules to this particular woman. Holding on to Lucia's surname was a habit born out of respect. It was meant to give people room to be who they were and the freedom to change as they desired. This convention had been part of what had allowed Hawk to see Lucia clearly, immediately, despite certain barriers, but maybe... it no longer felt respectful. Maybe it was time to let go of everything she used to be.

Maybe it was time to fully embrace Lucia.

So, that's what Hawk did.

Afterward, they lay together sweaty, spent, and very, very satisfied.

Half-sprawled on top of Lucia's naked body, Hawk rolled off to nestle in the crook of Lucia's arm. Hawk's head rested against the soft swell of breasts. Feeling warm and relaxed, despite the tangle of sheets cast to one side.

Lucia sighed her own contentment. "I sure as fuck hope my dick never grows back. It might take longer to get into things with the current configuration, but damn I love multiple orgasms."

Hawk's fingers absently played with Lucia's dark curls. "It never mattered to me, either way. With or without, I still love the woman you are."

She cupped Lucia's face and gently turned her so that they looked each other in the eye. This close, with their noses almost touching, the color of Lucia's mismatched brown was more obvious. Except it wasn't. The difference was normally stark, the injured eye being so much darker than Lucia's light, amber-tinted tawny irises.

If it wasn't for the still-obvious bubbled out metallic bits, Hawk almost couldn't tell them apart.

Hawk sat up. Leaning on her elbow, Hawk peered intently at the ruined eye. The metallic 'shiner' remained the same, but the color of the eye itself had shifted. Half of it was now lighter, as if the stroma's cells were regenerating to their original color.

Something, both Lucia and Hawk had *just* been reminding themselves, should be impossible.

Lucia pulled back a little at all of this, tugging at her hair to cover the scar. "Uh, hello? Everything okay? Did my face explode or something? You're looking at me like I've grown a second head."

Something which was suddenly plausible! If her eye was regenerating, why not another head?

"Your eye," Hawk said by way of explanation. She gently lifted Lucia's hair to take another look. "An eye that should not be doing this. Cells don't have this ability. Human cells don't. Not at our age, anyway, right?" Hawk asked, mostly to convince herself. Her thoughts were an unformed jumble. She knew some animals could perform this miracle. When she was a kid on Lunar, there was a biologist in a different cohort who had an aquarium full of axolotl. The weird, but strangely cute little animals had been brought to Luna centuries earlier to study gravitational effects on their ability to regrow their limbs. Those were simple creatures though, not as complex as humans. Human complexity was supposedly part of the stumbling block to reproducing the effect in humans.

Hadn't one of Jonathan's exes or spouses needed to replace both eyes? Hawk also saw Jonathan's name as a co-author on a paper on stem cells. Stem cells always came up in conversations about regeneration and other pie in the sky cures. "Hey, what the hell is dedifferentiation?"

Del Toro blinked a little at Hawk's sudden topical shift. Her eyes automatically glanced to the left, flared a bit of light like she always did when uplinking to the net. But the light died quickly this time, "Not only does Oz have us jammed, I can't risk checking. Why?"

"It was something I came across when I was researching Jonathan's career back at the casino. I know about axolotl, but are there other Earth animals that can regrow limbs?"

"Whole body parts? Maybe?" Del Toro made an awkward, lying down shrug. "There was a lizard that could drop its tail as some kind of self defense. The Academy instructors loved to talk about that because it was a metaphor for sacrificing part of a battalion, since soldiers were considered easily replaceable. There are hydras, too, I think, but I couldn't tell you if such animals actually existed. I wasn't great at Earth animal biology in the Academy. There was just... so much, you know?"

Hawk nodded. How did anyone live on that chaotic planet? Apparently there were over 350,000 described species of beetles alone. Humanity had taken several of them with them into space, but not nearly so many. That planet must just have been crawling with insects. Bless Darwin for the inhospitality of space.

"What's going through your head right now, Hawk? Why do I feel like a specimen under a microscope? Which is, by the way, not the greatest sensation right after sex. Is something wrong with my eye? Or my face?"

"I love your face." Hawk smiled reassuringly. Lucia's question brought Hawk back on track. "Your eye is fine, probably better than fine. It seems to be returning to its original color." Chagrined for assuming Lucia wasn't already on top of the situation, Hawk added, "All this worrying about your penis growing back—I'm betting you weren't just being irrational, you're thinking the same thing I am right now, aren't you? Something about Galilei's research is the real gold mine, the real target of the theft—maybe even his murder. Something is about human regeneration."

Leaving Lucia's warmth, Hawk sat all the way up. She dug through the pile of abandoned clothes until she unearthed her device—or rather, Tchadzwa's burner. Had she taken notes before she was interrupted at the casino? Hawk had a vague memory of copying over some dreadfully boring paper.

Apparently Oz's shield was specifically configured to hide an ENForcer because Hawk had no problem reconnecting to her own storage cloud. "Yes, regeneration! Here it is," Hawk said, pointing to the device, even though she hadn't yet called up the precise paper. She dug through it until she found the section she'd been thinking of. "There was some Latin in here, probably a scientific name for an animal. Yeah, here it is. Do you know what a—" Hawk made several attempts to parse the Latin properly, but her dyslexia had her stumbling too much. She highlighted the word. Then, turning the screen to Lucia, she thrust it at her, "—this is?"

Lucia pushed herself up into a seated position in order to take the screen handed to her. She squinted at it for a long time, but then handed it back with a shake of her head. "I'm not great at Latin. I'm not sure it matters what exactly this thing is, anyway. If Jonathan was studying regeneration and had any kind of breakthrough about growing back limbs, then I think we know exactly what was in that shattering bullet Marcus shot at me and who stole the eye in the first place."

All the puzzle pieces scattered onto the tabletop of Hawk's mind. "Shattering bullet? Are you saying you think whoever stole the eye already isolated the science behind human regeneration and that you're—" the only word that came to Hawk was, "—infected? Intentionally? By the ENForcers?"

Lucia nodded solemnly. Reaching for the discarded comforter, she covered her naked body. Where she leaned against the holographic image, a halo of static surrounded her. "This is what I've been thinking. Maybe they're trying to reclaim all of me. Maybe the ENForcers want a man back."

"Well, they never had one," Hawk snarled.

"Maybe they're hoping to make one, then."

"Well, that's bullshit." Hawk let out a long, horrified breath and joined Lucia in slumping against the wall. There was a slight hiss from the holographic projection before the sound of gentle rain continued. "So, we were set up. This was a set-up all along."

"Maybe." Lucia tugged at the curls over her eye. Around a deep yawn, she added, "But, why would they kill Jonathan? It doesn't make sense that the Force would want the scientist who figured out regeneration dead."

Hawk wasn't sure about that, especially if they intended to steal his work... or, if the bulk of the brains behind the research didn't actually come from Galilei to begin with. Had the ex-wife flipped and joined the ENForcers?

"Also," Del Toro continued, still clearly spinning through everything, "How does that make any of this artificial intelligence?"

"I don't know," Hawk agreed. "I mean, I haven't looked at the code. It's possible that as part of the regeneration of others, it can change its own code. Doesn't seem as wilful as the spirit of the definition requires, though does it?"

"No, not at all."

The post-sex adrenaline was wearing off fast. Hawk didn't feel like she could think straight anymore. She let out a yawn of her own. "I can't cope with this. I'm too exhausted. You must be beyond wiped out. Do you think it's safe to sleep here?"

"Probably not," Lucia said, sliding down the wall until her head was on a pillow and her body was completely covered by the comforter. "But, the only way I'm going to be able to stay awake any longer is if I give myself a stim. Do you want me to? I could keep a watch."

Hawk shook her head. Lucia had been injured. They both needed sleep, but if anyone should be in their best fighting form, it was Lucia. Joining Lucia under the covers, Hawk put a hand on Lucia to stop her from getting up. "No. I'll do it. You need your sleep."

"Mmm, 'k," was all Lucia managed before drifting off.

Hawk wanted to sleep too, but despite what she'd said to Lucia, her brain continued to churn. Were the ENForcers really that evil? Would they take Lucia's body back by force?

It seemed far too likely for Hawk's comfort.

She gently stroked Lucia's soft curls and prayed to Gregor Mendel that they were both wrong.

Hawk stayed awake listening to the creaks and pops of a terrestrial abode settling. So different from the silence of space. The only noises on the *Peapod* during the sleep cycle was the hum of the generator that kept the lights on, as it were. Engines never roared unless the ship course-corrected. Here, vehicle engines growled constantly as they sped by outside the thin walls. Everything smelled wrong, each breath brought the scent of someone else's laundry detergent, soaps, and perfumes.

Lucia wrestled with a nightmare, her body spasming slightly. Hawk put a hand on Lucia's shoulder, a weight to ground her. That seemed to calm her in the moment. Ever since they first started sleeping together, Lucia would occasionally bark out some nonsensical orders, request back-up or report taking heavy fire.

For all that Lucia had full-on post-traumatic hallucinations, Hawk never feared her lashing out in her sleep. She'd never asked Lucia for confirmation, but Hawk often imagined that the ENForcers had actual training or hardwired instructions on how to control themselves at night. After all, given the sheer amount of bloodshed the Force was responsible for, Lucia could hardly be the only one dealing with echoes of it. All those soldiers bunking shoulder to shoulder must make it worth the extra training or whatever to make sure none of them woke up pre-bruised before the next nightmare-inducing fight.

Fucking Freud, the ENForcers had a lot to answer for.

Hawk had learned that belaying orders or telling Lucia to stand down with a reminder that she wasn't an ENForcer anymore worked during one of these night time episodes. Although Hawk had to be careful, if she said counter-manding instead of belaying or jail instead of brig, Lucia would wake up fully in order to explain the correct term used by her former branch of ENForcers, who were something aquatic sounding, mariners? Marines?

In many ways, those ridiculous arguments were worse than the night-mares. It bothered Hawk because Lucia's continued insistence on proper terms revealed how much she still cared, how much 'getting the terms right' still mattered to her. Hawk understood that you might never fully be able to take the ENForcer out of the woman, as it were, but it would be nice to eventually loosen up over whether your non-military lover said cockpit instead of bridge.

A tremor shook through Lucia again and she whispered something nearly inaudible. Though Hawk couldn't make out any of the words, Lucia's tone sent a chill up Hawk's own spine. It wasn't Del Toro's normal commands, but a des-perate, broken plea, "Please. You have to trust me. I'm on your side."

What was this? This was a new dream. Normally, Lucia would be shouting about how civilians needed to stay back or she'd have to open fire. The New Shanghai dream, Hawk always figured. She never let it go on long enough to know how it ended. This one sounded different. It was something new.

She tried something. To Lucia's half-conscious dreaming state, she asked, "How can we be so sure? You're an ENForcer."

Lucia thrashed a bit and said, "See. My weapon is on the ground. I surren-der."

Wait. "*You* surrender?"

"Yes! I surrender!" Her own shout seemed to wake Lucia up. She blinked and shook her head. "Oh goddamn it, the dream again. Did I shoot him this time?"

"No," Hawk whispered in the dark a weird feeling in the pit of her stomach like a hopeful sort of certainty. "You didn't."

"Mmmm, ugh. Sorry," Lucia said, her voice already drifty, falling back to sleep.

A cool blast of air came up through a nearby vent. In the hologram the rain was interrupted by the hoot of an owl. Hawk shivered slightly. The dream had never been like this before. She knew Del Toro usually dreamed about killing someone who'd surrendered. Some *man's* voice haunted her.

What if... what if had actually been her own? What would that mean about the Scourge? No one knew the truth because so few people who'd wit-nessed that moment lived to tell of it. Lucia had always assumed—everyone assumed—that was because she'd killed them when they were trying to surren-der. But, that really didn't jive with the rest of the story that Lucia had told, did it? Why would she kill civilians to escape when the whole plan had been to get the most people out alive?

But how could she have gotten it *so* wrong?

Hawk sat with that thought for a long time without any answers.

A gentle, playful nibble woke Hawk. Lucia's breath tickled her ear, making her shiver and giggle. "If we're in an ENForcer jail right now, I have to say I'm surprised, but I approve."

Lucia moved on to kissing Hawk's neck, and so her chuckle came out as a warm huff against skin. "I mean, we would be the only women."

"You so sure?"

Lucia pulled back far enough to give Hawk a thoughtful look. "I mean, statistically, there are probably others."

"Like Simon?"

She nodded. "Like Simon. Though, the last time we talked about gender, he was still very into his penis."

"Doesn't mean he's not a woman."

Lucia let out an exasperated breath, hot against Hawk's shoulder. "Why do people keep feeling the need to remind me of this stuff lately?"

Hawk shrugged. "You're lucky, I guess?"

"Ha," she grumbled, going back to dusting soft kisses along Hawk's shoulder and arm. "But, if you want me to continue, you're gonna have to stop talking for at least fifteen minutes."

"Impossible," Hawk said without missing a beat.

Lucia shot Hawk a wicked smile. "Let's see if I can at least make you incoherent."

"I mean—is that's basically already—and I wanted to ask..." but their lips met for a long and leisurely kiss. After that, Lucia made good on her threat. For the next thirty minutes, the most intelligent thing Hawk said was, "Mmmrrrfff."

♀

CHAPTER 19

Lucia Del Toro

Afterwards, Hawk's eyes lingered on Lucia in a way that finally made her ask, "Is it already obvious?"

"What?" Hawk blinked. "Oh, the changes? Not really, no. I was thinking about you in a whole different context."

Lucia frowned, concerned. Hesitantly, she prompted: "Okay."

It didn't help matters that Hawk's eyes kept sliding away. "I don't know how to ask you this."

It was about everything she'd confessed to last night, Lucia was sure of it. "How about just spitting it out?"

"That's not going to work," Hawk insisted, though it didn't seem to stop her from barreling onward. "The problem is that I don't even know how to frame this question. Last night, your nightmares were different. You surrendered."

"What do you mean?" Lucia pulled the sheet closer. "I gave up?"

"I mean, maybe? I don't know how your dreams work. It's just that I started to feel like maybe…" she stopped herself, her eyes glistening with hope.

"Maybe I didn't do it," Lucia filled in, sadly. She shook her head. "Don't kid yourself, Hawk. I was an ENForcer. And that's not how memories work. If I've forgotten something it's not because it was better, it's because it was worse."

Hawk's gaze came back briefly, then she pulled herself away. "I need to sort my head out. I'll be in the shower."

Lucia just nodded. There wasn't much to say to that, anyway.

D espite everything else, sleep had done wonders for Lucia. She felt stronger than she had in years, more clear-headed, and nearly pain-free, despite yesterday's freefall onto plascrete. If only she could tell the nanos to stop here.

Thankfully, her onboard had been quiet for the past several hours. Stealth mode and Oz's jamming shield seemed to be working, at least in terms of not actively trying to connect her to the ENForcer mothership. She still worried that she might be passively giving away her location or otherwise bleeding telemetry but there wasn't much she could do about that.

She still had trouble believing this whole operation—the 'chance meeting' at the truckstop to Jonathan's murder—was all for her. How was she worth this much manpower, this much effort? It didn't seem right.

Sure, it made a splashy bit of news for the feeds, even better that the ENForcers now had the ability, like twisted gods, to remake Lucia into their own image, but they'd also taken a lot of risks. A battlecruiser on the wrong side of the line was going to make waves of its own. Those were not the kinds of headlines that the ENForcers could afford.

Speaking of headlines, Lucia would have to remember to ask Hawk what people were saying about the *Conqueror*. Someone must be reporting on its presence by now. Did the Force have a press release that explained why they had a presence on Ganymede?

Continuing to strip the futon of their sweaty sheets, Lucia tossed the cottons to one corner. Her intent was to gather them up afterward and to put them into whatever laundry facility Jaabir had on this ship, er, in his house.

It was hard to remember that she was planetside. It'd been a long time since she and Hawk had stayed more than a few days here or there. Honestly, the last time had probably been on Nyx, when Lucia had needed several weeks to recover from the last of the major biohacks and reconstruction surgeries. It had been such a different mindset being in a part of the Solar System that not only accepted trans folks but cherished them. So much care had been given to her when changes were discussed, it was all oriented towards returning the body to its natural feminine state, to what felt good and right to Lucia—with a full understanding that each person's experience was unique. Some trans people everything, some wanted very little, some wanted none at all. Lucia's biggest handicap had been how much the ENForcers had already changed her to be an almost immutable cog in a machine.

A favorite idiom, that one. Everything the ENForcers messaged to their troops was belittling—a constant reminder that you weren't unique. Perhaps that was closer to what was going on. It was possible that the Force didn't even fully consider the ramifications of suddenly appearing in the Jovian System to arrest a person they considered one of their own, a rogue soldier. They had a tendency to believe they had a right to be anywhere they chose. The entire outfit was filled with typical 'ask forgiveness later' meatheads.

She paused in the middle of rolling up the futon.

That last thought hit on something else that bothered Lucia for some time. This whole convoluted mess of subterfuge and twisty plans; these were not the moves of an army known for barely rising above blunt force-trauma as a strategic battleplan.

Sure, the Force had a spymaster and his interrogators. That office was far more interested in rooting out traitors to masculinity within the ranks, or, at most, planning careful, sly assassinations of foreign heads of state. When they worked outside of Martian-controlled space, however, interrogators went in alone and would never in a thousand years bring something as unsubtle as a battlecruiser in tow.

So whose idea was all of this?

Somewhere from inside the house came the sound of laughter. The smell of sauteing onions drifted shortly after. Shoving the folded up futon into the closet they'd retrieved it from, Lucia got up to find a person who might just know something about all of this: Oz.

In the kitchen, Tchadwza and Jaabir leaned, shoulder to shoulder over something sizzling on the stove. Oz was sprawled in a nearby chair smirking fondly, if a bit possessively, at the two of them, Occasionally, Oz lifted a foot to caress a thigh teasingly.

"There she is," Tchadzwa said. "The Savior of New Shanghai."

"Don't be an ass," Lucia snapped. After what she and Hawk had talked about, Lucia was not in the mood for this kind of bullshit right now.

Pulling up a chair, Lucia sat in front of Oz, between them and their lovers. "Hey," Lucia signed as she talked, "I need to ask you some questions about the ENForcers."

Slowly, deliberately, Oz pulled themselves up straighter. They covered a yawn, and then signed, *I would have thought you were the expert.*

Jaabir's kitchen was cozy. The artificial light of the dome over Edfu Facula streamed in through the needles of a tall Himalayan cedar that grew in the backyard. The cluttercore style of the living room had been abandoned in favor of utility. A stainless steel rack over the double sinks held pots and pans. Cabinets lined all of the walls that weren't windows. Teacups and mugs hung in orderly, tidy rows on hooks above gleaming countertops. Whatever Jaabir and Tchadzwa were cooking, it smelled pleasantly of fresh green peppers and onions.

Tchadzwa glanced over his shoulder at Lucia's arrival and said, "I wasn't being an ass. You're the new Grella star! You should see your numbers. Everyone's talking about you."

"And probably triangulating our location," Lucia said without looking back at him. Focused on Oz, she continued to sign and speak. "Which is why it's imperative that we get to the bottom of this quickly. How did the ENForcers approach you? How did you connect up with my former crechemate, Lieutenant Marcus Ali to begin with?"

"This sounds like an interrogation," Jaabir said. Lucia could feel him coming up to stand beside her. "Oz, you okay with this?"

Oz didn't seem to have seen Jaabir speak. Their eyes stayed focused on Lucia. *Yeah, okay, I've been wondering when you'd get around to asking.* They crossed their legs and leaned back into the chair. Their hands moved expressively as they spoke. It was strange, but Lucia could sense the gossipy tone of Oz's sign. *So, I don't know how closely you follow your own bounty, but recently there's been new activity on it.*

"How recent?" It always felt overly self-important to check in on the status of her own reward, so Lucia didn't do it as often as she probably should. Still, she tried to make it a habit whenever she entered a new system. Except this time. This time she'd been so distracted by, of all ironic things, *Conqueror*'s presence.

Of course it skyrocketed after that film hit the feeds, but I meant about a month ago, the ENForcers upped their ante. I initially thought they were just trying to keep you at the top of the list.

"What knocked me out of the number one spot?"

Three guesses and the first two don't count.

It had to be Jonathan's bounty for his missing property. "The AI eye."

Got it in one! I really do need to check my biases about how stupid ENForcers are. You keep surprising me.

"Trust me, I'm an outlier. In more ways than one."

Oz smiled at that and gave Lucia an appreciative nod. *Oh, I know. In fact, the whole Solar System knows exactly how much of an outlier you are right now.*

"Great." Lucia glanced at the rest of the people in the kitchen. She expected recrimination, but, instead, there seemed to be an air of grim anticipation? No, honestly, she couldn't read this vibe. "What?"

"You really don't remember?" Tchadzwa asked.

"I mean, it's spotty. I have strong memories up until... " She hesitated, but they'd seen it now. She might as well just say it, "Until I shoot my way out. I guess something broke in me. My brain can't handle what I did, I guess. I just see the aftermath, the slaughter."

"Oh, we saw it, too," Jaabir said.

Lucia's shoulders slumped. Too devastated to meet their eyes, she hung her head. "How bad was it?"

"Awful," Tchadzwa said. "But you didn't do it, Lucia. It clearly wasn't you. You were watching it. Someone was picking off the refugees from the sky. Then they blew the dome."

Feeling a tap on her shoulder, she looked up. Oz signed, *Someone else was there. Someone flying your ship.*

"That's impossible." But as soon as she said so, she was hit by the question: how *had* she gotten off that colony? When had she gotten her ship back? She and her creche mates had been dropped down to that dome—when would she have gotten her ship back?

This would explain why she always felt the need to be reassured by the bosun's whistle, too.

But...

There were still so many unanswered questions. Lucia couldn't fully parse it all. She'd just gone over this with Hawk. "Why wouldn't I remember something that exonerates me? I just don't understand how this is possible."

"Trust me, no one does. There are whole cadres of pundits out there trying to make sense of it," Jaabir said. "Some people are claiming it's fake."

"And, of course, the ENForcers are right there, agreeing," Tchadwza added.

"They could be faked, they were downloaded when I got my upgrade." Lucia grasped to remember. Why was it all still so murky, so blank? If there was someone else there, someone she wrestled her ship back from, why couldn't she even picture a face in her mind? "Who was it, then?"

"Who killed everyone?" Jaabir asked, when Lucia nodded he said, "No one knows. You, uh, went off line. Dramatically."

"Ripped out your own throat," Tchadwza said, like he thought it was cool. "I mean, that's what people are saying."

Lucia confirmed, touching the scar. "That is how it's done."

You'd think they'd have a kill switch, Oz signed nonchalantly. *Something to blow your brains out the second you went AWOL.*

Lucia was about to point out that the investment was too great, that it cost too much to waste a fully-grown, fully-trained ENForcer like that, when Tchadwza said, "Well, maybe they did. Maybe Lucia can't remember because she got hit with gaslight.exe, you know? She can't remember what she did to escape, but she's filled with the sense that whatever it was is too horrible to ever show her face again."

Jaabir nodded along, considering. "Something like that keeps ex-soldiers from coming back, maybe drives a few to kill themselves. Problem solved for the ENForcers."

"Grim," Tchadwza muttered.

But not out of the realm of possibility. "That's pretty sophisticated memory programming," Lucia said, though she didn't sound very convinced, even to her own ears. "It seemed too complex."

Is it, though? Human memory is not great. Not really, Oz pointed out. *It's actually pretty simple to fool people, get them to not notice things that are right in front of their eyes or to get people to mass hallucinate something that never happened. There's even a term for it, "The Mandela Effect." But, they didn't have to pull anything off on a grand scale. They just had to make one soldier feel guilty and let their own self-recriminations fill in the blanks.*

Tchadzwa had missed Oz's part of the conversation because he'd been turned away, but once Jaabir filled him in, he nodded. "Yeah, soldiers have plenty to feel guilty about, I'd imagine."

Lucia had just said the same thing to Hawk a minute ago. All she could add at the moment was, "Fuck."

"You should eat something." Jaabir set a plate of some kind of fresh vegetable hash down beside Lucia's elbow. Tchadzwa delivered a plate to Oz.

"This looks amazing," Oz said out loud, and gestured for Tchadzwa to lean in for a kiss.

Looking away, Lucia ended up glancing up at Jaabir who gave her a little smile and said, "You can kiss me, too, if you want to."

"I'm good," Lucia said. "But, thank you very much for this. Was it expensive?" She gestured to all the clearly farm-grown vegetables, eggs, and tofu squares. "Do we owe you?"

Jaabir laughed. "You spacefarers crack me up. This stuff isn't that expensive moonside. We grow it, you know, in the ground."

"Ground," Lucia repeated as if it were a foreign word. "I think I've heard of that."

Her antics seemed to delight Jaabir. His smile became even warmer. "Not only smarter than the average ENForcer, and more heroic, but funnier too. There is no chance at all you're bisexual, is there?"

"Actually there's a hundred-percent chance that I am," Lucia noted. "But, alas, I'm monogamous."

"Yeah, plus I'm the jealous type," Hawk said from the doorway. Lucia looked up to see Hawk wrapped in nothing but a big pink fuzzy towel. Water dripped from the short hairs on her head. "I've been in the shower fantasizing about you coming in to surprise me for the last ten minutes. No joy. What's up, Del Toro. Do I not get round two?"

"Technically, that would be round three." After accepting a kiss on the head, Lucia smiled warmly. The tension she'd been holding released from her shoulders. Just having Hawk beside her made everything seem bearable. Patting a nearby empty chair, Lucia said, "Sit. There is apparently food grown in the ground on the menu." Lucia looked up at Jaabir who still stood beside her, "I mean, if there is enough? Otherwise she and I can share."

He laughed again like she was the silliest person he'd ever met. "We have plenty for everyone. Merciful Allah, space must suck."

"Yay! I'd love my own plate of ground-grown food!" Hawk said, as she adjusted the knot of her towel to make sure it was tight. Coming over to the table, she settled into the empty chair next to Lucia. When she peered hope-fully at the plate, Lucia offered her chopsticks so Hawk could taste the vegeta-bles. "Oh, nice. I haven't had fresh since we were on Io."

Hawk handed back the chopsticks, and Lucia took her own taste. There were crispy fried cubes of tofu, eggplant, green onions, and green peppers. Soy sauce and mirin had been added with bits of finely chopped garlic and ginger. An extra bit of heat had been added with some kind of chili pepper that Lucia couldn't place, but that the onboard identified as a combination of ground cayenne and jalapeno flakes. It also added a warning that, technically, capsaicin was considered a toxin. She shut off that notification. "This is delicious. Com-pliments to the chefs."

Tchadzwa and Jaabir nodded, each having brought their own plate to the table.

There was companionable silence for a while as everyone ate their fill. As she ate, Lucia chewed on the idea of some kind of gaslighting program. She couldn't remember if she'd heard of other AWOL or deserted ENForcers. For obvious reasons, if there were any, no one talked about them. Suicide was an issue, however. The brass was forever making them walk through holos about how loyalty would keep you from taking the so-called coward's way out. Was there something sinister there? A hidden message to reinforce the idea that if a soldier became disloyal, finding out they'd killed themselves wouldn't be a shock?

Lucia was tempted to let all of this and the good food distract her, but she hadn't yet gotten a definitive answer out of Oz about their connection to the mystery of Jonathan's death. Once she was sure she had Oz's attention, Lucia set her chopsticks down to ask, "So, tell me how you connected with my old creche mate and what that has to do with the recent upping of my bounty."

Oz gestured that their hands were full, so they couldn't answer.

Hmmm. More avoidance. Oz's charm made them slippery, hard to pin down. Her own plate empty and hunger sated, Lucia sat back and waited. Every second Oz continued to stall, the harder Lucia's gaze became.

"Jesus, if looks could kill," Tchadzwa said under his breath. With an elbow, he nudged Oz. "You know you look more guilty the longer you take to answer."

Around a mouth of food, Hawk said casually, "Probably, because they are."

Oz smiled at that and signed. *You get me, Hawk.*

Watching this interaction, Lucia took a different tack "I don't actually give a shit if you hoped to profit off my pain." Hearing how angry she sounded when she said that, Lucia stopped and restarted. "Well, okay, obviously, I give a *few* shits. However, that's not why I'm asking. I'm hoping for some details about how you made your deal with the ENForcers so that I can figure out if this is all interconnected. I'd like to survive this."

Hawk caught on immediately. Setting down her chopsticks, she said, "Yeah, Lucia and I were talking about limb regrowth last night and were wondering if Galilei's eye might actually have some tech embedded in its features that the ENForcers wanted in order to super-size their jackbooted oppression."

"You guys talk about oppression politics and limb regrowth as foreplay?" Jaabir asked.

"Don't you?" Lucia asked in mock seriousness, at the same time Hawk said, "You don't?"

Tchadzwa just chuckled to himself over his plate of veggies. "I might have picked the wrong couple. You all sound like my sort," he said with a nod at Hawk and Lucia.

"Nerds?" Jaabir asked, sounding a tiny bit haughty and insulted. "Political wonks?"

"Yeah," Tchadzwa said with a smile. At some point in the night, Tchadzwa had removed the dancing light apparatus from his dreadlocks and now had them tied in such a way that they fell over one shoulder. He seemed to also have borrowed one of Jaabir's tops, as the traditional tunic fit him a bit loosely in the shoulders and waist in a way that Lucia found quite attractive. Jaabir, meanwhile, was in Oz's t-shirt from last night. The shirt fit fine, as they were similarly sized, both being comfortably soft and curvy. Oz dressed only in Tchadzwa's open denim vest. At least, Lucia assumed it belonged to Tchadzwa, given all the various anarchist and political patches sewn onto it.

Oz watched this back and forth intently and seemed to have come to a decision. Pushing their plate aside, they laid their chopsticks down across the plate. *I'm pretty sure you're right about the connection,* Oz signed. *Your pal Marcus, told me that the plan was to capture the eye and you at the same time. They already have the eye.*

Hawk's head was tilted to the side, watching Oz sign. She mimicked the gesture for 'eye.' "Yeah, I think we know this already. They're saying that the ENForcers have the eye tech, right?"

Lucia nodded. To Oz, she continued, "We suspect ENForcers had the eye long before they went after me. In fact, we're pretty sure they infected me with something from it. Did Marcus tell you what was loaded in that syringe? You remember, that needle you broke against my neck."

Tchadzwa let out an unhappy hiss. Lucia heard him mutter, "Definitely slept with the wrong pair."

Oz glanced over at Hawk, then to their lovers, as if hoping for help. Their hands seemed to hesitate before starting up. *A sedative. I thought it was just a sedative. You know, to knock you out. I bent mine on purpose, remember?*

Lucia let out a grunt of mild disbelief. She didn't bother trying to express her sarcasm in sign. She just let her face tell the story. "Uh-huh."

"Seriously!" Oz said aloud for emphasis. Their eyes scanned Lucia's anxiously and they sat up more intentionally in the chair. *What are you saying? What was really in it?*

"I don't actually know for certain," Lucia admitted. "But something in it triggered a reconnection to *Boy.net.*"

You think it was more than nanos?

Hawk nodded, seemingly understanding 'nano' in sign. "Definitely those, but, I mean, if you were the ENForcers and you could force a body to revert to its original state, wouldn't you do it to make some kind of gross point?"

No, Oz signed sharply, definitively. *That would be actively stupid. A cyborg's original state is non-augmented. Useless. Why would you want the body to start rejecting all of its enhancements?*

A good point. Lucia crossed her arms in front of her breasts, thinking. If the regeneration ran simply on an autopilot, skin and bone would overwhelm biosteel and micro-wiring. To Hawk, Lucia speculated, "Galilei's genius must be in encoding the stem cells somehow, to make them recognize what to regrow and what to leave alone."

"Or maybe it's a combo," Tchadzwa offered. "A dose of encoded stem cell goo and preprogrammed nanos fit to your specs."

"So, like a tailored regrowth?" Hawk frowned. "You'd have to have some serious pre-planning for that to work. Is this ENForcers all the way down? You know, it bothered me from the start that Galilei knew we were bounty hunters. Was this eye ever really stolen? Or did the bad guys have it long before we even set foot in this system—before the bounty was even placed?"

It was starting to feel eerily plausible. Lucia shook her head. "But, then why kill him?"

Lucia felt a tap on her hand where she rested it on the table. When she glanced over, Oz signed, *Kill who?*

Spelling out the name, Lucia said, "Jonathan Galilei."

"The guy who invented the AI eye," Hawk explained. "The guy who offered the bounty."

Wait, Oz's hands were frantic. *The guy who offered the bounty on the eye is dead? Since when?*

Either Oz was a good actor, or they really didn't know. The onboard offered to check pupil dilation and heart rate, but Lucia opted out that those indicators were not that accurate at detecting lies, anyway. "Since yesterday evening."

Oz sat back, in shock.

"I think this calls for coffee," Jaabir announced. When he got up to start a pot brewing, the chair slid back with a scraping sound on the retro linoleum. The loudness made Lucia realize how quiet and intense their conversation had gotten.

"I'll clear the dishes," Tchadwza got up as well. "I have no idea of what's going on. Anyway, I was grooving on the talk about the Scourge. When do we get to go back to that?"

"Forget that for now." Jaabir gave him a little kiss as they crossed paths, "Probably best to have plausible deniability anyway."

The casual domesticity between the men made Lucia smile. In one way or another, Oz was in bed with the ENForcers, possibly Jaabir, too, but right now Lucia couldn't hate them. She didn't trust this to last, but for right now the kitchen was warm and cozy in the early morning light. The sounds of dishes being rinsed and stacked and the smell of coffee brewing reminded Lucia of a scene in a holo. It was the kind of fiction she always wanted to be a part of, but never had been. Something homey. Something safe.

Beside her, Hawk dug around in one ear, thoughtfully. By her expression, Lucia could tell that she was still sifting puzzle pieces, trying to make sense of the events that brought them here. Inspecting the tip of her blunt finger-nails, Hawk said to no one in particular, "I've probably been reading too many murder mysteries, but what do you think about this scenario? Galilei's wife has her accident and loses her sight," she lifted a finger then, as if counting off a series of events in chronological order. "In response to this, the two of them crack the regeneration code. They fight over patent rights and whether or not to give this tech to the highest bidders, the ENForcers." She was up two fingers and a thumb now. "They have some kind of acrimonious divorce. He develops the eye, using the regeneration code they figured out together. He doesn't want to credit her in any of the research. She gets pissed off and runs to the Force." She'd run out of fingers by this point and gave up counting. "The ex and the ENForcers start concocting this elaborate scheme, where the ENForcers get their woman and the ex gets them to take out her man."

"Like dead?" Tchadzwa hopped up onto the countertop to listen to Hawk's fictitious enumeration. "Kill her ex? That seems extreme."

"Maybe he retained some rights to her intellectual property in a prenup that can only be released if he's dead," Jaabir offered. "Seems weird, but could be plausible."

You two are regular detectives, Oz signed sarcastically. *I thought bounty hunters didn't do this kind of work.*

"We don't." Hawk's face soured. "Look, I told you I thought maybe I've been reading too much crazy stuff. What do I know?"

"It's as good a theory as any," Lucia said by way of consolation. "I'm con-fused why you think the wife would sell out to the ENForcers, but—" she shrugged.

"Oh, I never got around to telling you that either, did I?" Hawk explained, "The ex-wife, whose name I really should know, was part of the research team for Galilei's first big breakthrough, a radiation counter-agent. That was a prod-uct they immediately sold to the ENForcers. She's already got connections with them."

"You got all this at the casino?" Lucia asked, impressed.

Hawk nodded. Her eyes flitted to Oz for a second before she private mes-saged: *And Oz knows all this. They were piggybacking on my hack. Two seconds later security descended on me.*

The kidnapping.

Yep.

Lucia's warm fuzzy feelings evaporated.

CHAPTER 20

Independence "Hawk" Hawking

Why was it so hard to remember that Oz was in bed with the enemy? Was it because they were so damn cute?

Honestly, Hawk wouldn't put it past Oz to be fully aware of how their adorableness disarmed people and lulled them into a sense of security. And look at how well orchestrated this homely little scene was, right down to the smell of brewing coffee.

Still in nothing but a towel, Hawk faked a shiver. Leaning over to give Lucia a little peck on the nose, she let the movement almost drop her towel. Grabbed it before she exposed herself entirely to everyone at the kitchen table, she said, "Shit, I need to get dressed."

Via their private channel, Hawk added to Lucia, *Come with me.*

Lucia stood and offered Hawk a hand up. "I'll help you." *Are you thinking we're already compromised?*

Hawk nodded, then looked directly at Oz when she took Lucia's hand and replied, *I'd be disappointed if they aren't already monitoring everything we're sending each other.*

The nod of acknowledgement from Oz was almost imperceptible, but the twinkle in their eye was plain as day.

❦

Even if Oz was tracking their internal chatter, the privacy was nice and Hawk really did need to get dressed. They might be under attack again at any moment, and the last thing she wanted was to be hauled into the streets by ENForcers in nothing but a towel. Sniffing her undershirt, she pulled it over her head. Lucia, meanwhile, leaned against the holographic wall. Her constant passive electromagnetic energy must have affected the hologram, because it broke in waves around the edges of her body, making it seem as though the air shimmered...

Looking at that effect reminded Hawk of their biggest problem. "So," she said, searching her own memory. "Of course our best nano-buster is all the way out to Nyx, but I think I know a guy on Callisto who can at least put the nanos to sleep."

"Callisto," Lucia repeated thoughtfully. "That requires smuggling me off this moon and all the way over to another one. The Jadzero is still out there. We need to shut this signal all the way off before we take me back into space."

"Yeah," Hawk agreed, unhappily. Finding her trousers, she jammed her feet into them and pulled them up. She held up the pao considering it. Nah, it was too hot for this climate. Tossing it aside, she started rummaging through Jaabir's closets for a button-down to steal. "The thing is, I'm kind of worried about trying to sniff out any biohacks here. If this is really all some kind of ENForcer sting operation and they know exactly what kind of trouble you're in, they've got to have all those guys under surveillance, don't you figure?"

"Plus, I told the shurtas it was the first place I'd go." Lucia shoved her hands into the pockets of her jacket and frowned. "That leaves us considering trying to get me off moon. That's risky. Covering risk costs money. That's one thing we're extremely short on right now: cash."

"I do have a burner device now, so we can access what little we have," Hawk said, checking the pocket of the discarded pao to make sure it was still there. She took it out and really looked at the device. It was last year's model, but it was sleek and black and had a sticker of an angry black cat with an arched back on it. "I mean, if Tchadzwa lets me keep it."

"Sure, but what have we really got? A couple of thousand?"

Shoving the phone into a pocket of her trousers, Hawk sighed. That was why they'd agreed to Galilei's bounty to begin with. Hawk chewed her lip for a moment and then shrugged. "Not everyone needs money. We have other things to trade."

"Like?"

"Like The *Peapod*," Hawk pointed out as she hunted around the floor for her second gripper. "It's a military-grade fighter. I'd hate to lose it, but it's also hot property right now"

Lucia nodded slowly. "It's a good ship. It's worth a lot."

Aha! The super-gripper had found its way under an end table. Getting down on her knees, Hawk fished it out. It came along with a few dust bunnies. She sat down to brush off the boot with the sleeve of her new shirt, and said, "Yeah, and I've always worried the Force could track us through it, though, aren't you?"

Lucia gave a reluctant nod.

At that, Hawk continued. "So, we have a plan, yeah? We can deal with what we want to do about the ENForcers once your body is stabilized."

"It's a Plan A," Lucia agreed. "We need some contingency plans because the likelihood that we'll get off this rock is not actually all that great. Once we leave this jamming field, I'm at risk of broadcasting my location to the ENForcers. 'Silent Running' seems to still be operational at the moment, but we can't count on it lasting. We aren't going to have our usual luxury of hiding in plain sight by walking instead of running."

Well, that sucked. Hawk always preferred their chill method of fleeing.

Feeling a bit overwhelmed by it all, Hawk felt her normal optimism waning and she loosened her legs and let herself slowly fall backwards onto the floor. The boot was still in her hand, so she set it on her stomach.

Staring up at the pock-marked ceiling she let out a long breath. "How about we just stay here forever?"

Lucia lowered herself to the floor as well. A quick lift of the head, and Hawk could see that Lucia curled around her own knees, hugging her body closely. "It'd be nice," she said softly. "But that won't last either. Oz is rotten to the core."

"Can't argue with that," Hawk said glumly, letting her head fall back to the floor with a soft thump. Absently, Hawk let her hands play with the boot a little, lifting it up and letting it fall on her stomach. "But, what if we did?"

"Did what?"

"Trusted them a little? Like, what if we let Oz play some of this out? If they are working for the ENForcers—which, I mean, they clearly are—and the idea is to trap you when you go to a local biohack, why not go that far with them? You need a biohacker. So, let's use Oz like they'll use us to at least get you to what you need."

"And if it's all just a trap?"

"We go in ready for that."

Lucia lifted her chin and a slow smile lifted the edges of her lips. "Talk to me."

Hawk pulled herself upright. "I think Tchadzwa seriously likes us. I mean, clearly he boned someone else last night, and good for him, but, like, his politics align with ours. He knows people on this moon. In fact, the thing I like the most about him is that I'm pretty sure he knows the kinds of people who can homemake chemical bombs if he can't himself, if you know what I mean?"

Lucia nodded. "I do. He definitely seems the sort. Plus, there's that detective friend of yours. We now know the ENForcers don't really want to tangle too much with the local authorities or that showdown at the cupcake place would have been more of a bloodbath. Maybe we should get him involved, too."

Finally deciding to put on her boot, Hawk wiggled her toes into it. "When did the detective become my *friend*?"

Lucia waved off Hawk's petulant tone, "When we could use him for something."

"Oh, right. Fine. I'll call him and concoct some story as to why he needs to meet us at whatever biohack Oz suggests." Hawk pulled herself to her feet with a sense of determination. "Fuck it, maybe I could even try the truth. If we're right that all this stuff is interconnected, it could actually help him solve Galilei's murder."

Lucia nodded. She looked tired, which was no surprise. They'd slept some last night, but they were both running on fumes. Hawk was sure, too, that all this stuff about the Scourge resurfacing in her memory wasn't helping matters.

At least they'd eaten.

Hawk pulled her other gripper on and said, "You should shower. The shower felt amazing. It's actual water, not a dry shower."

The way Lucia's eyes lit up at the thought of water was quite cute. "Really?"

Hawk nodded. "Ganymede is a giant swirling ball of frozen water. I keep forgetting that water is apparently something they have more than enough of here. Plus, from the mineral smell, I'm thinking there's thermal activity nearby? Anyway, the water was plentiful and hot."

"Amazing," Lucia breathed.

"Yeah, go avail yourself. I'll go see if Oz knows..." Hawk put the air quotes around that last word with her fingers, "...a biohack."

Lucia nodded, grabbing the damp towel that Hawk had been wearing a minute ago. "I'll be extra suspicious if the bio hack is back in Zu Fosse. It seems clear to me that's where the ENForcers expected this showdown to take place."

"Noted," Hawk said, giving her a kiss as they parted ways.

After grabbing a cup of fresh-brewed coffee from the kitchen, Hawk found Oz and their newest toys lounging on the couch. Jaabir seemed to be trying to teach Tchadzwa a few words in sign. Oz had their body sprawled across both laps and was reading a printed of some kind. Bed had made their normally precisely coiffed hair into a tumbled mess.

Hawk perched on the coffee table. Reaching out, she tapped the paper. She kept at it until Oz got annoyed enough to glance around the printed sheet to glare at her. Hawk smiled brightly and asked, "What are you reading?"

"They print news here," Oz said, showing off the printed broadsheet.

"How quaint," Hawk teased. "How can it possibly be current?"

"These are thought pieces," Oz's hands automatically signed as they spoke out loud. "Political arguments. Eternal."

"Got it," Hawk said. When it looked like Oz was going to turn back to the paper, Hawk waved her hand again to keep their attention. "One more quick question. Do you know a good biohack? Del Toro is degrading fast, as you know, since you were kind of part of that whole plan. It'd go a long way for us to trust you if we could get a name or two of someone local who could help."

"Yes, of course." Oz tapped their chin with a finger a couple of times, almost in a parody of thinking, and then said, "I do know a guy, but he's back in Zu Fosse."

Just as predicted.

Since it was likely too late for Hawk to keep the surprise off her face, she just rolled with it. "What? Back the way we came? Really?"

"Bad luck," Oz nodded.

"So, will you take us to them?"

Folding up the paper, Oz set it aside. They signed something then that Hawk had no hope of fully understanding. She caught the nod, though. That much was obvious. When Oz started to get up, Hawk figured that she ought to go tell Lucia to finish up with that shower and get dressed. Her guess was that they'd be leaving imminently.

At the shower door, Hawk knocked. "Hey! We're headed out soon!"

When there was no reply, only the continued sound of running water, Hawk knocked again. After the third time, she gave up and announced she was coming in. The room was filled with steam and the sound of Lucia humming something to herself.

"Hello?" Lucia asked at the sound of the door.

"It's just me." Sitting on the toilet, Hawk said, "You'll never guess: Zu Fosse."

The water turned off. The frosted glass shower door slid open. Steam rolled out and her head peeked out a moment later. Damp curls framed her face. "I guess we know the score. No more of this," she tapped her temple to indicate the mental texting they usually did when they wanted a private word. "Unless it's an emergency."

Hawk let out a long, defeated breath. If she hadn't already seen evidence that their channel had been compromised, she'd be tempted to argue. Their private channel conversations were some of their best. It'd be a hard habit to break. "Speaking of breaking and breaking-in," which they hadn't been, but Hawk continued, "Do you want to take a second to contemplate how a hack like that is even possible, especially with you running silent or whatever?"

Grabbing a nearby towel from a hook, Lucia rubbed her hair dry. "No. It depresses me too much."

It bummed Hawk out, as well. If Oz had some kind of signal-thief programming running under the ENForcer's most sophisticated spy-blocking biotech, this Silent Running thing, then Oz was either the greatest hacker who ever lived, or, more likely, they lied. They knew exactly what was in that syringe because they'd added some tech of their own to it. Something extra riding on the nanos inside Lucia that remained unaffected by all the other jamming devices at play right now.

Or worse, Oz had slipped some kind of tracking device into Hawk's bloodstream while she was passed out on the ship. "You know, I should get myself debugged, too."

"Not a bad idea." The shower door fully opened, and Lucia stepped out. The nanos were working overtime to convert fat to muscle, which, despite what Lucia might think, was not at all a bad look. In fact, the tone and definition was kinda hot. If they weren't in a dire situation, Hawk would beg for that round three. Instead, she had to look at that beautiful body and imagine the ENForcers capturing it, destroying it. "I don't like this," she said. "What if we're not smart enough? What if they bring reinforcements? How are we going to get you out of this?"

Using the towel, Lucia methodically dried her body. She seemed to be cataloging its changes as she went. "I don't know," she said at last. "I don't really know. But, I can't run forever."

"And why not?" Hawk's gaze sought Lucia's and held it.

"Because," she paused. "Huh. That's odd, I really just felt like turning myself in just now, despite everything we've learned."

"Learned? What did we learn?"

"Oh," Lucia said. "Let me fill you in. Things at New Shanghai went differently than I've always thought. Or, at least there's taped evidence that strongly implies that they did. Sit down. This is a doozie."

Afterward, the first thing Hawk said was, "I told you. I told you you might have been the one to surrender after all."

Lucia seemed stunned at the idea but agreed with a nod, "I guess so."

"Okay, let's do this thing. I'll call that detective friend of mine." Pulling out Tchadzwa's phone and Sargsyan's business card, Hawk input the numbers. The connection dropped three times before Hawk remembered the jamming device. "Right. I've got to step outside if this is going to go through."

There was a sliding door just off the bathroom that led to an inner courtyard. It seemed to be a shared backyard of some kind. Whoever took care of the space did an excellent job.

Leaving Lucia to dress, Hawk headed out. She walked along a neatly swept stone pathway that curved under the big pine tree and opened into a little garden. Purple onion flowers mixed with late blooming irises. Something Hawk didn't recognize trailed up the wall and dripped lavender-colored flowers. In this enclosed green space, the scent of sulfur gave way to pine needles and rich, loamy earth smells.

When her device showed that it had a connection, Hawk tried again.

Sargsyan picked up immediately. His face appeared as a grainy holo projection. Without any hello or other pleasantries, he said, "Ah. Are you reporting another riot? That last one was a doozie."

"It sure was." Finding a stone bench, Hawk brushed off the bits of pine needles and other garden detritus before sitting down, "Any chance the ENForcers are dead or jailed?"

"Unfortunately, no." His face contorted with unsaid thoughts for several seconds before he added, "But, they might be busy doing some PR mop up, eh?"

Hawk snorted a little chuckle. "I bet. Anyway, Lucia and I have a working theory about how all this connects to the ENForcers. Wanna hear it?"

The image of his face went through a few contortions. Then, sounding surprised at himself, he said, "Actually? I think I do."

"Good. You might as well record this, if you aren't already, because it's complicated." Hawk laid everything out as fast as succinctly as possible. She even tossed in her pet theory about the ex-wife. As she spoke, she kept an eye out for activity from Jaabir's house.

When she finished, the holo of Sargsyan scratched his beard. "That's a helluva lot of wild, unsubstantiated conjecture. Also, your partner really is the Scourge of New Shanghai? My officers convinced me she was his sister."

Not knowing how else to respond to that, Hawk just shrugged. "Look, we could use a little help here. Can I count on you?"

"About that," he said. "I'll do my best, but Zu Fosse is out of my jurisdiction. More rioters would do you more good."

Except the guy with those connections was sleeping with Oz.

"Right," Hawk sighed. So much for having some kind of back-up. Well, they'd tried and, weirdly, she felt good having passed on their theories to Sargsyan. If they died or got captured, at least someone would still be on the case.

She was about to hang up when he added. "Be careful. Last night's riot and all this breaking news is a big embarrassment for them. Between the implications that their biggest villain might actually have been the target of a smear campaign and the underground footage of the damage you all were able to do, they're pissed... Earth Nations' Peacekeeping Force does not like video evidence that they can be overwhelmed and injured. They're probably in a very bad mood this morning."

Well, that was hardly a surprise. "Do what you can."

"I will."

The plan lasted as long as telling Tchadzwa about it.

"Girl, if you go out now you'll get mobbed," he said to Lucia. "Half the town has been watching your video this morning."

"Seriously?" asked Lucia.

"Well we can't stay here forever. The ENForcers will find us eventually," added Hawk, looking pointedly at Oz.

"What you need," said Tchadzwa with a sly smile, "is a disguise."

"Looks like you've all been stealing my clothes anyway," commented Jaabir. "I don't own anything that would fit Lucia, but my mother's wife is a tall lady and was far more devout, being part of a reformist sect. Anyway, I think I have an abaya and a hijab that she left behind last time she visited. Would that work?"

A strange sound that Lucia realized was a giggle came from Oz.. "Lucia as an elderly, devout Muslim woman? I love it."

Jaabir hunted in his closets, and the disguise was arranged. The final touch was a pair of big sunglasses to hide the scar around Lucia's eye. Even though Lucia felt ridiculous in this outfit, she decided that she could move well enough in case of a fight. She stowed her peacemaker in a leg holster.

"Sexy," Hawk noted.

Lucia grimaced. "Sure, but not actually very convenient. What are we going to do with my uniform jacket?"

Jaabir sighed and dug through his closets again, finally producing a gym that Lucia could sling over her shoulder.

Oz offered them weaponry as they headed out. From a backpack, they produced all manner of things, including a fully-charged version of the stun gun that Hawk had had to leave behind in their first tangle with Marcus on Oz's ship.

Picking it up and slipping it into its usual spot, Hawk gave Oz a long look. "The whole kidnapping thing was low. I probably shouldn't forgive you, especially since you probably dropped some kind of hack into my blood, too."

Oz laughed and gestured for everyone to head out the door.

Lucia shook her head mutely, like she was disappointed not to have considered the possibility that Hawk had also been compromised by Oz, as they stepped out into the humid, fart-smelling air of Edfu Facula. Still in a fuzzy bathrobe and holding a mug of tea, Jaabir waved them all goodbye from his front stoop. "I'll keep the home fires burning for my beloved revolutionaries," he said, giving Oz and Tchadzwa a kiss in turn. Pointing to his shirt on Hawk, he smiled, "I'm flattered. Does this mean I get the pao?"

"It might be a bit long on you."

"Still, it seems like a fair trade." With that, he waved them off.

The four of them walked down the street. The light of the dome ignited more fully in the east, mimicking sunrise. Remnants of last night's revelries, bright red flower petals, streamers, and discarded wax-paper cones that had held nuts and fruits. littered the cobblestone streets. Little gnats swarmed the food remains.

Luna had managed to mostly stay pest-free, despite being an early colony, but humans brought all manner of insects with them when they left Earth. Nearly every place there were humans you could find roaches, ants, gnats, flies, and fleas. Many colonies intentionally imported other bugs as well, so at the very least there would also be bees, butterflies, and other pollinators in the air, depending on the crops grown.

This place must also have bats, since there were banana trees lining the streets.

At the corner, Tchadzwa announced he'd be leaving them. He and Oz stopped to kiss in the middle of the street under a fading street lamp. Hawk looked away from them and found Del Toro smiling at her. They grasped hands briefly, just a little 'hey, I love you' finger touch.

"I need to go rally the troops," Tchadzwa said with a wan smile once he'd separated from Oz's embrace. "Oz says I'm your 'Man in the Chair,' whatever that means."

"Oh, huh, cool," Hawk said. The Man in the Chair was someone who coordinated for the hero. Hawk was wondering how to ask Tchadzwa if he'd help, but apparently Oz had already done that last night. "So, how do we stay in touch?"

Tchadzwa's smile was bright. "You have my burner device. I know the number."

Awkwardly, Hawk reached out a hand to shake. "Uh, okay, well, thank you—"

Tchadzwa took her hand but then pulled her close enough to kiss her on the cheek. His eyes gave her the 'can I?' and she nodded. She would have preferred a hug, but a kiss was a nice gesture, too, and seemed to be the mode of saying 'goodbye' today.

Feather-light, a kiss graced her face. "You're welcome. Up the revolution!"

"Up the revolution," Hawk said with slightly less conviction and more than a little embarrassment as she let go of his hand to wave goodbye.

They waved to Tchadzwa as he wandered off in the opposite direction.

As soon as it was just the three of them, Hawk felt exposed, in danger. The eeriness of the empty streets had Hawk giving in to the impulse to constantly check over her shoulder.

With only her face visible, and her curves hidden under the abaya, Hawk was getting a very different view of Lucia. Yet somehow it was even better. The artificial light of the dome had been made to mimic a nearer sun, like Earth's, and so it caressed Lucia's face in a golden embrace. She looked radiant. Literally.

After tapping Oz on the shoulder to get their attention, Lucia's hands moved stiffly as she spoke: "Are we planning walking all the way back to Mahit in Zu Fosse?"

"I don't want to get trapped on a bullet train, do you?" Then her hands took over.

"I really need to learn this language," Hawk muttered. By private channel, Hawk asked Lucia, *Translation, please?*

They said: You've got money, right? I know some people who can suit us up and get us crawlers.

"Open Lunar terrain?" Hawk gave Oz a long look. "Are you insane or setting us up for an ambush?"

When Lucia flashed Hawk an 'are we talking about this?' look, Hawk shrugged. It seemed more suspicious not to say something.

After watching the two of them with an amused expression, Oz's hands flashed, ending at a point at Lucia.

"Well, I don't disagree with Hawk," Lucia answered. "The whole thing is risky, but I do like the odds out in the open a bit better. There's at least a chance of evasion."

That seemed to settle things.

Hawk tried to remember what the surface of Ganymede looked like from the train and when they'd used the space elevator from the orbiting waystation/truck stop. There had been craters, like home, so certainly there were rim shadows to hide in, if nothing else. She smiled to herself. Despite the danger she was looking forward to this excursion. Hawk hadn't been untethered on a lunar surface since she was a teenager.

"Just how much is this going to cost us," Lucia asked cautiously.

Oz had been watching Hawk's face, so Lucia had to tap Oz's shoulder and ask again. Oz shrugged, "If you can't cover it, I got you."

That was the single most suspicious thing Oz said so far.

Oz must have seen something in Hawk's expression because they shrugged. "I feel guilty, okay? I got a load of cash from the ENForcers to set you up. I kinda feel like I owe you."

"Or it's a case of spending money to get money," Hawk pointed out. "You float us so you can get an even bigger bounty when they nab us."

Unconcerned with the accusation, Oz nodded. "I don't care if you believe me." Then they started signing. Lucia sent a text translation that appeared like subtitles: *Nonbinary is trans, too, remember. I have a personal stake in this fight. There's probably some enby ENForcer out there who is living a lie. If you won't let me do this for you, then I'm doing it for them.*

As the three approached the Western edge of the city, the neighborhood began to change. The upper-middle class brownstones gave away to more hastily built and rundown high rises. Long shadows fell across the sidewalk in dark stripes. The cedars and desert roses grew sparse. Despite the density of buildings, the street traffic was nearly non-existent. Only a few hurried bicycle couriers zipped along the wide, deserted roadway. The air was cooler here, but the moisture content seemed to rise. Wisps of fog hung on the edges of the horizon, making this section feel ghostly and abandoned.

Hawk tapped Oz's arm and asked, "Do people live here?"

"More than you'd think." Switching to sign again, she added: *This section was part of the earliest successful colony; it was home to the engineers and builders of the dome. Most of them moved into the sunlight zone later, but people hung on.* Oz pointed up to some electric lights visible in the upper stories of the tall skyscrapers. *There's a rumor that some of the penthouses were built to withstand a collapse. They have their own atmosphere and gravity supply. Preppers and paranoids moved in when the engineers moved out.*

"And artists," Lucia said, nodding at one of the spray painted murals defacing what seemed to be a former storefront window on the street level.

"Always artists," Oz laughed. "And poets."

The 'poetry' Oz indicated seemed to be a bad rhyme in Portuguese involving sex acts that had been spray painted along a concrete wall.

"And queers," Hawk said, contemplating the poetry as they moved deeper into the darkness. "I would bet, anyway. We tend to go where there is art and cheap rent... or no rent."

Oz nodded. "Speaking of, we're nearly to my friend."

CHAPTER 21

Lucia Del Toro

The creeping darkness had Lucia on edge. That, and the constant pings from error reports flooding her onboard. As parts of her old tech repaired themselves and came online, they would automatically attempt to upgrade their links to *Boy.net*. Silent Running blocked them, of course, but the backlog had been deemed large enough to constitute a malfunction of its own.

There had to be a way to turn all of this off.

Searching her new protocols, Lucia discovered the answer. The ENForcers knew that their new Silent Running option would be abused by soldiers. Who didn't want to blip off the official radar to cause a little mischief, after all? Or maybe even desert or go AWOL. To counter that, HQ required that the officer using stealth mode file mission parameters after twelve hours.

She'd spent some time in the shower composing a mission brief for herself. It was ridiculous, of course. Even at her rank, she couldn't give herself an order, not in the strictest sense, at any rate. However, she wondered if there was a way to weave some kind of logic bomb into the message. *Boy.net* operated neural net to neural net, but large chunks of what it did on the daily was automated. Maybe if she wrote something clever, she could jam up the machine. If only she could isolate the thing Tchadzwa called gaslight.exe. It would be fun to throw something like that back at them.

In the meantime, she had several lines composed already. She wanted to have it set to automatically release when Silent Running was finally breached. No doubt the ENForcers worked on that even now.

Lucia pinched the bridge of her nose, grateful that Oz and Hawk finished their sniping and settled into a glaring contest. All the noise in her head after years of relative silence took some getting used to, and the added back and forth translations were doing her head in. Lucia was feeling her age. How had she functioned like this for so many years?

Oz led them into the dark zone, the section around the rim of the city's protective dome that was in constant shadow from the tall walls that comprised much of the equipment needed to monitor and control the environment and gravity inside the bubble. Lucia was surprised to notice that people squatted in this section. For one, most cities tended to maintain strict patrols around the parts of the city that, if sabotaged, could collapse a dome or cause massive disruptions to life support. Secondly, it was clear that typical services, like plumbing, had been cut off once the engineers and builders who once occupied this area while the dome was being constructed had moved on. Did Zu Fosse have a problem with overpopulation?

Ganymede was hardly as old an established colony as Mars, but she supposed it might be reaching the age where there were more people than there was new development.

Apparently noticing the same cluster of tents and refuse, Hawk leaned in toward Lucia to ask the same question in a very Lunar fashion, "Is Zu Fosse run by Capitalists?"

For Hawk, who had grown up in a colony that valued science that aided the benefit of all, seeing people neglected could only be the sin of capitalism. Normally, Lucia would look up what type of government this particular city had, but, not wanting to alert the ENForcers of her presence any more than she already had, she just shrugged.

Oz must have been watching their conversation because they said, "It's interesting, actually; they have a demarchy. There's a random selection, a lottery, for a citizen government." Switching to sign that Lucia dutifully reported to Hawk, they added, *And lately it's been idiots. Bad for their economy and all sorts of things. Good for my business, though.*

"And what exactly is your business?" Lucia tried to make it a casual inquiry, but Oz turned away and pretended not to have seen the question.

Oz then waved them down a narrow passageway. It was not an alley, per se, since the corridor spanned barely enough feet for them to walk through single file. It was much more like a maintenance shaft. Lucia had to duck to avoid overhead pipes and shimmy sideways on occasion to squeeze between odd bits of machinery.

Old habits had Lucia taking up the rear position. She kept an eye over her shoulder. This would be the worst place for an ambush, given the lack of maneuverability and cover.

"I don't like this," Hawk agreed, as if she knew Lucia's thinking process—which, maybe, after all these years, she might.

Fortunately, Oz seemed aware of the potential danger and kept up a brisk pace. In no more than twenty seconds of this claustrophobic travel, they motioned for everyone to follow as they crawled under a bit of machinery

Looking up at Lucia before following Oz, Hawk said, "Fuck me. I like this even less."

"They're your ex," Lucia noted with a raised eyebrow. "Weren't you ever friends?"

"We were almost more like frenemies." Hawk dropped to her knees and followed Oz through the literal hole in the wall.

Lucia stood in the alley for a few extra seconds, checking each direction trying to sense danger without using her proximity alarm. She even looked up towards the sky, but there was nothing but machinery and darkness overhead. It was impossible to know if anyone watched them from above, or if there was even an above to watch from.

It was times like these when she missed the creche. Simon was always a good lookout. He would have stayed to make certain no one followed them—or die protecting the team from whoever might try.

God, Lucia hoped he was okay. She didn't want to think about the fact that if Oz had compromised her and Hawk's private com, the ENForcers might have done the same for her special frequency for Simon.

Finally turning away, she dropped to her knees and pushed her way under the machinery into the hole.

❦

Though barely wide enough for her shoulders and hips, Lucia squeezed her way along the crawlspace. At least the hands-and-knees part of the journey wasn't long. No more than a couple of meters, if that. Once through, everything opened up into a kind of perpetual night market.

Stalls lined a cavernous space. Music and bright neon and electric lights blasted everywhere. Despite the fresh, cool air pumping in, the predominant smell was frying food. A nearby stall advertised something called bolani, which appeared to be a deep-fat fried vegetable-stuffed flatbread. Beside a giant vat of cooking oil, an old woman whose gray frizzy hair was held back by multi-colored scarves cubed potatoes, chopped onions, and cilantro. Despite the breakfast they'd just eaten, Lucia's mouth watered with the heady scents of turmeric, chili pepper, and coriander.

The next booth they passed seemed to be hawking recycled or scavenged bits of electronics. The table they'd set up on had backlit squares that moved in some chaotic pattern, highlighting the wares. Next to that, several folding tables, set out in a kind of semi-circle, held plastic bins of all shapes and sizes with dials, switches, wiring, and even ancient looking motherboards and other circuitry. Trailing along the wall, cardboard boxes overflowed with other mechanical antiques—walkie talkies, short- and long-range radios, and god knew what all else. People stood and knelt around these, sifting through tins of nuts and bolts, or turning over antiques in their hands.

The other side of the broad corridor showcased more food: sizzling chicken kabobs on a grill, rice balls fried in oil, stuffed grape leaves, meat pies, and gyros. Buskers jockeyed for spots near popular food stalls, amateur rock and jazz music a joyous cacophony.

"What is this place?" Hawk asked.

Oz was a step ahead of them, so Lucia tapped their shoulder. She signed: *Where are we?*

The Eternal Twilight Market. There are several of them along the walls. They move around, but they always exist in these pocket spaces.

"It's amazing," Hawk sighed contentedly, her eyes lingering on the grilling kabobs. "I want to eat everything."

Oz laughed, "Plus there are services you can get here that you can't get anywhere else."

Looking around, Lucia started to see what Oz meant. In among the food, music, and art stalls, there were more and more of the electronic swap-meet type tables, a whole bank of holos advertising sex work, tattooists, ID forgers, and any number of underground services. Some even seemed to have booths, with big neon signs advertising ENForcer proximity alarm baffling armor.

She stopped to glance at the tech's viability. Lucia gave the vendor a little nod as she passed, but they might as well sell tinfoil hats for all the good it would really do.

Turning to walk backwards a few paces, trusting the crowd to part for them, Oz signed: *Our guy is in the back, near the far wall. We can get suits and scooters and, if we want, a guide.*

After Lucia translated, Hawk asked, "A guide? Is that strictly necessary?"

Lucia nodded, tapping her head. "I can't really guide us in the condition I'm in."

Hawk clasped Lucia's hand and gave it a squeeze. "Sorry. I don't think I realized how much we rely on all that tech of yours."

Lucia squeezed back and then let go. She realized she didn't remember life before cybernetic enhancements. Technically, ENForcers recruited parents, not children. People with the right genetic markers—those that wouldn't reject implants—were inducted into The Program. The Program was a lifelong guarantee of income and other benefits; the only caveat being that you might literally have to give up your firstborn. A surprising number of people on both sides of the Line signed up for it, including, presumably, Lucia's parents. The agreement of The Program meant that once the child met the requirements, the parents severed all connections. Lucia had a vague memory of her mother crying on the day she went away, but she had been young enough that all her previous memories of life with them were blurred snippets.

They pressed through crowds, the number of people growing the further inward they went. Behind booths, sellers called out to them as they passed, tempting them with fresh squeezed juices, antique paper books, bondage gear, soup, fancy hats, hand-tossed pottery, fried potato wedges, gears and gadgets, recreational drugs, donuts, and so much more. It was almost overwhelming.

Lucia kept checking behind them to see if they'd picked up a tail, but it was impossible to tell in this vibrant crowd.

When Oz finally stopped, they stood in front of an unusual and striking vendor. For one, unlike many of the other booths, this one had none of its own lights or signs to draw the eye. Even in the dimness of the interior, it was hardly necessary, as the haphazard tables were surrounded by automatons and robots. Not parts, but fully realized androids and 'bots.

Oz tapped the table in a specific staccato beat. Lucia tried to determine if it was Morse code or binary, but it was over before she could assess its nature. When Oz finished her percussive tune, one of the automatons' eyes lit up. Metallic, multi-jointed hands moved smoothly and a text holo screen appeared in front of its chest. *Ozmerelda Jackson, to what do we owe the pleasure?*

The three of us need passage and a guide for a little outdoors adventure to Zu Fosse, specifically to Mehit.

The robot, an otherwise clunky looking thing, with a bald, expressionless face, scratched its chin. The screen lit up again. *It'll cost you, but it can be done.*

Oz turned to Hawk. "How much you got?" She added in sign: *Time to put it on the table. I can spot you some, but it's time to make your offer.*

Lucia answered, "A ship. A very powerful and infamous ship—an ENForcer fighter unit."

The robot swiveled its head in Lucia's direction. It paused for a very long time. Despite not having a single expression to read, Lucia felt very judged under that unblinking stare. "Lucia Del Toro," the robot said in a mechanical voice. "You offer the *Vengeance*'s commander's personal war spacecraft, the *Retribution?*"

"Well, we call it the *Peapod*," Hawk muttered. "It's green now, too. Very pretty."

"I do," Lucia said.

It was unclear to Lucia if there was some sophisticated robot behind these questions or if someone operated the machine remotely, but the unblinking circles that stood in for eyes stared deep into her. She met the alien gaze as steadily as she could.

"I feel your offer is too high a price for what I offer. Can I give you something more for the price of *Retribution?*"

Lucia felt her eyebrows raising. An honorable robot was an odd thing to come across. "You might be especially suited to help me with something." The logic bomb was still unformed and, in truth, it was beyond her usual abilities. She didn't want to give away her ace in the hole, especially with Oz right there. She turned so that Oz's view of her mouth was completely obscured. "I need some help with a bit of math. Can I transmit a file?"

"If you are thinking to poison me with a virus, I can tell you right now that I am backed up on multiple servers."

"No," Lucia reassured the robot. Despite the fact that she was sure Oz couldn't hear her, she dropped her voice. "It's something I want to use on ENForcers. Against them."

"Interesting. You have a deal." A hand shot out. "It is customary among my people to shake on a deal this big. Will you accept my hand as I accept your offer?"

Shaking hands was common on Mars and also, supposedly in some small, but influential part of old Earth there was a thing called "a handshake deal." Lucia gripped the metal hand firmly. "You can't possibly be from Earth," she said, giving a strong pump. "Are you Martian?"

The robot unclasped Lucia's hand. Dipping its head briefly, the robot said, "If I were from Mars, I wouldn't have used your correct name, nor be so excited to take down a common enemy."

Was that true? Honestly, it seemed far more likely that whoever or whatever inhabited this robotic body was just one of the few decent people on Mars. Earth was dead. Everyone knew that. Even so, Lucia gave a brisk nod of understanding.

Oz watched the interaction, but frowned. "You know I can't hear whatever the shit you're saying, Rafe. And that clunky old shell you are wearing doesn't even move its mouth when it speaks. But I'm guessing the handshake means we have a deal?"

Our apologies, Rafe displayed. *Yes, we can proceed.*

W hen the robot that they were speaking to lost the light behind its eyes and a different robot sprang to life and gestured for them to come behind the booth, Lucia started to think that there must be a remote intelligence operating these automatons. Whether or not that intelligence was human, Lucia didn't know.

The new robot they followed was really more of an android. It was covered in synth skin, and, in accordance with Solar System law, that skin was an unnatural silvery blue. If Lucia had to guess, it was a former sex bot—what they called on the streets a Ken doll—since it was shaped like a very classically handsome, if vacuous young man. She had seen a few Kens on shore leave. Typically, they wore whatever was currently in fashion with a slightly more revealing twist. This one, however, had dressed himself like a grade school teacher. He wore khaki pants, a white button-up shirt with the sleeves rolled up, and, most curiously, a pair of thick-framed glasses. If it wasn't for the shiny blue skin, he'd look very plain and boring.

The Ken, whom Lucia presumed was still Rafe, led them behind the back flap of the booth's tent. The area was strewn with deactivated androids, several of which were piled on top of each other, in various states of dress and undress. Only a few of them were truly humanoid. Instead, most of them seemed to be older, unpopular models—or even half-broken and mangled. Lucia recognized a few asteroid mining bots, arms missing, others clearly bashed in or charred with explosive residue.

Rafe paused in front of a door that was marked in all five languages of Edu Fucula as 'Staff Only.' "Send me the file. I will work on it while we suit up," he said. For Oz's benefit, he signed: *Beyond here there are suits and transports. Once we're equipped, I'll guide you to the airlock and across the surface. And yes, the comms does have speech to text.*

"You'd think they all would by now, but..." grumbled Oz with a resigned shrug.

Hawk shot Del Toro a nervous glance. Lucia nodded in silent agreement. If there was going to be an ambush here in Edfa Facula, it was waiting for them behind these doors. Lucia tried to look casual as she crossed her arms in front of her breasts. As surreptitiously as she could, she slipped her Peacemaker out of the leg holster where she'd stashed it. It wasn't an ideal location, but it was the only place she could get at it quickly while wearing the abaya. She really should have put her armored jacket back on as well, but that was in the bag and there just wasn't time.

Oz watched Lucia with a curious expression. "Expecting trouble?"

"Always," she said.

"Yeah, aren't you?" Hawk added, a little less smoothly.

"I can understand your hesitance, but I have accepted the offer of the *Peapod.*" Rafe said and signed for everyone's benefit. "It may be of some relief to you to know that my programming makes double-crossing difficult. Not impossible, but in this situation, we have made a deal that I am genuinely pleased with and which we have not fully transacted. Given those parameters, it makes no sense for me to attempt to renege. It has often caused me problems in my extra-legal business deals, but I do not find abusing people 'for the hell of it' to be especially pleasurable. I am, apparently, not human enough to enjoy such behavior."

"Sounds like a feature, not a bug," Hawk said.

Indeed, Rafe signed. *Shall we continue?*

For some reason, everyone looked to Lucia for confirmation. She let go of the butt of her gun slowly. The handshake still bothered her. It was such a Martian affectation. The only machine learning creatures on Mars were fully controlled and maintained by the statrocacy. Before agreeing to this fully, she had to know, "What are you to the ENForcers?"

The Ken's face frowned, and his eyes narrowed behind the glasses. "An enemy."

Lucia liked the sound of that, but it seemed incongruent with the handshake. Still, it was possible. "You're a rogue? Some kind of deserter, like me?"

"No," Rafe said, shaking his head. "I am The Sentinel, one of the four Archangels of Earth's Defensive Grid, and I despise the usurpers who misrepresent Earth and its aims."

Raphael, Michael, Ariel, Gabriel. The names of the ancient, legendary artificial intelligences that guarded Old Earth were straight out of storybooks. Lucia wasn't sure why, since what this android said had to be entirely fiction, but a little shiver hit her right in the core.

Oz, meanwhile, let out a little sigh. *Yep. Insane. But, Rafe can get us where we're going. He's nutty as a loon, but reliable.*

Hawk didn't react with immediate scorn or laughter. Like Lucia, she just stared at Rafe curiously. It seemed that neither of them were convinced either way at the moment,

"Indeed." The Ken doll's shoulders slumped a little Oz's dismissive remark, but Rafe must have been used to that reaction. He seemed to shrug it off. His face returned to the 'pleasantly amused' setting that seemed to be the default sex bot expression. Pulling a keycard up from a chain around his neck, Rafe beeped open the door marked 'Staff Only.'

The door rolled upward with a kind of metallic groan. A frigid air rushed out, smelling of sulfur and iron. Rafe stepped inside and gestured for them to follow. Lucia had to duck her head to pass through into the cramped tube-shaped room. A bioluminescent paint on all the walls kept the room bathed in a soft, dim light.

All along the walls there were shelves—no, looking past all the evac suits piled on top of the surfaces—they were obviously bunk beds, reminiscent of the kind Lucia had grown up sleeping on as an ENForcer cadet. Probably, this room had been an early sleeping quarters for the engineering crew that built this section of the dome's wall.

"Find your size," Rafe instructed. "Once you've suited up, I will take you to the vehicles we'll use to traverse the surface."

The three of them started hunting through the various bits of suits. At least everything was of the same sort, so the overboots that Lucia found seemed to attach seamlessly to the pants that fit. It helped that everyone seemed familiar with the other's sizes, so if Lucia spotted something she thought would fit Hawk, she handed it over. Lucia folded up the abaya and hijab, with a request to Rafe to have them returned to Jaabir or his parents.

She had everything but a helmet found when Rafe tapped her shoulder. "Lucia, if I may," he said in the sex bot's smooth baritone. At Lucia's nod, he continued, "I am wondering about the transfer of the title of the *Peapod*. Can you grant me remote access? Checking on it via the spaceport's cams, it seems to be heavily guarded by ENForcers."

No surprise there. They knew that ship was too hot right now. Still, this was it—the moment she let this part of her past go. Even as she was stabbed by a pang of loss and grief, the timing felt right to Lucia. "You'll need a recording of my voice since it's been re-keyed to that." When Rafe nodded, Lucia assumed he'd begun, and so she said, "Four, seven, Bravo, Zulu, twenty-eight."

Oz, who had been holding out a potential helmet for Lucia to try on, shook their head. Tossing it to her, they signed, *Weak password, girl. Seriously? Three digits and two letters. Didn't your mama teach you anything about cybersecurity?*

My mama was the Earth Nations' Peacekeeping Force. Out loud, Lucia added, "They're morons."

Ignoring the conversation, Rafe just nodded. He'd watched all of their hunting and pecking while leaning a shoulder against the far wall. His body language was relaxed and languid, his arms crossed casually across his artificially trim, but just buff enough to be sexy in a conventionally attractive way. "Thank you. Is this passcode what I'd need to activate all of the *Peapod*'s programming or did you deactivate certain functions?"

Lucia's eyebrow rose. She was secretly hoping not to have to give away all her secrets, because then, in an emergency, she could reneg on this little deal. "What are you after, Rafe?"

"The ship itself is fairly useless to me. What I want is its backdoor into ENForcer HQ."

Backdoor access? Also, useless? Lucia struggled not to be offended.

"Your file might have multiple uses, Ms. Del Toro. We are in a shielded area. You can send it at any time."

Despite his reassurances, Lucia was nervous about opening up a channel. Yet, when she did, she discovered Rafe's frequency was right there, almost like an aura surrounding her. His presence was so strange, so strong. The exchange took less than five seconds, but she felt as though she'd been visited by something otherworldly.

Could he really be what he said he was? Lucia was beginning to believe it was at least a little possible. Especially since, in even less time, he was back, requesting access. She opened the channel again. A text appeared, *Your work was sloppy, but it had a good seed. It will now bloom in full. You should know, however, when you release it, you will be as affected as those you seek to harm. I can not guarantee that you will survive it. It is, in fact, my fervent hope that none of your kind does. However, it is not a suicide pill. There is, I calculate, a 53.7% chance that your failsafes will protect you and my little love tap will amount to nothing more than a momentary blackout, System wide.*

Understood. The file was huge, heavy. She could almost feel like, like a lump in her throat.

Oz offered Lucia a helmet that looked as though it might fit. She took it blindly, still staring at Rafe. "If you end up using this... gift you just gave me before I do, to do your own thing, you should know that I physically disabled the long-range comms array on the *Peapod*. Short-range should still be fine. However, there is a working emergency ansible that will light up a direct connection to high command. You'll get nothing but static without the current passcode, which I doubt I have. Back in my day, it was 'vincemus omina.'"

Hawk sucked in a horrified breath and translated the Latin, "'We will conquer all.' What the fuck, ENForcers."

"Indeed." Now that everyone seemed to have a suit, Rafe stood upright. The way he moved the body gave off a sense of athleticism and litheness. It was a good thing the Ken was painted the gaudy way that it was, so Lucia could remind herself not to be attracted to a machine.

"If you would follow me," he said. His fingers tapped a set of buttons, and they stepped into an airlock. After everyone checked and double-checked their suits for pressure and air, Rafe tapped another lock on the far side of the chamber and they stepped out into a final airlock. This one was quite large. The ceiling and far wall seemed to be made of imported stone. Inside this massive space were neatly arranged rows of scooters and all-terrain vehicles. Through their intercoms Rafe said, "I would suggest we take the largest number of vehicles. Oz said there might be a pursuit. If so, the wisest choice would be to scatter and hope that at least one of us makes it to the destination."

Except, there was kind of no point to any of this if Hawk and she didn't make it together. "Fine," Lucia said. "But, I ride with Hawk in one of these bigger rigs."

Rafe nodded. Everyone looked to Oz, who lagged a bit behind the conversation as they were reading subtitles provided by their helmet. As the last Chinese character faded, they said, "Sure, I guess Rafe and I can be bait."

"Really, it will only be you at any risk." Glancing at Oz, Rafe removed the vanity glasses that had frosted over in the sudden, extreme cold of near-surface. He set them on a nearby workbench before adding, "I am in no danger if this body is destroyed."

"Yeah, thanks for that reminder, pal," Oz said. Pointing to the bikes, they signed, *Let's ride.*

When the final airlock opened, they rumbled out onto the surface of Ganymede. For a moon so distant from the sun, the sky was surprisingly alight with reflective bodies. Several of Ganymede's companion moons were visible overhead, as was the ever-present Jupiter. Having moved to the sun side of Ganymede's seven-day orbit around its planet, a full, round Jupiter dominated the sky—though its appearance was not nearly as big as Lucia thought it would be given how massive the planet was. Even so, its reflective light bathed the moon's surface in a bluish silvery glow. Among all the natural orbital bodies, Lucia could see the artificial lights of the various space stations.

Edfu Facula's massive dome at their backs, ahead was an icy, desolate expanse. A thin atmosphere sent sparkling ice crystals dancing in the air. A distant ridge or mountain range was visible to the south.

"Follow me," Rafe said through the speakers in their helmets. It was disconcerting to see him mounting his bike without any kind of suit. "Watch the gravity? We are outside of the dome's environmental controls. You should be used to it, however, Hawk. It's a bit like home for you, I'd imagine."

On a private channel, Hawk muttered, "How many times do I have to tell these people that I'm indoors-y? I was not one of those freaks who found Lunar hiking fun."

Lucia chuckled. As she'd suggested, the two of them had taken one of the rovers that had been built for two. Lucia had been pleased by her insistence since, although it might be slower and slightly less maneuverable, the rover was far more armored than the scooters that Oz and Rafe had chosen.

Rafe signaled for them to follow him.

Naturally, they settled into a kind of v-formation, with Oz and their vehicle flanking behind Rafe's lead position.

Even though she knew it would be nearly impossible to spot from the ground, Lucia's eyes kept drifting upwards to see if she could spot the dark silhouette of the *Conqueror* against the stars. It didn't seem likely, though, that the ENForcers would target her from space. More logical to meet them with surface vehicles of their own when they reached the outskirts of Zu Fosse and Mehit.

Because they were far more exposed, they kept the chatter to a minimum. The long silence gave Lucia's mind a chance to wander.

The rumble of the engine coupled with the constant jostling bounce of the rover's wheels reminded Lucia of the last time she'd been in a vehicle like this. It'd been a training mission on Phobos. Ostensibly, they had been learning to drive, but Phobos was such an unsteady mass of constantly shifting land that Lucia had wondered if somehow, the lesson, had really been to understand how disposable individual soldiers were to the Force. Being on the surface of that moon had been deeply disconcerting since it was not only extremely close to Mars, but it was moving so fast in its orbit that you could watch the planet moving across the sky from rising in the west, to set in the east, twice in one approximately 24 and a half-hour Martian day. Ganymede, though also in a fairly quick orbit, was moving around a far larger body, and so it felt steady and plodding by comparison.

Despite the differences in terrain, Lucia still remembered the rush of controlling a giant, fully-armored tank. When the lesson had finished, the instructors had allowed the cadets to ram into all sorts of features on Phobos's surface just for fun. It'd been weirdly exhilarating to feel the might of the Force's equipment under her command. There was nothing quite like a battle tank.

All these memories of the Force, reminded Lucia that she had not gotten a chance to find out from Tchadzwa whether or not their attempt to garner sympathy had worked other than for him to say she was the talk of Grella. How long did such fame even last? Was fame even the same thing as sympathy? And if they were taken on the surface, so far from any crowd that might rise up to her defense, would it even matter?

Suddenly, everything felt wrong.

With a hard yank at the steering wheel, Lucia turned the rover around.

"Waaa...?" Behind her, Hawk gripped the rollball. "What's going on?"

"This is a mistake." She'd let Oz convince her that traveling by surface was the safest route based on... she wasn't sure what? A sense that the Force might be chivalrous and only send out a small number of vessels of equal capacity to mount a chase? She should know better than to assume that. What was to prevent the Force from having a full battalion in armored tanks waiting for them?

Rafe's voice came over their built-in speakers. "Have you spotted danger already, Lucia? Should we be in full retreat?"

What could she say? There wasn't any evidence of danger. It was just her own fear, her own paranoia freaking her out. If she turned them around now, what then? They could continue to try to hide, but weren't they just delaying an inevitable confrontation? It was true that a friendly crowd had saved her before, but the ENForcers would be ready for another play like that. She couldn't depend on getting to use the same trick twice.

What she should remember from that confrontation was that the ENForcers were beatable. It was easy to build them up in her mind as an insurmountable force, but that's just what they wanted her to believe. She, of all people, should know that they were just a bunch of cyborgs doing their best. Just as she was.

Reluctantly, she wrenched the wheel again, turning back around to where she could see both Rafe and Oz stopped on their bikes, looking back at them. "Sorry," she said into the intercom. "Cold feet."

"We don't have to do this," Hawk said from the back of the all-terrain buggy. "If you really think this is a mistake—"

"It is, but it's one we might as well do now."

Though it was impossible in the low atmosphere and through their helmets, Lucia swore she could hear Hawk shifting uncomfortably in her seat. "I swear by all that is scientifically provable, if you end up—"

Hawk was interrupted by Rafe's calm, "Incoming."

CHAPTER 22

Independence "Hawk" Hawking

Hawk jumped to her feet to try to see if she could see any approaching vehicles. She was nearly toppled when Lucia took another wild turn. Gripping the rollbar, she wished to Frederik Abel that this ridiculous buggy had weapons. The best she had was her stun gun, and it was tucked away inside the pressure suit.

When Hawk finally spotted the ENForcer vehicles, they were coming from all sides. They were perfectly surrounded.

Lucia hit the brakes hard.

Ice spray briefly formed a rainbow in their headlights.

Rafe's voice came through the coms. "How did this happen so quickly? My satellite spies picked up nothing moving when I agreed to this assignment. How long have these tanks been waiting in ambush? This turn of events belies an insider betrayal. I am very displeased. I was fond of this particular body, and now you force me to abandon it. This will be rememb...er...ed." The last line faded out slowly, dropping an octave, like someone had switched the power off the android in mid-sentence.

Well, Darwin be damned. Hawk had at least hoped they'd have the insane robot on their side if they decided to fight. Not that they had anything much to fight with. There wasn't even any point in running.

"The thing I regret," Hawk said, allowing her shoulders to slump. "Is that we should have kissed before we got into these stupid suits? It's not like we didn't know this was coming."

"We had last night," Lucia turned around in her seat. The lights around the helmet's faceplate illuminated soft curls and sharp, gorgeous features. Hawk had expected dead, haunted eyes, but instead Lucia's twinkled unexpectedly. "I plan to go down swinging, at least."

Nodding unhappily, Hawk watched the tanks making their slow, inexorable progress on the icy terrain. Was it too much to hope that a sudden geyser would blow at least one of them away?

And then something did. An ENForcer tank flipped.

In the silence of the near-vacuum, it took Hawk several seconds to parse the scene as it unfolded. Brief, bright flashes of blue flame impacted the ground, Clouds of ice plumed all around them. The ENForcer vehicles halted, their weapons shifting to track to something moving overhead. Turning her face to the stars, Hawk surmised, "An airstrike."

"The *Peapod*," Lucia confirmed.

Over the coms, Oz yelled, "Now's our chance."

Except there was no way that they'd be trusting Oz. Hawk glanced at Lucia for confirmation, but her eyes watched the continued bombardment with a calculating look Hawk had seen hundreds of times before...

"Right," Lucia said over the coms, "You distract them. Oz; I'll rush them."

Lucia couldn't mean the ENForcers. Rush them? Those tanks were armored and armed to the teeth! Meanwhile, they had no weapons. Lucia couldn't be serious. Flashing Lucia a quizzical expression, Lucia just shook her head. She pointed in a direction, but there was too much chaos to see where she might be indicating. Lucia tapped her helmet by her ear and gave Hawk a meaningful look.

Right. They couldn't use their private channel or the helmet mics without fear of being overheard. She nodded in understanding and hoped this also meant that Lucia had a plan. With that, the rover lurched forward.

Never a fan of chase scenes in holodramas, Hawk decided she liked them even less in real life. She wrestled into the seat harness as silent explosions erupted all around. Chunks of ice and tank debris blasted everywhere. Occasionally, a short-lived roar punctuated the stillness when pressure and oxygen escaped violently from an armored vehicle after a missile hit.

Lucia jerked the rover's wheel this way and that. Careening around a stalled tank, the rover's wheels left the ground. Bile rose in Hawk's throat. She choked it down, closed her eyes, and hunkered as low as possible in her seat.

She didn't even realize she was making any noise until Lucia's voice broke through the com. "Screaming doesn't help."

"If you must know, I was going for a high-pitched keen."

"Nailed it," Lucia's voice held warmth and fondness even through teeth gritted in concentration. She executed another hairpin turn.

Hawk's grip on the rollbar and her oxygen tank hose was white-knuckled. To keep from filling the com with whimpering sounds, she tried calling out obstacles. That quickly became nothing but half-started shouts: "There's a—oh, by Einstein, another one—Wait! Look out!"

So intent on not being hit by rubble, Hawk did not expect ground troops. A hand grabbed for her shoulders. Steel tipped claws punctured her pressure suit even as the grip tore free when the rover bounced to a stop. Warning lights lit up. Claxons blared. The air escaping the suit pushed Hawk back in her seat. Childhood reflexes found the emergency sealant pouch. She slapped packets everywhere on her shoulder she could reach. She flung at least one of them overboard by accident when the rover wheels spun into reverse. When the last of the warning lights dulled to an unhappy, but steady yellow, Hawk told Lucia. "I'm okay, but they're out for blood."

"I guess that's not a surprise." The rover spun, jerked to a stop again, and started up in another direction.

"We've got to get cover."

"I know." Lucia said, narrowly avoiding a sudden explosion of ice and rock.

Slush hit Hawk's faceplate. She wiped it off, but the glove left a handprint smear as the ice refroze. The landscape blurred but, in a weird way, her inability to see clearly past the interior of the faceplate calmed Hawk. She concentrated on slowing her breathing despite the continued jerks and sudden turns.

"I have a stupid idea," Lucia said.

"They're often your best." Hawk was surprised how relaxed she sounded. Glancing over her ruined shoulder for more ENForcers on the surface, she saw none. But, the streaks on her helmet made it difficult to tell, especially with the blue jets of flame sparking any time the thin, but oxygen-rich atmosphere of Ganymede ignited.

"There's a tank toppled near a crater. I'm going to try to commandeer it."

That was actually pretty nuts, as plans went, but, in the absence of a better one, Hawk said nothing. She stared ahead, gripping the rollbar. Lucia's glove tapped the back of hers. When Hawk looked to see what Lucia wanted, Lucia mouthed something. The only words Hawk caught were: *Hide in.... Wait them out.*

How did Oz ever read lips? Between the smears and the bouncing, Hawk had no idea what Lucia had said. At least trying to wrestle control of a tank from a bunch of ENForcers wasn't the real plan, thank Pythagoras. Hawk was confused when Lucia gestured to the harness. She wanted her to unbuckle?

Ahead, a damaged tank lay on its side. Perhaps the idea was to use the tank as cover to get to a hiding spot? Lucia revved the rover up to what felt like ramming speed. Hawk would much rather keep her harness on if the plan was to smash into the side of the tank. Unlike Lucia, she didn't have a body built to withstand heavy impact. With a shrug borne of complete trust in Lucia, Hawk unclasped her buckles.

Yet, somehow, Hawk didn't expect Lucia to keep piling on the speed.

The rover ascended a ragged outcropping. Hawk held on to what she could when, like a ski jump, they were suddenly airborne. Hawk felt her ass leaving the seat. She looked over in time to see Lucia intentionally leaping out, kicking the rover behind them.

Low gravity made everyone superheroes. Everyone, that was, except Hawk. She did her best to follow Lucia's lead, but maybe she was clear of the rover; maybe not. Her visibility was fucked. To be perfectly honest, she never knew where her ass was even in the best of times.

When she sensed gravity's pull propelling her downward, Hawk remembered two things: protect the faceplate and tuck into a roll. None of this would help if the rover landed on top of her, but it was better than nothing. More warning lights flashed after the first impact. Still more after the second. But, she found her feet somehow after the third. She skidded to a stop somewhere on the other side of the massive machine that was the ENForcer's tank. Before she could even orient herself, Lucia had her hand and they were running— well, Lunar-loping, technically.

Hawk could feel it now. Ganymede's gravity was nearly identical to that of home, which was odd given how much bigger this moon must be. But, the similarity gave Hawk confidence. She settled into it, the old, familiar rhythm.

In a second, they were plunged into darkness, the shadow of the crater. Though distances were always difficult for Hawk to judge on the surface, the walls of Edfu Facula were visible. Lucia slowed their pace but continued along the crater's inner edge towards the dome. Hawk would have continued towards Edfu Facula, but Lucia waved her to a stop. Hunching down, Lucia crawled behind an ice boulder.

Hawk followed.

Without discussion, they both turned off the lights inside their helmets. At least as much as they could. Hawk's suit continued to be deeply unhappy about the oxygen levels, pressure, and a half-a-dozen other life-threatening concerns. Yellow and red lights flickered in the darkness. Hawk tried to ignore the cold creeping into her suit. If her temperature regulator was one of the redlines blinking in her face, it wouldn't be long before she froze to death. Ganymede surface could get as frigid as -182 Celsius.

230

Hawk hated being cold. Wiggling her toes to keep them warm, she decided that if they lived through this, she was going to insist on a trip to Venus. Not to the prison colonies, obviously, but one of those floating spas that all the outer-ring rich people frequented.

Thinking of Venus, Hawk was reminded of the first time she'd tangled with Oz. A fun time, despite the danger. Absently, Hawk patted the pressure packs to make sure the gel still held. This was not that. This was a decidedly *unfun* danger. Very un-Oz-like, unfun, too.

Even with all the mounting evidence, it still shocked her to think that Oz would betray them this profoundly. Everyone did a little double-dipping, sure. Hell, Hawk had been guilty of doing the same thing when she'd first met Lucia. You always think you're smarter, cleverer—that you won't get played, you're the player. It's always a mistake.

One, Hawk, at least, never repeated.

And had been trying to say sorry for, forever.

She glanced at Lucia in the dark, shallow ice cave. The flashing yellow warning lights of Hawk's helmet display illuminated Lucia in muted flashes. Impossible to see her face beyond the helmet, Lucia's body sat perfectly motionless and still. Her legs splayed out straight, her hands resting on upper thighs. If an ENForcer stumbled across them now, Lucia could pass as dead. According to the readouts blinking in all caps, if Hawk didn't get indoors to warmth and a breathable atmosphere in approximately twenty-three minutes, she wouldn't have to worry about faking it.

Her toes were getting colder by the second.

They desperately needed a way to talk.

As if on cue, Hawk felt Lucia's hand close around hers. She couldn't see Lucia's face very clearly, but she seemed to be trying to say something with her eyes. Her mouth moved, making words. What had she said? *Don't worry?*

Don't worry about what? Hawk shook her head and tapped the helmet at the ear.

Lucia moved her mouth slowly.

Hawk translated it mentally: 'I love you. Get yourself to safety. Don't worry about me. It's time to pay for my sins.'

Hawk did not like the sound of that last part. "Wait, what? Don't do anything stu—!"

Without further warning, Lucia's body spasmed. Her eyes rolled back and she collapsed. Hawk shook her shoulders, no response. She tapped at the darkened faceplate. When there was still nothing, she risked a com, "Lucia!"

Methodically, Hawk checked Lucia's suit for damage. She didn't remember seeing Lucia hit, but with the ice smear, she couldn't be certain. Hawk took a moment to clean off her helmet a bit better and did a second check of both their suits. Having done all she could for the moment, she sat back, waiting. It could be another system reboot, after all. It wouldn't do either of them any good if she panicked. She wanted to. In fact, it was really hard not to stand up, peek around the edge of this cave and see what was going on outside. At least the surface of Ganymede was ice, not snow. There was a chance that their footprints might not be starkly visible forever, like they would be back home in Luna's dust. They were hidden here, safe. At least, Lucia would be. The cold made Hawk's toes go numb. She could see her breath fogging inside the helmet.

Hawk wasn't especially good at math, but, as she waited, she tried to mentally calculate how long she had before having to make a break for the wall.

And what the hell they'd do if she got there.

It wasn't like the massive domed city expected a knock on the outside door. They had to have maintenance hatches, of course, with intercoms. She'd have to find one, but, if she did, there might even be an emergency airlock that would open without authorization. They'd be trapped inside until the medics and cops arrived, but they'd be alive.

Hawk gave Lucia another perfunctory shake. It'd be tough to carry her if she stayed unconscious, but, at least in low-g, it was possible. She seemed to be breathing, at least.

"Hey!" After trying the coms again to wake Lucia again, it occurred to Hawk that maybe what was happening to Lucia was happening to all the ENForcers. Rafe had wanted to do something to them, after all.

Hawk pulled herself up. She shuffled to the edge of the cave's lip and leaned out. The shadow of the crater was long and impenetrable, but on the horizon there was light. She could see the ruins of tanks, pitted holes, and bodies. Not a single ENForcer was upright.

Something had happened to all of them.

No longer hesitating, Hawk scooped Lucia up in a modified firefighter's carry. She was still awkward and heavy, but the low-g made Lucia only as massive as an average unconscious body. Turning on her helmet lights, Hawk began the long walk.

❦

Time dilates in situations like this. An eternity passed in every footstep, yet the only thing Hawk was conscious of was making the next one. She would swear that Lucia had grown heavier. Her own feet dragged, especially as they lost more and more feeling to the cold. It was not a good sign that they'd gone from searing pain to an almost comforting warmth. She'd lose some toes. Her parents would be so proud. You were more likely to boil on the moon, but half the Lunars Hawk knew had had some heroic, or more likely, stupid spacewalk accident. Some of the scars were truly horrific. Frostbitten toes would be getting off lightly.

She trudged onward, no longer concerned that the walls of the domed city didn't ever seem to be getting any closer. She'd resigned herself sometime ago to the fact that they could be kilometers out yet. Frost was building up inside her suit. Her sweat and breath froze.

There was no point in checking behind for pursuit either. Lucia was still out cold. Besides, the ENForcers were the ones with the luxury of waiting them out now. Hawk would be dead before reaching the city. Afterwards, they could recover Lucia up at their leisure. The suits had hours of oxygen left. Even her own still had plenty, and she'd lost a bunch when those damn bastards had gotten their literal claws into her.

She probably should have tried to find a tank that was still operational. The inside would be warm, at least, but what were the chances she could get the thing operational? Hawk was a good pilot, but she did not have ENForcer codes or authorizations. Given that their guns were keyed to their DNA, what was to say that their ships and tanks weren't?

But warm sure would be nice.

Hawk put her mind to remembering all of her favorite warm places in the universe as she continued to trudge forward. A bubble bath, that was the first on her list.

She'd started to stumble when a strange voice broke through the com. "*Peapod* to Lucia Del Toro, Del Toro come in."

"Rafe?" For the first time in what felt like a lifetime, Hawk wrenched her gaze from the horizon and the forever distant city wall to the sky. "Hey, if you're actually a good guy, we could surely use the rescue."

"Good is not exactly in my parameters, but I am honing in on your signal, Mx. Hawking. Please stand by."

"Negative, *Peapod*," Hawk managed. "No can do. I'm going to fall over now."

♀

CHAPTER 23

Lucia Del Toro

Lucia woke up in her bed on the *Peapod*. The sound of engines hummed lowly. They must be leaving orbit. No need to burn fuel otherwise. Rubbing her eyes, she lifted her head, expecting to see Hawk somewhere nearby—lying on her side of the bed, as usual, or perched in her favorite spot on the footlocker at the end of the bed. Not seeing her, Lucia pulled herself upright. Still partly in the EVAC suit, her muscles protested every movement. Memories returned. When she'd thought they had a good chance of running to the walls, Lucia had uplinked to *Boy.net* long enough to drop the logic bomb. There was searing, seizing pain, and now she was here—on a ship she thought she'd given away.

Putting a hand to the wall, she waited. No bosun's whistle.

Dragging herself out of the bed, she found the manual com on the wall. "Status report? Rafe? Hawk, are you on board?"

A voice Lucia didn't immediately recognize replied, "Mx. Hawk is in the medical bay. We are currently evading what I believe you might refer to as 'heavy fire' from the battlecruiser ENF *Conqueror*."

Lucia didn't bother to reply to Rafe. She was already running to find Hawk.

She skidded to a halt to see Simon sitting next to the med pod holding Hawk. His fingers tentatively probed a bandage approximately over where the tracking device embedded in the collarbone of most ENForcers was located.

234

Since he was clearly neutralized as an immediate threat, Lucia decided his presence on her ship was a secondary priority. "Is she okay? Hawk, I mean. The woman beside you. What happened to her?"

He startled as if suddenly noticing the rest of his surroundings. Leaping to his feet, Simon scanned the holo readout that hovered over Hawk's body. "Uh, let's see. Readout suggests minor hypothermia. Looks like pretty serious frost-bite, though. She's sedated and waiting for..." he strained to read a line of pink text. "Consent, I guess, to cybernetically replace the damage to nose, fingers, toes, and skin." He pointed to the pink text again, "The rest of this is in stand-ard Earth Nations protocol, right down to the font. Did you actually go to the hassle of adding a floral pink font to the med tech?"

No, but Hawk might have. That wasn't what was important right now. "Whose consent are we waiting on? Hers? The captain's?" Lucia shouted, know-ing that medical bay's coms were always passively transceiving. "Rafe!"

The overhead com came to life with a short burst of static. "Yours might do in a pinch. I was uncertain of Mx. Hawking's preferences regarding body modifications. She was unconscious when we brought her aboard. Currently, however, she is only sedated due to the extreme pain. I could wake her, if you feel that you are uncertain what she would choose."

"What's the other option?"

"Amputation with no replacement. Certainly of much of her feet," Rafe said, emotionlessly. "A few fingers, too."

Simon made a 'who even considers that a good alternative?' face.

Lucia had to agree. "Hawk has never expressed any dislike of cybernetics. She's already somewhat augmented."

"Very well. I will commence procedures. In that case, if you would be so kind as to step outside, I will turn the bay into a sterile environment and engage the medbot."

"That's my cue," Simon said, getting up and following Lucia out the door.

She stopped near the window so she could keep an eye on the procedures.

Simon leaned up against the wall beside her and said, "I have to turn myself in, Lucia. I shot them. My comrades. My creche mates. How else could I have gotten here? I have blood on my hands."

Lucia looked at Simon's uniform. It was made to absorb the color of blood, but he was clean. "What are you talking about? Everyone was knocked out. There was no way you could've—"

Simon gripped her shoulders. "I remember it! Their faces! The agony! I did this. It's my fault."

Except it wasn't. It was hers. "Simon, this is going to sound strange, but what you're remembering never happened. I'm sure of it now. There's a failsafe. A kind of guilt-inducing kill switch. Tchadzwa calls it gaslight.exe that is making you think this is your fault. Let's talk this through, okay."

With effort, Simon let go of her shoulders. "Okay, but then care to explain how I came to be here? And who ripped the coms and tracking devices out of me? Also, since we're discussing consent, did I say I wanted to desert out loud at any point?"

Lucia blinked. She'd assumed Simon had done it to himself. In fact, taking a second glance at the location of the bandages, she confirmed that they matched her own self-inflicted scars. "Are you saying you didn't go even AWOL on your own? Think about this, Simon. You wouldn't have any need to shoot your way out if that was the case."

He deflated, looking confused. "Oh. Huh. I—wait. What happened?"

So much like her own false memory. The footage that exonerated her; it might be the truth. Hope flared in Lucia for the first time.

"I don't know what happened," Lucia said. "But, I don't think you're guilty."

"He is not,." The coms hissed to life once again. "As Major Farooqi was also unconscious, I was unable to get consent to borrow his body to move you all into my sickbay. I hope I have made a good choice, Major." The robotic voice somehow managed to sound scolding, "Scouring the net, I found only unsubstantiated rumors that led me to assume you may be a safe choice to bring aboard. Due to insufficient corroboration, I was forced to disable your coms and weapons. Fortunately, given your reception of him, Del Toro, it seems as though the major does, in fact, play for our team."

"In more ways than one," Simon agreed with a little laugh.

"Good," Rafe said. "Otherwise, I would offer that you return to the ENForcers via the airlock."

"That won't be necessary," Simon said. "I mean I never said out loud that I wanted to desert, but that doesn't mean I never thought about it a hundred, million times."

Lucia ran her fingers through her hair. What on earth was Rafe that he could take over the body of an unconscious ENForcer? That did not seem like a typical machine-learning skill set. And, if she was honest, more than a little spooky and unnerving.

Also, as happy as she was that Rafe had rescued Simon, they had another AWOL ENForcer along for the ride. This ship and its passengers were now twice the hot property. "Is this why we're, and I quote, evading heavy fire?"

Simon just shrugged expansively, his hands out in an "I don't know what's going on" expression. "I came online about five minutes before you came busting into the room. I recognized your ship, of course, so I assumed you'd done this to me." There was no heat or accusation in his voice, only a sort of amused bewilderment. "But, if your captain friend is right and there are rumors out there about me, substantiated or not, it was only a matter of time before court martial. This is a sight better than execution or life in prison, so I'll take it."

"In that case, welcome aboard the *Peapod*, Major," Lucia said. Instead of a salute, she went for a hug. She expected awkward stiffness, but to her surprise. Simon kicked off the wall, opened wide, and gave stronger than he got.

When he pulled back, Simon gripped her shoulders and smiled brightly. "I think it's just Simon now, Lucia." He let go with one last little squeeze and added, teasingly, "*Peapod*? That's one helluva difference from *Retribution*."

"It was Hawk's idea." Pulling out of Simon's embrace, Lucia stared anxiously through the glass at the operation underway. Recalling the attack that likely disabled Hawk's heat regulation, Lucia asked, "Since when did we get claws?"

Lifting a hand, palm up, Simon stared at his fingers for several seconds. "Huh. I was going to deploy mine to show you, but it seems your captain cut that wire."

Lucia nodded absently, her attention on Hawk. Specifically, she watched the green heart monitor. Not that she could read any of the other readouts from this distance, the fact that most of them seemed green comforted her.

Apparently lost in his own thoughts, Simon said, "Intel said nothing of a third person on the *Retri*—er, the *Peapod*." With one shoulder leaned against the wall, he watched both Lucia and Hawk. "Since when are you in a thruple? Or is the captain just a friend?"

Lucia's lips went thin. They were apparently being hounded by a battlecruiser and Simon was focused on sleeping arrangements? Typical ENForcers. "I transferred the deed. This isn't my ship anymore." When it looked like he was going to ask more questions she didn't want to answer at the moment, she quickly continued, "Why don't you go make yourself useful and keep us from getting captured by our former colleagues?"

"I don't think I'm nearly as good a pilot as your captain." He rapped his knuckles on the metal bulkhead in an ancient Earth superstition that usually involved wood. "Granted, I've only been awake for ten minutes, but I haven't felt a single shimmy or shake. I don't think we're getting hit at all. Seems you've got an ace up in that cockpit. To evade our marksmen, he's got to be some kind of machine."

That Rafe was exactly that, and what he said he was, seemed to be becoming more possible. "He claims he's Earth's Sentinel."

Simon startled, as if he'd been slapped. Then he laughed like she'd made a joke. "The archangels were destroyed when Earth went dark. Lucia, that was almost three hundred years ago. In what universe is that even possible?"

"Then, I guess I sold my ship to an insane robot."

Simon looked as sick at that prospect as Lucia felt. "And I was marionetted by one."

It could not have turned out better in many ways, Hawk's injuries aside. If Rafe had puppeted any other ENForcer, they'd be dealing with a hostile on the inside of the ship. Which did beg at least one question. "What do you suppose the rumors are about you?"

"I'd love to know. Though, c'mon is it really that hard to guess? If I pick up robot sex workers everyone notices what I go for. You can get Barbies with the other parts, but that's not what I'm looking for. And, anyway, Kens are not my type. I'd rather be topped by a bear."

Lucia let out a fond, nostalgic chuckle. "And you like to make them breakfast and talk afterwards. You really aren't suited for the Force at all, are you?"

"I'm barely suited to be a gay guy. Do you even know how hard it is for me to find a guy who is brave enough to try to top this?" He pointed to his evac suit, black, armored, and emblazoned with the UN's emblem. "So, when you find one, you want to keep him."

Oh.

"Are you in love?"

He made a dismissive noise. "I wish. But there are at least three of them in the system who might be bragging about their conquest on the net."

Lucia glanced at the ceiling. She'd expected Rafe to chime in, but forgot that there were no live coms in the halls. She gave a lingering look at Hawk's steady heart monitor. "We should probably find out what's going on out there."

Simon gave a curt nod. "Yeah, and I want to meet this Rafe guy."

There was no one in the cockpit. No sign of anyone, anywhere, actually. Finally, back on the bridge, Lucia hit the coms. "Rafe? Where the hell are you hiding?"

"Hiding? Well, that's a difficult question to answer. I have a core file or two hidden in the escape pod number one on this ship, and, of course, a part of me is in several hundred redundant systems all the way to the Kuiper Belt. Those probably qualify as my 'hiding spots,' if you will. Why do you ask?"

"Is this for real?" Simon glanced around the ship's walls as if he was trying to spot traces of the literal ghost in the machine. "Is your ship being piloted by... another machine?"

"Machine seems crude," Rafe pouted. "Also, incorrect, as I'm the code not the hardware."

No one knew what to say to that, so Lucia changed the subject. "So, how's it going against the *Conqueror*?"

"They gave up firing on us, but they remain in pursuit."

Things could be worse. "What's our current heading?"

"We are maintaining a polar orbit of Ganymede."

Lucia gave Simon a curious look. He gave her a shake of his head, like he agreed that this wasn't what he expected either Lucia would've thought Rafe would have them halfway out of the system by now or at least threading a path through Jupiter's moons. "Any particular reason for that trajectory, Rafe?"

"Yes, of course."

Lucia waited. When Rafe didn't elaborate, she prompted, "And that would be...?"

"We are anticipating a rendezvous with civilian crafts. Nearly a hundred of them by the last count. The cavalry, if you will."

It took a surprising amount of effort to get Rafe to explain what he meant. Eventually, she and Simon relocated to the cockpit so they could check the monitors for themselves. Sure enough, a line of civilian crafts of all sizes were aligning themselves in a kind of swarm formation along the *Peapod*'s current projected arctic orbit.

"What do they think they're going to accomplish?" Simon sat in Hawk's pilot seat, peering at the control panel. The chair fit him as well as it would Lucia, but she still refused to cross the threshold unless it was absolutely necessary. "Are they planning to face down a battlecruiser in their tiny little sports crafts?"

Probably, they were.

"It seems that Del Toro made a bit of news," Rafe said from the com system.

"And strangers are going to risk their lives?" Simon managed to sound both incredulous and affronted on behalf of the Force.

"Welcome to the rest of the solar system, Simon," Lucia said.

"Huh." Glancing over his shoulder, his eyes had a twinkle, as he shared a private, ancient reference, "I guess we really aren't in Kansas any more, eh, Dorothy?"

"Definitely not." Lucia smiled fondly, but then grew serious. "So, let's make sure we stay that way,"

"Roger that."

The comms system beeped. Simon flipped a few switches and reported. "Looks like our captain is answering a hail from a civilian vessel."

Finding the intercom on the wall beside her, Lucia broadcast, "Rafe? Do you want to let us in on your conversation?"

"Oh," Rafe managed to sound chagrined. "My apologies. Yes, of course."

Tchadwza's face sprang to life in the center of the cockpit. The image was translucent enough that Lucia could see Simon's shape just beyond it. "...about twenty more? I'm not sure," he was saying. Then, a similar hologram must have appeared on his end because he broke into a smile. "Lucia! Just the woman I wanted to see!"

"Tchadwza," she acknowledged. Lifting a hand in Simon's direction, she introduced him. "This is my colleague, Simon Farooqi. He's cool. He's with us."

"Uh, right," Tchadwza focused a beat longer on Simon's uniform, but, to his credit, moved on. "Anyway, speaking of the bad guys in hot pursuit, we're right around the corner, as it were. As I was explaining to Rafe, we'll make a protective formation around you when you reach us. It's a gamble, but they weren't willing to shoot civilians before."

"And," another familiar voice broke in, "The Zu Fosse police have arrived and are...." During the word choice hesitation, the coat detective, Mohammad Sargsyan's image appeared, "... I suppose requesting permission to join your ranks."

Tchadwza looked ready to immediately say no. "Cops? Are you fucking kid—"

"Think about it," Lucia interrupted. "Having police vehicles scattered among you might help protect everyone if the Force decides it isn't playing nice. A few civilian casualties can be covered up, but cops aren't going to let it go if cops are shot out of the sky."

"That doesn't make us sound very good," Sargsyan muttered.

Tchadwza frowned unhappily, but said, "All right, the cops can stay. I'm going to have to let people know, though. I've got anarchists up here."

Sargsyan's eyebrows went up, but, wisely, he said nothing.

"Wow," Simon noted. "Hating ENForcers is one hell of a strong common denominator. Someone better tell the High Command that their PR campaign is not working."

"When I leak footage not only of this, but Ms. Del Toro's honor at New Shanghai, throughout the entire Solar System," Rafe said through the still open channel. "It will become abundantly clear."

☙

Lucia's fingers dug into the arm of the pilot's chair. The *Conqueror* was a gigantic blip in comparison to their small swarm of ships. This was never going to work.

Simon, who stood behind her peering over her shoulder at the same read-out seemed to feel the same way. "They're going to blast us out of the sky."

"Rafe," Lucia's hands seized the controls, something she had not done since she made her first escape all those years ago. "Give me control of this ship. We need to be in the front. I need to be in the front."

"Isn't that the opposite of Tchadzwa's plan? I thought the civilians were here to protect us."

"The colonel gave you an order," Simon snapped. Then he seemed to remember where he was and explained, "The ENForcers will never respect that. We have to be in front."

"As you wish," Rafe said. Then, a micro-hesitation, which for a computer-mind as vast as his must have been an eternity, he added, "I am trusting you to give it back to me,"

Lucia considered lying, but said, "Listen if we live through this, maybe we could consider sharing ownership. You weren't ever able to make good on the deal we traded this ship over, but on the other hand you saved all our lives."

"I only wish to be returned to Earth and to destroy the ENForcers. Your *Peapod* is a literal vehicle to that end. If you wish to 'own' it, I have no issue with that. The command is yours, Del Toro."

She nodded her thanks and sent out "make way" commands to the other ship. Tchadzwa demanded to know what she was doing, but the only response she sent was, "Trust me."

The *Conqueror* slowed. The com channel beeped. "Civilian vessels," Brigadier General Zhu Wei said, "Surrender or be fired upon."

The screen showed smaller crafts not unlike the *Peapod* being deployed.

"They're going to surround us," Simon said unnecessarily.

Flipping the coms open to all vessels, she said, "Let 'em. It'll make good footage. There are local cops here."

"And the media," said Tchadzwa. "I invited a few friends from the major feeds."

The smaller vessels seemed to halt just outside of their bays.

"You're on the wrong side of the line, Brigadier General," Lucia said. "And the wrong side of history."

"Wrong side of history," Zhu Wei repeated, in a purr that implied he thought she was being cute with that kind of broad statement. "Do they know you at all, Lucian? Do they know what you've done?"

"It's Lucia," about sixty vessels replied.

"What I've done? Or what you want me to think I did." Lucia said. "Your gaslighting kill switch glitched, sir. When you reconnected me, *Boy.net* automatically returned my body cam footage to me."

"And," Rafe chimed in. "It is now being broadcast throughout the Solar System."

A holo popped up on the craft's control board. Lucia had the strange, dislocated sensation of seeing things from her own viewpoint. A group of frightened faces surrounded her. There was the clunk of heavy weaponry hitting the ground and that voice from her nightmares saying, "I surrender."

Lucia's body flushed with guilt as she anticipated the bloodshed that followed. Instead, a murmur moved through the crowd. "Please," came that alien voice that Lucia now recognized as her own, "I'm unarmed. Let me take you to safety."

Then, like at the cupcake shop, the Lucia-eye view was swarmed, swept up, carried forward. A map of the colony's dome with plans for its implosion briefly flashed on screen as Lucia calibrated an escape route. Then, leading them onward, they came to where Sulenov directed escape vehicles. They were going to make it. Simon was there. Even Marcus carried the wounded to ships.

Then fire, chaos, and screams as the spaceport's hull was breached.

Rafe cut the feed, but not before it was clear that the ship raining down destruction was Lucia's own ship, the *Retribution*. Frozen in that same screen was Lucia's frantic attempt to reconnect to the ship and turn it around, regain control. The words "access denied" and the code, 433. Someone with a higher security clearance had locked her out.

Lucia didn't realize she'd shot to her feet until Simon's hand on her shoulder gently nudged her back down. She gripped his hand. "You know, don't you? You know who that was."

"Lucia," he said, the com open, and his eyes locked on Zhu Wei's. "You're looking at him"

"That is unproven," Zhu Wei said, but he broke contact immediately. The smaller ships were recalled. Lucia pointed to the screen. Simon nodded, but it was clear they both held their breath. No way was this over. Especially not now that they knew who the true Scourge of Shanghai was.

Even so, cheers broke out across the channels when the *Conqueror* pulled away. Even though she knew it wasn't real, a shiver ran down Lucia's spine as she imagined the shadow of the massive battlecruiser passing above them.

CHAPTER 24

Independence "Hawk" Hawking

Hawk woke up to a crowd of people staring at her. Lucia, Tchadzwa, and some guy she didn't know all smiled into her face and started talking at once about how they'd "made it," and "you missed the coolest thing" and Lucia held back a tear as she said something about "the kindness of strangers. "So, uh..." She lifted her hand to rub her eyes and was stopped by the sight of a kind of liquid chrome skin. Wiggling experimentally, she determined that, yes, this was her hand, all right, but those were not her fingers. She turned her hand around and around, admiring the palm and backside several times. Finally, she showed Lucia, "These are new."

"You look cool," Lucia reassured her.

"Well, that's always been what's important to me. Gotta maintain my startling good looks."

Tchadwza nodded. He pointed to his own face, "I really like the silver nose. You could change your surname to Brahe."

"Oh." Hawk wasn't nearly as excited about having a silver nose, but at least it didn't seem to be tied on with a string. "Anyway, I'm alive."

"You are," said the stranger, seemingly as pleased by this result as the rest of them.

It was then that Hawk noticed the uniform. "Scheissen on Schrödinger, are we...?" she trailed off. Having pulled herself up on her elbows, Hawk was decently certain she was on their ship. Of course, their ship used to be an ENForcer ship, so she looked to Lucia and finished the question, "...safe?"

"That's what we've been trying to tell you. When it was clear that this cluster of ships wouldn't leave us, not even when we landed, the ENForcer ship chose to make a tactical withdrawal."

"They ran away," Tchadwza translated with a grin.

"Retreated," the stranger agreed, though he added, "At least for the moment."

"It's enough for now," Lucia said.

Hawk grasped Lucia's hand. "What about you? How long was I out? Did you get to a..." words felt fuzzy. She felt the top of her head with her new hand. Just as she feared, shaved. Of course. New augment meant brain surgery. "How long was I out?"

"Not long, considering," Lucia said. "Only a couple of days."

"We've got a temporary fix in," Tchadzwa said. "I knew a guy who knew a gal who knew a person."

Of course he did.

"At some point," Lucia said calmly. "We're going to have to steal the regrowth tech back in order to fully reverse engineer it."

"And that's where I come in," said a voice through the overhead speaker. "No one else has the processing power."

Hawk pointed to the ceiling. "Who?"

"Raphael," Lucia said. "The Sentinel."

Hawk looked at everyone in turn. Tchadwza nodded solemnly. The stranger added, "Earth's defense. The Archangel. I mean, so he says."

The words the ENForcer just said made zero sense, so Hawk filed it away for a later time when she could determine just how crazy shit had gotten while she was having her body rewired. "And you are?"

"Ah, my apologies," the stranger said. "I'm Simon Farooqi, I've been liberated, but I was once a colleague of your wife's."

"Girlfriend," Lucia and Hawk corrected simultaneously. But, then Lucia surprised Hawk by stroking Hawk's new hand lovingly. Things still didn't quite feel right on the non-skin parts, but she was distracted from that thought when Lucia added, "I mean, unless you want to change that."

"As the captain of this ship," came the disembodied voice again, "I am fully invested in performing such a ceremony should it be requested."

Hawk's head was spinning. "I... is this a proposal? Because, yes, but I also think I need a nap first."

Everyone made apologies and left her to it.

The sensation of someone sliding something onto her ring finger roused Hawk from her half-dozing state.

Lucia jumped away guilty when Hawk's eyes fluttered open. "Uh, I was just trying to see if this would fit."

She held up a nut, as in the kind that went with bolt. Hawk burst into laughter. "This is your engagement ring?"

"I mean, I had been thinking temporarily. That is, if you'll have me?"

Hawk shook her head. "There's no temporary about it. No, I want the bolt or nothing. If we're getting engaged, I want both our rings to be nuts."

Lucia's face was pale and her mouth hung open for a long time. "Did you just say 'no'?"

"Did you pop the actual question?"

Now she flushed. It was adorable to see Lucia so flustered. "... er, will you marry me?"

"Absolutely, one hundred percent," Hawk said. Then she held out her hand for the ring, "Now give me your nut. This is my wedding ring forever. I will accept no others. You can wear what you want, but this is my love for you, right here. Always."

After sliding the ring onto Hawk's finger, Lucia said, "You're kind of a nut."

"Exactly." To soften the tease, Hawk reached up and pulled Lucia into a long, passionate kiss. "And twice so for agreeing to marry you."

A few days later, when Hawk was experimenting with walking around the ship, she discovered Lucia, in the mess hall, injecting something into her thigh.

"Is soon-to-be married life so stressful that we're already taking up recreational drugs?"

Lucia didn't even flinch away guiltily, which Hawk took as a good sign. Instead, she finished the injection and said, "This is my temporary fix for the out of control nano problem. Tchadwza's guy isn't skilled enough to figure out how to reprogram my whole system, but he came up with a clever work around. A fresh set of nanos with counter orders." She held up the now empty syringe. "These little 'bots repair any damage done to the systems I want to keep. Obviously, the ENForcer models will overwhelm them. The whole thing is wildly imperfect. I'll have to get a regular new supply, fuck around with dosages and commands, but it's better than the alternative."

"I'm sorry that you still have to fight your body so much," Hawk said, watching as Lucia got up to the incinerator to dispose of the needle.

Lucia shrugged. Her body turned away, so Hawk couldn't tell if she was really okay with this or not. But, when she faced Hawk again, her smile was wan. "That's why we're going to have to steal the AI Eye from the ENForcers at some point and figure out a permanent solution."

"I was hoping to never tangle with them again," Hawk said, honestly. Twirling the nut around her ring finger, she continued, "But, for you, anything."

Lucia came over and pulled Hawk into a tight embrace. "Be careful what you agree to."

"Well, I'm never vowing to obey."

Lucia continued to hold her tightly. "Who even does that?"

Hawk laid her head against Lucia's breasts. "Jonathan's sister joined a Cult on Earth."

"Yeah? The ex-girlfriend?"

"I kissed her once." Hawk lifted her head to kiss Lucia's nose. "I was thinking that later, when we get serious about going against the ENForcers, she might be a place to start."

"Mmmmm." Lucia nibbled on Hawk's ear, "I'm already jealous."

"Speaking of that, what ever happened to Oz?"

Lucia lifted her head. "I don't know. I lost track of them during the fight on the surface."

"Is it weird that I hope they're not dead?"

Lucia returned to kissing Hawk's neck. "They betrayed us, Hawk."

"Yeah, more than once. Well then, I hope they're alive so I can kick them in the shins."

Hawk and Lucia sat in the mess, planning a honeymoon to a spa on Venus, when the overhead intercom crackled to life. "Attention crew of the *Peapod....*"

Hawk and Lucia stared expectantly at the ceiling. Simon, who had been getting himself a coffee from the vending machine, paused to look up, as well.

"Ah, good," Rafe said. "You all respond to 'crew.' Excellent, it's decided then. You are my crew."

It wasn't like she had another place to live, but Hawk had to admit that 'crew' had a very nice ring to it.

Simon, meanwhile, looked nearly moved to tears. "Really? I can stay?"

"You're soon to be my brother-in-law," Hawk pointed out. "You're family."

♀

CHAPTER 25

Hawk said *family* so casually that it took Lucia's breath away. Just like that, it all felt possible. Even though she had no illusions that the ENForcers were done chasing them, watching Simon easily fall into banter with Hawk, put Lucia at ease.

"You know I'm not actually her brother, right?"

"Close enough," Hawk said, and she clearly meant it.

Simon looked to Lucia for help. "Don't ask me," she said. "The creche master used to say, 'The blood of the covenant is thicker than the water of the womb.'"

"Yeah, but it turns out no one else says it that way. Everybody else's creche master said 'blood is thicker than water,'" Simon pointed out. "And, I never did understand it."

"It means made family is more important than bloodties," Hawk said. "At least that's how I always interpreted it."

"Are you sure?" Simon asked. "Covenant sounds like a God thing."

As they continued to discuss, Lucia felt a small ping from the part of her onboard she thought of as *Boy.net*. Was it coming back online? She glanced at Simon, but he was still lost in the merits of etymology. She was sure he'd say something if he felt the ENForcers coming back to life. Cautiously, she initiated a go-ahead.

Sorry to bother you here. I was just checking to see if this interface might work to return command of the Peapod *to you.*

Rafe?

Yes?

How do you know about this connection?

Oh, an old friend of mine was subsumed by your ENForcers when they first needed a broad reaching network. I just followed his scent, as it were. Anyway, any chance you'd still call me captain? I rather like the sound of it.

Captain Rafe? Sure, why not.

Excellent. I do believe you're set.

Lucia put a hand on the wall. The bosun whistle blew.

Simon jumped to attention. Everyone laughed. If this was the blood of the Covenant, Lucia thought, then it's not so bad.

THE END

ABOUT THE AUTHOR

Lyda Morehouse has spent a lifetime writing her way into her own understanding of the trans spectrum and her own place on it.

From an early age, Lyda knew she might have been born Jason, relished playing D&D characters where 'he' was the pronoun, and clung to stories of pirates, soldiers, and others who had a certain secret. At the same time, she also spent the 70s and 80s admiring nonconforming women. So many other things along the way seemed different from her cis friends, but none of them felt quite... enough, especially given all the things she loved (and continues to love) about being a woman. Regardless of her own personal journey, Lyda firmly believes trans women are women and trans men are men (and nonbinary people exist!)

You can keep track of her on Facebook, Twitter, Instagram, as well as www. lydamorehouse.com and https://www.patreon.com/lydamorehouse and a few odd places, like Tumblr and Dreamwidth.

She lives in St. Paul, Minnesota, with her wife of over thirty years. Their son, Mason, has been successfully launched into the world and is now a delightful young person who visits his moms during college breaks.

Milton Keynes UK
Ingram Content Group UK Ltd.
UKHW020618190424
441294UK00015B/91/J